Fantasy

-Beyond a Veiled Reflection-

Book Two
Anachronistic Dimensions

Christine Church

© 2018 Christine Church

ISBN: 978-0-692-16865-3

Beyond a Veiled Reflection
Anachronistic Dimensions, Book Two

Grey Horse Press

www.christinechurch.net
www.facebook.com/fatetruevampires
www.twitter.com/christinechurch

Praise for 'Beyond Every Mirror'
Anachronistic Dimensions Book One

"An intriguing start to a promising new series." -KIRKUS REVIEW

"I have never read anything quite like it and I loved it. Brilliant and well written. Superb!! And the writing style of the author was amazing."
Rabia Tanveer, Readers' Favorite

"Fans of Lord of the Rings, Diana Gabaldon, Anne Rice, and all fantasy novels will really enjoy this book! Truly one of the best books I've ever read!" **Bonnie, Amazon Customer**

"All the strands of plot come together to deliver a cracking denouement."
Book Viral

"Emotionally involving. A really impressive start to a series." **Online** Book Club

"I have never read anything quite like it and I loved it. Brilliant and well written. Superb!" **Reader's Favorite**

"A wonderful love story. Like a dangerous but beautiful animal, this romance novel comes with some nail-biting moments that are definitely worth reading. I recommend this book to vampire fans." **Benjamin Ookami**

Other Books by Christine Church

Beyond Every Mirror
Beyond a Veiled Reflection
Beyond Broken Glass (2019)

Fate of the True Vampires series

Sands of Time
The Early Scrolls
Blood Moon
Love's Tragedy
Children of Blood
Blood Hunter (2019)

Nonfiction

Housecat: How to Keep Your Indoor Cat Sane & Sound
Indoor Cats
Your Outta Control Cat

PRAISE FOR BEYOND A VEILED REFLECTION
Anachronistic Dimensions Book Two

Three-Time 5-Star Reader's Favorite

"This is definitely one of the best and most entertaining fantasy romances I have read..." **-Rabia Tanveer**

"A wonderful story full of excitement, action, and heart-felt romance." - **Grant Leishman**

"Betrayal, heartache, manipulation, and dangerous revelations will keep you turning the pages of this unique novel." **-K.J. Simmill**

"Yet another masterpiece from the creative mind of Christine Church" – **CrazyCat Lady**

"Excellent descriptive writing style combined with great storytelling." - **Itinerant Writer**

"A must read." **-MIMA48**

Prelude

Dane Bainbridge died under the heat of a desert sun. At the moment of death blackness surrounded him and the pain of life vanished. Then came the light. Beautiful azure bound his body-less mind. And everywhere flowed water.

Peace.

All the troubles, tortures, fear and worry drifted away on the tides. He could have remained there forever. But soon there was something else. Red. Just a color, but not a color. Hair. Red hair. A word.

Meirah.

The word drifted through his unconscious mind, but he didn't know what it meant.

Kaeplan.

Yes, that was a name he knew all too well. Kaeplan had killed him. They'd been fighting for centuries. And it was Dane who lost in the end.

But, if Kaeplan was here, then he must be dead too. But, where were they? Heaven? Hell? Or some other place? Hell. If such a place existed, they both deserved its fiery end.

So, even those from other dimensions went to Hell. But then...what was Hell but another Dimension in the folds of time. Just as Mikaire had been. Just as in Almareyah.

Someone was speaking. He couldn't yet hear the words. He blinked open his eyes. That's when he saw it. Just a sliver at first, but it grew into a ball of bright white light. Not Heaven, for if he had landed there, Bruce would be chastising him for his disbelief.

A face came into focus then, blocked out the light. She was beautiful with long brown hair that perfectly framed a sculpted face, high cheekbones and big brown eyes. She drew closer to him, and behind her he saw another. Both scantily clad.

As beautiful women closed in around him, Dane reveled in the paradise of his own thoughts.

A dream.

He tried to move, to reach to them. But the pain returned. His back aflame, his arms ached, legs stiff and sore.

Hell hath no fury... And the blackness returned once again.

April 2015

"What makes a desert beautiful is that somewhere it hides a well."
-Antoine de Saint-Exupery

Heat penetrated his flesh and exposed areas burned as if rancorous flames licked at him. Not even the sweltering air of the Red Dust Mountains burned so fiercely. But where was he?

Obviously, the planet was the same, for even the power of Sakkana and the Main Mirror could not transport one to a new planet. If there even was such a thing. And it was the desire to know that raised his body from the searing sand, made him move forward.

Meirah always believed there were other planets that housed beings like themselves. But her delusional obsession with the Mortal Dimension had brought her books from that world which told lies. She, being as naïve as anyone he'd ever met, believed them. And that was one thing he loved about her, had always loved about her. She plagued his mind even now. So clearly he could see her before him, as if she stood there at that moment. Her long ginger hair hung loose and waved in the breeze to supple thighs. She wore the dress—the one she'd worn for the celebration of their engagement, which had never taken place.

She was mean to be his.

That damned mortal. For 12 human lifetimes the beast

possessed her heart and never let it go. And now she was with him—somewhere within the vast Mortal Dimension. And the time had come to find her. But for now, he did not even know where *he* was.

One step. Two steps. At first, he counted them, but lost his number at somewhere over a thousand.

Hunger burned in his gut. But this vast wasteland of sand held naught with which to drink. The few creatures he came upon confused him. Small and unlike anything of existence in Mikaire.

He took a chance, reached down and quickly grabbed a small hairless thing with claws and a long tail. Tiny legs. More like an insect, he doubted the miniscule body held much blood, but he was desperate.

He was about to pierce it with a fang when the jointed tail arched up and the barb at its end punctured the skin on his hand.

He dropped it quickly. "Ow! Ye shite!"

He put his hand to his mouth when a droplet of blood appeared. The wound stung as if being bitten by a Mikairian bee.

Holding his injured hand with the other, he walked onward.

-Two-

Dec 7, 2016

"Come with me, where dreams are born and time is never planned." -Peter Pan

Dane
Aiken, South Carolina

He scarce heard the soft feminine brogue that tried to draw him away.

"Dane, wake up."

A voice, lenient and familiar and distant. He wanted to stay where there was no pain, no anguish. Just love and acceptance. And sex. But the voice called to him once more and the ground began to quake. What fresh hell was this? Shaking. Shaking.

Leave me alone!

"Dane *please*! Please wake up!"

The paradise around him crumbled and thus began his ascent into the real world. He groaned as the waking world attempted to claim him. Mentally, he shoved it away, needing to remain in a place that was fun and safe. He waved his arms about to dispel the voice that drew him away from bliss.

Up, into agony.

No. No more.

Pain sliced across his left cheek, his arms pinioned. Something held his body down yet brought his mind aloft.

"*DANE!*" The voice shrieked. "*Wake…Up!*"

His eyes blinked open. Above him blurry red flames circled and danced. No, not a blaze, but something much worse. An angry pregnant wife with fiery red hair, fangs…and a temper to match.

Forcefully, he croaked, "Meirah, what f—" His words were abruptly stifled.

"Dane! By Sakkana's power, I thought ye was dead!" She sounded both relieved and irate simultaneously and he wasn't sure how that was possible.

He closed his eyes again. "I was. Go away," he croaked.

He tried to roll to one side, but he was crushed by a powerful force—a ginger-haired Mikairian with hormones that made her stronger than she was normally—and that was a lot! She was not going to let him go. He opened his eyes again.

"Get yer arse *up!*" she snapped in his face.

Everything in his bedroom whizzed by as he was forcefully hoisted; the king-sized bed he shared with his now furious wife, the Louis XVI armoire, the antique bureau with a larger than life gilt framed mirror, French double doors to a balcony that allowed in far too much sunshine.

Before he could fully process the situation, he was sitting on the bed by no power of his own, feet planted on the floor. Meirah gripped his hands, held him up. His stomach knotted. He lowered his head to avoid the spinning room. One bare foot kicked an empty wine bottle, sent it spinning into the lion's claw foot of the bureau.

"Oh, no' again!" Meirah sighed.

As he was hauled to his feet his stomach surged. He swallowed hard. In no time at all, he was in the adjoined bathroom, shoved to his knees on hard tile, head bent over the toilet. The speed at which Meirah moved and positioned him was all he needed. What was left of several bottles of wine came up and out. Meirah had his hair in her hand. This was nothing new to her now. But how could he tell her the truth? She was aware he'd begun once again to drink. But she didn't know why.

Once he stopped heaving, pain clawed his scalp as Meirah jerked him backwards, planted his naked ass painfully onto the bathroom floor.

"Ow!"

He reached up, grabbed a towel off the sink, wiped at his mouth and sweat-soaked face. Finally she released his hair, the damp wavy strands of black falling over his shoulders like wet noodles on a hot day. He leaned back against the wall and rested his forehead on his arms, crossed over bent knees.

"Dane…" Meirah's voice calmed, finally. The screeching had given him a headache. "Dane, look at me."

Slowly he raised his head and saw, through sweaty strands of hair and half-closed lids, his wife crouched before him. Even with all she had been going through, her beauty still radiated. Her hair hung in a neat braid to her thigh, but fly-away strands had come out of the binding and danced about her face. Intense emerald eyes stared at him, wide with anticipation.

He sighed but said nothing. The look in her eyes, the confusion on her brow. He knew her well enough now to know what it was she thought.

"Tell me what is goin' on," she said simply. "Is it the nightmares? Have they returned? I remember what ye went through. Ye know I'm here for ye."

He knew that well. She loved him. Hell, she had given up her entire world and existence for him. And he could never repay her.

She'd stayed with him through the nightmares a year ago.

He'd done quite well—surprisingly well—after the entire incident in Mikaire. With Meirah at his side, his life was completely different. He'd found it simple to quit drinking, he had no desire for another woman, and it appeared he'd finally 'grown up;' his partying days were behind him. Music was his career and not a way to meet 'tail.' Music and Meirah together aided in his sanity and in keeping the memory of the tortures away.

But, that all lasted only one year. On the anniversary of the day he'd been taken into Mikaire he'd begun to have horrible nightmares that he'd returned to Mikaire, only Meirah was the wizard and she watched his death with glee.

He'd awakened from the dream so frightened that he had fled downstairs, grabbed a sword off the wall and threatened to kill Meirah with it when she followed behind to see what was wrong. After that, he had gone back to drinking heavily. Meirah learned all too quickly then what it was to be wife to a drunken rock star.

The nightmares had lasted several months—until the anniversary of the day Mikaire died to be exact. And then they were gone. Just like that.

Ever since then, Dane dreaded December. His birthday, his kidnapping. The horrible dreams that refused to let him forget.

Now December was upon him again and something new had begun to transform him from loving husband and sober rock musician to the alcoholic sex-fiend he'd been before he met Meirah—or rather, before he knew of their past lives together.

These dreams, however, were different from those of a year ago. These were dreams of peace and serenity, and most of all, scantily clad women. Now he drank to bring the dreams on rather than make them go away.

Meirah stared at him, expecting an answer. He had none; at least nothing he dared tell her.

He attempted to lift himself from the floor, but his limbs rebelled, collapsing like the spaghetti Meirah once endeavored to cook when she'd wanted so desperately to fit in to his world—soggy and lifeless.

Once more, her strength became his aid. She placed a deceptively fragile-looking hand under his arm and lifted him to his feet, more gently this time. When the room ceased its movement, he walked to the sink and splashed cold water on his face, wet and slicked back his hair, ran a finger through the damp waves, then brushed his teeth.

He still had no idea what to tell Meirah as he warbled back to their bedroom and sat on the bed to slip into a pair of jeans.

She followed, of course, still waiting on her answer.

He looked up at her. She crossed her arms over her chest; such an intimidating figure for such a petite girl. The long yellow tunic-like shirt she wore covered most of her buttocks, her black cotton sweats tight. Those thighs. For a moment, the blood rushed from his brain to his genitals and in his mind erupted a thought of her lying naked beneath him. That coupled with the images in his dream brought an immediate response.

"Dane!" She glanced down at the bulge in his jeans. *"No' now.* Please. Speak tae me!"

7

"I don't know what to say, Meirah. It's not something I can control, or explain."

"Have the nightmares returned?" She dropped her arms to her sides, her face softening along with her voice.

"Yes. No. I don't know. It's not the same as last time. Images. Feelings. There's water, and floating. Peace... then it changes and I am in a sort of paradise—"

"Wi' other women," she scoffed.

What could he say? He'd have to lie. When it came to women, Meirah was the jealous type. She knew his past, but that only made things worse.

"No," said Dane. "Not like that. I really can't explain it, hun. It's just a dream." He stood and kissed the top of her head. "C'mon. I'm sure Edna has breakfast ready."

"Breakfast was three hours ago." she muttered.

"Lunch then," came his quick retort. He strode as quickly and smoothly as his condition would allow toward the door.

Down in the kitchen, Edna was in her usual spirits. "Welcome back ta the livin', Mr. Dane," she smiled.

But Dane was not in the mood, so instead he let escape a grumble that would put the Grinch to shame. He caught the look Edna and Meirah exchanged among one another. Since Meirah had come to live with him, even before their wedding, the two women had formed a bond that was based solely on their judgement of his lifestyle. Long ago he had learned to live with it.

"What's for lunch?" he asked Edna coldly.

"A tuna sandwich."

"You know me too well." Dane frowned.

"I know y'all have work ta do. Bruce wants the new song done *today*."

When Dane worked at the piano, a tuna sandwich was his meal of choice. No fork or utensils to get in the way of his concentration.

"Fine."

He headed off to the music room he had built the year before. He knew with a wife and baby on the way he would no longer be able to work quietly in the parlor. Bruce had taught him that well enough. A sound-proof room was a necessity. Though the baby was not yet born, Dane needed the solace more desperately now.

And so he closed himself into the room and locked the door.

Meirah

Though she stood at the far end of the mansion, Meirah cringed when she heard the music room door slam, her husband closed within.

What in the name of Sakkana was happening? Nightmares were not new to Dane. Getting him to open up about them, however, was.

Once he had she always understood—recollections of his tortures in Mikaire, suffering by the hands of both Kaeplan and Sakkana. And Kaeplan taking her from him. This, she had learned, was normal behavior for humans who had been through trauma.

Meirah ambled into the den, lifted an empty bottle from the table. Alcohol. Dane had once again begun to drink. As a Mikairian, alcohol had been foreign to her. No such drink existed in the time dimensions, at least it hadn't in Mikaire. Only blood was consumed, and water on occasion.

But Meirah had learnt all too quickly what alcohol was—and its negative effects on humans. Married to a rock star, as Dane's profession was called, taught her much she'd never experienced—nor imagined.

"Y'all okay, Mrs. Dane?"

The voice startled her, so lost she was in worry.

"Aye, I believe so." Meirah set the bottle back on the table and turned to Edna, who stood framed by the arched doorway. She held a plate with a sandwich on it and a glass. Dane's lunch.

"Would you like ta bring this to 'im?" she asked softly, holding up the plate.

Meirah shook her head. "I do no' think I should."

"Well, go into the kitchen. I'll be in ta fix ya some vittles."

Meirah nodded and moved toward the kitchen as Edna headed up the stairs.

Several moments passed as Meirah sat quietly on the tall chair she had long learned was called a stool at the island table, lost once again in contemplation. Edna returned, sans plate, but with the glass still in her hand. She walked to the sink, dumped its contents and placed the glass in the dishwasher.

Meirah knew what that meant. He did not take the glass—more than likely he was drinking his alcohol. She sighed. Edna removed a covered glass container from the cold box humans termed a refrigerator. So complicated, this dimension, so many words to learn.

Dane's housemaid placed the container in a small box called a microwave. Usually, Meirah would watch in fascination through the small window as the food spun round and quickly heated. But this day, melancholy replaced her normally quizzical nature. She worried over Dane as Edna removed the container and placed its contents on a ceramic plate, set it before Meirah.

She lifted the fork, held as Dane had taught her near two years before, and stabbed at the meat, stared at it. She'd needed to learn to accept solid food to integrate into human society. As a public figure, Dane—accompanied by his wife—often attended parties and gatherings with many other humans who were not privy to who she was—or her diet. In time, she developed her favorites and Edna's meatloaf was one of many.

Indiscretions in her behavior were easily explained off—she hailed from a remote island off the coast of Scotland and did not always understand American culture. The previous year, Dane had flown her to Scotland to study the culture. Most spoke in an accent similar to her own speech. Natives questioned her birthplace, of course, and many spoke in such a way that even she could not always understand them. But she had studied the language and culture, and outside Scotland no one knew the difference.

"I know y'all likes my meatloaf," said Edna, sitting across from her.

The statement was true enough, but not that day. The scent reminded her of years past, when a fire had spread through the forest outside her village in Mikaire. Many animals were killed, burnt alive. The smell had overwhelmed, nauseated, and she had grieved at so much loss, not only of life, but food for Mikairians. Meirah dropped the fork onto her plate.

"Are ya not hungry, Mrs. Dane?" Edna asked, watching her.

"No' really, I guess."

Edna stood. "Do y'all want some o' the blood then?" She started for the refrigerator where they stored bottles of animal blood acquired from a person known as a butcher.

"No' really, Edna. I think…aye, I need fresh today."

Edna glanced to the window. "But it's daytime."

Meirah always hunted at night, avoiding the prying eyes and curiosity of humans.

"I shall be careful." She stood. "I promise."

Edna nodded and removed Meirah's untouched plate.

"My apologies, Edna," said Meirah.

"No. No, I understand. Y'all be careful, sweetheart."

Meirah slipped out the back door, not bothering to change into her 'hunting attire.'

As she strolled toward the path to Hitchcock Woods, she stopped and turned her gaze to the rear of the mansion and the music room Dane had closed himself into.

"What are ye thinkin', my love?" she whispered. "What are ye doin'?"

She had not drunk from him in two years, since the night she'd followed her instincts to the east—his parent's home—and thus to him. The power of his blood had long vanished from her veins and with it her ability to sense him.

With a sigh, she turned away and dashed into the solace of the forest.

Dane

His hands hovered over the keys of the electronic keyboard, in a silent room laden with foam walls, that boasted nothing but a few amps, a sound mixer and several microphones.

Before Meirah, inspiration came from the pain and anguish within—then from Meirah herself. Now, however, his mind was a blank, at least where music was concerned.

Wine. He needed a drink.

Dane rose and moved to the small fridge he'd placed in the corner for drinks. Inside he found a stock of bottles; several bottles of water, and rum that had been there close to a year. He grabbed up a bottle of unopened red wine. Nothing fancy like the French wines stored away in the hole of his tiny wine cellar. Just—wine.

The cork screw he used to open the bottle left a clean imprint in the dust when he lifted it from the top of the fridge. No need for a glass. There were none to be found in the room anyway. Straight from the bottle, that was his preference. He brought it to his lips, but almost dropped it when the buzzer sounded, alerting him to someone at the music room door.

The 'RECORDING' light was not lit, which indicated he was not be disturbed. He took a swig from the bottle, pressed the intercom button.

"Leave me alone, Meirah! I'm working."

But the returning voice was not his wife's.

"Your tuna sandwich, Mr. Dane."

He stashed the wine bottle behind an amplifier, though why he didn't really know. It was, after all, his house! What was it about women that made him feel guilty in his own home?

He opened the door, grabbed up the plate and muttered, "thanks." A flash of his long-time housekeeper holding out a glass of soda swept his vision as he slammed the door. Rude, he knew, but Edna would understand.

He set the sandwich down and fetched the hidden bottle. Once again at the keyboard, he stared at the keys, picked at the bread crust. Habitually, he picked up the sandwich, intending to hand it to Wolfe, his loyal Doberman, when his heart clenched. The dog had passed months before and Dane often forgot that his companion for the past eleven years was gone. He tossed the uneaten sandwich back onto the plate.

Tired of trying to make sense of the dreams and nightmares, and still reconciling the loss of his dog, Dane took a long swig from the bottle before placing his fingers on the keys. *Time to work*. Bruce was a beast when a song was due for recording before a tour and Dane was not in the mood to deal with his lead guitarist's wrath.

Meirah

Within the blue sky she saw his eyes. In the black forest his long jet hair, and along the sinewy trail, his slender yet perfectly muscled body. It wasn't Dane Meirah saw, however, but a noble knight she had known long ago—Sir Kori Blackmore.

Of all his incarnations, she missed him most of all. Untainted by years of death and rebirth. Raised in a time when chivalry lived and men fought beyond inner need and emotion. When weakness was frowned upon, Sir Kori existed in a time that most closely resembled that in which she had been raised.

And though Dane was Sir Kori—or had been—living the life of a modern celebrity inevitably altered some aspects of who he had once been. By human years, Sir Kori died centuries ago, but to her he had been gone just over a Mikairian decade.

How different would her life be if she had saved the knight? She wondered. None of Dane's subsequent incarnations would have existed. There would be no Dane Bainbridge, the rock star, who turned to alcohol when times grew rough. Though she could not know for certain, she doubted the knight she had first fallen in love with would allow such weakness to befall him.

She loved Dane with all her heart, yet she could not help but wonder…

A symphony of voices brought her back to Hitchcock Woods and the present. Along the winding trail she traversed, several humans idled along. They were headed straight toward her. Their rants, raves and laughter were so loud even a deaf human could hear them coming. She dashed into the cover of shadow produced by the dense flora.

Unaware of her presence, they traipsed by her hiding place. Two young women and two young men. Teenagers. She watched from behind a large oak as they passed. One of the boys gleefully took the girl beside him around the waist, kissed her. She slipped on a moss-covered rock, lost her footing. With a whoop she went down. Worried, her male companion bent to her, expressing concern.

Meirah shook her head. Humans. She turned to disappear into the wood when the wind shifted direction. Over the scent of perfume and male body sweat, wafted a scent so enticing that it drew her back. Peering through the cover of brush, she watched as the girl who had fallen held her knee, her companions pining over her well being. A small crimson stream ran down her leg. *Human blood!* Normally Meirah could ignore it, but her mental state had rendered her weak to its enticement.

So busy they were aiding the girl, they did not notice her silently and slowly slink up behind them. So much blood, so sweet. So...necessary. Meirah's mind could think of nothing else. No consequences. No worry. Just simple and feral need. Only a few yards away now. Meirah could taste the warmth of the girl's blood in her mouth, flowing down her throat. But then voices sounded behind. More loud humans taking advantage of a warm day. They drew her from the stupor as the breeze rustled trees and brush and sent away the delicious aroma.

Realizing how close she was to the teenagers with more rounding the bend behind, Meirah bound into the wood so quickly the humans turned to see what had rustled the air before the others came into view, rushing to offer aid.

Distanced from the scent of the humans, Meirah leaned her head back against the smooth bark of a large cypress tree and closed her eyes, breath hard and fast. Nothing such as this had happened before in the years she had lived in this dimension. Too close! She conjured no images in her mind as her hands shook and she pressed her palms together to quell the movement.

But an image did appear behind closed lids. Sir Kori. She tried to change it, to see him as Dane Bainbridge, her husband, but the knight persisted. His eyes, so light blue boasting silver specks as to seem transparent, stared up at her as he lay on a marble floor, dying. The spark in those eyes dimmed and fogged over like a cloudy bleak day.

Meirah opened her own eyes to whisk the image away with the whispering wind, but in it she heard his name. *Kori!*

Her face wet with tears, she swiped at them in frustration and moved deeper into the forest where no humans dared tread. The wooded floor was thick with brambles, bushes, tall grasses and weeds. Emotions of fear and confusion swept through her and she found herself running. Faster and faster. Needing to get away from Sir Kori, his image and the remembrance of his death. So quickly she ran she hardly noticed the enormous animal that bolted nearby. She pulled out ahead of the beast and darted into a thicket. The scent of its blood pounded through her and she needed to take it, to *kill* it! Still as a lion stalking a zebra, even her breath halted instinctively. She had become the ultimate predator.

She listened, intent. The hooves crunched on dead leaves and she easily pinned its location in reference to hers. Silently, she crept, her feet bound by the dexer-hide boots she had been wearing when she crossed into the Mortal Dimension. They allowed her stealth no human-made footwear ever could. No beast could detect her. No animal in this world, however…

As the hoof beats halted, she parted the brush to see, and gasped! It stood still as a rabbit detected by a hawk, gazing in her direction. A massive rack of horns, brown-ticked coat, large humped withers.

A dexer!

Only yards from her refuge. Meirah was taken aback. How could the largest animal in Mikaire have followed into this dimension undetected?

Only but once had she taken down a dexer, drunk of its blood. One step in her transition into womanhood.

Kaeplan had been so jealous!

Kaeplan!

What or whom else could have followed her through the Main Looking Glass the night Mikaire died? Regardless, she couldn't abide the presence of such an anomalous creature as a dexer being seen in this dimension. Thus far, she had seen nothing on the television box, nor heard of anyone spying such a beast. Now she had reason to kill—a crime in Mikaire. A daily occurrence in this world.

As she had in Mikaire, she scrambled up a large oak tree, using its coarse bark and branches as footholds. She perched high above the path the dexer was following. And, as she expected, it moved on, walking slowly, guarded, beneath her lookout, towards the watering hole beyond.

Meirah edged out onto a thick branch, breath held. The substantial forest canopy gave the illusion of early eve and offered her fair protection. Even donned in a yellow tunic, she knew none could see her.

The dense brush below rustled angrily. Meirah readied herself. The animal came into sight below… The enormous horns, the ticked coat. She leapt, landed square onto the animal's back. Reaching to grab the hump as it faltered then righted itself, Meirah found only massively muscled withers. Her hands took hold of the thick fur. Realization struck her as she leaned in for the kill bite to its throat. This was no dexer, but a larger than normal buck deer. As the animal parried, frightened, she lost her grip and landed with a hard thud onto a thicket of thorns. The deer took off in the other direction and disappeared into the shadowy wood.

Meirah rose up slowly, untangling herself carefully from grabbing vines and prickers. She felt little pain, but upon inspection, she found her tunic torn at the sleeves and back, her breeches soiled. No major injuries marred her flesh, only a few scratches, one that bled through the cloth on her arm. The water hole was close and so she made her way to it.

Splashing water on her wounds staved the bleeding, though she found herself quite thirsty now. Water would have to do.

Squatting, she dipped her hands into the cool ripples, brought it to her lips. Water quenched the dryness in her mouth, but did nothing to fill the empty need for blood. She reached down for more…

A reflection along the surface caught her eye and stayed her hands. Something stirred. A ripple on the surface grew to ensconce the entire pool. An image materialized. Red hair. Meirah's hands, held just above the surface, trembled. Her heart skipped.

No! It couldn't be…

His image appeared in full then as the liquid ripples smoothed and cleared.

Kaeplan.

Meirah released a screech of utter terror as she scrambled to find her feet. She bolted into the wood, toward the mansion and the safety of the mortal world she had previously been desperate to escape.

-Three-

May 2015

"Continents drift. And so do hearts."
-John Mark Green

Kaeplan

Two days. A week. He couldn't be certain of the passage of time as he walked, growing weaker by the day. But what constituted a day in this dimension? He did not even know what dimension he had landed in.

By day, the brutal sun beat upon his exposed flesh. By night the air turned bitter and frigid. Naught around but endless dunes of sand. No shelter. No food. A barren wasteland lay in every direction.

As Kaeplan fought to find footing up yet another steep dune of yielding dry earth, a strange hissing sound from behind called his attention. He turned to find a dark wall blocked out the sun beyond. It moved and swirled and was headed straight towards him.

A sandstorm. They occasioned the Red Dust Mountains in Mikaire, but not so large. Instinct screamed at the need to find shelter that did not exist. He dropped onto the hot rolling sands and covered his arms over his head as the storm washed over him. Particles struck him like stones, tearing at his already tattered tunic and his flesh.

By the time the storm passed, he was buried. He remained still, even as the hiss of storm and wind dissipated. Sure the pain of pelting sand was well gone, he dug out. The warmth of the earth engulfed him.

And from that day forth, he buried himself during the frigid nights, allowing the warm sand to cradle his aching body.

More days and nights came and went, all the same in a world that never changed. Climbing from his ditch took all Kaeplan had left in him—and twice as much time. By now he had convinced himself this place must be an unclaimed dimension; one which no wizard had yet created. But, how did the sand and tiny animals exist if none had created them? It appeared as if a wizard had begun construction of a dimension but gave up before finishing. He knew of no such dimension, but then he had not seen them all. No one had. They existed in every moment of what mortals referred to as *time*. Unclaimed time slots held no notice in the Mortal Dimension. That moment merely skipped past. Only dimensions that fell, such as Mikaire had, created a ripple in the Mortal Dimension—a chaotic void, until such time it settled and became once again unclaimed time. And this dimension, beyond whichever time portal it existed, held naught on which to survive. He was sure he would die here.

Every step to get his feet beneath him was an agonizing burden. His boots had worn through and filled with hot sand from the holes at the sides, exposing calloused and welted flesh. With no repast, he did not heal as before. Periodically his feet bled and pained him more and each time he worried no more blood ran through his sunken veins. Though Mikairians were long-lived, he troubled over how much longer his heart would continue to beat under the stress of no sustenance, extreme heat and cold, and little rest. Even the sweat that had once soaked his clothing had ceased, which told him how dehydrated he had truly become. Even water, though it would not satisfy his hunger, would aid him during this road of his miserable journey.

Crouched on hands so sore even the soft sand beneath them cut like sharp pebbles, and knees raw where his breeches had torn, he managed to crawl forward, low as the belly of a pocturn. Except, unlike the small Mikairian critter whose large belly always dragged the ground, he had no stomach left. His arms like twigs, red hair matted and scorched, he could crawl no more than a few feet until even his shoulders could hold him up no more. He dropped into the fiery granules face first. Laboring his head to one side, he spat dust from his mouth. His tongue had swollen and became as dry as the landscape around him.

Just give up. Die already.

But he did not die. He lay unmoving under the squelching sun, flesh burning to painful welts. Open and exposed, Kaeplan prayed to the closest being to a god he had ever known...

Take me, Sakkana. Please. End my suffering.

But Sakkana was dead—murdered by that beast of a human who had stolen all from him—his love, his life.

This was Kaeplan's last thought before the pressing heat took over his conscious mind. Dark fell upon the world as he lay there, his awareness of the nighttime cold dim. Consciousness waned and waxed. But as he awaited death, a scent reached him... blood. It filled his senses like a welcome sign, and signaled his brain to awaken.

He forced his eyes open. The icy air of night settled over burnt flesh and came as a measure of relief. Though relief was a grave misconception, it was the blood that raised him from certain demise. Through the ringing in his ears came a sound. Distant at first, but nearing. A scuffling. Behind his line of sight. A whoosh then a thunk. Whoosh. Thunk.

Near his head.

Go on, he thought in delirium, *Eat me. Kill me.*

Sniffing. The creature assessed this odd lump of a being lying in its path.

Whoosh. Thump. Whoosh. Thump.

The creature came into sight before blurry vision. Short front legs, long back legs, a ticked brown coat. And blood—a lot of blood, pumped by a quick heartbeat. The critter half-walked, half-hopped near Kaeplan's face, sniffing at him. Its curiosity could mean its death—and his life.

He needed, however, to catch it. He drew in a deep and silent breath, allowing into his dying body its life essence.

Near his hand now.

He would have but one opportunity.

One last attempt at saving himself.

Fear and hope raged in his mind. Catch it and survive. Miss and die.

Drawing on the last of his reserve, he snatched outward... and caught the beast by the scruff of its neck. It screeched in surprise and fear. Kaeplan pulled it to himself as it struggled to free itself. Large back legs with thick sharp claws dug at his arms, but he did not let go. Pain could be ignored. Hunger could not.

Kaeplan's fangs pierced its fur and flesh. Blood—life-saving blood—poured into his mouth, onto his swollen tongue and soothed down a sore throat.

Bitter. Warm. Perfect.

He drank until the well of blood ran dry. The limp creature shrunk in his hand and he released it to rot in the desert. A crime in Mikaire, killing the animal one drank from, he hoped this dimension did not as well persecute for such an infraction.

Kaeplan threw his head back, drawing in a deep breath, allowing the strength of the crimson repast to refill withered veins. At long last, he pushed himself to his feet, still hungry but renewed enough to move on. One painful step...and another. Perhaps more of these animals existed beyond.

"Thank ye, Sakkana," he whispered.

He blinked to clear the haze from his eyes, and followed the tracks made by the animal. Where there was one there had to be another. If only to find it before his strength ran out or the winds covered the tracks, whichever came first.

Watching the movement of the moon, he discerned that another hour had passed. Then the sun. He welcomed the warmth as the fiery orb peered above the dunes, casting an orange hue over the wasteland.

And the trees just over the next hill.

He picked up his pace, sheer will keeping the excruciating pain from knocking him down yet again. Trees meant water. And water meant more critters from which to drink.

Stumbling up and over the next dune, Kaeplan spied an oasis. Though he didn't think he had it in him, he ran. The area came upon him like a small verdant paradise. Shade. Water. Food. Unable to keep his feet any longer, he tripped on a root and went down—and landed in a pool of water.

Creatures of many shapes and sizes scattered in surprise.

He sat up, waist-deep in liquid that cooled burnt flesh and eased pained knees, hands and feet. And he laughed like a Young

One with a new toy, shaking his head, soaked red hair tossing about, flinging droplets everywhere.

He took in the luxury of the shade, drew a satisfying breath, and gazed down. He gasped at the reflection on the surface before he realized the sunken skeletal being with darkened red flesh smeared with dirt, and matted disheveled hair was his own. Not wishing to see himself in such a poor state, he cupped his hands and dunk them into the pond, brought the liquid to parched and swollen lips and drank. Not his drink of choice, but the moisture penetrated dry muscles and squelched the need on his tongue. Water was a necessity for all living beings, even a Mikairian. Generally, he received enough of the life liquid in the blood he drank. Between the water he now consumed and the small amount of blood he had managed to squeeze from the hopping creature, Kaeplan's veins returned to life. Though still weak and horribly starved, he found within enough strength to catch more animals once they returned.

He climbed from the water and sat on a patch of soft grass at the pond's edge—and he waited. His thoughts turned to Meirah as he sat there, avoiding his own sad reflection. She was all that mattered now. He closed his eyes, allowing her image full reign of his mind's vision. He wondered where she was, what she was doing—where she had landed when she jumped through the Main Looking Glass. Was she in the same barren land as he? Worry overcame him then. Would she find what she needed to survive? He could not sense her, for he had never taken of her blood. He needed so desperately to see her that when he opened his eyes, her face stared back at him from the water. A thin veil of reflection.

A delusion of the mind. Or was it?

He reached towards her reflection, but as his hands neared the water, she vanished.

"Meirah!" he called, voice rough and dry. He pulled back, let the water settle. The only reflection now was his own sad face.

He sat back. Could he have actually seen her? Water could easily serve as a portal to time dimensions… and with enough blood—human blood—and strength, his powers would strengthen and he could find an empty slot in the fabric of time and create a new dimension—his own dimension!

Gazing at the sparkling pond, hope and renewal filled his

heart.

"I shall come for ye, Meirah. I shall break the portal that separates us—and you shall be mine at last."

-Four-

December 7, 2016

"The reason for anger is always fear."
-Eloise Lownsbery

Meirah

The woods—the world—passed by in a blur as Meirah rushed towards the estate. She did not slow even as she reached the back door to the mudroom. She reached for the doorknob, but missed it. Moving at such lightning speed prevented her from trying again and she hit the wood and glass door head on. It exploded with her force. Fortunately, the kitchen door was already open.

Her first momentary awareness was of two cats that scurried in a panic from the room. She ran, panting and crying into Edna's arms. She could have knocked the older woman down, but she stopped short as the warm meaty arms surrounded her in maternal comfort.

"Mrs. Dane... what is wrong?"

Edna held Meirah close, letting her weep as words, incoherent even to her own ears, spilled through her panic.

"Okay. Okay... shhh. Mrs. Dane, please sit..." Edna guided Meirah into a chair at the table in the breakfast nook, then pulled a chair close, sat and took Meirah's trembling hands in her own.

Meirah focused on her breathing, calming herself enough to speak.

I-I saw him," she huffed. "He is here!"

"Who did ya see?"

"K-Kaeplan!"

Dane

Relaxation washed over him. With an entire bottle of wine running through his veins, Dane at last finished the song the band needed for their upcoming tour.

He opened the studio door in time to hear a loud crash coming from downstairs.

"What the f—"

Meirah's panicked weeping voice cut off the expletive.

Dane sprinted down the hall and the wide staircase, skipping one or two steps, suddenly sober with adrenaline, in his rush. As he rounded into the kitchen, the first thing he saw was the open back door, wood and hinges splintered, glass littered the floor. Horrible images stampeded his imagination when he caught sight of Edna and Meirah sitting in the nook. Meirah was clearly upset.

Dane rushed to his wife as Edna stood, allowing him the seat she occupied. Edna moved to the kitchen door, brushed away the debris with her foot, and closed the door, thus preventing any cats who might return to the kitchen from escaping, as she went to get a broom and pan to clean up the mess.

Dane took Meirah's hands into his own. His wife's face was red and damp with tears, emerald eyes red-rimmed.

"What happened?" he asked, frightened at the possibility of what could cause such fear in his steady, strong wife.

"Oh, Dane," she wept. "I s-saw him. I saw Kaeplan."

Dane's chest tightened, his mouth went dry. "*Where?*"

"I-In the water. The r-reflection… clear as my own," she choked.

Dane leaned in as Meirah's arms enveloped his neck. He pulled her petite form into his lap and held her close. She shivered uncontrollably.

Under normal circumstances, most would dismiss her accusation as unwarranted paranoia. But, as he himself had experienced the true magic of time dimensions and wizards who required human blood to keep their worlds alive, worry plagued him. Could she truly have seen the enemy they both believed dead?

His nightmares, in which Kaeplan played a prominent role, were all too real in his mind. He thought of his most recent nighttime escapades—paradise and hell. Heat, sand, even water…and death!

Then the women came and all was paradise. If the past had taught him anything, however, it was that Kaeplan's presence brought him nightmares from past lives. The timing coupled with the reoccurrence of such nightmares couldn't be ignored.

Dane stood, lifting Meirah into his arms. He carried her upstairs as she pressed her face into the crook of his chest as if in hiding. Once in their bedroom, he placed her onto the California King bed, grabbed the blanket from the foot of the bed and pulled it over her, tucking it about her shoulders, then sat beside her.

She stared up at him, emerald eyes still glistening with moisture and terror.

"It's ok, Meirah. I'm here. You're safe." He stroked her forehead and her hair gently, lovingly.

Eventually, her lids drooped and her eyes closed. He remained until her breathing slowed into slumber. He kissed her forehead then stood. Carefully as not to wake her, he silently exited the room. Bruce would arrive soon, wanting the song he had written.

-Five-

December 18, 2016

*"A great marriage is not the union of the perfect couple,
but an imperfect couple who accepts and embraces each other's
flaws." -Unknown*

Dane

"Take me wi' ye!" Meirah pleaded, pacing the bedroom as Dane packed clothes into the suitcase open on the bed. "I do no' want tae be alone!"

Dane folded yet another black tee shirt into the case. He sat on the bed, patted the spot beside him. Meirah complied, sitting where he referenced, hands in her lap like a child about to be scolded.

Dane reached over, took her hand and brought it to his lips. Emerald eyes turned a sideways gaze to him. He kissed each of her slender fingers until he saw those eyes soften, then he spoke, keeping his hand in hers, softly caressing the delicate flesh with his thumb.

"Meirah, sweetheart," he cooed, being deliberately charming. "You hate being on tour with me. Remember?"

Her eyes pooled with tears and then disappeared behind lowered lashes. She nodded slowly. "But I was new here then," she countered quietly. "So many places. So many humans. The scent o' their blood—I can control it now. Ye were so busy, I scarce saw ye. I do no' want tae be alone here."

Dane released a breath. How could he make her understand, to remember what she had gone through with last year's tour? Her fear of seeing Kaeplan again played in her mind and caused her to forget. He knew this. He knew *her*.

"I worry," he said carefully, "of a repeat of last time. Neither of us can go through that again."

Meirah squeezed his hand. "But it willna, I promise."

A tear ran down her cheek. His heart broke for her, but he needed to be tough—for them both. "How could it be different?" he asked sincerely. "Nothing's changed. There will still be women—"

"I know!" she interrupted. "I promise no' tae be jealous this time."

"You *bit* a fan, Meirah!"

"But she kissed ye—in front o' me." Meirah defended weakly.

"And I've explained more than once—it means nothing to me. She wanted an autograph, an innocent kiss. It happens all the time. I won't be able to concentrate with you there. This is my career. Women are drawn to rock stars," he attempted to explain so she would understand, though he'd had this conversation with her on several occasions. She would be fine at first, but then a fan would come along and chaos ensued. He seriously doubted her jealous nature had disappeared in a year. If anything, she had become more protective of him.

"As Sir Kori I was like a rock star of the time. Women wanted me then, too. But I was loyal to Julianna's memory—just as I am loyal to you now."

Meirah nodded. "I willna bite anyone. Ye have my word."

Dane shook his head. "You'll be happier here—with Edna and the animals. You can care for the horses, ride every day. You'll be safe, and you won't feel alone. I will call every day, promise."

She began to weep then, her body trembling with emotion. Dane tried not to let this sway his decision. He reached around her shoulder, pulled her close.

"Meirah. By now you know my life on the road. You'd still be alone, just as last time. I have to work. No distractions. And Caitlyn will not be there this time. No wives or girlfriends will be present to keep you company."

He purposefully neglected to inform her that Bruce and their manager, Gary, forbade any significant others on this tour. Too much drama had interfered the last time. They needed to concentrate on their music and the new line-up.

"Meirah," he whispered as her tears flowed free and strong. "You have to skip this tour. Maybe you can come on the next one."

Though he doubted it—unless Meirah could truly control her jealousies. No one could abide the same shenanigans as last time when a fan had visited his hotel room for an autograph, an innocent kiss on the cheek. All she had wished for was to meet her favorite celebrity, but was met by a jealous Mikairian wife. In a rage, Meirah had grabbed the poor girl away and sunk her fangs into the fan's throat. If Dane had not interfered when he did— yanking Meirah off the girl—Meirah might have taken her life. Fortunately, no law suit had come of it, but the girl did go to the media. They'd had a field day with the story.

Rock Star Holed up with Vampire Bride.

It had taken Dane and Gary much anguish and headache to tone down the rumors—and months before the media found something more interesting to focus upon.

Now, however, Meirah refused to give in. "And what of yer nightmares?" she wept.

He knew well the true reason for her desperation. Kaeplan, or whatever it was that had spooked her eleven days ago, convinced her he lived, crossed into the Mortal Dimension behind her, and would take her away. Since then, she had hardly left Dane's side. She accompanied all rehearsals, recording sessions, parties and even small errands. No longer did she hunt, nor ride the horses into Hitchcock Wood. She'd become his constant shadow.

He released her and stood. He decided to utilize the method he'd heard from so many who were annoyed at Meirah's constant clinging, distracting all. *Tough love!*

"Meirah... This is my *work*! If I worked a nine to five job you'd not be able to accompany me. This is no different. *Let...it...go!* You cannot come this time. Period!"

Oh, the guilt that ran through him at that moment.

Her cheeks, already red with tears, grew several shades darker. Flames burned in the once soft verdant eyes.

"*Fine!*" she bellowed, scaring Lucy, who slept on the pillow. The cat bolted into hiding under the bed. "Go then! Enjoy your tour and your women! If Kaeplan comes tae take me ye will be sorry!"

Then she was gone.

Words unspoken sat upon his open lips. He stood to retrieve her when the blast of the limo's horn sounded from the drive. He needed to go. With a heavy heart, he grabbed up his travel bags and moved downstairs. He would call her when he arrived in Vegas.

He gazed out the limo window as it pulled down the drive, hoping to see Meirah looking out a window but she was not there. He ducked back into the limo when view of the mansion disappeared, guilt plaguing his every thought.

-Six-

"Guilt is anger directed at our ourselves—for what we did or did not do." -Peter McWilliams

Dane was dreaming of Meirah when the thunk of the landing gear shook him half-awake. He tried to stay in the dream a bit longer, to be with his wife, but apparently that wasn't to be...

"Wake up, Sleepyhead," said Bruce, sitting beside him, shaking Dane's shoulder as the plane descended into McCarran International in Las Vegas.

"Yeah. Yeah. I'm awake," he snapped.

"Grumpy Gus. Are you going to be like this through the whole tour?" Bruce smirked, one dark brow raised inquisitively.

"Only if you're lucky," Dane grumbled.

Once within the airport, Dane removed his cell phone from his pocket. The time read *10:33pm*. He'd updated the phone to Pacific Time before they'd left, so he knew it was *1:33am* at home. He opened his contacts and tapped on Meirah's picture.

One ring. Two rings. Three. Four.

"C'mon, Meirah, pick up," he whispered into his cell. "Pick up. Pick up." As if he could mentally will her to answer. But then...

"This is Meirah...um...I am no' here. Oh, I might be here. Maybe I can no' answer now. Call back." BEEP.

"Meirah, sweetie," Dane said, not even sure if she remembered how to check messages. "Please call me."

"C'mon, Dane. Let's go. I need sleep," said Bruce.

"Yeah, ok," he muttered before hanging up the phone and placing it back into his pocket. He followed the others to the buses, which had driven to Nevada ahead of the band.

Meirah
South Carolina
December 19, 2016

She stared at the small screen on her cell phone, which Dane had bought her six months earlier. Music played from it—a song from Dark Myst that Dane had written for her—and on the screen was his name and the time: *1:33am*. With a sigh, she tapped the red ignore button and tossed the phone beside her on the bed. She picked up her book and continued to read.

Sitting alone with only a couple cats for company on the large bed that Dane called a California King, Meirah tried to concentrate on the words she had already read twice. But, after reading the same paragraph three times with no comprehension of what it said, she gave up. She put the book aside and flicked off the bedside lamp.

The bed was too large and cold without Dane's warm body beside her. Since she arrived two years prior, she had never slept without him. Even on the nights when he would fall asleep downstairs in front of the television box, she would wake and head down to him. He would follow her upstairs and they would make love before falling asleep wrapped in each other.

Even last year, when he had gone on tour, she had gone along and his warmth was always there, even on the tour bus, though the bunk was small and close she did not mind.

But, now, as she moved to place an arm around him, she found herself grasping only empty bedsheets.

And no sex!

His appetite was as insatiable as her own. In Mikaire a united couple could mate only once, unless a baby was not produced. Twice if needed to get pregnant. This was the law in the small dimension of her birth. But, here, they could make love anytime they wished and with Dane it was so perfect, so pleasurable, she never denied it.

She missed his hard-muscled naked body beside her, his soft breath as he slept, even his luxurious hair tickling her face when she curled close behind him.

Sometimes, when she was sound asleep, he would press his arousal against her until she woke, she would always roll to him and take him into her. And again in the morning, in the shower, when he came home from rehearsal, and of course before sleep. Two or three times a day was never too much for either of them. Everywhere and anywhere.

Was he wanting her as badly right now, she wondered. She knew about masturbation. Dane had taught her that she could pleasure herself, just as he could, when need arose. But she had tried and it simply was not the same and held none of the desired effects.

Meirah tired herself out with her emotion, and when Dane's cat Lucy curled up close to her, offering a bit of warmth, only then did she finally fall asleep.

Dane
December 19, 2016

He awoke at 10am and tried Meirah one more time. Still no answer. He suspected she was ignoring him. Still angry. However, to be sure she was ok, he phoned Edna, who reassured him "Mrs. Dane was fine," they were out shopping, and he should give her some time. He decided he would wait a day, hoping she would cool off and answer.

He had little time all day to think on it much, however, as the entire day from there on forth was booked with interviews, going over the line-up and rehearsals, sound checks, as well as some last-minute recording.

December 20th, 2016
5:00pm Pacific Time

Sound check that afternoon went uneventfully. Everyone, including the orchestra, arrived on time. They chose several songs, including one of their new numbers that included a twist away from previous routines. Rather than his usual dance and swordplay alone, as he'd always performed, Dane shared the stage with

Sabrina, the head violinist who'd been with Dark Myst from the beginning.

The song began with her electric violin playing out a haunted melody, then joined by Bruce's metal guitar riffs.

Sabrina stepped to her mic as the music toned to a more melancholy level. Her rich soprano voice told tale of love lost in an era gone bad by nuclear war. On cue, Dane stepped up to his mic and sang his part about waiting for his love, for as long as it might take. They rehearsed not only the song, but the movements and choreography as well.

More than once during the song, Dane caught Sabrina gazing over to him and offering a wink in his direction. He returned a smile, thinking nothing of it.

7:56pm Pacific Time

The venue was packed to capacity. Backstage, the cacophonous roar of thousands echoed throughout each hallway and room.

Dressed in his stage costume, Dane remained in the dressing area just a bit after the others. He held in his hand his cell phone, staring at the screen, hoping to see a missed call from his wife. Nothing.

Outside the closed door, chants and stomping feet shook the arena. Two minutes until showtime. He should be near the stage entrance with the others. Instead, he stood with his finger hovered over the contact picture of Meirah. He drew in a deep breath and tapped the button. He listened intently as the phone rang. Disappointment surged through him as her phone went to voicemail. He hung up.

A knock sounded on the dressing room door. "Thirty seconds, Dane."

Distracted by worry, he hardly heard. What if Meirah was right? What if Kaeplan had come through, was alive, had found her? He would call Edna.

"Dammit, Meirah. You're not here and you still manage to distract me!"

He searched for Edna's number in his contacts when another, harder knock sounded. "Time, Dane!"

Frustrated, he tossed his phone onto the sofa and rushed out of the dressing room just as the melody of Bruce's guitar, Adrian's drums and Stephan's bass crashed together for the first song. He ran out onstage, cape billowing behind him and grasped up his mic just in time to belt out the first line of the first song of the evening. The crowd went wild and he was lost in the music.

Meirah
December 20, 2017

In the first dream, Sir Kori came to her. He was locked in his cell in Mikaire, pleading as he once had, for her to free him. The hand that held the key trembled as she fought to fit it into the lock, but it resisted her attempt to turn it.

Behind her, footfalls sounded, descending on her. She turned, expecting the night Prison Master, but instead Kaeplan stood there, red hair matted with dirt, amber eyes aflame.

"I told ye no' to touch it," he said. "The armor o' the knight. I warned ya."

Meirah shook her head. "Ye were no' there!"

"I will be…" he grinned. "The mortal will only cause ya pain in the future. Come back wi' me, tae my dimension. Ye're mine, Meirah."

She spun away and the dream took her elsewhere—beneath the scorching sun of the Red Dust Mountains in Mikaire. The Main Looking Glass towered before her, its surface flickered and sparkled like the waves on a great lake. She reached a hand towards the glass-like surface. Her fingers made contact, but did not penetrate the portal.

She jerked back, fingers dripping. Water. But how…?

Looking back to the Mirror, a curious image shimmered on its surface.

Dane! He reached for her, face twisted in fear and anguish.

Her heart raced with need. She dashed towards the portal that separated them, leapt into it. Pain. Her body felt it would break in two. But water surrounded her then, took her into its depths. She thrashed to find the surface, yet was drawn deeper underneath a watery cage. Her lungs burned with the need for air. She would drown.

As she readied to take that last breath, for she could hold it no longer, a hand plunged through the water's surface, grasped hers, dragged her up from impending death.

She landed hard on wet sand, coughing liquid from her lungs.

Strong but gentle arms reached beneath her body, lifted her against a warm chest.

"Oh, Dane," she choked.

Then she gazed up to look into his silver-blue eyes—and was staring into the amber eyes of Kaeplan.

Meirah awoke screaming. Lucy skittered from the bed as her wails filled the mansion, reaching the ears of no one.

The sudden music startled her—the cell phone. *Dane.* *10:56pm.*

She grasped for it, but her hand hit it awkwardly and sent it flying off the bed and under the antique bureau.

"*Shite!*"

She scurried out of bed, dropped to the floor and reached beneath the dresser as the phone sang. Out of her reach, she called out, "Dane, wait!" as if he could hear her. But the music stopped then.

She rose to her feet, grabbed the first thing she saw—a sword—from the wall. Using it as an extension of her arm, she stretched once again beneath the furniture. The sword hit it, sent it spinning out from under the bureau to rest against the armoire.

She snatched it up, hit the redial and waited, trembling as it rang and rang. No answer. When his voice message came on she hung up.

 -Seven-

June 2015

"A hunter must stalk his prey until the hunter becomes the hunted. Then the prey becomes the predator. Then the predator and the hunter fight. -Unknown (movie quote)

Kaeplan

Reluctant to leave the oasis, Kaeplan remained there for a week. Plenty of the long-legged hopping critters came to the water hole, offering him enough blood to survive, even heal, but only human blood—and a lot of it—would spark the Wizard within.

Many nights, as he lay under the sand, fear plagued his mind that he would never find a human in this dimension, in whatever time it existed. No human blood meant he was stuck here forever, existing on animals, his Wizard powers lost forever.

On the eve of his seventh day at the immutable oasis, Kaeplan awoke to a scent he had not experienced in far too long. His stomach grumbled and ached with need. He extracted himself from his nighttime grave, exposing himself to the rigid night wind. However, the scent grew stronger above ground. Then the voices reached him. Did he dare hope?

Kaeplan crawled to a copse of palmetto bushes and hid behind wide leaves and palm fronds. Carefully, he parted them, allowing him a clear view of those whose blood had awakened his need.

Dressed from head to toe in loose linens he counted five as they rode in on the most odd-looking of beasts. Long gangly faces, crooked sinewy legs and a hump that put a dexer to shame. No antlers or horns. When they came to a halt, he saw one of the beasts carried no rider, but was burdened only by many packs.

One released a bellow that made Kaeplan cringe, as it stopped, dropping to its knees to allow its rider to dismount. But it was not the beasts—which smelled terrible—whose blood roused his senses. As the breeze brought the rider's scent towards him, the sweetness near made him swoon. Yes, he had experienced that delicious aroma before.

Human blood!

He was not sure which offered him the most relief and exaltation; the realization he was indeed in the Mortal Dimension, which meant Meirah was within his reach, or the knowledge humans would feed him tonight, allowing his Wizard powers to surface at last.

But to take them all; that was his dilemma. As they unpacked the humped beasts, he could not help but notice the swords that glinted in the moonlight attached to each human's hip.

Patience.

When the time was right, he would take them one by one until he'd fully consumed their lives. Not yet, however, and so he waited.

By daybreak they had set up a camp of sorts—strange structures made of a light material that fluttered in the breeze. He watched their activities from the depths of his own shelter of fronds and brush. They hunted the same hopping creatures he had been feeding from. Rather than consume the blood, however, they placed skinned carcasses on sticks over the fire to cook the meat, which they consumed heartily. So much work for a small meal.

Night came on quickly in the desert and all but one disappeared within their shelters, set in close proximity to the others.

The lone human sat by the fire, his attire hiding his visage. In his hands he grasped a weapon, but Kaeplan did not know what manner of protection it provided.

A guard, though what threat they expected he did not know. They were not aware of his presence and the animals posed no danger.

The night grew cold. Kaeplan longed to burrow beneath the warm sands, but the idea of human blood was far too enticing, even though he had not fed all day. Besides, he needed the cover of night if he was to take so many unawares.

He hugged the trees and brush closely, moving silently closer to their shelters… and the guard on duty. He closed the gap between them relatively quickly. His timing needed to be precise. Take out the guard in silence, then the sleeping humans would be simple to dispatch in their singular sleep quarters. He was sure, with his stealth, speed and awareness, that his plan would be a success.

Keeping to the shadows away from the fire, he slunk to the side of one of the shelters and remained tight to its shadows as he moved around it and came up behind the guard. He drew in a deep breath then moved in, quick and silent.

He wrapped one arm around the guard's waist, taking him by utter surprise. Startled, the human reacted immediately. He raised the weapon—a gun, Kaeplan realized. He had seen them in Meirah's books from this world. Kaeplan reached out with speed no human could match and wrenched it from the guard's hand. He tossed it far, heard it land with a thud on the dense sands outside the oasis.

Though dressed in many layers of cloth, Kaeplan found the throat of the human easily. He pressed its head to the side, moved in to drive his fangs into the pumping vein. With surprising speed and conviction, the human spun on him. The sharp blade of a knife glistened red in the light of the fire.

A sharp pain cut across his chest. Kaeplan stumbled back, releasing the human.

The man let out a high pitched bellow. A war cry. Kaeplan heard the rustle of the shelters, footfalls, voices. A language he did not understand.

Run!

Instinct forced him to break away and he bolted to the cover of the trees and bushes. The human voices grew in number and volume. All had awoken, emerged from their shelters. They spread out and like bugs seeking food, they swarmed the area. Kaeplan was now their prey.

-Eight-

December 20, 2016

"In my nightmares, someone else is calling me theirs."

Dane
Las Vegas, NV
8:02pm

Cacophonous bellows shook the arena. Yet he could not see the audience. The stage lights were dimmed. Dane stood on the platform behind the wood and steel head of one of the two dragons that faced each other on either side of the stage.

The spotlight, hot and bright, came up then, nearly blinding him, and he peered down. The stadium still black, an occasional truss spotlight sliced across thousands of indistinct faces and bodies, already on their feet, leaping, cheering, hollering.

The usual routine, yet tonight nothing felt typical. Guilt plagued his heart, and this usually exhilarating routine seemed more of a chore. She had not answered his calls, none of them. Angry or not, Meirah was not petty, nor did she hold grudges. The ego and actions of humans was not in her nature.

As the platform lowered, Dane forced her from his mind. No place here for distraction or lack of concentration, lest he disappoint thousands of paying fans. He forced the excitement of being onstage, the music, the love from fans take him away from his concerns, as ever-growing as they were.

Adrian's heavy fast drumming followed by Stephan's driving bass, and the nerves that plagued Dane's gut became a welcome and familiar feeling. More like home than even his estate, or hotels or the tour bus. This is what he lived for!

No longer did Dane utilize the pseudo chains and bare torso of the past. The scars from his torment in Mikaire forever altered his stage presence. His new costume, still black and adorned with a shredded-hem cape, now allowed only a view of his unmarred chest. On his arms leather bands hid the marks of the knife that bled him. His back was covered as well, hiding the scars from a flogging meant to punish and humiliate his act of defiance and self-protection.

Though still apprehensive of heights, no longer did the platform that raised him above the audience make his stomach twist.

If not for the nightmares and paranoid episodes that followed, he might need to thank Sakkana for giving Sir Kori ever-lasting life.

Bruce's guitar hit the first hard note simultaneously with the landing of Dane's platform. He leapt forward to his microphone. But he wasn't alone…

Unexpectedly, and veering from the well-practiced routine, Sabrina stepped forth, following his steps, to *his* mic, abandoning her own. Together they began the song, faces unnecessarily close, like two lovers meeting after a lengthy absence. So close, he could smell her perfume over the usual scents of sweat and machine-made smoke. What was she doing?

When the pyrotechnics exploded, signaling the end of the song, he moved away to her mic. The lights went down and the audience exploded.

The next song began with resounding cheer and applause, and when the lights rose, she was there again—singing so close their mouths nearly touched.

Dane danced across the stage, in an attempt to make this variation from routine appear normal, to his own mic. She followed, her colorful dress flowing with her supple moves, exposing legs so well-shaped Dane almost missed the chorus. He turned his gaze to the audience, the dragons, the stage castle behind them—anywhere but on her. This was no turn-on, he was outraged.

The lights dimmed for the next song and relief flooded him as he moved to his piano and sat for the next song, a ballad about a woman named Lorna scorned by love. He hoped Sabrina's charade was over. She grabbed up her violin from its place by Stephan's now empty and darkened drum riser. The tune was a duet accompanied only by piano and violin. More classical than rock.

Dane cracked his knuckles and placed his fingers on the keys, began to play as a spotlight shone down only on him. He became so engrossed in the song, he was almost startled when the crowd roared at a moment when they were normally silent. He gazed up and across the piano to find Sabrina sitting seductively on his Steinway, naked legs fully bared. As she wasn't too close, he let it go.

She played her part beautifully and the audience went dead silent. But then she began to sing...perfect, except... Dane swore he heard the name Meirah when she sung about Lana. Had Sabrina just changed the name purposely? He continued on, convinced he was hearing things until the next chorus. He was sure this time— she sung "Meirah" where the words called for Lana. Rage broiled within him at such audacity. His concentration faltered for only a moment, but experience allowed him to hide it well. Relief washed over his anger at the song's finale. Sabrina took her place in back with the orchestra and Dane once again held center stage—alone and much relieved.

The moment the last encore finished, Dane ran offstage, snatched a towel from a stagehand, and wiped the sweat from his face and hair. Sabrina, cleaning her electric violin, sat at the far end of the backstage area. Dane walked over as she packed the instrument into its case. This was his band, his show. Such nerve she held at varying from the routine.

Sabrina looked up as Dane approached. "Oh, Dane. Hi," she said, smiling.

He, however, was not amused. "What was *that*?"

"What was what?" She bit her lip innocently and offered a small grin.

"You know what," he snapped. Her actions onstage were bad enough, but to pretend nothing untoward had taken place... "Why did you change the choreography? And you changed Lana to Meirah! What the fuck, Sabrina, was all that?"

Deep red lips parted to speak when the band's manager, Gary, strolled over. He wore a larger than life grin on his face.

"I don't know why you two changed the routine," he said. "But the audience *loved* it! Keep it up."

He sauntered away before Dane could contest.

Sabrina stood, lifted her violin case, blew Dane a kiss and strode off, proud of herself.

Meirah
12:01am
December 20, 2016

Meirah sighed as she settled into the hot water. A bath. That was just what she needed now. After numerous nightmares and missing her husband, the relaxation would do her well.

The tub seemed so large without Dane to accompany her. She reached to the switch to flick on the spa. The water bubbled comfortingly around her. She was not sure how long she had sat in the tub, for her mind drifted.

The water had grown cold. She flicked off the spa and the water went still. More relaxed now, her hand ducked beneath the surface to open the drain. When she saw his face, she halted, fear staying her movements.

No…!

Kaeplan stared up at her from the water, her hand began to tremble moving the water, causing small waves. Still he was there—and he looked directly at her as if he saw her, watched her, naked in the tub.

She panicked, pulled the drain lever. As the swirling water made its way down like a liquid tornado, she screamed. Kaeplan had not disappeared.

"NO!" she screeched, leaping from the tub. She slipped on the smooth floor and went down awkwardly, one leg still over the tub rim, the other out in front of her. She scrambled to remove herself, falling onto the tiles like a wet fish. She grasped at a towel, wrapped it quickly around her body.

As she lay on the floor, her breath came hard and fast. How could Kaeplan visit her in her tub? She had fallen asleep. Perhaps she had dreamt him? Yes, that must be it. But, she had not been asleep at the pond in Hitchcock. Why and how was he there?

She reached up, grasped the edge of the tub, lifted herself. Slowly, shaking, she peered over the edge. The water had emptied. No one was there. Just an empty jacuzzi. She sighed.

That was enough for her! Fearfully, she rose to her feet and dashed into the bedroom. She felt completely exposed. Though logic told her he was not there, still she felt Kaeplan's eyes on her. Quickly, she donned her night dress and ducked into bed under the thick coverlets. But sleep did not find her. She was too frightened. She dared not ramble through the mansion…what if Kaeplan had materialized there?

Pulling the blankets over her head, she knew she could no longer be alone in this big house without her husband.

-Nine-

June 2015

"I'm just suffering from extreme hunger."
-Brian Spring

Kaeplan

From within his shelter of sand, Kaeplan heard the footfalls of the humans all around him. The muffle of the strange tongue, the smell of human blood as if it seeped through the soft earth.

An hour or more they searched. Though the language was foreign, their frustration at not finding the beast in which they searched for was clear and obvious.

All talking began to fade as they gave up their search and rambled back to their shelters. Kaeplan realized then they would be on high guard. He needed to alter his strategy. These humans were a bit more cunning than he had ever given them credit. He needed their blood desperately—he would not survive much longer without it.

He dragged himself from the ditch, shook and brushed the dust from his hair and clothes.

The oasis was dotted with a wide variety of tees, but their trunks were too slender as to provide much in the way of shelter.

The sky, speckled with stars and a bright moon, swept light along the vast landscape. Though human eyesight was not as superior as his own, too much light from above would reveal him easily.

Kaeplan considered waiting another night, but the he risked the chance the humans would move on, taking with him what could be his only hope. The emptiness grew within him, both physically and mentally. His mind had begun to swim like Sakkana's srependile.

Sitting amongst a copse of dense brush, he concentrated. He would need wits and strength if he was to take so many humans—and he could certainly not take them all at once.

Drawing in a deep breath, he prepared himself and stood. A plan came to mind and he had but one opportunity to make it work.

The human's shelters were situated fairly close together yet far enough apart he felt he could make his way behind, and take one at a time. Remaining crouched, he slunk from one copse to the next until he had made it around and behind one of the small tents. Hugging the fragile structure, he could hear the human within snoring.

Asleep. Perfect.

Kaeplan dropped to the ground and crawled through the sand like an insect. The shelters being temporary, gaps beneath allowed a perfect and obscure entrance inside. He slithered beneath the shelter wall. The man slumbered on a blanket set on the sand. No beds. The human was fully dressed in heavy robes against the chilly night, though he had removed the head dressing and his long black hair splayed about the rolled blanket beneath his head.

Kaeplan stiffened as the man stopped snoring, let out a grunt that resulted in the expelling of gas from his body. The human rolled to his side, head bent at an angle, which revealed the dark skin of his throat.

With swift yet silent movements, Kaeplan slunk to him and in one quick motion he placed a hand over the man's mouth. No more warning cries.

The black eyes flew open. Before he could resist, however,

Kaeplan found the artery pumping hard with fear and before any struggle could ensue, Kaeplan's fangs sunk easily into the soft flesh.

So long ago had Kaeplan tasted human blood—not since Dane's tiny drops had entered his mouth two years past. And though this human's blood did not carry the same strength, with each warm mouthful he felt his energy renewed.

In Mikaire, only Sakkana had been allowed to drink from a human, to take life into himself. Kaeplan had survived until now only on the blood of animals in his now destroyed home dimension, yet never allowed to take enough to end the animal's life.

But he had been born to rule his own dimension—born to be a wizard! Taking the life of a human was a necessary step towards this goal.

Kaeplan reveled in this first human kill—every drop a succulent life-assuring nectar. As he filled himself with the blood of this man, his veins expanded, each muscle taking in the nutrients needed to invigorate him, to offer the strength he required to one day possess the magic of Sakkana.

Kaeplan's body lightened and grew heavy simultaneously. He flew as if he possessed wings. The perfect drug. But then the human's heart stopped beating and the succulent blood ceased its flow. Kaeplan pulled away. The human was dead, and no one heard, no one was the wiser. His plan was successful. Time to move on to the next.

By the time he had drunk from the last sleeping human, only the guard remained. But he now possessed the vigor to take him easily. His weapons were no match for Kaeplan's heightened power.

In an audacious move, he stepped from the last tent, grabbing up a sword that lay beside his last victim. To say this human was startled would be an understatement. He moved quickly towards his weapon. But to Kaeplan, body pumping with the blood of the guard's companions, his movements were slow and sluggish. He slashed the sword once. The guard went down, grasping his throat which pumped blood that spewed out uncontrollably.

Before the food could be lost in the sand Kaeplan dropped to his knees, placed his mouth over the gaping wound and drank quickly, draining the guard who had fought him earlier in the evening.

The heartbeat died fast. Kaeplan rose up and closed his eyes, reveling in the power that coursed through him. The wizard within had been born.

-Ten-

December 20, 2016

"Stop cheating on your future with your past."

Dane
Las Vegas, NV

Chains encircled his body. His arms were bound. He struggled but the cold metal tightened painfully around naked flesh. Panic overcame him and he screamed out in frustration, waking himself in the process.

"Son of a bitch!" Dane exclaimed as he untangled his body from the hotel sheets and tossed them aside.

He sat up, dragged his hand through his hair, still damp from his after-concert shower. His mind was hopping, worry over Meirah preventing restful sleep. After the concert, he'd checked his phone and saw a missed call from Meirah. But he had been onstage. By the time he was able to return the call, there was once again no answer. She could have been asleep as the time, even on the east coast, was late.

He needed to speak with her, to apologize for being so brash before leaving. If she had only understood that he didn't always have control over the rules. The decision to not include significant others on this tour had not been made by him, and he had to abide. Besides, he'd also agreed to it, and figured Meirah would be okay with staying behind; she'd seemed so unhappy on the last tour. And she probably would have—if only she hadn't seen Kaeplan!

He reached to the bedside table, flipped on the light and grabbed up his cell phone. One more try. He pressed Meirah's contact number. The phone didn't even ring—her voice message came up immediately.

"Shit, Meirah, what the hell is going on?" he said to the phone. Either her phone was off, the battery had died or…

The only other thought was too horrible to think about.

Rising, he padded to the hotel suite's bar, opened the small fridge. He'd requested it be stocked with rum and red wine. Situated within were several small bottles of rum and one bottle of Chardonnay. Yuck. One wine he despised. And the rum bottles were so small he could drink all five and feel nothing. He grabbed one of two full-sized bottle of vodka. Not really a vodka drinker, especially without orange juice, he figured beggars can't choose. It would have to do.

He twisted off the top, tilted the bottle to his lips. The burn cascaded like an acidic waterfall into his stomach. His nerves calmed a bit. He sat on the edge of the bed and chugged.

A soft knock sounded on the door.

Dane glanced to the clock. 3:15am.

Who in the hell…

Sighing, he set the bottle on the nightstand—or at least he thought he did. The bottle hit the carpet with a dull thud, precious liquid spilling out into the fibers.

"*Shit!*"

Another knock.

Leaving the bottle, he stood and moved to the door. "Who is it?" he snapped, rather than look through the peek hole.

A muffled feminine voice came through the door. "Sabrina. Can we talk?"

Dane snatched his robe from the hook by the door, threw it on, tied the sash. He took in a deep breath before opening the door. "It's late, Sabrina, can't this wait?"

"No, please," she said, her voice soft and seductively.

There was no way to deny her sexual allure as she stood posed in the hallway, donned in a hotel robe identical to his own. One perfectly shaped bare leg exposed as she stepped forward and sauntered passed him into the room.

"Come on in," he said sarcastically, and released the door, letting it close on its own.

"Oh, Dane, such a waste." She bent and lifted the vodka bottle from the floor.

"What do you want, Sabrina?" He followed behind her.

Spying what little remained of the clear liquid she drank the rest before helping herself to another bottle from the bar's refrigerator.

"Did you come here in the middle of the night to drink my liquor?" Dane asked, unable to hide his annoyance.

"I don't have a bar in my room." She popped open the cold bottle, moved to the bed and sat on its edge.

"Come. Sit. Have a drink." She scanned the crumpled sheets snaked around the edge of the king-sized bed. "I see you can't sleep either."

Dane sat on the bed, keeping a few feet between them. She handed him the bottle.

He took a quick sip. "You came here because you can't sleep and… what? Thought you'd drink *my* booze to help you?"

Sabrina crossed her legs, the robe falling away, exposing both bare legs up to her thighs. Dane took a long swig.

"I wanted to apologize," she said, reaching for the bottle.

"Apology accepted. Now… take the bottle and go drink it in your room."

"I'm serious, Dane." She chugged at the bottle. "I'm sorry I changed the choreography. I felt the audience would prefer to see us singing a love song together—lips to lips."

Dane shrugged. "Apparently you were right. But this could have waited."

"No," she said abruptly. "It couldn't. I couldn't sleep until I apologized." Another swig of vodka, and she whispered, "Do you forgive me?" She sidled a bit closer to him and handed him the bottle.

He drank a hearty mouthful, trying to ignore such perfect

sexuality only a foot away. The drink coursed nicely through his system. "Of course I forgive you. Pleasing the fans, isn't that why we do this?"

Closing the gap between them, she took the bottle, bent to his ear and whispered breathily, "I promise to make it up to you."

Her breath in his ear. The alcohol running rampant through his system. He quickly placed both hands in his lap to hide the erection no longer hidden beneath his robe.

Sabrina placed the half empty bottle on the nightstand, leaning over him as she did so, her robe opening at the top just enough for him to see faultless breasts, large and alert.

She tilted her head up to look at him. "There's no need to be ashamed." Gently, she took his hands, moved them aside, exposing him completely through the part in his robe. "No need at all." She leaned forward then and took him full in her mouth.

"Ohhhhh, God!" Dane dropped onto his back on the bed.

No, I'm married, he wanted to say, but the words never left his lips.

As her warm, moist mouth overtook him, he tried to resist. Feebly, he pushed at her shoulders, but she had him in a sexual stranglehold he was helpless to resist.

Meirah

She always loved flying, but without Dane at her side it did not hold the same appeal. The human beside her slept soundly and all the better, for when he was awake he stared incessantly at her.

Earlier in the flight, she had kept her gaze away, looking out the window at the night sky.

"Hello," he had addressed her in a raspy voice.

Congenially, she turned only to mumble a quick. "Hello."

"What's your name?" he asked.

Though normally she was quite friendly and enjoyed socializing with the humans of this world, this man smelled of the cigars humans sometimes smoked. She had learned many things the last time she had gone on tour with Dane, and that was one of them—among others. It made her nauseous.

"Meirah. My name is Meirah Bainbridge," she had told him

before turning back to her window. But he was not done talking.

"I like your accent," he said. "Where ya from?"

"Scotland," she answered without turning back. In two years, it had become her natural response, where in the past she'd started to say Mikaire. Now 'Scotland' came naturally from her lips.

"Nice country, I hear."

With a sigh of contrition, she turned back to look at him. Though she had seen many variations of humans in this realm, this one was not pleasant to look upon. His bald head reminded her of Edna's boiled eggs—a phenomena she found quite enigmatic as none in Mikaire ever removed, cut, nor lost their hair. Nor did they grow hair on their faces, not even the men, and this puzzled her most of all. This man sported a full face of it—a beard, Dane had once explained.

In his various incarnations, Dane had grown hair on his face, but not by his accord. The time variation between Mikaire and this world caused a quicker aging cycle and the hair and he had always grown hair on his face, lacking the proper tool to remove it. In his own realm, however, he remained for the most part, shaved close—except on a few days when he had been drinking heavily, then he would grow what he referred to as a 5 o'clock shadow. Meirah had no idea what that meant.

The egg-headed man beside her was speaking. "What part of Scotland are you from?"

Meirah tried to recall the names of towns she and Dane had visited in Scotland. "Uh…"

"You can't remember where you're from?" he asked rather rudely.

Meirah merely wanted to be left alone. In a magazine she had read about a technique called a diversion tactic. Worth a try.

She forced herself o look the stranger in the eye. "Why d'ye have no hair on yer head?"

He ran a meaty hand over his bald scalp. "I shaved it off."

"Why?"

"Umm," he stuttered, clearly taken aback. "I don't know. No one in Scotland is bald?"

"No' where I hail," she responded. "Nae."

"And where is that?"

And they were right back to where they had begun. Her

diversion failed, she fished her mind for an answer. "Ye'd no' heard o' it."

"Try me."

Meirah glanced out the window, momentarily distracted by the sky so dark yet so blue during the day. "Uh, Skye!" she answered, proud of herself.

"Oh, the Isle of Skye," he said with a smile. "I've heard of it. Never been there."

Meirah flashed a quick grin and turned back to the window. Apparently, he took the hint, for he closed his eyes and fell asleep shortly after that.

The clouds below flashed with lightning that lit them like strange mountains. She usually marveled at how solid they appeared so high above the ground. Now, however, she found little pleasure in the view.

She had behaved so deplorably towards Dane before he left. She knew the decision to leave behind wives was not out of his doing. Just like a job, there was always another to answer to. Dane had left the house without their usual kiss and show of affection. Even if he was merely going on errands or to rehearsal, never before had they parted in anger.

So frightened she had been after seeing Kaeplan in the tub, and at the concept of months without Dane, she had allowed her fear to manifest into anger. Unacceptable. Though she would not be able to tour with him, she needed to see him, to apologize, to feel his arms around her, his lips on hers.

And so, she had asked Edna to help her buy a plane ticket with the small plastic card Dane had left for her.

Edna had refused. "Meirah, sweetheart, call Mr. Dane first," she had recommended.

"Nae. I wish tae surprise him. I know this world relies upon written conversation and its technologies of which I am unaccustomed, but it is all too impersonal. Too easily misunderstood. Too easily come and gone."

In all honesty, she had feared he would not answer, bringing her worry to its peak. She was being daft, she knew. But it was how she felt.

Edna had furrowed a confused brow at her.

Meirah simply offered a shrug. "*Please*, Edna! I need tae see my husband. I miss him somethin' terrible."

Edna hugged her then and when she pulled back her maternal gaze struck Meirah's tense one.

"Ya must get used to this world, Meirah," she said softly. "Even if Mr. Dane isn't there." Her small mouth pursed and she dropped her gaze. "My apologies, Mrs. Dane."

Meirah tilted a glance to the older woman. "Do ye no' think he will be glad tae see me?"

Edna's face softened. "Oh, darlin', I am sure he will be."

"Will ye help me?"

Edna nodded.

Rather than booking the flight herself, Edna felt it best to show Meirah how to look up the airlines online and find a flight direct to where Dane was staying. Dane had left his band's itinerary, hotels, stops, show times, etc. Meirah knew from her last exertion being on tour with him that, barring an emergency, they followed the schedule strictly. The printed itinerary stated they would be in Las Vegas, Nevada, four different dates, so a week there. And so that was where she headed.

Once she arrived at McCarran International Airport Meirah's excitement grew, along with her apprehension. She feared he would be angry that she had followed him. But as she entered the airport, her fear turned to excitement at seeing him. He would understand, she convinced herself. He always did.

The desk clerk was a tall man with hair so short his ears stuck out hideously. On his lip he sported what she assumed to be a mustache, but it appeared more of an ill caterpillar. Why, she wondered humorously, were so many human males unattractive?

"May I help you?" he asked, in a monotone of boredom.

On the schedule Dane had left for her was a note that explained the band, orchestra and crew usually booked one or two entire floors in each hotel they stayed at, hence his name would not be available. For the first time, however, she noticed the note he wrote for her of an alias he left at each hotel desk in case she needed to contact him for any reason other than private cell. If only she had seen it before.

Beside the Las Vegas hotel name he had written the name of Jonas Graham, one of his names from his past lives.

"May I have the room number for Jonas Graham, please." She said to the clerk.

The clerk looked her over suspiciously, studying the loose red tunic she wore over tight black leggings. With a shrug, he gave her the room number.

"May I get a key?" she asked. "I wish tae surprise my husband."

He grabbed a plastic card from under the desk and handed it to her. What was it with this world and cards? She took the card key and headed towards the elevator.

Dane

He tried to resist, but Sabrina was insistent—and incredibly beguiling. As a man with a sexual addiction away from his wife, a woman like Sabrina easily tore down the barrier of his fidelity before his mind could catch up to what was truly happening. Justifying the act of a mere blowjob was simple and that, after all, was not cheating. But as her advances brought him up farther into the throes of sexual ecstasy, his convictions weakened then fell altogether. Just as he reached the point of climax, however, she stopped, leaving him with a carnal need to finish.

Dane was well aware of the sexual manipulations of women— leave them unable to resist and desperate for more.

He let Meirah enter his mind—what little mind he could conjure—hoping guilt would overcome desire. But the thought of his wife, her beauty and his desire for her only left him needing more.

Making love to Meirah was the single most pleasant experience, mixing love and desire until his need for relief became unbearable. Two nights without sex that, with Meirah, was several times a day, became too much.

Sabrina knelt and straddled him. With seductive moves meant to tease, she unbelted her robe. Slowly drawing it aside, revealing skin of alabaster and breasts so pert and perfect he almost finished without her. The sex-addict rock star that existed before Mikaire returned full force.

Sabrina dropped her robe, tossed it casually aside. She gripped his robe then and lifted his body up, meeting her lips to his in a passionate kiss as she pulled his robe away and tossed it atop her own. He wrapped his arms around the most perfect female body he had ever touched.

Just this one time, the sex-addict within screamed in desperation. The husband in him, loyal and loving, faded into the background. When their heated bodies pressed flesh against flesh, any resolve that might have existed melted away.

In response, his kiss grew deep, his hand reached between them, found her smoothly waxed heat, moist and ready. Easily, he rolled her over on the bed, simultaneously moving atop her. Like a well-played symphony, their bodies came together in perfect synchrony.

Sabrina opened herself to him, wrapping long slender legs around his waist. His hand probed her feminine heat, fingers teasing her in expert rhythm, his tongue probing her mouth. She moaned against his lips, ready.

Pulling up, he grasped her wrists in his hands, pinned them above her head, holding her captive to his desires. Her beauty and warmth called to him and he could wait no longer. The tip of his erection teased her opening, until she was wet and hot.

"Ohhh, Dane, please," she begged, and her words only made him want her more.

A small sound at the door went ignored—he heard it as in a dream. Another moan of pleasure, of need. He pressed just the tip of his manhood into her, more teasing. And, as he prepared to thrust her hard, his mind screamed.

No, this is wrong. He paused. She wriggled beneath him.

"Ohhh," she cried. "Don't stop!" Her voice was that of a Siren whose song rendered him helpless to her.

She pulled her hands free, grabbed his ass cheeks and pulled him in.

So wet with desire he slid into her, and from the heat that surrounded him, he moaned.

"Oh, Meirah!"

Before Sabrina could react, the hotel door opened, spilling light from the hallway over them.

The spell snapped.

Footsteps moved towards the bed.

A gasp.

The door closed, and in sheer dark Dane reacted quickly, rolling off Sabrina, grabbing up a sheet and drawing it over them both.

He was about to chastise whomever dared disturb them when a lamp flicked on. He was temporarily blinded, throwing a hand up over his eyes, blinked quickly.

"*What the F—*"

And then he saw her. Meirah! She stood beside the bed, emerald eyes wide above the hand that covered her mouth.

Sabrina broke the silence. "Who the hell are you! How *dare* you..."

A flash through Dane's mind reminded him they had never met. The last tour, Sabrina had remained with the orchestra, in the background, before personal issues forced her to leave early.

Meirah's flaming stare moved to Sabrina and then to him. Their burn pained him in ways he could not comprehend. Her normally smooth complexion twisted in an expression of shock, hurt and disbelief.

Within, Dane's voice screamed for forgiveness, but his thoughts never reached his mouth. Nor could movement reach his limbs. He was frozen in this terrible moment, unable for the moment to see it as reality.

The entire scenario lasted no more than a few seconds, yet ran through his mind in slow motion, making the staring match seem eternal.

At last the words reached his tongue. "Meirah! Please—it's not what it seems!" Lame. It was exactly as it appeared. "W-Why are you here?" As if those words would make this awkward situation any better.

But his wife remained silent, chest heaving in anger and emotion. Her eyes darted back to Sabrina, then to Dane again as if she were trying to process the scene before her. Dane doubted this sort of thing ever happened in Mikaire despite their "one-time" sex law. Guilt hit him as it never had before.

Meirah lowered her hand, opened her mouth as if to speak. All that came out was a squeak, and then she spun and vanished from the room in her typical Mikairian speed. The door was closing before any human eyes could grasp her departure.

Dane leapt from the bed, snatched up his robe and threw it on as he darted towards the door.

Behind him, Sabrina finally spoke. "Dane! Where are you go—" He slammed the door behind him.

Meirah was already at the elevator when he caught up to her. The doors opened. She slipped in, quickly began pressing buttons. Just as the doors closed, Dane reached a hand between them. They opened again. He entered and let the doors close behind him. Before the elevator could move, he slapped the STOP button. The car jerked.

Meirah turned on him. "*Leave me be!*"

"Please! Let me explain—"

"Nae! Ye think me daft?! I know what ye were doin'... *How could ye!*"

Dane placed a hand on her shoulder.

Before he could blink, she grasped his hand, twisted it behind his back.

"*Do no' touch me!*"

"Meirah!" he cried, tears streaming from his eyes, more at the agonizing pain than fear or guilt. "You're breaking my arm..."

"Ye're lucky if that is all I break!"

Agony spread from his arm through his shoulder and neck. The elevator car began to darken as his body reacted to the pain. He would lose consciousness soon, or she would kill him. Either way, he deserved it—and she possessed the power to do it.

"M-Meirah," he tried in a last attempt at reason. "N-Nothing happened."

She released him with a shove so fierce he slammed into the back wall of the elevator car, the force nearly knocking him unconscious. He crumpled to the floor, arms covering his head instinctively.

"I know what my eyes saw!" she screeched at him.

Gradually, the world came back into focus. Using the wall for support, he lifted himself back onto his feet, wincing.

"Ye were matin' wi' that woman." Her tone softened, her voice sallow. Tears filled her eyes.

Dane's heart seized in sorrow and fear. Would he have continued had Meirah not showed up when she did? He didn't have the answer. Sabrina played on his weakness for sex—played him as well as she did her violin. Several times, he reminded himself, he had tried to stop. Or was that a justification of his guilt?

Through twelve reincarnations he never hated himself more than he did at that moment.

"Meirah," he stated softly, "I cannot express how sorry I am. I know these are mere words but I have nothing else to offer. The dreams—memories—it all returned. I couldn't sleep. She came to me. I was vulnerable. I'm only human, Meirah. We're flawed. We make mistakes. We're weak. Please—I am truly sorry."

She looked at him then and hope entered his heart.

"*This* is why ye refused tae bring me on tour wi' ye!"

It wasn't a question.

"*No*...! Meirah... no... I never... this wasn't... no..." He wanted to express words that would make it all better, but they tangled on his tongue.

Fire returned to Meirah's eyes. He had seen her angry, even hurt, but not like this—her body trembled as if holding back rage and a desire to kill. She stretched out an arm. He winced, unsure if it was to kill or hug him. Instead she hit the OPEN button.

"I need time." At least her voice had calmed.

The doors slid open—and standing in the hallway was Sabrina, wearing the robe identical to his, hair mussed from their encounter. Waiting. Watching.

That was all Meirah needed.

"*Get out!*" she growled, baring intimidating fangs, reminding him she was not human, but a deadly race from a different dimension.

Her fist was too fast for his mortal eyes to see. Dane's torso exploded in agonizing pain as Meirah's hand hit him dead center. He flew backwards, hitting Sabrina so hard she slammed against the hallway wall with a grunt and crumpled to the floor. Dane landed atop her.

As the elevator doors closed, Meirah spoke, her words sending shockwaves through Dane's heart.

"We are *done*!" Then she was gone.

Dane just sat there, in shock and pain, staring at the elevator door, crumpled against Sabrina behind him. Weakly, she shoved at him and in his state he fell on his side to the floor beside her. By this time, others had trickled from their rooms out into the hallway. All of the band's entourage, crew, band members and orchestra, swarmed around them.

Before Dane could clear his mind enough to process all that had happened, Bruce was crouched before him, shaking his head.

"You did it, didn't you?" he accused. "Cover up, you whore!" Bruce grabbed the hem of Dane's robe and flipped it over Dane's junk, which he had not even realized was exposed.

Dark Myst's guitarist did not offer any words of comfort; he merely stood and walked away. Adrian reached a hand to Dane and helped him to his feet. His chest felt as if he were having a heart attack and deep in his mind he hoped Meirah had not damaged him permanently; physically or emotionally.

It was then he realized Sabrina was no longer there. He would need to speak with her at some point, but at present, all he could do was lick his wounds and move forward with hope that Meirah would forgive him, somehow. To lose her would be like death. He limped off to his room to be alone, passing one pitiful expression after another.

-Eleven-

August 2015

"You basically only discover a new thing once."
-URS Fischer

Kaeplan

The humped beast let out a bellow as Kaeplan dragged it by its lead up a giant dune. Below, many dotted lights lit the desert like a mirror image of the stars above. Electricity. Meirah had read it in one of her many books. He had not believed it at the time—to harness the power of lightning? Only the Mortal Dimension possessed it.

"Where are we, girl?" he asked the beast beside him, wishing she could offer an answer.

He had not believed civilization could exist in this vast wasteland, but there it was, sprawled out beneath him. A village.

Two months had passed since he left the oasis. Two months of walking, searching. The Mortal Dimension ran on a faster timeline than Mikaire had and he continued to age as a Mikairian. Two months here and he was no more than a couple days older. This allowed the human blood to remain in his system much longer than it would in Mikaire—and gave him the strength to continue on easily.

After he had dispatched the humans at the oasis, and took his fill of their blood, he released to the desert all but one of the humped animals. He stole the human's clothing, set fire to their shelters, their bodies and all possessions except what water he could carry. Such satisfaction he had taken in ridding the vile humans of their lives and watching their bodies burn.

He had packed this one beast with blankets, all clothing save that which he now wore, and allowed her to lead him along on his journey. She seemed to know the way so he gave her free rein—and she did not disappoint.

He kicked her forward and together they made their way towards the lights. Down the last dune where he hoped to never again need to go thirsty or feel the burn of the sun on his flesh.

The village was fairly large, when compared to those in Mikaire, and the buildings, rather than made of stone and wood as they were at home, were constructed of what appeared to be the sand itself.

He urged the beast along, its cloven feet soft even on the packed dirt road between strange homes that glowed with an unnatural light. No flickering of candles or lanterns; simply a consistent burning that illuminated the smooth walls in a set of off-white. As it was evening, some of the houses were dark. But as he lumbered slowly along, human silhouettes occasionally passed by or appeared in the windows. A few of them stepped out to watch this stranger who meandered into their town. He could smell their blood, wafting on the breeze, hear the beating of their hearts. Like a feast of grand proportions. Excitement fluttered his insides. With so much blood, he would be a Wizard in little time, able to find and create his own Dimension.

Not yet, he reminded himself. He would need to know where he was, the lifestyle of these humans, and to fit in among them so as not to draw unwanted attentions.

Beyond the row of homes he came to a split in the road. He halted the humped beast. To his left, more of the same. To the right a variation; a string of lights and wooden signs that hung at the front of each building. Businesses. At least one appeared open. He turned the animal toward it.

He heard them before they came into sight. Three men and a boy, dressed similarly in long light-colored robes and head wraps, rounded a corner and halted in their tracks the moment they saw him. Unafraid, he rode over to them.

The tallest of the men spoke to him in the same language as the men at the oasis. He merely shook his head. In the dark and with his head and face covered by wraps against the desert winds, they could not discern he was not of their land.

His lack of response drew them in closer. Again, they attempted to converse with him. "Um—" he stuttered. Silence would get him nowhere. "Do ye speak Mikairian…eh…I-I mean…" what exactly was the language called in this Dimension?

Before the word came to his mind, the boy spoke. "English?"

Kaeplan nodded. "Aye. English."

"I speak English," said the boy. "I learn in school."

Kaeplan gazed about at the expanse of road, the mud buildings, a land unfamiliar. "Where am I?"

The boy's dark eyes squinted in confusion. He turned to an elderly man beside him. They exchanged a few words before the boy shrugged, looked back up at Kaeplan.

"You are in Egypt. You are lost?" His accent was heavy, speech difficult to fully comprehend.

Kaeplan nodded. "Aye… yes."

"You not know where? Why?" The boy moved in, but the younger man grabbed his arm, holding him back.

They were leery of him, Kaeplan thought quickly. "An accident befell me," he lied. "I found myself here."

Again, the boy conversed in his own tongue to the others.

When finished, he said merely, "Follow."

Kaeplan rode and they walked until they came to large estate surrounded by fertile grasses and trees. He scented water nearby… a lot of water. This was no mere oasis, and as he followed along he saw in the distance the shimmering outline of a vast river. More lights lined its banks, reflecting like a mirage. Cities, villages and towns sprang up around it. A life source.

The humans led him to a ramshackle barn made of stone and wood. The roof was thatched and looked in desperate need of repair. They halted before it, and the boy approached Kaeplan.

"You and camel," he said, motioning to the barn. "Sleep there."

At least he would have a roof over his head—and now he knew the beast was called a camel.

-Twelve-

December 20, 2016

"There is no pain so great as the memory of joy in present grief."
-Aeschylus

Dane
Las Vegas, NV

Careful not to aggravate the pain in his chest, and the bruise that began to form there, Dane threw on a black shirt and jeans before grabbing up his shaving supplies, shampoo, conditioner and other toiletries, tossed them into his black travel bag with no concern for organization. He hurried into the bedroom and placed the small black leather bag beside his open suitcase on the bed with its sheets still tangled and strewn about from his night of failed passion.

He picked up his clothes from the floor and bureau, tossed them unfolded into the case. He had just thrown the last single sock he retrieved from under the bed into the suitcase when a knock came at the door.

Meirah!

He rushed to the door, heart pounding in fear and hope. He paused only a second, then opened the door, ready to issue an immediate apology.

Bruce didn't wait for Dane to respond. He pushed passed him into the room. Dane turned quickly, and winced, placed a hand over his chest. Meirah's hits were formidable! He closed the door and followed Bruce into the room.

Bruce turned on him in an instant. "What's this?" He motioned to the suitcase and travel bag on the bed.

Spotting yet another sock poking out from under a pillow, Dane snatched it and flung it into the suitcase. "I'm leaving!" He closed the case and latched it.

"Excuse me?" Bruce grabbed Dane's arm as he reached for the suitcase, forcing him to spin around.

"OW! Jesus Christ!" Dane grabbed his chest again.

Bruce released him. "We have a tour to finish. Or have you forgotten?"

Dane snatched a lone hair tie from the dresser, pulled his hair into a ponytail. "I haven't forgotten, but I have to find Meirah." He lifted the cases, ignoring the pain the movement caused, and started for the door.

"*Dane!*" Bruce bellowed. "*Stop!*"

Dane sighed, turned, and looked at Bruce, who crossed his arms over his chest with an air of supremacy.

"Bruce, I *have* to go! I need to fix this." Within his breast his heart nearly pounded from his chest. His hands shook and he fought to keep tears from rolling down his face. "*I cannot lose her!*"

Bruce dropped his arms to his sides. "Let her go for now, Dane. She's upset. If I've learned anything about women, it's that they need time to cool off when they are angry. Give her that time."

Dane placed the suitcases back on the bed. "Maybe that's true for *human* women. May I remind you Meirah is *not* human?" The agony in his breastbone reminded him of such.

"But she is still a woman," said Bruce softly. "She will go home and be there when you return."

"In *two* months? *No!* I need to find her *now*! You don't know Meirah. She said it was over and Meirah never says what she doesn't mean. She doesn't react like human women."

Bruce rubbed a hand over his close-cropped beard. "We have one day off tomorrow. Call her. She'll be home. Or call Edna. She'll make sure Meirah stays home until our break, then you can go."

"Bruce, that is not for three more weeks! Even if she does go home, Edna cannot stop her if she wishes to leave."

"And you think *you* can?" Bruce snapped, his gaze falling to Dane's hand that subconsciously rubbed at the wound.

"I-I have to try!" Dane's voice caught and a tear trickled down his cheek. He wiped it away quickly, turned from Bruce, reached for the handle of his suitcase, but Bruce caught his wrist before he could grab it.

"Listen, Dane, Sabrina is gone."

Dane yanked his hand from Bruce's grasp. "*What?*" He coughed and winced yet again. He wondered if she had cracked something.

"That's what I came to tell you. She *quit*! Now we've lost our best violinist... and the new line-up."

Dane turned on Bruce. "And this is *my* fault?"

"Well, it's certainly not mine—or anyone else's!" Bruce's face twisted and Dane saw the irritation he had been trying to hide.

Guilt, anger, pain, worry all congregated in Dane's gut like a nuclear bomb.

"*MY* fault?! *She* came to me!" Dane barked. "Did you hear her change the words from Lana to Meirah? Did you see her stay at *MY* mic!"

"Yes, we all noticed, Dane—and it worked—until you and your cock fucked it up! Just can't keep it in your pants, can y—"

Bruce never finished his sentence.

Dane's fist connected with a sharp crack to Bruce's nose.

Dane gasped for breath at the movement.

Bruce grabbed his face. "Damn it! You broke my nose! What the *FUCK* is the matter with you!" Red crimson trickled through Bruce's fingers.

Blood. Meirah. Everything reminded him. He snatched up the cases in one hand, hurried to the door, whipped it open—and halted.

Once again, a small crowd had gathered in the hallway. Closest to the door, Adrian glanced at the cases, a look of bewilderment crossing his genderless features. "Where are you going?"

"I need to find my wife!" Dane snarled, not wishing to be disturbed. "I'm sorry, this can't wait."

Adrian opened his mouth to speak, but said nothing when he saw Bruce in the doorway, blood covering his hand, dripping onto his white robe.

Dane shoved through the throng of orchestra, crew and band

members alike.

"Stop him!" yelled Bruce, voice muffled in pain.

Dane was at the elevator when Adrian caught up to him.

Dane spun on him. "No!" He growled, causing the drummer to take a step back. "You're *not* going to stop me!"

"What happened, *Curva*?" Adrian asked, voice soft as if trying to dispel Dane's fury.

Dane said nothing at the Romanian nickname Adrian had long ago dubbed him. Though he had hardly heard it since marrying Meirah, right now he felt he deserved to be called a whore.

"Go away, Adrian." He looked beyond the tall slender figure wearing only shorts, toward the small throng that had followed to the elevator. A few remained behind to tend to Bruce, the rest stared at Dane as if he donned three heads.

Dane wished the elevator would hurry up when the band's manager Gary parted through the crowd like Moses at the Red Sea. He approached Dane, his round face red with anger.

"We have a tour to finish!" Gary stated authoritatively.

"So I heard."

"Dane, we have a tight schedule. You cannot leave." Always the corporate man—all business. "I don't know what happened between you and Sabrina, but she quit and went home. We can replace her songs with the old line-up, but we need *you!*"

"Oh, really!" Dane's eyes burned fierce and angry towards Gary. "Then I quit too!"

Gary's small hazel eyes widened. "You can't quit!"

As if purposely timed, the elevator door opened. Dane stepped inside and pressed the lobby button. "Watch me!"

As the doors closed, the last he saw was a dozen open mouths and shocked stares.

Meirah

The tears, the fear, the anger all coalesced within her until she felt naught but confusion. She had felt these emotions before, but one at a time. Together, they overwhelmed until her stomach ached, her hands trembled, tears spilled down her cheeks. *Dane.* How could he?

Her mind obsessed over the details of the night, particularly the scene she had witnessed. So badly she had wanted to see Dane, to apologize, to hold him close, to let him know she understood his decision to leave her behind.

She would sneak into his room, slide into bed beside him, hold him, kiss him. Her desperation, she knew, was not acceptable in this world of hidden emotion and false truths. But in all his lives, Dane had never lied to her. He was her rock, the one she counted on most. The other half of her.

As she walked down the busy brightly lit street, passing humans everywhere, she began to doubt her decision to leave. She passed a couple holding hands, speaking quietly, offering kisses. She could smell the human blood everywhere, hear their beating hearts, but she felt no hunger. None but her hunger for him.

He had been so sincere in his apology and insistence that nothing had happened, nor would it have. She knew of his insatiable appetite for sex. Perhaps without her there he lost his convictions, and needed to...

To what?

All she had wanted was one night with him... She had snuck in, the room was dark, which she expected. Her superior eyesight allowed her to see at night, for hunting animals. So unlike humans.

She had moved into the bedroom as the door closed behind her. Then she saw them. Naked. Kissing passionately, Dane atop this stranger, her long legs wrapped around his waist... Just as she had so many times with him. And the moans.

She was well aware of his past. He had explained many times how his career made women want to bed him. But he had sworn to her no other woman would share his bed again, ever—except Meirah. His appetite for sex was insatiable, but he had told her he could take matters into his own hands if necessary.

Lies!

And suddenly she realized that the one human she had placed all of her trust into was no longer reliable. She was alone, all alone, in this strange world. Like a lost child, frightened and wishing for the safety of her mother's warm arms. But her mother had died long ago—along with everyone she ever knew.

At that moment, she wished she had never hopped the wagon into the Red Dust Mountains to see her first human—Sir Kori

Blackmore, who had remained faithful to his wife Julianna to the end of his life. If only Meirah had listened to the voice that told her not to touch the human… If only she had walked away.

Anger pushed aside the pain, she was torn in two—*Stay. Leave. Love. Betrayal.*

What she needed now was to get far away. Away from Dane and his crazy lifestyle. Away from humans. Alone with nature as her company.

In Mikaire she had her secret cave. But where would she go in this vast world? Returning to the mansion was no option. He would surely find her. And at that moment, she felt, for the first time, hate towards Dane Bainbridge.

-Thirteen-

December 22, 2016

*"Out of the fires of desperation burn hope and solidarity." -Sharan
Burrow*

Dane
Aiken, SC

He didn't bother calling home. Even if Meirah was there, he
didn't want to alert her that he was returning. If she was angry, she
might be gone before he could speak to her.

Evening had recently fallen and he stood outside the fence
even after the taxi's tail lights faded into the fog. What if Meirah
wasn't there? Sometimes not knowing was preferable to the truth.

Minutes ticked by as he drew in the courage to finally punch
his key code into the lock and push open the tall wrought iron gate
overgrown with ivy that hugged its sinewy tendrils around each of
the gate's black bars.

He grabbed up his bags and walked the path towards the
driveway, staring up at the gothic mansion, its crenellated towers
and turrets towered into the cloudy sky. Thunder rumbled in the
distance and the occasional flash of lightning lit the stones of his
home as if daylight had momentarily sprung.

He searched the many windows for any lights that might be
shining. Edna would not have gone home yet, but he saw no lights
on. Still early, he thought.

He had his key in his hand when he approached the double
front doors, decorated as Edna did every December with massive

wreaths. He never cared much for holidays—until Meirah. She adored the lights of Christmas, the decorated trees, the music, and he had wanted her to experience the entire world around her, to which she always displayed the utmost exuberance.

Standing before the wreaths now, however, made his heart ache and his stomach twist. He felt like a stranger at his own house.

Though he'd eaten nothing in 24 hours, he felt no hunger, only a desperate and burning need to see Meirah home and ready to forgive him. Or at the least ready to talk!

Drawing in a deep and staggering breath, he opened the door and stepped into the foyer. Usually, he would remove his sneakers out of habit, place them with all the other multitude of shoes and boots lined up along the walls of the entry. But, with no pause other than to drop his suitcases, he continued through the French double doors into the gallery.

The mansion was dark save for the small night lights built into the base of the walls, giving the room an eerie ambiance he had never noticed before. He gazed up the wide staircase—more night lights illuminated each step, but the upstairs was pitch. Then down the hallway, to each door.

Finally, he called out, "Meirah!" Only his voice, echoed off the walls, returned to him. The house at that moment seemed too big, too lonely, particularly without his dog.

Meirah, please be here.

The only sounds were of pipes expanding and contracting in the walls, of the wind outside whistling dissonantly around the structure and into the tall arched window to his left; its sheer curtains fluttering like something out of a ghost story.

Perhaps she had gone to bed, he thought, hope screaming in his heart. He began toward the staircase when he caught the sight of a light coming on down the hallway, in the kitchen.

He started toward it, pleading with himself that Meirah would appear. Instead, a stout older woman, gray-streaked hair pulled in a bun, emerged.

"She is not here, Mr. Dane," said Edna when she saw him. Dane's heart dropped. Edna rambled on..."Did ya's not see her? She was so determined to get ta ya. I tried to stop her, but...well, ya knows yer wife. There's no stopping her when she's determined—"

"*Edna!*" Dane screeched, halting her ramble mid-sentence. "Something horrible has happened."

A look of horror flitted across Edna's pudgy face. The gray eyes grew wide and her hand came up to cover the gasp.

"She left, Edna. She's gone!" Dane swallowed hard the lump that formed in his throat at his own words.

Edna shook her head slowly, the wrinkles of her 60+ year old face squished together. She lowered her hand. "Oh my! This is all my fault, Mr. Dane. I tried to make her stay here, I did! She was so insistent... Oh Mr. Dane I—"

"*Edna! Stop!*" Dane threw up his hands in frustration. "This is not your fault. It's mine. She did find me. She found me and..." Dane trailed off.

His housemaid's expression morphed from fear to accusation. "What did yas do?"

"I fucked up this time—*big!*" Tears escaped despite his best efforts to hold them in. "I've destroyed my entire life!"

The maternal in Edna always knew when to show itself. "Come." She placed a gentle hand on his arm, led him to the den around the corner. He sat on the sofa with her gentle guidance. She flicked on the Tiffany lamp.

"I need a drink, Edna, please," he begged. He'd ordered one glass of wine after another on the flight back to South Carolina, but all it did was get him home without freaking out.

"I'll get yas somethin'" She patted his shoulder and rushed back to the kitchen.

Alone, thoughts came unwanted to his mind. If Meirah had not come home, where was she? He knew her better than anyone. He'd dared take Bruce's suggestion that she had come home. *Fail.* Now he hadn't a clue where to look next. He gazed to the den's stone fireplace; empty, cold, forlorn. A mirror to his soul.

Emotions, fear, worry, and physical illness overwhelmed. He'd not slept in more than 30 hours. Exhaustion knocked at his brain and body. His mind wanted to shut down. To feel nothing. To hear nothing. See nothing. To no longer exist. But he would not sleep until he found his wife.

Edna returned moments later with a glass of wine in one hand, the bottle in the other. She knew him well. He took the glass and downed the red liquid in one long swallow, placed the glass on the side table. Edna handed him the bottle. He didn't bother refilling the glass. Straight from the bottle—he guzzled nearly half of it in one long pull.

By this time, Edna had taken a seat beside him on the large plush microfiber sofa. Dane chugged the wine as his eye caught the side window, the dark night beyond. Lightning, sharp and bright, illuminated the room, then a crash of thunder followed immediately behind.

"Terrible storm comin'," said Edna matter-of-factly.

"Good! Let it come." Dane brought the bottle to his lips. The alcohol was finally beginning to have an effect, especially on such an empty stomach. His heart slowed, hands no longer trembled. He sighed with relief.

"Tell me what happened." Edna picked up the empty wine glass, gently took the bottle from Dane, and poured herself a glass. Dane had never before seen her touch a drop of alcohol. This worried him all the more. Edna was a rock. And if she needed a drink, he knew her genuine positivity had slipped.

Exhaling, he told her about the concert—and Sabrina—how she had changed the words to the song, remained near him, came to his room, seduced him. And how Meirah had snuck in.

"I was going to stop, but she saw us... and that's what she believed to have happened. She was so angry..." Dane pulled up his shirt and Edna gasped. Direct in the center of his chest the bruise had spread and become an ugly variation of yellow, purple and black. "She is a fierce one when mad."

"Meirah did *that*?" Edna asked. "She hit yas?"

"I tried to stop her. She wasn't about to be stopped." He pulled his shirt down.

"Let me ask ya..." Edna took a sip of wine. "Would ya have continued had Meirah not arrived?"

Dane was aware that Edna knew the answer. "No! I mean, yes, I tried to stop but she played me better than her violin! She knew my weaknesses, she's known me for years, seen me with other women. I'm not sure what changed. Maybe she always harbored a need to share me. Perhaps she was jealous of Meirah and decided to act once Meirah was not there. I can't be sure of her motive. I may never know." He looked over to Edna. "She quit the band.

And so did I."

His friend and housemaid for the past decade—who had seen and experienced it all, caring for a rock star and his home—for the first time gazed at him with wide hazel eyes of surprise.

"Y'all quit the band?"

"I was desperate, Edna! Bruce, Gary, Adrian—they all wanted to keep me from finding me Meirah!"

Edna placed a loving hand on Dane's shoulder. "They don' understand it all. They know the story—of Mikaire and your past lives, but they were not there."

"Oh my God," Dane blurted, suddenly recalling. "I hit Bruce! Broke his nose!"

Edna chuckled. "And about time, too!"

Dane looked at Edna, surprised to hear her words. "He blamed me, Edna... for everything. I just needed to find Meirah. I still need to..."

"Never ya mind him, Mr. Dane."

"But I quit the band... oh my God what did I do? That band... music... is as much a part of who I am as Meirah!"

Edna shook her head, momentarily closing her eyes. What was in her mind Dane didn't know, but she continued, "They need ya Mr. Dane. This will all get worked out, don't yas worry. Focus on Mrs. Dane right now."

"Where could she be?" His words came out in a hiccup of fear. "If she didn't come home, then where did she go?"

"Well..." Edna took a sip of wine, sinking into the sofa. "What do we know of her? Her likes, loves, hates?"

Leave it to Edna to find reason in a sensitive conversation.

"Right now she hates me," said Dane, wiping tears off his face.

"No, she could never hate ya. She's just upset. I reckon she mighta gone to see yer parents in Connecticut."

Hope touched Dane's heart for the first time in two days. "Edna, you're brilliant. And they say southerners are daft."

"Only ones who say that are Yanks." Edna offered a grin. "Mr. Dane. I need to get home." She placed the half empty glass of wine on the table. "Call aroun'. And call the credit card company. See if there is a charge for another plane, or bus or any form of transport, and where to... If nothin', then she is most likely still in

Vegas. And don't worry on it… Mrs. Dane loves ya, even through yer indiscretions. She'll come 'round."

"Thank you, Edna." Dane leaned in, gave his housemaid a quick peck on the cheek.

She patted his shoulder and stood. "Ya'll find her. Everythin' will work out, ya'll see."

Once Edna had gone, Dane pressed the contact for his mother in Connecticut.

"Dane!" his mother answered. "So surprised to hear from you. Aren't you on tour? What's wrong?"

"Mom, listen. Is Meirah up there?"

Silence ensued or a few seconds. "Um, no. Why would she come here? What happened?"

Hope faded. He explained to her all that had transpired in Vegas, leaving out no detail. Normally, he'd show discretion when talking to his mother, especially where women were concerned. But he saw no need. If Meirah had gone there and asked his mom not to tell him…

"Mom, please. If she's there or been there, tell me."

"I'm sorry, sweetheart. She's not here. I haven't heard from her at all. Why don't you come home and—"

He cut her off. "I'm sorry, mom. I have to find my wife." He hung up.

Dane grabbed up the bottle Edna had left on the table and sunk his body into the plush sofa. Other than his cats, none of whom were in the room at that moment, and his horses who were in the barn, he was completely alone. Edna was gone. He had no band, no wife and he sat all by himself in a mansion worth several million dollars that could house five families.

At one time that was enough. Fame, money, music and women. He had been so busy he never realized he was lonely— until he was dragged through a portal in his mirror, sucked into a dimensional world that existed within one moment in what people referred to as time. Even he still had no explanation for its existence. There he had met Meirah, and his entire life changed.

Dane lifted the wine to his mouth and drank the entire contents until not even a drop remained. He stared at the empty bottle. Alcohol. His one constant companion through it all. He had quit drinking for Meirah; he had no longer needed its crutch. Now he felt as empty as the bottle in his hand. Frustration roared. Anger spilled into him, at himself, at Sabrina, at everyone.

"Fuck this!" He threw the bottle into the fireplace. It exploded in shards that rained on cold embers.

Shards. Mirrors. Meirah.

He'd lost her yet again. Just as he had in a dozen deaths and reincarnations. Only this was worse. He'd had her. He'd had everything. One incident, one night of indiscretion and weakness he lost it all.

A crash of thunder outside startled him back to where he was, to a reality he didn't want to know. He needed to call the credit card company for the card Meirah carried. But, for now, Dane Bainbridge prayed to a god he didn't believe existed.

-Fourteen-

June 2016

*"Every day is a journey, and the journey itself is home." -Matsuo
Basho*

Kaeplan

Nearly a year, but finally it happened. After depleting nearly an
entire Egyptian village of its citizens, then traveling the Mortal
Dimension in search of more, he had successfully opened a portal,
and now he stood within his newly created Dimension—his own
portion of time. Most of what he knew he had learned from
Sakkana, as well as the mistakes the Wizard of Mikaire had made.

All around him nothing yet existed. Only sky and sand. No
forests, no barriers, no mountains, nothing living. He needed to
bring in humans from the Mortal Dimension, the largest
dimension, the one in which all others stemmed, in order to begin
his creation of this new world and make it as he saw fit. Once
finished, he would bring Meirah to him. And he would do what he
wished to make Dane suffer for taking her from him.

He possessed enough power to create a home, but citizens,
loyal followers, required much more. He had to return to the
Mortal Dimension, find humans with strong blood and put them
through the test required to build his strength to its fullest potential.

He knew not what powers he yet possessed. Sakkana had
possessed the power to reincarnate the one human he had
discovered who held the strength to keep him and his world alive,
to renew his Dimension each year. But his was a rare power not
shared by wizards who ruled other dimensions. Each held magics

unique to themselves and their worlds.

Kaeplan held no delusion he would develop this power, but once he discovered his own potential he could work with it, build it, to get what he wanted... the most powerful dimension in all of time.

His mind turned to Meirah. She *would* be his! They would rule together. Unlike Sakkana, Kaeplan refused to rule alone. Uniting with Meirah would assure a powerful place for him amongst the time dimensions She, after all, had been the daughter of an influential member of the Committee—as all Committee members in Mikaire held the power within to rule a dimension if they so wished. He and Meirah, being the only two to make it out of Mikaire alive, was fate. She was never meant to unite with a human, and he had every intention of reversing this tragic and erroneous destiny.

Perhaps, he thought, one day, he could become the most powerful wizard ruler of all the dimensions. A lofty goal for sure. All the layers in time would be his to do with as he pleased. But that dream was far off. One victory at a time. And so, with the power to do so, he began to build his castle and plot the barriers that would take him anywhere in his world he wished to go.

- Fifteen -

"A man who has never made a woman angry is a failure in life." -
Christopher Morley

Meirah
December 22, 2016
Las Vegas, NV

She had never known such anger. Such hurt. Such fear. Even watching Dane's past incarnations die before her in Mikaire did not hurt in such a way.

She held no desire to return home to the mansion, nor to be in this strange world any longer. Nothing made sense to her here. Once, she believed only in Dane and his loyalty to her. And with him, all she saw was happiness and it pervaded her world.

Though she had seen on television the violence humans could inflict on one another, on their own world, she felt protected against it. Dane was by her side—her knight, her love. He would always protect her from pain and fear. Now she felt open and exposed, and utterly alone.

But, alone at the moment was preferable to facing Dane and what he did. He would want to talk, to apologize… as if that made a difference. He would say nothing was going to happen between himself and that other woman. How could she believe him? How could she bring herself to believe anything he ever said again?

So, she walked onwards. Until the lights of the city disappeared and the noises of traffic and humans faded into the distance. Once she had realized how far she had walked, she stopped. Everywhere around her she found nothing but vast expanses of sand, rocks, strange plants and dead grasses. Her first reaction was to run back to the lights, the humans. To call Dane to come and get her, go back to where she had once felt safe.

"Buck up, Buttercup," she told herself, using an expression she had once heard on television.

She did not need Dane, and she most definitely did not need his lies. She would walk on and see where this land brought her. Eventually, humans would come along for her to feed upon, then she could build a home for herself and her child. Dane never needed to know where she had gone.

Serves him right! Let him suffer.

That was as her mind told her. She ignored the voice of her heart, however, which told her otherwise.

Dane

Out in the stable, a black Andalusian gelding shook the water from his body and mane before continuing to munch at the hay hanging in a net before him.

Through the back door of the mansion, rain water trailed through the kitchen and soaked the hallway carpet. Lightning streaked across the dark midnight sky, each flash sparkling off empty wine bottles strewn about on tables and floors. In the master bedroom, water pooled at Dane's booted feet and dripped from his hair where he sat bent and exhausted on the large empty bed.

Following Edna's advice, he had checked with the credit card company and found no charges since the one for Meirah's plane ticket to Vegas. That fact alone should have meant she was still there, but she was smart and might have anticipated him tracing her. She carried cash, and so he deduced she could have come home even though she was not in the mansion. Meirah loved nature and Hitchcock Woods was her nighttime hunting grounds. It was the one other place he could think that she might have gone.

As he did not possess her speed and prowess, the quickest way to get there was by horseback. So, he'd run to the stable and removed Camelot from his stall.

His blood running with liquid courage, Dane had not even bothered to saddle the horse. He threw on its bridle and hopped bareback onto the tall black animal, kicking him into a gallop through the drenching downpour. Heavy hooves splashed and kicked up explosions of water all around and behind them as they turned onto trails familiar to them both.

Fortunately, Camelot did not spook at crashing thunder and sharp flashes of lightning, the horse was in it for the run, and Dane was too desperate and inebriated to care about the weather.

As a knight in 17th century England, jousting and other games from the back of a horse were regular occurrences. Before Mikaire, he'd never known why he was such a natural rider. He'd never taken a lesson in any of his previous lives—courtesy of Sakkana. Just as his prowess with a sword came to him naturally, riding horses was a skill cemented within him from his very first life as the knight, Sir Kori Blackmore.

A knight who had perished in a time dimension called Mikaire, where he had inadvertently cursed himself to never love another woman in the Mortal Dimension. Though he hadn't known it, forever would Meirah be the only woman he could ever love. And he would rather die than be without her.

Now, she was missing—lost in a realm of humans she didn't understand and vast lands she could never comprehend. Though worry touched him that something terrible had happened to her, he knew her well enough to know this unlikelihood. Meirah was a survivor. But he couldn't help but fear those she might encounter. In the two years since they'd destroyed Mikaire together only to be separated by the Main Mirror, she had crossed the unfamiliar world alone to find him.

If it weren't for the alcohol coursing through him, he'd be a basket case. But one thing he did realize…

The time he'd been avoiding had finally come. Keeping this from the media had been in the back of his mind these past few days. They would get hold of the news that he left the band and took off after his wife. Reporters were experts at digging into the personal lives of celebrities. He'd been fortunate the last time, when he'd returned from Mikaire, that his fabricated tale of an unresolved kidnapping had become a cold case and forgotten.

The details of his indiscretion, he was sure, would remain unclear. But they would have a field day now that his wife was missing. The straw, however, had just broke the camel's back and the reality remained—he needed help. He snatched his cell off the bureau and punched in the numbers 9-1-1.

-Sixteen-

December 24, 2016

"For me, my awakening came when I was kidnapped." -Patty Hearst

Meirah

Exhaustion. Hunger. Anguish. Cold. Meirah lay beneath the open stars, sprawled on the sand, trying to sleep, but unable to do so. She had walked through a night and a day. And night descended once again. Sleep should have come immediately. The day had been so hot under the burning sun, nights contradictorily cold.

The plan had been so clear in her mind. So simple. If only she could find a forest, trees—shelter. And blood. In this vast wasteland of sand, sharp plants and rock formations so tall they reminded her of the Red Dust Mountains, she had found nothing on which to feed. No animals, no humans. Only insects and snakes and other critters far too small to feed upon. She could no longer smell blood of any kind, anywhere, only the dry air and the occasional flower that grew off some of the needle-pointed plants. And that worried her.

She began to feel she had made a mistake. She knew the Mortal Dimension was immense, she had learned that when she arrived from Mikaire and walked most of the way to the east coast to find Dane. But then there had been plenty to feed upon, shelter to keep her safe.

Now, lying on warm sand with a chilled breeze as her only company, she began to wish she had gone home, where Edna would have blood waiting for her, or she could hunt in the woods.

She missed Dane and her life with him more than ever now, though inner pain and anger still coursed through her shrinking veins.

As the dark cold night gave way to the pink hue of sunrise over the rocks and sand, Meirah forced herself to her feet. Drawing in a deep breath of courage and reserve, she walked on, heading towards the rising sun. At first, her destination was a mystery to her, but subconsciously she became aware that she was heading back to the Atlantic Ocean—to South Carolina. To home.

She had gone a mere ten feet when a sharp pain within her abdomen halted her. Instinctively she grabbed her belly and double over. Within minutes, the pain faded. Taking in a few more deep breaths, she continued along.

Several yards and the pain returned, sharp and encompassing, dropping her to her knees. The baby! But she was nowhere near ready. By mortal time she had three more years, which put her at the human equivalent of just over a month along. Too soon. Something was wrong.

Squatting on the dusty ground, she cried out. "Dane! Please, help me!" Though she was all too aware he could not hear nor sense her.

Lack of nutrition had begun to take its toll not only on her, but their Tiny One as well. They would both die out here in this land of eternal nothing if she did not find blood and shelter soon. But, as the sun burned its path higher into the sky, no sign of anything other than that which she had seen for days spread out in every direction.

Her emotional anguish aided in keeping her weak. The last time she traversed the lands to find him, her love and devotion kept her going, kept her alive. Their baby then was naught more than a tiny cell that needed little of the nutrition it required now.

If she did not get to blood soon, she would lose the one thing she had to live for. With that in mind, she rose to her feet. She had to save her baby.

Half a day passed as she struggled to continue on, fighting through the pain that came and went. And when she saw ahead a pool of water surrounded by green plants and trees, she was sure she was hallucinating.

She picked up her step, determined. It was no illusion and she ran to the water hole, dropping to her knees at its fertile edge. She reached her hands into the water, cool and clear, and drank. It wasn't exactly what she needed, but it certainly aided in staving off the thirst and the heat, so she crawled into the cooling pool and sat emerged to her chest, leaned against the bank.

So relaxing, she let her body sink. The pool was not terribly deep, but she allowed the pull of the water to drag her under until even her head was submerged.

Vaguely was she aware of the weightlessness as she sank deeper into the cooling bliss. Her mind drifted away, farther and farther until blackness surrounded her completely. So lost was she that she took a breath... pain!

Coming awake suddenly, she was no longer in the water but on a sandy embankment. She coughed and gagged liquid from her lungs. She turned onto her back, taking in deep and labored breaths. But as she blinked her eyes open, above her stood a silhouette—no features save the long wavy hair framed by the bright red sun behind it.

Meirah coughed out one word. "D-Dane?"

"Hardly!" said the silhouette sarcastically. He sat back and the silhouette that was her rescuer came into view.

Kaeplan!

Meirah sat up quickly. "W-What...?"

"Ye'll be alright now," he said lovingly, and the past crashed in to greet her.

She stood, still wobbly, but managed to keep her feet beneath her. Kaeplan reached to grab her, to steady her, but she shrugged away before he could touch her. She stood staring with wide emerald eyes at what she was sure was an illusion—or worse, she had drowned and he was there in the next world as well.

"Meirah, please." He stepped towards her, one auburn eyebrow rising pleadingly. "I will no' harm ye."

"Am I dead?" she asked, fearing the answer.

Kaeplan let out a small chuckle. "Nay. Ye're verra much alive—thanks to me."

She stared at him in disbelief, from the leather boots and beige breeches, to the white linen tunic and long red hair that hung in wet strands over his shoulders, soaking his tunic. She had wished to see a familiar face, but…

She looked around. A lake of pure blue spread out beside her, mirrored by the azure of a cloudless sky.

Oh my God, Dane!

The thought of what Kaeplan had done to her husband punched her in the gut. She squeezed her eyes closed, then opened them. Kaeplan stared at her in silence.

"Where are we?" she demanded. "How did I get here? What did ye do wi' Dane?" she blurted all at once.

"Whoa!" Kaeplan raised a hand to halt her tirade. "One question at a time, my darlin'."

"I am *no'* yer darlin'!" Regardless of what Dane had done, he was still her husband.

"Meirah, I can explain all," said Kaeplan, who she still was not sure was real. "But ye must come wi' me."

"Where?" she asked suspiciously. Once again, she gazed about. Water, sand and trees.

"Ye've forgotten already," said Kaeplan, shaking his head.

"What did I forget?"

He reached a hand out to her. "Please."

She paused a moment, sighed.

Oh what the hell… I'm dead, dying or asleep anyway…

She placed her hand in his. Gently, he led her towards the trees. As they passed the first row, those closest to the water, the scenery changed and they were walking on a packed dirt road. Meirah halted, forcing Kaeplan to stop short. She looked at him with wide eyes.

"A barrier! We just crossed a barrier. Where are we? How is this possible? Mikaire is gone. Besides—she looked around again—this is no' Mikaire."

"No," said Kaeplan with a broad smile. "Welcome to Almareyah. This is *my* land. My Dimension." Pride beamed on Kaeplan's face.

Meirah stood astonished. "Y-Yer a W-Wizard?"

"Aye!" Kaeplan nodded.

"B-But…*how?*"

"Meirah—" he drawled out her name. "Every member o' the Committee was chosen by Sakkana because they held Wizard potential."

She turned to him in awe and surprise. "Even my…"

"Aye, Meirah. Even yer father. But ye killed him, and all the others, so…"

Meirah's mind spun and she squeaked out, "b-but… how did ye escape Mikaire?"

The grin faded then, and his features grew dark. "Did ye think yer *mortal* could kill me so easily?"

"Ye leapt through…? Just as we—"

"Aye," he interrupted. "I did. The verra last window. Now, please come wi' me so I can show ye aroun'."

Slowly, unable to think, she nodded. He moved on down the path and she followed obliviously.

The world was most different from Mikaire. Mostly sand, as she had experienced in Nevada. Except for the occasional sand-built hut and trees.

"I leapt through the Main Looking Glass," said Kaeplan, "right after ye. Only I came out in a land of sand as far as the eye could see or the body could walk. I was sure I would die there. Nothin' to eat. Jut sand dunes… everywhere."

He went on to explain how desperate he was to find her, and that need alone kept him alive. He had not known at first that landed in the Mortal Dimension until he came across the oasis— and the humans.

"I saw ye in the water—later on. Just a wee bit o' water and there ye were."

"I didna imagine that?" she said.

This time it was Kaeplan who stopped. "Ye saw me too?"

Meirah nodded slowly. "I was… in the bathtub. I thought I saw ye, but…" she shook her head

"Do ye know what this means, Meirah? I saw ye, I conjured ye. I wasna a full Wizard yet. We are bound, don' ye see? We were meant to be one after all."

Suddenly, a thought came to her and she called out, "Dane!"

Angrily, Kaeplan said "Don' say that name!"

"No… can ye no' see…he had been havin' bad dreams. Seeing tortures again. From Mikaire, so we thought, but… they were no' the same."

Kaeplan grew silent, nodding his head as if it suddenly made sense.

"In past incarnations," Meirah continued, "he saw Sakkana and previous lives. Somehow he knew I lived. He was connected to Sakkana and to Mikaire, and hence to me."

Like a strong wave it hit her. "Ye're goin' tae take him as Sakkana did!" She backed away slowly.

"Nay! No, Meirah. I have ye now. Ye came *here*. Ye found *me* for a reason. He led ye to me. Can ye no' see... *He* is the catalyst! All this time I thought he stood between us, but I was wrong—he was meant to have ye so he could lead ye back to me!" His words were sharp in desperation for her to understand how he saw this convoluted situation.

But, he made sense and she could see it! She did not *want* to, but she did, and confusion circled her mind like drowning in a whirlpool. Though she and Kaeplan had been destined in Mikaire to unite, she had fallen in love with a human—Sir Kori. Every step from there on had led her to this moment, and to Kaeplan.

"Listen, Meirah," Kaeplan's words interrupted her thoughts, but did not dispel the perplexity. "I know ye carry his Wee One inside ye, but the Dimensions don' lie. All o' it. His lives, you, me... It was all put into place so ye could find me here—so ye can be my queen. Mikaire fell so we could finally be one."

Meirah nodded slowly. Not that she agreed, but between Dane's deception ultimately leading her to the desert, and the oasis... It was too much to think on all at once.

"Perhaps—I-I canna be sure."

Kaeplan placed his hands on her arms and gazed deeply into her eyes. "See it, Meirah... All of it. Years to us—meant to bring ye here to me. Ye can be queen beside me. Ye were ne'er meant to live in the Mortal Dimension. That was merely a bridge over time to bring ye here."

"Ye always wanted me..."

"Exactly. But if we had united in Mikaire we would be slaves to Sakkana. He knew I was the strongest of all, the one best suited to Wizard my own Dimension—wi' *you* at my side!"

Sakkana had been the insightful Wizard, able to manipulate the rebirth and reincarnation of humans. Had this all truly been planned centuries past by mortal time?

"Give me a chance," said Kaeplan. "Ye'll see! If ye do no' see it, ye can return to the Mortal Dimension. Back to yer human."

Meirah looked to Kaeplan, deep into his eyes. "And ye'll keep this word?"

"Aye. If ye see what I have to show ye, and ye do no' see what I do... still wish to return to yer human, I will take ye back myself."

Meirah nodded. "All right. Show me what ye need then."

Dane

Intermittent red and blue lights flashed against the lace curtains in the parlor where Dane sat, a glass of wine trembling in his hand. He needed more, but didn't feel it would look appropriate to chug from a bottle of booze before the cop who stood before him. Bad enough he had to clean up all the dozens of wine bottles, pull his hair back and shave before they arrived. He dressed in a neat light blue button-down dress shirt—of which he left only the top two buttons undone—a pair of un-holey jeans and sneakers.

The older police officer, whose name badge said 'Walowitz' was perhaps mid-30's, a bit large, his uniform tight over a stout belly, held a clipboard and pen. The other, younger and more lean, stood nearby in silence.

"Tell me, Mr. Bainbridge," said the police officer with the clipboard, a disapproving look on his round face. "Where did your wife go missing?"

This was tougher than Dane thought it would be. Did he tell the truth? Lie as he had when he was 'kidnapped' into Mikaire, or some variation in between? Desperation told him this was the time to be honest... or at least in part.

"Well," he began, taking a sip of the wine. "My band was on tour—in Vegas. Um, she flew in to surprise me."

Walowitz stopped writing, raised a brow. "Did she go missing in Vegas then?"

"Well, yeah, but I was sure she'd come home. I returned to look for her, but she isn't here."

"How long has she been missing, Mr. Bainbridge?"

Dane paused a moment. "Uh...what day is this?"

Walowitz sighed. Dane knew he was being judged. *Drunken rock star loses wife, can't recall the day.*

"Perhaps you should put down the wine, Mr. Bainbridge," said Walowitz. "And it's Thursday."

"Um…Tuesday night. Yeah, Tuesday night." He took another sip of wine, not caring if the cop judged a man for having a drink when the woman he loved was nowhere to be found.

"Did you call everyone, make sure she didn't go and stay with a friend or relative?"

"Of course I did," Dane said, trying to keep his patience in check. "She has no relatives in this dimension!"

Walowitz gazed up from his clipboard. "Excuse me?"

"I-I mean, she's from Scotland, but has no living relatives. I am all she has."

Walowitz gave him a look as if to say 'poor woman.'

"I love my wife," Dane defended, even though the cop had said nothing. Most policemen hated rock stars and Dane was tired of being looked at as if he was harboring a drug ring in his basement.

Walowitz went back to jotting notes on his clipboard and the scratch of the pen was beginning to get on Dane's nerves. He drank more wine, finishing the glass as Walowitz looked back at him.

"Tell me the whole story. She met you in Vegas, then what?"

"We had a bit of an argument and she took off."

"What was the argument about?"

"That's personal," Dane said, really not feeling the need to divulge his affairs.

Walowitz lowered the clipboard, rolled his eyes. "Look, Mr. Bainbridge, we can't help you without all the details. Please… everything that happened."

Dane paused, looked at the empty glass in his hand, wishing it would magically refill. "She came into my hotel room and saw…she saw me with a bandmate."

"Man or woman?"

"Woman! I'm not gay!"

Walowitz cleared his throat, then went back to scratching in the clipboard. "So, your wife walked in on you having sex with another woman, got mad and left…"

"No! I mean, yes, but no. We didn't do… anything. But Meirah thought we were."

"So you and this woman..." Walowitz looked to Dane and gestured for a name.

"Sabrina."

"So, you and...Sabrina were doing nothing and your wife thought you were cheating on her?"

Every question felt to Dane more of an interrogation on him than an attempt to find Meirah. "We were..." Dane tightened his grip on the empty wine glass. "We were in bed, naked, yes, but not doing anything. I mean, we started to, but I stopped it because of Meirah."

"Because your wife caught you?"

"No. I stopped... Look, Sabrina came to me! She tried. She's very seductive and beautiful."

"And you couldn't help yourself, so you removed your clothes and climbed into bed with her, but did nothing."

This man's facetious contempt flustered Dane's mind, making him say the wrong things, making him look and feel more guilty than he already did. He desperately felt the need to exonerate himself. "No, I was in bed—alone! I couldn't sleep for fear of the nightmares."

"Nightmares...?"

The younger cop motioned Walowitz over to where he stood in the arched doorway of the parlor. They began to speak quietly. Dane took that opportunity to rise, excuse himself for a moment, and headed to the kitchen where he filled the wine glass. When he returned Walowitz was back to his original position by the sofa. Dane sat and took a long drink from the glass, then set it on the table beside him.

Once Dane settled, Walowitz spoke. "You're the rock star who was taken and tortured a couple years back? The culprits were never found?"

And there it was! His past once again haunted his life. "Yes."

"Are you sure she was not taken by the same perps who took you?"

"I'm positive. It's not possible." He rubbed at the white gold wedding band as if, like a genie from a bottle, Meirah would appear.

"How do you know? Could they have returned to take *her* this time?"

Dane pondered for a moment. Meirah had seen Kaeplan in the pond's reflection. Could it be he returned somehow? Could he… "No!" he said aloud, not meaning to speak his thought. "No, they didn't, I-I don't think…"

"Mr. Bainbridge, I want to help you, but you need to disclose everything. Do you know who took you? Are they making you keep quiet?"

Dane slowly shook his head. "I just want to find my wife. If it will help you find her, then I guess it's possible." Not that he felt they could even catch Kaeplan if he had survived Mikaire and made his way into the Mortal Dimension. And he absolutely could not tell them the truth.

"Ok," started Walowitz, "let me get this straight. You were kidnapped two years ago, no ransom note, nothing. They tortured you and eventually returned you with no reason you can recall, and then they disappeared. And you have no idea who they were? Now your wife is missing after catching you with another woman in Vegas. Is this correct?"

"Yes… " On its most basic level it was truth.

"Give me your wife's description. What was she wearing… every detail."

Dane grinned thinking about Meirah, and his answer was a bit too honest. "She's the most beautiful woman in this world!"

"In *this* world? How about any other?" The officers exchanged a quick grin.

Anger rose in Dane's chest. The love of his life—the woman he'd died a dozen deaths for—was missing, and they mocked his word choice!

"Yes!" he snapped. "In this world or any other!" He drew in a deep breath, then described her appearance, what she had been wearing when last he saw her.

Walowitz cleared his throat. "Ok, Mr. Bainbridge. We'll put out a missing persons report. But I suggest you speak with the Vegas police and file a report with them as well."

"I will."

Dane stood and walked the police officers to the door.

"We'll be in touch," said Walowitz as Dane opened the door for them to exit. Flashes from cameras blinded him. *Shit, the media!* They received info on their police scanners and simply couldn't resist. He watched Walowitz and his partner fight through them, saying "No comment" and "please leave the property" at the ruckus of questions tossed in their direction. As they moved in on the doors towards Dane, he slammed them closed, locked them.

-Seventeen-

"Anything can happen, so you have to control your attitude and stay strong." -Jason Day

Kaeplan and Meirah

The castle was the most luxurious place Meirah had ever seen. Much larger than even Sakkana's had been—built of limestone, like the pyramids she had seen on television and in pictures.

She had learned much about the mortal world by watching the television box. What a magnificent invention. All of Dane's televisions were huge, but her favorite was in what he referred to as a Home Theatre. The screen covered one wall, just like going out to the 'movies,' which she had done several times with Caitlyn (Dane never went to the theater, he said, because he had one at home and did not need to worry about being recognized and interrupted). This brought the world to her as if she were there. Her favorite shows were what humans called documentaries.

The Mortal Dimension boasted civilizations that dated back tens of thousands of years. She wished she could visit them all, but Dane worked so much, they had not had the chance. Though she had accompanied Dane on tour only months after they had united, they had remained within the United States and a country called Canada. They moved from place to place so quickly, she had little time with which to visit these places.

Occasionally, however, they would get a day off and Caitlin, or Dane if he had time, would take her to see places of interest. But no pyramids and no castles like this one, or those she had seen in Scotland, which was the only 'vacation' she and Dane had taken.

She had hoped for many more.

Kaeplan led her onto a portico that overlooked sprawling green lawns, gardens and many trees. He sat on a stone bench and motioned for her to sit as well. She took the seat across from him.

"Well..." said Kaeplan, who stood before her, "do ye like it?"

"It is magnificent." Though her heart ached for Dane, and yet chided him for his betrayal, she smiled sincerely. A sudden flutter of movement within took her by surprise. "Oh..." She placed a hand on her belly.

Kaeplan was at her side in an instant. "Are ye alright?"

Meirah nodded. "Aye. I felt...something."

"Are ye in pain?" he asked sincerely.

"Nae, it is gone now. Just a ... a movement."

"Ah..." Kaeplan returned to his seat. "The wee one inside ye. It's grown a bit since ye've been here."

"But, I've only just arrived."

"Aye. Do ye no' remember Mikaire...the time ran faster than the Mortal Dimension, eh?"

"I am well aware, Kaeplan!" She felt a slight annoyance build, yet it felt familiar, almost...comfortable. "I conceived in Mikaire, so the babe was growin' by Mikaire's time. In the Mortal Dimension, I have a few years to go." She spun her wedding ring around with her fingers, a subconscious habit she had picked up when anxious.

"What is the time here?" she asked.

"Well," Kaeplan sat back in his large chair. "This dimension is no' as fast as Mikaire, but as I figure it, about a week has passed in the Mortal Dimension."

"Oh, by Sakkana's power, I have tae go back!" She stood quickly.

Kaeplan was once again at her side, his hands gentle on her shoulders. "Meirah, please. Sit. Almareyah may be a bit faster, but ye're back in a magical realm—just as ye were born to...Just as ye're meant tae be. Yer child will grow as time has meant it. The Mortal Dimension is too fast for our kind. They age and die so quickly. Don' ye want yer wee one ta live longer than that? If the babe is born in mortal time, it will be mortal and age as such."

Meirah thought about that a moment. She had not known a lot about how the times worked between dimensions, but she did know mortals aged by mortal time, and those born to time dimensions aged by their own dimension's time. It had always confused her, so she had avoided any more knowledge than that.

"So, if I stay here until the baby is born," she started, "then return to the Mortal Dimension, my child will age by this dimension's time?"

"Aye. In four days, a bit o'er a week will have passed. Yer mortal will wait. Isna worth it tae have yer baby live longer?"

Meirah remained silent, deep in thought. It was hard to make such a decision. Remain here, away from Dane until the baby is born?

"Meirah, look..." Kaeplan drew her attention away from her thoughts. "Ye'll give birth in less than a year and a half here... almost three in the Mortal Dimension. I wish I could have taken Mikaire's time, then ye'd give birth so much quicker, but Mikaire's time is in chaos. There have been ripples all over time, in the mortal realm too... they just do no' know what it is. They think they see ghosts or UFOs," he chuckled. "But a chaotic timeline is the fault. I'm sorry, Meirah. This was the best I could do."

"But Dane... He will be frantic."

Kaeplan sighed and paused as if in thought before saying, "How about if we send him word that ye're here, ye're safe, and the reason ye're stayin'. If he loves ye, he will wait."

"*If* he loves me?" Suddenly she was defending the man who had forsaken their vows.

"Ok, aye," said Kaeplan quickly. "He loves ye. Then ye know he'll wait. Particularly if he knows ye're doin' this so yer babe can live longer, do ye no' think?"

A bit over a year. Not too long, she thought. If she stayed in the Mortal Dimension, she'd not give birth for close to another 3 years, and people were already beginning to talk, what with Dane being a celebrity and all. This would cut the time in half. Dane would come up with a reason why his wife went away and came back with their child. He was quite good at... lying. Meirah shook the word from her mind. No, he would be an amazing father. He always beamed when they spoke of the baby. He had said he wanted their child to grow up with Bruce and Caitlyn's son, aptly named Dane; born when Dane was imprisoned in Mikaire and presumed dead. Little Dane would be five when her child was born; this way, their baby would only be a bit younger, closer in age. Meirah found herself smiling. They could be the family she and Dane always dreamt of having.

She looked seriously at Kaeplan. "And ye'll send word regularly so Dane knows I am safe?"

Kaeplan grinned. "O' course! Anythin' ye wish!"

Meirah nodded. "Aye then. I shall stay."

-Eighteen-

January 5, 2017

"Where you used to be, there is a hole in the world, which I find myself constantly walking around in the daytime, and falling in at night. I miss you like hell." — *Edna St. Vincent Millay*

Dane
Aiken, SC

As he came awake, he blinked slowly, trying to focus against the bright light that shone in his face. In its center, a silhouette. Someone stood above him.

"Meirah?" he asked, hopeful. He reached out his arms towards her. "You came back. Oh, I missed you. Do you forgive me?"

The silhouette closed in on him, grew wider, morphed. "Meirah?"

Then he heard a voice. Not a Mikairian accent but a southern drawl. "Mr. Dane, are yas okay?" Edna stood above him where he lay on the sofa.

He pulled his arms back and shook his head slowly.

Edna's brows furrowed in concern.

"Edna. Where is Meirah?" He glanced around the den where he had passed out the night before. Reality crashed down on him then and an ache formed in his gut. Two weeks. Meirah still had not come home. No word, nothing. He had contacted the Vegas police, left a report. Nothing.

He attempted to sit up, but his head ached, nausea filled his gut and he moaned. Edna reached down, took his hand and helped him to sit up. She handed him the glass in her other hand that he didn't notice was there. Clear, bubbling liquid.

"What is this?"

"Alka-Seltzer. I figgered ya'd need it."

His stomach knotted and he drank the horrible contents before setting the empty glass on the table. He was soaked in sweat, his hair matted and dripping. He ran a hand through it to smooth it. His bare chest was wet, as were the jeans he had not changed out of in a week. Yet he felt cold.

Edna sat on the sofa beside him. "Oh, Mr. Dane. Ya look terrible... so pale and..." she crinkled her nose. "Y'all could do with a shower."

"What's the use?" He swallowed back the nausea, but couldn't swallow back the worry over his wife.

"For one, ya stink!" stated Edna bluntly.

"What time is it?" Dane asked her.

"Two in the afternoon. Quiet as a mouse I'm tryin' ta be, but I can't vacuum with y'all lyin' here. At least go ta bed so I can get my chores done."

He merely shook his head. He couldn't bring himself to go into his bedroom without Meirah there.

"Then at least go sleep in one of the spare rooms?"

Dane opened his mouth to speak but was interrupted by the jingle of his cell. He kept it charged and close by at all times, just in case. Last week, the Nevada police had called him to say they had found a trail leading to a small body of water in the desert, but the trail led to the small pond and went cold from there. They couldn't be sure if the footsteps belonged to a man or woman. They would call him if they found more.

Dane snatched his cell off the table and looked at the screen. *Adrian.* He had heard nothing from anyone in his band since the night he left the tour.

He pressed the green answer button. "What do you want, Adrian?"

The Romanian accent on the other end sounded annoyed. "No need to bite my head off, Dane."

"What do you want?"

A sigh, then, "I am worried for you. Have you heard from Meirah?"

"No. I don't want to talk about it. Is that all?" Dane didn't care that he was rude.

"Dane, we need to talk."

"What about?"

"Have you forgotten the band?" Adrian spoke softly.

"I quit the band, remember?" Somewhere deep within he was glad to hear he was still needed back in the band, but he was torn between that and his fear for Meirah. And she won—she always won.

"I had hoped you'd changed your mind," said Adrian. "Please come back. It's not too late to finish the tour, Gary canceled all the dates, refunded money, but said he would reschedule. We lost a lot of money, Dane."

"Go back to your private life, Adrian, and I'll go back to mine."

A Romanian curse sounded through the phone. Dane hung up, not wanting to hear more. Edna was staring at him, one gray brow raised.

"What!" Dane snarled.

"Ya know I'm not one to tell yas what to do, Mr. Dane—"

"That's *all* you do, Edna!" Deep down he regretted the words immediately, but offered no apology.

"Fair enough," said Edna. "but you know I care for ya. In all these years I've only had yar best interest in my heart. Y'all are like a son to me."

Dane remained silent.

The knock on the door just then was quiet but obvious. Dane leapt to his feet, despite how terrible he felt.

"Meirah!" He dashed toward the door.

Edna rose off the sofa. "Mr. Dane—wait! It's not her."

Dane cocked his head at her. Something was up and he was determined to find out what it was. He turned quickly, but his toe caught on a table leg. "Shit!!" Limping, he continued towards the door, a line of curses following him... and Edna on his heels.

The disappointment he felt when he opened the door could not be explained... nor could it be contained. "What the *FUCK*?!"

On the landing stood Adrian, Stephan and Bruce.

"How the *hell* did you get past the gate?" he snapped. *"What do you want?"* He addressed Adrian, knowing he had called from outside the estate.

Before anyone could speak, he spun on Edna. "*You* did this!"

His housemaid wrung her hands together and swallowed hard, yet spoke despite. "Y'all need to work this out."

Dane slammed the door shut in their faces. "I will deal with *you* later!" he shouted at Edna, and stormed into the parlor, not even feeling the pain in his toe.

He should fire her, right then and there, he knew. But if he had to be honest with himself—and he did—he couldn't. Since Meirah's disappearance, and without his bandmates and friends, he'd never felt more alone. He actually missed them and needed to talk to someone from the outside world. But anger and pride would never allow him to show it. Shivering, he grabbed a blanket off the back of the Victorian sofa and wrapped it around his shoulders.

He heard the door open. *Oh God, Edna let them in.* He pulled the blanket over his head as if he could disappear. Footfalls entered the parlor. Many footfalls.

"Go away!" he mumbled from under the blanket.

But they didn't go away, and when he poked his head from under the blanket, he could see through unwashed black locks, his bandmates taking various seats around the room. Adrian sat on the sofa beside him, Stephan the large stuffed chair near the fireplace. Bruce, however, remained standing near the arched doorway.

"Alright," Dane conceded. "You're here. Say what you must then leave me be!" He flipped greasy hair from his face and sunk into the sofa, wrapping all but his face into the blanket like a protective cocoon.

The three men glanced at one another as if deciding who would speak first.

"*Well?*" Dane said impatiently.

Adrian, being closest to him, cleared his throat. Nervously, he twirled at a long lock of flaxen hair. "You are not out of the band," he stated distinctly. We talked. You are irreplaceable."

Dane glanced to each of the men he had known and worked closely with for over a decade. No expression other than a need to clear this up and get on with their careers. He shook his head. "None of you understand. I lost her once—"

"And you got her back," interrupted Stephan.

Adrian spoke next. "Do you remember what I told you in the bus last time you lost her?"

"Yes," Dane said quickly. "Your boyfriend killed himself!" Harsh words, and Dane knew it.

Adrian's blue orbs widened.

"Oh, c'mon Adrian…" Dane continued. "We all know you're gay! Stop trying to hide it. We don't care. You're an exemplary drummer."

Adrian's pale cheeks turned a bright red.

Stephan weighed in. "He's right, Adrian. We've known for a long time. After all these years together, you can't hide it." Stephan pulled his long red ponytail over his shoulder, played with it. Apparently everyone was nervous at this intervention.

"This is not about me," said Adrian softly, lowering his head.

"No, it's not!" Bruce finally spoke. "Adrian, Dane told us the ultimate secret when he revealed where Meirah came from—do you think your private life matters?"

"I suppose not," said Adrian, face hidden beneath strands of long blond hair. "But please keep this between us. I do not need the media getting hold of it."

"Do you think," started Stephan, "that in this day and age, a gay drummer will be front page news?"

Adrian's face turned a shade brighter than Stephan's hair.

Dane pulled the blanket tighter around himself. He still shivered, but within the fibers confining his half-naked body he reveled in the warmth.

After what seemed an eternity of silence, Dane spoke up. "Are we done? I'd like to go back to sleep now."

"You don't handle emotion well," said Stephan. "You're killing yourself—again. How long do you think you can do this?"

"And what is *that* supposed to mean?" Without waiting for an answer, Dane looked over at Bruce. "What if this was Caitlyn?"

"I'd be frantic trying to find her," answered Bruce honestly. "But I would *not* hole myself up in the house, drinking myself to death. Look at yourself, Dane. You're gaunt and shivering, though it must be 80 degrees in here. Have you even eaten anything? Left the house? What good will you be to Meirah when she returns?"

Dane shrugged. "*If* she returns."

"She will," Adrian weighed in. "She did last time."

"Last time," said Dane, "she barely escaped Mikaire and landed in the Rocky Mountains. She didn't catch me naked in bed with another woman!" He'd never regretted anything more. And he knew that if he could go back in time...

He dropped the blanket and sat up straight. "Oh my God!"

"What?" asked Stephan and Bruce simultaneously.

"Time! Mikaire was a dimension in time. Don't you get it?"

Adrian, Bruce and Stephan looked to one another then back to Dane in confusion.

"The nightmares! My nightmares... They changed. Water. Meirah said she saw Kaeplan in the water."

"Elaborate, Dane," said Bruce.

"He's alive! Kaeplan is alive! I don't know how, but he came here to this dimension—he has her!"

"The man she was to wed in Mikaire?" asked Adrian.

Dane nodded. "It all makes sense now. Kaeplan came through. Oh my God, he has her!"

"You can't be sure of that," said Bruce.

"But I can! In all my recent dreams there were reflections... water. Meirah told me there were many dimensions that existed through the veil of time that this world is unaware of... Mikaire's portal was mirrors. Water can be another."

"How can you find her if this is true?" asked Stephan, skepticism and hope touching his voice.

"I have to return to Vegas! I need to follow the trail the police mentioned—find the pond. It's a portal, I'm sure of it."

"I will go and help you," said Adrian in an animated tone. "We will get your wife back."

"Me too!" said Stephan.

All three of them looked at Bruce then. He rolled his eyes. "This is a long-shot, but if it gets Meirah back and the band together again, I will go too."

Meirah

The tears dried on her face only to be replaced by new ones. She sat on the bed within the chamber Kaeplan offered to her. It was a beautiful room, as large as she and Dane's bedroom at home. Gold and silver chandeliers graced the ceiling. The bed boasted a soft feather mattress, tall wooden four-poster style with mosquito netting tied to each post. Bamboo shutters adorned the windows, and the furniture was an ornate Egyptian style beautifully marked with Egyptian carvings. Hieroglyphs, she knew they were called. Marble statues stood around the area, of Bast, Athena, Odin, and many other variations on ancient human gods. Sheer curtains fluttered in the breeze. She felt like a queen from an old human culture.

Though Kaeplan made every provision for her comfort, deep within she missed Dane and the familiarity of his presence in her everyday life.

Repeatedly, her mind replayed their last encounter—the woman she had found him with—the fight they had. Though the feelings of betrayal still rumbled in her churning gut, it had faded considerably. He had told her nothing happened, that he had stopped the inevitable progression of sex and she wondered now if her eyes and fears had belied what her heart told her was truth. She regretted having been so rash in her decision to leave.

"Oh, Dane," she cried to no one, "what have I done?"

This was a man who had died a dozen deaths for her, endured unspeakable tortures and sought her until she was once again cradled in his arms.

Two weeks in the mortal world, yet she had been in Almareyah barely a week. Kaeplan swore he had sent word to Dane of her whereabouts and plan. He had promised to leave a portal open in the event Dane wished to join her. A nice gesture, but had he kept his word? For the first week and a half she had convinced herself the time variation was to blame. Now, she began to have regrets, second thoughts.

As she prepared for bed, she decided she would ask Kaeplan come morning.

Kaeplan

He peeked into her chamber on his way past. She slept peacefully, breast rising and falling gently, lengthy red hair falling over the pillow to spill off the bed, nearly touching the floor.

"Ye shall be mine, forever," he whispered. But he knew for that to happen he needed more than a mere gaining of her trust here. He could not take the chance that she would ever again lay eyes on her mortal.

He closed the door silently and moved down the corridor to the far wing of the castle. After several turns he came to the hallway that went nowhere—or so it seemed to anyone other than himself. He stopped at the large tapestry that hung on the wall. The window above the hanging gave the wall a solid appearance.

He moved the tapestry aside. To any eyes but is own, only a stone wall existed there. He pressed both hands to the cold stones of the wall. The door appeared; wood and iron. Only his touch could reveal it. He pressed the latch and allowed the door to open inward. He crossed the threshold, closed the door behind him.

Kaeplan followed the extensive stone steps down into darkness. Only when he reached the first landing did the flickering light of a torch illuminate the next set of stairs. Though he could see well in the dark, some light was necessary for full vision.

Three floors below the castle, deep in its bowels, he came upon the large chamber, lit by more torches.

Lenophis stood by the first torch as if knowing his Master would arrive at that moment. The slave bowed deeply.

"Is it ready?" asked Kaeplan.

"Almost, my Master."

"Let me see," Kaeplan responded.

Lenophis bowed again and moved towards the door at the far end of the vast, nearly empty chamber. He pressed on the door, which opened with no protest.

They stepped into the dank room, smaller than the previous, and the moisture of the chamber hit him like a wall. He had found no need to create temperature or climate control in here. Droplets of dew dripped down the walls and off the ceiling. Perfectly uncomfortable.

Two servants halted in their labors and bowed to their Master.

The slave Aropheus looked eagerly at Kaeplan. "It is nearly done."

"Excuse me?" barked Kaeplan.

"It is nearly done…er…Master."

"Must I remind ye who rules this dimension?"

"No, Master. I am sorry."

Kaeplan sighed. He insisted all his workers call him Master;

one of the few things he brought with him from the Mortal Dimension hailed from several of what was called movies. In the mortal world the act was called B&D. Bondage and Discipline. He liked the sound of it, though mortals saw it as a form of sexual pleasure, he saw the servitude as respect for those higher up than themselves. Most of the superiors in the movies had been women—a Dominatrix he believed they termed themselves. He knew, however, that he would utilize its concept as a non-sexual way of controlling all in his world—and in his own dungeon.

As torches around the chamber were lit, Kaeplan smiled. The mortal world may have developed bondage equipment by their own imaginings, for their own pleasure, he had taken it one step farther.

He studied each piece of equipment, inspecting them for accuracy and the need to intimidate. On the far wall was what he referred to as a Rack. In the Mortal Dimension, this torture device was created to stretch a man until he tore apart. His, however, was built for a different purpose. The cell was nearly finished. It could easily fit two humans as long as one was hung from the chain and manacles on the wall. The cell in Mikaire had offered too much freedom and the mortal had taken full advantage. No more. To the right, against the next wall was an Iron Maiden. Intimidating in appearance, it appeared more of a coffin than the body shaped device he had seen in a museum of torture in the Mortal Dimension.

Thus far, all was exactly as he planned. Feeling pleased with himself, he moved on to study the whips, bonds and other equipment he had ordered for his dungeon, when suddenly his mind was distracted by a tickle in his brain that ran down his spine.

"Finish up. I will return," he ordered the workers. Someone was tripping the magic spell of a portal and his mind alerted him to a presence.

-Nineteen-

January 7, 2017
"In time and with water, everything changes." –Leonardo DeVinci

Dane, Stephan, Bruce & Adrian

It was a long hot walk into the desert. Dane wore his usual jeans, a tank top, a ball cap to keep shade on his face and his ponytail from whipping into his face. He should have worn a light long-sleeve shirt, as his shoulders turned red by the minute.

The other three were a bit more diligent with their attire, particularly Stephan, who burned easily due to being a redhead. His long-sleeved loose white shirt flapped in the wind, along with his hair, which was tied back but so long it still whipped around into his face. He spent most of the walk brushing it back. Adrian had the same issue with his blond locks, also tied back, but half way through the trip he stopped and pulled it up into a man-bun. Most of Bruce's hair was by now stuck in his beard.

All of them wore small backpacks filled with bottled water, protein bars, and in Dane's case, a bottle of wine... just in case.

The path was mostly blown over, but the four men followed the description received by the police in the direction of the pond where they had stated the footprints led to. The area was a bit like an oasis; a small water hole surrounded by grasses, some bushes, cactus and a sparse mingling of palm trees.

Dane and his band mates circled it several times, even walked through the water, but saw nothing of importance. No sign of anyone having been there.

"Dane," said Bruce, standing on the opposite end of the small pool of water, "this is not a pond but a puddle."

"It doesn't matter! I was dragged through a mirror in a bureau. Magic can't be explained. No different than your belief in God and the Bible."

"This...puddle," Bruce argued, "hasn't been here for thousands of years and is believed in by millions!"

"How would you know? Have you been here that long?"

"Well, I do know—"

He was interrupted by a shrill whistle. Both looked over as Stephan removed his two fingers from his mouth. "*Stop it* you two! This argument got old years ago!"

The arguing was replaced by contemptuous glares.

"Look, Dane," Stephan weighed in, once again pulling hair from his mouth and tossing it back over his shoulder only to have the wind whip it back again. "There's nothing here but an old puddle. I'm sorry, but there's no sign of...anything. It's been over two weeks. Wind and weather washed away any footprints the cops saw."

"Doesn't mean she wasn't here." Dane sighed.

"True, but there's nothing here now."

"You guys go home then," said Dane. "I'm staying here."

"And do what? Sit by a puddle?" Annoyed, Stephan finally followed Adrian in pulling his hair up onto his head.

"If I must!" He removed his backpack and set it in the sand, reached in and pulled a bottle of spring water. He opened it and drank.

"This was such a waste of time," snapped Bruce under his breath.

"At least it got him to shower and leave the house," said Adrian in a small voice.

"That's about *all* it did." Bruce started towards the others from across the water. "Let's go, I want to get back to Caitlyn."

Bruce was half way across the water, which was surprisingly deep, up to his knees, when Dane saw it. Just a flicker at first, water rippled unnaturally around his legs.

"*Bruce!*" Dane called out. "Get out of there, *quick!*"

The stubborn guitarist stopped. "Why? Have you—"

He never finished his sentence. A face appeared in the water's ripples—a face framed by bright red hair. *Kaeplan!*

Bruce dropped as if sucked suddenly into quicksand. He screamed in surprise and thrashed to remove himself.

Dane reached for him, his feet at the edge of the water. "Grab my hand!" But there was at least a foot between them.

Adrian splashed into the water to aid his friend, who was sinking rapidly.

"Adrian! No!!" Dane screamed. His words echoed on empty air as Adrian went down with Bruce.

From the shore Dane and Stephan reached, scrambled and fought to grab hands, hair, anything, to rescue their friends. But then they were gone.

The water bubbled and churned, then grew quiet.

"NO!" Dane sloshed into the puddle, thrashing his hands in the shallow and empty pool. "No! No! No!"

A hand from behind grabbed his shirt and pulled him backwards onto the land. He spun on Stephan, panic pounding in his breast. "We have to get them back!"

"They're gone, Dane!" Stephan choked. "There's nothing there."

"Did you see?" Dane grabbed Stephan by the arms. "Did you see him?"

Stephan nodded, shock registered clearly on his face. His russet eyes were wide. His breath came short. Hands shook.

"Oh my God, Stephan. He has them. Kaeplan took them."

Dane's legs gave out. He plopped into the wet sand beside the water bottle he had dropped, the clear liquid dribbling onto the earth. He grabbed it up and drank the rest, gritty sand washing over his tongue along with the liquid. He barely noticed.

Stephan dropped his backpack beside Dane's and sat beside his friend. "I kn-knew you hadn't lied about M-Meirah..." His voice quivered. "But...but part of me didn't want to believe such a thing existed."

"He was after *me*! This is all my fault."

"No," said Stephan softly. "It's not."

Dane looked up through wet strands of hair. "How can you say that?"

"They chose to come, just as I did."

"If I had gotten here first," Dane countered, "Kaeplan would have what he wanted."

"You could not have known."

"He's going to kill them," Dane wept. "None of this would have happened if I had not slept with Sabrina. Meirah would be with me, we'd be on tour and all would be as it is meant."

"Kaeplan would have found another way. You know this."

"He would have taken me when he was ready."

"And where would that have left Meirah? She would have followed. He'd get her no matter what…"

"But Adrian and Bruce would be safe."

"From what you've told me, he was out for revenge. He'd probably have taken us all. Now you have an advantage."

"What advantage?"

"We know he can get through a portal by water into this world, right?"

Dane nodded.

"We find another body of water. Let him take us together. But we'll be ready… aware. We need a plan. Once we're in we can get everyone out, including Meirah. You bested him before. You can do it again… With the four of us and Meirah, it's a sure thing."

Stephan's confidence gave Dane a mote of hope, but deep inside he knew how impossible any plan they devised would be. In Mikaire he'd had Meirah, who knew the world, where and when to move, where to hide and how to get out. Even then they barely made it. How well would she know this new dimension? And would she want to return after what he had done?

Reaching in his backpack, Dane's hand touched the bottle of wine and his fingers wrapped instinctively around it. But he let it go, and pulled another bottle of water instead. "Wherever they went, Meirah is there."

Stephan's face was more pale than usual.

Dane reached into Stephan's pack, pulled a bottle of spring water, handed it to him. "We wait. Kaeplan saw me, he had to—I saw him."

Stephan took a sip from the bottle with shaky hands. "We can't sit here forever."

"It's me he wants," said Dane. "I'm sure of it. He will return for me."

"Today?"

"Probably not. If Mikaire taught me anything, he will imprison them then use them—and Meirah—to get me to go to him."

"Then you fall into his trap, too. And there's no guarantee he will let the others go." He drank some water. "We need a better plan than just sitting here, Dane."

Dane thought for a moment, sipping the water and wishing it was the wine. "Well…any body of water should serve as a portal. Just as Meirah could see me through any mirror. I need to be prepared—and armed. The next time he comes to get me, I will be ready!"

"I'll help," said Stephan, though his words held more conviction than his tone.

Dane shook his head. "No. I understand these dimensions. I can't risk you ending up there, too. It's better I go alone."

"But, you will need—"

"Stephan! You don't know these realms. Sakkana was very powerful, enough so that he could renew my life as many times as he wished. There's no telling what powers Kaeplan possesses. Stay here, go home. I'll keep you informed."

"But—"

"No! I appreciate your loyalty, but I need someone on this side who knows what's going on. I'll go home and wait for Kaeplan to find me."

"You're going to sit by water the whole time?"

"Perhaps," said Dane, "but I doubt I'll need to. He can cross into this world. He knows where I am. He'll find me."

Both stood and lifted their backpacks. Walking away was difficult. Not only was Dane sure now that Kaeplan held Meirah, but now his friends too. But he had the advantage of having lived a dozen lives in a magical time dimension. As much as it hurt and fear ran rampant within him, memories of his tortures in Mikaire foremost in his mind, hope had been sparked. And Dane was ready to face his foe once again.

-Twenty-

Almareyah

Kaeplan

He could work with this variation from his original plan. He had hoped to snatch Dane, but the two mortals close to the human would do well.

When he had felt the alarm in his mind—more of a tingle really—which alerted him to human presence near the portal where he had taken Meirah, he'd wasted no time. He'd expected some random human. The pond in the desert was one of many in which he had placed a location spell. Any human presence would alert him and more than once the alerts had ended in disappointment. Random humans here and there. Some he had taken for food, others he ignored.

At all times he kept at least two guards by the Main Portal in Almareyah, and he surely needed them for the two humans he had just received. One sported what humans referred to as a beard, the other so pretty he thought at first he'd captured a female. But as they struggled with the guards, it became apparent they were both men.

They were easily subdued, chained so quickly their fight was a joke to Kaeplan. Though human bodies were inherently weak, their blood could hold the utmost strength. He wouldn't know until he had put them through his tests then tasted the liquid nourishment that ran through their veins.

With each guard holding one of each of them, the bearded one fought most fiercely. As Kaeplan approached, however, he went still, a snarl on his ugly human face.

"My, my," Kaeplan sniggered, "Such arrogance!"

"We know who you are," said the pretty one in an accent that reminded Kaeplan of a movie he had seen in the Mortal Dimension.

Kaeplan reached a hand to him, flicked at some of the hair that hung over his face in dripping blond strands.

"I thought ye were a lass when ye first came through," said Kaeplan abrasively. While in the mortal world, Kaeplan had seen men such as him—too pretty to be male. Others, he had learned, once were.

"Such an anomalous world from which ye hail. Lads who resemble lasses, lasses who look like lads. I do no' think I will ever understand."

The bearded one began once again to struggle. Kaeplan moved to stand before him, a snide grin on his face. "Ye'll never defeat my guards. Ye're but a human. Weak. Ye're all weak."

"If we're so weak," said the human, "then why do you need us to survive?"

Kaeplan tilted his head. "I'm impressed. Obviously ye're human friend Dane told ye all about Mikaire."

The pretty one spoke next. "He did—and all about *you,* Kaeplan!"

"I am at a disadvantage then. Ye know my name, but I don' know yers."

"Adrian Ionescu," said the blond quietly. Such a delicate voice. "And he is Bruce Beaufort."

Bruce snapped a glare at Adrian. "Don't tell this *beast* who we are!"

"What difference does it make?" Adrian replied.

Kaeplan nodded. "Hm, I like ye, Adrian Ionescu," he said, trying to mimic the accent. "I might just have tae let ye live a wee longer."

"If you're going to kill us," said Bruce, "Just do it!"

Kaeplan tilted his head towards the bearded one. "In a hurry to die... *Bruce?*"

Silence.

"That is what I figured." Kaeplan turned to the guards. "Take them tae the dungeon."

The guards bowed to their Master then dragged both men outside where a wagon, hitched to two black horses, awaited. They were tethered to it, then dragged along behind. Kaeplan preferred juspettes, but in his rush to create this world, he'd taken the short route and merely copied human beasts. Creating his own beasts of burden, as Sakkana had done, would take much more power and time. Camels were too slow and ornery. Horses served his purpose just fine.

Deliberately had Kaeplan built the dungeon near the Main Portal. It wasn't long before they crossed the barrier into his Kingdom. The back entrance was hidden, as were all entrances to the dungeon, by trees, bushes and magic—lush vegetation as he had seen in the mortal world in a place called the Amazon. He had built his entire world based on what he had seen and experienced there. And he would keep building until his was the largest and most powerful dimension of them all.

Once within the hidden gates to the castle, the wagon halted. Kaeplan hopped out and watched as the humans, still bound, were dragged inside, panting, sweating…exhausted. Another guard, positioned at the entrance, took care of the horses.

Within, a single torch lit the dungeon. The humans would be more submissive if they could not see well. Yet another weakness with which to take advantage. And, as he'd expected, they allowed the guards to lead them into the dimly lit chamber.

Inside, they stopped, turned to their Master for instruction.

"Put that one," Kaeplan instructed, motioning to Adrian, "in the cell." He turned to the other guard. "That one in the Iron Maiden!"

Apparently, the human knew of this device, as he began once again to struggle—fiercely. Once Adrian was locked away, the second guard rushed to aid the first. Each grabbed an arm and dragged Bruce to the large upright rectangular box, the only opening a single slit at face level. One guard opened the box, the other shoved Bruce in, then the door was slammed and locked.

From within, Kaeplan heard the human's sigh. He approached. Only Bruce's eyes were visible.

"Did ye think," Kaeplan chuckled, "that I would copy this human device exactly? No…I left out the spikes. Ye'd have bled out too quickly. What a waste. Comfortable, is it not?"

No reply. Just wide eyes.

"Hm." Kaeplan moved away, letting the human mull in his misery.

He approached the cell where Adrian had been chained, arms outstretched, to the far wall. "Open it," he instructed.

"Yes, Master," His guard, Yeholi, bowed quickly before unlocking the iron-barred door.

Kaeplan stepped inside and approached Adrian. He looked him over. Pale for a human, thin and tall, with flaxen hair, once tied up, fell now straight over bony shoulders and down his back. His clothing had dried from the trip through the water portal, but sweat offered a bit of damp to his chest.

"Are ye sure ye're a male, Human?" he asked, a snarky grin on his face.

Kaeplan received no reply.

"I suppose I shall have to find out for myself. Need to be sure." Kaeplan drew the sword he always kept at his waist. Adrian cringed back against the non-yielding stone wall.

"Fear not," said Kaeplan. "I shan't harm ye. No' yet."

Two quick slashes with the weapon and Adrian's white linen shirt fell in a crumpled heap to the flagstones, revealing a pale chest, devoid of hair as Kaeplan had seen on other human males—including Dane.

"Hmm, no breasts like a woman," he teased, marveling at the humiliation in the human's face. "Only one way to know for sure."

Two more slashes of the sword's blade and the tight jeans fell as well, crumpled at Adrian's feet. The human closed his eyes, dropped his head as if to hide the humiliation behind his hair. Male for sure. Kaeplan smiled… removing the human's clothes was a ruse. Not to reveal gender, for he had long established Adrian as male, but to induce the ultimate humiliation—a most powerful weapon. Most humans took the privacy of their bodies so seriously.

Kaeplan reached forward and grasped a handful of Adrian's hair, jerked his head back and up to peer into the blue eyes. "Keep your head up…or I will nail it to the wall!"

He released the human and stepped from the cell, leaving him naked, save the shoes on his feet. A guard entered, gathered up

Adrian's torn clothing, exited. Soon, Kaeplan knew, the damp cold would penetrate this human's naked flesh. Punishment did not always need to include physical pain.

Satisfied, Kaeplan left the dungeon, leaving the mortals to think on their situation.

Meirah

She opened the door. Lenophis stood at the doorway, his drab robes of grey and white hung loose. Slaves attire.

"Yes?" she said coldly.

"Master requires your presence for breakfast." Lenophis moved aside and two female servants passed him and entered the room.

"Of course he does!"

Meirah closed the door in his face once the servant girls were in the room.

As per her routine for the past three weeks, Meirah sat at the dressing table while Keliah began work on her. Isophia prepared day clothes for her.

"What news without?" she asked the servant girls. They looked at each other but, as usual, said nothing, and went on with primping her.

Keliah brushed Meirah's thigh-length red hair with utmost precision before working it into a braid.

"The two of ye have ne'er spoken tae me," said Meirah, gazing into the mirror at the reflection of the both. Once more, they gazed to each other but spoke not a word.

Three weeks and no one but Kaeplan to talk to. How she missed Dane's conversations and Edna's uplifting views. *This is for the baby*, she reminded herself. Whenever she began to miss Dane, she pulled up the image of him and the other woman in the hotel and the spell of her love for him snapped.

Keliah wrapped the long braid onto Meirah's head and pinned it into place. Meirah stood and allowed Isophia to dress her in a floor-length silk gown of beige, light lace outlined the low neckline, revealing the tops of breasts that had grown bigger since her residence here. Even her belly now showed a slight bulge. She grinned and placed a hand over it as Isophia wrapped gold bands around her upper arms. On her feet they placed golden slippers. Meirah felt like a queen.

Once dressed and ready, the girls led her out of the room.

"I can find my own way," she said and picked up her pace. But they matched her stride. "I guess not."

Rather than leading her to the portico where they had always had breakfast, the girls turned down a different hallway. She had never been in the Dining Hall, but she knew this was the way.

They reached the over-sized blue and gold double doors and the girls paired off and away as a male guard, apparent by the uniforms of blue and white they all wore, opened the doors to allow Meirah entrance.

He bowed to her as she stepped inside. "M'Lady," he said then closed the doors behind her.

The Dining Hall was as ornate and large as the other rooms she had seen in the castle. Kaeplan had certainly spared no power in making it.

"Ah, there she is," said Kaeplan as he stood from the throne-like chair that resided at the end of a table so long it could easily seat twenty. On the walls were a mish mash of art, swords and paintings that looked as if they had been stolen from various eras of human history. This reminded Meirah of Dane's home. She sighed.

Kaeplan was dressed in fancy wizard robes, similar to those Sakkana had worn, except an off-white color hemmed in gold. A servant pulled out a chair for her on the side of the table closest to Kaeplan's throne.

"Thank ye," she smiled to the servant. But, as always, he merely nodded as she took her seat, then moved away and left the room.

The table was elaborately set with a wide array of dishes filled with many variations of human food. She knew the names of each and every one; eggs of all types, orange juice, bacon, sausage and even grits. Every dish was coordinated around a large sparkling silver candelabra, each of its dozen candles lit, creating a romantic ambiance. Heavy blue and white drapes closed out the daylight.

"This is different," she said, gazing around. "Human food? A huge Dining Hall? What's the occasion?"

"Do ye no' like it?" Kaeplan reached towards a ceramic pitcher, began pouring its contents into one of the many glasses set before her. Blood. She could smell it now. Human blood! She lifted the glass, sniffed it. Fresh, and warm.

Meirah gave Kaeplan a sideways glance. "Where did ye obtain this?"

Kaeplan poured himself a glass, drank it down in one long swallow. "Does it matter? Drink before it gets cold."

She took a sip. Sweet and delicious. She tilted the glass and drank half of it down.

"Good. Is it no'?" asked Kaeplan.

She took another sip. Like drinking paradise. "But only wizards can drink human blood," she said, though it was more of a question than a statement.

"Maybe in Mikaire that was truth. But no' here. Well...ye're an exception. You and I are the only ones allowed." He poured himself another glass. "Drink... before it gets cold."

Gazing warily at him over her glass, she placed it to her lips and finished it. Kaeplan poured the rest from the pitcher into her glass. So good, she finished it at once.

Meirah set the glass down. "What is wi' the human food?"

"Eat. I want ye tae feel at home. I am sure ye partook o' human food in the mortal world. This is a special occasion. I want ye tae be comfortable."

Meirah tilted a suspicious glance his way. "I have taken breakfast wi' ye for three weeks now... always animal blood and some eggs. What is this occasion of which ye speak?"

"Nothin' too special," he replied. "Try this... It is quite satisfyin' tae the palate." He removed the lid from one of the silver serving dishes, took up the spoon and scooped it into the bowl by her elbow before filling his own.

"What is this?" she asked cautiously. She sniffed at the dish. Unfamiliar but with a tang that made her stomach grumble. Or was that the baby again?

"'Tis a vegetable barley soup. In the time I resided in the Mortal Dimension, I had the chance to try many human recipes. I must say, at first it made me ill, but certain foods also cured my ills. And so I took to those. Try it."

Meirah spooned a bit into her mouth. The taste reminded her

of a few of the dishes Edna made; a slight kick of spices, and quite delicious.

"Mmm. Good." She smiled.

Kaeplan offered a wide grin in response. Something was different... His fangs. Were they longer? Sakkana's fangs had been the longest and sharpest in Mikaire. She could only deduce that, as wizards grew in power, so did their fangs. This would not matter except that it meant Kaeplan's powers were still growing and that made her a bit nervous. A wizard's power came from drinking strong mortal blood.

Dane!

Meirah dropped the spoon into the dish, some of the contents slopped out.

Kaeplan started. "What? What is wrong, Meirah?"

She glared at him. '*Where* is he?"

"Where is who?"

"Dane!"

Kaeplan placed his spoon into the dish. "I know not, Meirah. Probably taking his pleasure wi' another woman!"

Meirah stood so quickly, the chair she sat in fell backwards.

Kaeplan stood as well. "Meirah! What is wi' ye? I told ye the truth. Yer Dane is no' here!"

"Don' ye lie tae me!" She bared her fangs. "Yer teeth... Wizards only grow their fangs from strong human blood."

"Meirah, please." He lifted the chair, moved to stand by her. He placed gentle hands on her shoulders and guided her back into her seat. "Let me explain."

As he bent forward, a chain he wore around his neck fell from its hiding place beneath his robes. He grasped it and tucked it back away, but not before she saw the pendant; almost identical to the key to the Main Mirror in Mikaire, except the serpents had wings.

She sat, but remained tense, her hunger gone.

Kaeplan re-took his throne seat. "Do ye think yer mortal is the only human wi' powerful blood?"

"That is why Sakkana chose him—reincarnated him all those mortal centuries."

"Meirah..."Kaeplan reached a hand to place over hers, but she pulled away before they could make contact. He sighed and placed his hands on the table in front of him. "I promise on my own existence and the existence of my world, Dane is *not* here! I traveled the mortal world quite a bit. I found other humans wi' the blood I require. I swear this tae ye."

Meirah looked deep into Kaeplan's amber eyes. Usually, when he lied red specks would spark, yet nothing within spoke of deception. As far as she could see, he told the truth.

She sighed and sat back. "I believe ye."

Kaeplan smiled. "Here, try the eggs."

Once breakfast was over, Meirah returned to her chamber, escorted as usual by her two female servants.

As they removed her dress and prepared her for day/hunting attire, Meirah attempted once again to engage them in conversation. No reply.

Finally, she spoke bluntly. "Can neither o' ye speak?"

Both women lowered their gazes as if in shame. Meirah moved to Isophia and gently placed a hand beneath her chin, raising her face to look into her eyes.

"Can ye no' speak?" Meirah asked.

Isophia shook her head slowly. Meirah looked to Keliah. "And you?" Another head shake.

"Ye're both mute?" They nodded. "And this is as ye've always been?" More nods.

With great suspicion in her heart, Meirah asked, "Are all women in this world mute?"

The servants glanced to one another again before nodding.

Kaeplan had created a world of mute women! Complete subservience.

"Oh my God," she spoke the expression she had often heard in the mortal world.

"Please go," she said to them. "I need to be alone to hunt."

They bowed and left the room. Meirah sat on the bed in her hunting clothes; beige tunic with matching breeches and leather boots. However, she had no intention of going out to hunt.

Kaeplan had not informed her he had created a world of male domination, leaving women with no voice. Slaves! This was not a world in which she would be comfortable. There was more going on beneath his veil of deception. She knew that now. It was time to find out what Kaeplan was *really* up to!

Bruce and Adrian
Almareyah

Bruce stared through the tiny slit of the dark cramped box where he had been imprisoned for hours. His feet and legs had begun to cramp as he was unable to bend his knees, nor to sit. The Iron Maiden may be void of the spikes normally attributed to the torture device for which this box was named, but it held its own torments. He shifted his weight as best he could from one foot to another.

Only a single torch on the dank stone wall flickered and it had taken his eyes awhile to adjust. He began to understand, if only remotely, what Dane had gone through in Mikaire. But Dane had been flogged, beaten and tortured, and now Bruce prayed silently that same fate was not meant for him or his friend.

About twenty feet away, he could just see Adrian behind the bars of his cell, chained like an animal to the wall. His friend was slumped forward, naked, shivering—and bleeding from a deep wound in his arm. Adrian's blood trickled steadily like a leaky tap into a wooden bowl set on the floor to catch the crimson stream.

If it weren't for his memory of Dane's explanation for this abuse, he'd not understand why one of Kaeplan's minions had sliced Adrian open like a pig at slaughter, taken a pitcher of his blood, and placed the bowl to capture the rest. No sense in wasting food.

"Adrian!" Bruce called, his voice echoing inside the tight enclosure.

His friend, whose head was bowed, body so weak only the chains held him upright, groaned and forced his head up laboriously to peek through his hair. "Still here," he said weakly.

"Stay with me buddy."

"W-Why?" Bruce feared Adrian had begun to give in the blood loss.

Bruce guesstimated they had taken near half his blood.

"Because I need you. The band needs you."

"Wha...what band?" His head dropped again.

"C'mon!" Bruce needed to keep his friend talking, awake. "Dane and Stephan are still out there. They're working on a plan to get us out of here."

Silence.

"*Adrian!*"

The blond head came up slowly.

"Stay with me, buddy. I don't want to be stuck here alone."

"Why...are...they..." His head drooped forward again.

"*Hey!*" Bruce screeched from within his own hell. "I don't think they want you dead. So, don't die!"

The words had just escaped Bruce's lips when the dungeon door opened. He pressed his face against the rough wood to see better. One of the guards sauntered in, a woven basket in one hand. He opened the cell door and approached Adrian.

"Hey, you!" Bruce yelled at him. "Help him." He was ignored.

The guard pulled a large green leaf, similar to a palm frond, from the basket. He placed it over the wound on Adrian's arm. The bleeding stopped immediately. He then wrapped Adrian's arm with a long bandage from the basket and tied the ends. Taking up the bowl, he covered it with a cloth and placed it carefully into the basket. Bruce noticed something small in his hand, and when he reached up to Adrian's wrist, Bruce held his breath. The guard unlocked the shackles. A key! Adrian dropped like a rag doll onto the stones.

He lifted the basket and exited the cell, locking it behind him. But before he moved to the door, he glanced over at Bruce.

"You are next!" And then he was gone.

Meirah

Like a labyrinth that had yet to be complete, the castle hallways went everywhere and nowhere. Most hallways seemed useless, empty, dead ends. Others were lined with doors. She opened each one to find either desolation, or servant's quarters. Each hallway, no matter which direction she chose, always led either to the Portico, the Dining Hall or her own chamber. She was moving in circles.

Unlike the castles in Mikaire, which followed a logical sequence, this castle appeared as if it were still being constructed. Kaeplan had built a world and a home, but apparently had not yet come into his full powers to finish it. She wondered idly if she could use this to her advantage. Nothing came to mind presently, but...

She turned down the fifth hallway, and arrived at yet another dead end wall. Sighing, she stared at it long and hard. There appeared to be something different here. Nothing obvious came to her attention—at the least nothing that would stand out to someone who was not looking. But she had seen the same walls and dead ends so many times, each detail emblazoned on her memory.

She approached the solid wall and placed her palms against it. Cold hard stone. She repeated the motion a few feet down the wall, walking her hands up and down, when she came to a near invisible anomaly. Just a slight flicker, easily confused with the light from the torches, and a slender shadow where there should not be one. She pressed her hands against the shadow—and they disappeared before her.

She pulled back, a small grin touching her lips. "Ye sneaky bastard," she whispered.

A barrier. Kaeplan had placed barriers on unassuming walls, sure no one would notice.

She stepped forward, ready to cross into wherever this barrier led, when the sound of footfalls echoed against the empty corridor. She turned, setting her back again the wall near the barrier, and feigned straightening her tunic.

He came around the corner and halted when he saw her.

"Oh, M'Lady," he bowed.

Meirah straightened. One of Kaeplan's male slaves. Kaeplan may have been clever in creating his labyrinthine castle with its hallways to nowhere and hidden barriers, but he fell short in clothing design. All male slaves wore the same beige robes that brushed the floor. All wore their hair in long braids down their backs. This one's complexion was dark with black hair and deep brown eyes.

Once the slave arose from his bow, he spoke to her. "May I ask where you are headed, M'Lady? May I help you find your way?" His words were slow, careful, and touched by an accent she could not place.

Meirah wanted to tell him to go to hell. Instead, she said, "I seek Kaeplan. Do ye know where I can find him?"

"Mm, I am not sure, M'Lady."

Meirah nodded. "May I ask ye somethin'?"

He nodded.

"Where are ye from?"

A perplexed expression crossed his dark features. "I am from here, Almareyah, M'Lady."

"Ye were born here?" She cocked her head.

"Uh...I...yes," he stuttered as if not quite understanding the question.

"Have ye ever been tae the Mortal Dimension?"

"The M-Mor-tal... Dim—"

"Never mind. Please instruct me tae the exit. I am quite lost and wish tae hunt."

"Oh, I can lead you..."

"No, no, 'tis alright. Tell me where and I shall find my way."

The slave shrugged and proceeded to direct her.

"Thank ye, that will be all," she said dismissively.

He bowed once again and continued along the way he had been heading. Once out of sight, Meirah ignored—actually she forgot—his direction. When she was sure he was gone, she turned to the barrier, paused for a deep breath and stepped through.

She found herself in yet another labyrinth of hallways.

"Oh Jesus Fucking Christ!" she repeated a typical curse she had picked up from her husband.

This hallways went nowhere—on the contrary, it was one large triangle. At one end, a window high above let in tendrils of light, below it a large tapestry. Why would Kaeplan place a tapestry in a hallway beyond a barrier that went nowhere? He wouldn't. She knew then she was missing something.

She studied the wall around the tapestry for shadows that should not be there. The castle was full of wall tapestries, but something about this one stayed her, searching for an anomaly. It was a rather grotesque depiction of a human male, naked and bleeding from a gash in his arm. The silver-blue eyes of the man wept, then it hit her—his eyes were Dane's eyes. She swallowed hard. The man in the tapestry was clearly not her husband, only in the eyes... and his bleeding hand motioned towards the bottom of the wall hanging.

Squatting, she followed the hand's image to the bottom right corner...a tiny symbol, almost invisible. She gasped. The image was almost identical to the pendant key from Mikaire used to open the Main Looking Glass. Except the beasts wrapped around the small sword were not srependiles, Sakkana's mote beasts. No, these snake-like creatures had wings.

She had seen this image before... on Kaeplan's own necklace.

"Oh, Kaeplan, what did ye create?"

Meirah studied the tapestry more closely. Beneath the suffering mortal man with Dane's eyes, was the reflection of the same man reflected in a pool of water. A veil of blood spread out amongst the water's ripples. The knowledge struck her all at once—water. Kaeplan had pulled her into this dimension through the puddle at the oasis in Nevada. So, the portal was through water, the sword symbol—the key.

But what she needed was to find the main portal, the one through which he had brought her to this world. She tried to recall detail of her journey into this dimension, but she had been in such despair, and he had swept her off on the back of his horse so quickly, she had paid no mind to her surroundings.

She was sure now, however, that one of the barriers within the castle led to the outside, to the main portal somewhere. Kaeplan would not have created it far away. She would start mapping the castle in secret, marking all barriers until she knew every inch of Almareyah—Kaplan's dimension.

-Twenty-One-

January 9, 2017

"Try to be a rainbow in someone's cloud." -Maya Angelou

Dane and Stephan

"Where are we going?" Dane asked Stephan for the umpteenth time as they boarded the private plane.

"You'll see."

Same reply as the last time he asked. "Why is this such a mystery?"

"It's not'" said Stephan as he took the seat facing Dane and buckled up.

Dane sighed exaggeratedly. Stephan had called him to pack what he needed for a few days, but nothing fancy. He refused to answer Dane's questions. When the limo arrived to pick him up at his estate, Stephan was in the back. No matter how many times Dane asked where they were going, he received the same reply. Now, in the private plane the band hired to fly overseas or across the country, Dane still got nowhere.

"If it's not a mystery, Stephan, then tell me." One of the stewardesses set drinks on the table in front of them the moment the plane leveled off. "Thank you," Dane smiled.

At one time, he thought as she walked away and he watched her hips sway under the short black skirt, *I would have hit that!*

He turned his attention back to Stephan, hardly a picture with his pale and boyish slightly freckled skin and waist-long red hair tied back in a ponytail. But the women flocked to him on tours, as he was now the only eligible bachelor in the band, except Adrian, who always avoided the girls—and guys—who made passes at the band members. His life he kept so private, even the media never showed any interest in him. Although, he wondered, now that Meirah might leave him, would he be eligible again?

Dane shook away the thought as Stephan spoke.

"I don't want you to get too excited." Stephan tilted the champagne glass to his lips.

At first, Dane thought Stephan was talking about the stewardess, but then realized he was wrong. "Unless you found Meirah," he said, "I doubt I will get all that excited." Dane lifted his own glass; red wine rather than champagne. A list of all the band members' preferred food and drinks were kept in the galley of the hired jet.

"Well, no," said Stephan, his face turning a bit redder than usual. "I'm sorry to say I haven't found your wife, but I have an idea that just might lead us to her." He smiled as he sipped.

Dane downed the glass of wine, wishing he had the entire bottle.

"Just fucking tell me!" The stewardess was back, taking up his empty glass and setting down a fresh one. Good service.

"All right." Stephan leaned against the table, looked Dane in the eye. "We know the portal is water, correct?"

"Yeah, so—?"

"What's the biggest body of water in America?"

"The ocean."

Stephan slumped back in his seat and the amber eyes rolled, closed then re-opened. "*Fresh* water!"

Dane shrugged.

"Lake… Michigan." Stephan spoke slowly as if Dane were a child.

"Ok, I get it. So why such a big body of water? Adrian and Bruce were taken in a puddle in the desert. We could have just stayed there."

"You want to sit in an empty desert for days and nights on end?" The red brows rose. "There's camping at Lake Michigan. I rented an RV and a spot by the water. We will have warmth, food, shelter and a bathroom. It's winter. No one will bother us."

Dane shrugged. "I guess so."

"C'mon, Dane, it's brilliant and you know it."

The idea was a good one, but Stephan's ego needed no boost. "It's an ok idea."

Adrian and Bruce
Almareyah

His stomach wouldn't leave him alone. Though he couldn't discern day from night, Adrian guessed he hadn't eaten in close to a week. Nothing solid anyway. Once per day, by his best determination, one of Kaeplan's slaves brought water and a bowl of slop they called food. It kept him alive, but his needs ran more along the lines of a nice Cordon Bleu and roasted peppers.

He'd lost weight, but hardly required it. He could see his ribs more than usual and his arms were not much bigger than his drumsticks. He wish he'd had a set, then he could keep his mind busy drumming on the floor or bars.

At least they hadn't chained him to the wall again, and they finally brought him a blanket. He wrapped himself up in it, but still shivered as the damp cold had seeped into his bones. At the least he still wore his leather boots.

He guessed their intention was not to have him freeze or starve to death, but sometimes he thought he'd die of boredom. At least he had Bruce to talk to... until his friend went silent.

"Bruce?" he called out.

A weak barely audible voice replied. "Yeah?"

"Are you alright?"

"I've been better."

Just as they had drained him of most of his blood, they had done the same to Bruce. Leaf and all. Adrian looked at his arm where they had cut him. Barely a scar showed.

"Don't give up, Bruce," he said. "They don't want us dead."

"Not yet," came the soft reply.

Adrian felt for Bruce more than he did himself. Though the cell was small, he could at least sit and lie down. He had gathered up the sparse amounts of straw laid out on the stones and made himself a very prickly and uncomfortable bed. Bruce, on the other hand, had to remain standing—as much as he could.

A few times Adrian heard thumping and banging from the box they had referred to as an Iron Maiden. Before this, the only Iron Maiden he had heard of was a rock band from before his time. This one was a strongly built heavy wooden box that reminded him more of a tomb... or a coffin standing upright. When Bruce became too weak to stand, he'd start to go down, his knees and body crashing against its close walls.

"Bruce?" Adrian wanted to keep his friend awake, as he had done for him.

"Y-Yeah."

"How long do you suppose we have been in here?" *Keep him talking.*

No response.

"*Bruce!*"

"I...don't...know, Adrian. Too long." His breath came hard between words.

"Hang in there."

"T-trying."

They'd given Bruce slightly less food as they had to spoon it through the small hole. Most, he was sure, spilled inside, onto Bruce and the interior of his prison. By now he was sure it was rotting. All too increasingly was he aware of the stench building in the dungeon; a vile mix of mold, body odor, and urine and feces. He had a corner of the cell in which to relieve himself. He dared not think on how soiled Bruce must be, unable to get away from his own excretions.

"Dane and Stephan will find us, rescue us," he said, using the same encouraging words Bruce had when he was down.

"I-I hope they hurry," said Bruce. "Not sure how much longer I can stay like this..."

Adrian heard a thump and Bruce went silent yet again.

Meirah

The cave was damp and dark, green moss covered the walls and ground like thick carpeting from the Mortal Dimension. It squished beneath her feet and she found it quite soothing. She wanted to remove her leather shoes, but she had no idea what else this cave would offer, so she left them on and continued forward. The way narrowed slightly and ahead she could see the passage turned a corner, and beyond, sunlight trickled in and touched the wall. Finally!

After a week of secretly mapping the castle and every barrier she could find within it, she had begun to believe the castle was one large circle of labyrinthine barriers that led to other rooms, or nowhere.

Meirah removed the pen and folded paper from the hidden pocket within her hunting breeches beneath the green tunic that flowed down past her buttocks. She deliberately wore loose shirts of soft cotton, not only for comfort but to keep hidden the map and pen she kept with her on her excursions.

Kaeplan had taken much from the Mortal Dimension when he created this place, and it certainly made life easier. Pens were her favorite for writing poems and journal entries; so much simpler and easy to carry than quill and ink. Cotton rather than linen or hide was softer, warmer and so much easier to move about in when hunting, or to transverse corridors and down narrow passages.

Coming into the sunlight around the corner gave her hope at last. She began to jog until the cave opened up into a wide mouth. She picked up a run around the next corner where the sun was full—and halted quickly, for she almost ran straight into a barred door.

"Son-of-a-bitch!" she whispered to no one. Why did she think Kaeplan would make this easy?

She placed her hands on the bars and shook them. Solid. The only rattle was of the thick chain and the large lock that hung from one side, keeping the door well locked. Of course… Kaeplan wanted no one to get out, or in, unless he knew of it.

There had to be a way outside, to the main portal, for when he had brought her to the castle, though she paid no mind to the way, they had been outside before entering into the shadows of the castle walls. And they'd been on horseback. No caves.

Meirah folded her knees and flopped down to sit on the sandy ground. No soft moss here in this bright sunlight. Staring at the door, she allowed herself a moment to think on what she might have missed. The bars were made of a heavy iron, so there was no way to break or bend it. The horizontal top and bottom bars were thicker than the verticals that made up the door. Each bar was no more than a couple inches apart, and as slight as she was, even she couldn't squeeze through.

Sighing, she pressed her palms into the sand beneath her. It was then that she sat up straight, grabbing handfuls of the sediment and letting it sift through her fingers. She began to laugh.

"Can nae think o' everythin', can ye Kaeplan," she said aloud.

Crawling forward, she came right up to the door. The bottom bar was about six inches from the ground. She began to dig. Maybe she couldn't get through the door, but she knew she could get under it!

A half hour later, she had a hole big enough to squiggle through, and she came out on the other side. Dusting off the dirt from her clothes and hair, she looked around. She was in a forest of dense trees and brush. The ground outside the cave was mostly sand, but as she walked towards the trees, her feet crunched on dead leaves and hard packed soil. It was as if the castle and even the cave had been built in a desert and Kaeplan had chosen to plop a forest onto it. The trees were similar to those she saw in South Carolina and other states, yet also bore tropical fauna as well. It seemed almost odd to her after living two years in the mortal world, to see a palm tree beside a maple.

Carefully, she moved along, watching the greenery, for it grew quite thick with many black palms and their crazy long sharp thorns. She had not seen black palm before, but on television, so she knew of its dangers. The air as well changed gradually, from a dry heat to moist, sticky and extremely humid. A rain forest.

She had begun to wonder if Kaeplan had built villages, or had citizens, other than those within the castle grounds, when the fauna grew thick with not only the black palm, but every variation of thorny tree and bush she knew existed, and many she knew not. Avoiding the thorny fauna became impossible, and she winced with every scratch and cut to her flesh.

This had to lead somewhere special, she thought... why else would he not only have a barred door but dangerous plants protecting it?

Determination kept her going, despite the tearing of her shirt, cuts on her legs. No one except her would be crazy enough to weather this region.

But it paid off when at last the world around her opened up; not like a Mikairian barrier, but like coming to the end of a great wood into an area of populace. Before her stood buildings, roads…and people. She stepped from the forest of thorns and tread through sand once again. More desert. The air grew dry and, though hot, not nearly as within those trees. She sighed in relief as the wind fluttered through her torn, sweaty tunic.

She reached the road, made of white cobblestones, and followed it through what appeared a city; at least by Mikairian standards. She marveled at what Kaeplan had created here; apparently taking bits of what he had seen in the mortal world and placing them randomly within this place. She walked past homes and shops, each so unique as to appear mismatched. Some were built of simple mud-brick, others elaborate wooden structures and even large stone structures.

In her awe at the structures, she had not noticed the crowds of villagers watching her. But she felt eyes upon her at last and when she finally tore her gaze back to the present, she realized she had wandered into what appeared to be the center of town. Men, women and children alike had halted in their activities and stared at her with questioning, but she had no idea what the question, or the answer, could be.

The attire of these people was as varied as the buildings, but most were dressed in simple clothing; loose tunics like herself, robes and head dress such as those she had seen in the castle and even more 'modern' wear. Less common, but a few of the younger ones wore khaki slacks and button-front blouses.

As they all stared, she wanted only to disappear, for their interrogations had grown quite uncomfortable. Was it the scratches on her body from the thorny forest? Her torn clothes? She stopped, looking about as villagers seemed to appear from nowhere just to gawk at her. She opened her mouth to ask what was so interesting when she spotted the tapestry. Her mouth dropped open in disbelief.

Hanging on the outside of a stone and brick building, and as large as the building itself, the tapestry depicted a painted version of herself wearing the burgundy dress from Mikaire that was her celebration gown for her and Kaeplan's interrupted engagement. Beside her was a painted Kaeplan, in his wizard robes, smiling fiercely... and they were holding hands!

Suddenly feeling frightened and exposed, she broke into a run, forcing people to part quickly or be run over. Once away from the people and out of sight of that deplorable tapestry, she slowed, her breath coming hard and fast. Needing a place to rest, she sat on what she thought was a stone wall and leaned back against the wooden beam behind it.

She tilted her head back, closed her eyes, tried to concentrate on catching her breath. But before long, she once again heard the sound of voices, the shuffling of feet. Reluctantly she opened her eyes. Sure enough, the villagers milled into the open area before her, watching. She began to understand why Dane wore a disguise of brown contact lenses and a ball cap when out in public. This was getting creepy.

But when she tried to make eye contact with one of them; a male around her own age, who stood closest to her, he merely lowered his eyes, bowed his head. She tried another. Same response. No one spoke, they only stared until she looked direct at them.

Meirah had had enough! She stood and turned to seek a way out. The wood beam she had been leaning against caught her attention now and something about its placement did not seem right. It was just a tall and large plank of wood, surrounded by a small stone wall that seemed almost like a...platform. She gazed its length upwards. Just above where she had sat, attached to the wood with thick iron rings, hung chains and shackles.

Oh God, a whipping post!

"No!" she called out, recalling the flogging Dane had endured in Mikaire.

This place was a nightmare.

Once again, she took off. What direction had she come? She couldn't recall, she just bolted. She thought she heard someone yell, "my Queen!" but she ignored it.

She darted down an alley, determined to find solace from the masses, but she ran head-on into a line of drying clothes.

Untangling herself, she halted and peeked around the long

robes and bedding that were hung between the buildings. She was alone. Thinking quickly, she grabbed up the robe and head dress, throwing them on over her tattered clothing. The robe had a hood—perfect. She pulled up her red hair, which apparently gave her away more than her appearance. As she could see, none in this world boasted the red hair that she and Kaeplan shared in common. She pulled the attached veil over her face and cautiously exited the alley. Once back on the street, she walked quickly, looking at no one.

So distracted at avoiding recognition, she barely noticed when the terrain changed back to sand. Her shoes sunk in its depths and slowed her. She stopped quickly. The sun shone brightly in the cloudless sky and the heat, though dry once more, was unbearable.

Her memory decided at that moment to relay feelings and thoughts from the day Kaeplan had brought here to Almareyah. She had been wet from the portal of water, but barely noticed as she struggled against Kaeplan as he hauled her onto his horse. Had it been hot? Yes! Heat...dry heat. But as she had been wet, it had not penetrated her clothing as it did now.

She moved again, struggling with her footing, up a dune of shifting sand. Wind whipped the gritty stuff into her face and eyes, but she was sure she saw footprints. Most had been covered, but she was sure of it... footprints of people who passed through here recently.

She struggled up the mountainous dune and when she neared the top, something beyond flashed in her eyes. The dune was so steep, she used her hands to gain purchase in the unstable sand to reach the top. Once there, she stood and looked down on the structure in disbelief. It was so bright white, the sun glared off it like a beacon.

A pyramid—enormous and bright. Like those in Egypt, made of new limestone and illuminated with magical light.

Meirah half slid, half ran down the dune towards it. The structure was farther away than it appeared. She traversed the deep sand until she reached it. She followed the side until she came to a corner. She peered around—the front was marked by grand obelisks that flanked an entranceway of double doors decorated with lacquered dark wood and Egyptian symbols.

She approached them, staring in such awe she almost missed

the echo of voices growing louder from within its mouth. She ducked behind an obelisk and peeked out. Several male citizens dressed in loose white robes, some wearing sandals, others bare feet, exited through the wide arched mouth of the pyramid, speaking softly to one another. Meirah didn't recognize the language, but what she did notice was the smear of blood along the lips of the young male. He wiped it away with a cloth, casually like a diner wiping his mouth after supper. Meirah knew she needed to get in there without being recognized.

In the tapestry, her hair was bound tightly on her head. Now, she had a disguise. She pulled her long braid up and tucked it neatly into the head dress, then lifted the hood over that. The veil attached gave the final touch as she pulled it over to cover her face, so only her eyes could be seen. She removed her boots, hid them in the sand at the base of the structure. The sand was hot on her sensitive feet, so she rushed towards the entrance.

Keeping her eyes low, she passed another man, who glanced in her direction, but he did not seem to recognize her; he merely shook his head and continued on.

Once inside, the cooler air relieved. The short hallway was lined with torches. Seeing no one, she lowered the veil a bit to get a better view. A tall set of tan-colored doors stood before her. Emblazoned across it were words, written in many languages. On the top, written boldly in English the large letters read:

NO MORE THAN THREE SIPS PER
RESIDENT. VIOLATORS WILL BE
EXECUTED.
-Per the Almareyah Government

Meirah drew open the doors. The somber atmosphere and ambient lighting within was broken by the sounds of moaning. But it was the scent that caught her attention first.

Blood. Human blood.

She stifled her gasp with one hand as she moved to the center of the large room. Around one half of the circular area, poles were erected, and chained hands and feet to each was a person. And there were about a dozen of them. Some stood upright, others slumped against their chains. Beside each was an obelisk, about 3 feet in height with angled tops. Written on each was a number. From where she stood, Meirah could see each number. At first, she thought each body was assigned a number based on their location within the circle, but there was no correlation or logical pattern to them.

She carefully approached a young blonde female, scantily clad in only a bra and panties, who struggled uselessly against her bonds. As Meirah approached, her blue eyes grew wide with utter fear and her struggles grew fiercer, all the while slight moans escaped her parted lips. The number written on the obelisk read 2.

Meirah glanced about. No one else was in the structure at the moment. She moved in close, but the woman fought so violently against the chains, the echo bounced from the limestone walls and marble floor.

Meirah wanted to tell her to stop, that she wouldn't harm the girl, when a sudden bang from across the room silenced her. She glanced over. A castle servant in full robes entered the room from a heavy iron door on the opposite side, near the last row of humans.

He moved straight towards her. Though she was unrecognizable, her telltale red hair braided and well put beneath the stolen headdress, a veil across her face, still she backed away.

The servant was not approaching her, however. He stopped before the female and raised a small whip with a single leather strand and brought it down hard across her arm, leaving a welt but not cutting into the flesh. The girl whimpered but ceased her useless fight.

The servant looked at Meirah and she lowered her eyes instinctively.

"My apologies, Miss," said the servant in broken English. "She will not give you trouble."

Meirah said nothing.

"Are you all right?" he asked.

Meirah nodded, not daring to utter a word. She had seen enough mute women in the castle, and though she was not sure if female villagers were held to the same outrageous stifling of their voices, she took no chances.

The servant moved away, returning through the door from which he had arrived.

Meirah relaxed and let out a sigh. She once again approached the girl. No struggles this time, but her eyes were wide orbs of oceanic blue surrounded by clean white.

Making sure she was alone, she whispered to the girl. "I shan't harm ye."

Though her long sweat-soaked strands of hair were plastered to her throat and face, Meirah noticed marks on her neck. She moved the girl's hair back away from her neck... two puncture wounds marred the pale flesh. And on one arm, she saw two more at the wrist. Fang marks. They were drinking from her. The number on the obelisk became obvious now—this was the number of times she had been drunk from.

Meirah recalled the sign on the entryway door... *Three sips per resident.* The throat and wrist offered the most reward with the least amount drunk. It would not do to kill them too quickly.

"Are ye from Almareyah?" Meirah asked, but the girl only stared at her with those frightened eyes.

"Can ye speak?"

The girl shook her head, opening her mouth as if to say something, but only a stifled moan issued from her throat. Meirah noticed her teeth then; straight and white. She reached to touch the girl's mouth, but the poor girl cringed as if Meirah had jabbed her with a hot poker.

"'Tis alright." Meirah spoke in a soothing tone to calm the lass.

The girl relaxed, if that's what it could be called. She shook violently in fear, but her body no longer tensed against the bonds. Meirah lifted her top lip carefully. No fangs.

Human!

Kaeplan was allowing his citizens to drink from mortals... straight from the tap so to speak. This was an act strictly forbidden in most dimensions, and Mikaire had been no exception. Any Mikairian caught drinking from a human was executed. Wizards alone held the honor due to the strength in human blood. Kaeplan was breaking all the dimensional rules, but to what end? Had he hoped to create a dimension of potential wizards such as himself? Only human blood could create a wizard if it was in their own blood to become one. And, though Meirah had never visited another dimension other than her birthplace, she had heard this was a universal dimensional rule. Too many wizards vying for time would throw off the balance of timelines in the Mortal Dimension and possibly cause a catastrophic event throughout the worlds that existed on each plane of time.

"What are ye up tae, Kaeplan?" she whispered.

"I am sorry this happened tae ye," she said to the human girl. "I wish I could free ye, but I am a prisoner here as well, in my own right." As she walked away, the girl's desperate moans made her heart ache.

The next was a male. Again, he wore only a pair of white undergarments. More flesh to feed from. He was slumped forward against the chains, head bowed. She would have thought him dead if not for the soft breathing. The obelisk beside him read 15. Fang marks covered is throat, arms, and even his torso. He was unconscious, barely alive. She could hear his heartbeat, erratic and slow. She need not check his mouth, for the blood that seeped slowly from the freshest wounds smelled distinctly human. They were *all* humans.

Meirah gazed about the room. Behind the half-circle of prey humans she spotted a door. She approached. This was no hidden barrier. Above the door was written: CASTLE RESIDENTS & WORKERS ONLY. The door was odd in that she could see no visible handle. A hidden entrance that was not well hidden.

She peered around the top, sides and bottom for a way to open it, but once again the sound of voices interrupted her. She turned to see a man and a woman entering into the chamber. She moved away from the door swiftly, to the closest bound human, as if she was going to drink, and watched discreetly.

In a language she did not know, the man spoke to the woman beside him, but his tone and gestures were not pleasant. He shoved her forward, towards the man Meirah had just visited with the 15 on his obelisk. He continued to sprout what appeared to be curses and instruction in a harsh voice. Reluctantly, the woman leaned in to the half dead human, lowered her veil and bit into the man's arm. *Three sips.* The man yanked her away more harshly than necessary then moved in for his own feeding. From where she stood, Meirah heard the human's heartbeat slow and then stop as the villager pulled away. With his robe sleeve, he wiped away the number on the obelisk, and using a piece of chalk that hung from a strip of leather on the obelisk, he wrote a new number.

He shoved the woman towards the exit. They left with him spewing more harsh words at her.

This dimension made Mikaire look like a paradise!

Only moments passed after they left that Meirah heard the bang of the door on the opposite side of the room. Two servants entered, unchained the dead human and hauled him away. Two more servants came through the door as the others existed. They had hold of another man, dressed only in black boxers. He fought hard against them, but their strength was far superior. They chained him up on the dead man's pole, erased the number, and left. He stood looking around fearfully and curiously.

Meirah shook her head in disbelief at this unimaginable cruelty that even she never would have thought Kaeplan capable of, and moved back to the door with no handle. Feeling around its frame, she searched for a hidden latch, anything. She looked behind the tapestries that hung on either side of it. Nothing. Just a rectangular door with no way in.

Meirah stood bewildered. She stared up at the sign again. CASTLE RESIDENTS AND WORKERS ONLY. She was, for all intent, a castle resident.

She approached the door again. She had pressed the frame and sides of the door, now she placed her palms in the center and prepared to push.

She stumbled forward as the door simply vanished. She caught herself before falling, took a step, and found herself in yet another dark limestone hallway. What a crazy world Kaeplan had created—Sakkana's dimension had been straight-forward with solid doors and walls. Though not easily breached, it had been. Kaeplan meant to confuse to prevent mistakes of the past.

Meirah, however, knew him better than anyone. Soon, he would search for her; it took her over two hours just to find this place and she began to worry she would not make it back in time before he noticed her disappearance.

If she turned back now, she might just make the trip in an hour, now that she knew the way, and in her disguise she hoped to avoid detection. She could explore another day, on one of her 'hunting trips.' Much to her dismay, however, when she reached the door to the pyramid she found only solid stone walls. She was sure she had taken the correct path as it only went one way. She pressed her palms to the wall. Nothing. Yet another trick to keep one in without the means to exit. Turning, she followed the hallway—the only way to go was forward and hope she came to a barrier into the castle.

The hallway was bare and smooth, wall torches lighting the way.

"Creative ye're no', Kaeplan," she muttered.

If this dimension confused her so, an escaped prisoner from the Mortal Dimension would find himself completely lost. That is when she realized what appeared boring and unfinished held meaning after all.

In Sakkana's castle, Dane found his way out with her aid, though neither had traversed the path before. Almareyah, however, with its puzzle of halls, labyrinth-like passages and hidden barriers was impossible to solve for any, other than those Kaeplan entrusted with the knowledge.

Meirah pulled out her map and pen, jotted this hall and the door and the pyramid before it. THE ROOM OF DEATH, she labeled it.

Pocketing her precious map, she moved ahead, coming eventually to another handle-less door. With no hesitation she pressed her hands against it—and stepped forward into a new room so large she could not see the walls beyond.

The air hit her like a stone; hot and humid like the forest, yet the sand beneath her face reminded her of the desert. She was sure she had found the exit at last. Palm trees grew to great heights, fronds as big as a person grew everywhere, greenery, and even the horrible thorny black palm stood before her. She had no idea where she had come out. The wall with the door stood behind her, so she followed the path around the dangerous thorns, until she came to another wall in front of her.

"What the..." She gazed up the wall, and far above her head, she noticed an odd anomaly.

She was not outside after all, but in a huge room with light that appeared to be sun shining down from above. Another illusion.

Half way down the next wall, she noticed a path into the fauna and chose to follow it. She walked perhaps ten minutes when the plant life opened up to what appeared an oasis…

And in its center was a lake. Or at the least it gave the impression of a lake.

"The portal?" she whispered excitedly and ran the rest of the path to it.

As the sandy beach came to its end, her feet stepped on hard flooring. She looked down. Marble. Meirah stepped to the water. Though quite large in diameter, it did not appear to be deep. She could clearly see the bottom, blue, like a human swimming pool, but there was something interesting there. Painted on the bottom and visible beneath the warping waves was the symbol. The necklace—the same symbol on the tapestry.

Meirah chuckled. "Way tae give it away, Kaeplan."

She had no way to open the portal now. But her new mission became clear; get the key!

In Mikaire, even without the ability to open the Main Looking Glass portal, she could conjure Dane's image easily—and he could see her providing he was before a mirror. But what chance that he would be standing by water now?

No harm in trying. Meirah closed her eyes and thought of Dane. She opened them again, but the pool had not changed; just water.

She knelt down at the pool's edge and placed her hand on the water's surface.

Well, this is different.

The water was not water at all. The liquid beneath her hand jiggled with semi-solidity, like the Jell-O she had once seen in Dane's house. An illusion of water, cool to the touch.

"Oh Dane, where are ye…please!" The jelly-like water rippled.

"Oh my… Yes!" She closed her eyes again, placed both hands into the portal water, concentrated hard on her husband's face, the silver-blue eyes, the silky black hair, his body, all of him. She opened her eyes and gasped.

His image rippled and cleared, only an image but she saw him—and he was not alone. Long red hair, similar to her own. Her heart skipped, fearing he was with another woman. But as the second image materialized, she sighed in relief. Stephan was with him.

Behind them, she saw stars—night. Beside them, a pile of flaming logs; a fire pit. Behind that a bus, similar to the one they used when on tour except it was silver, and lined with windows out of which light glared. Dane and Stephan sat near the fire, talking. Camping? Dane hated camping. Though he loved animals, he was not a nature lover. Even the fully loaded tour bus made him want to stop at a hotel for room service and a real bed.

Campers often parked by lakes... water. And then she realized...

He was searching for her! Highly intelligent, Dane certainly would have discovered the portal lay in water. She needed him to see her.

Meirah stood and stepped into the jelly-water, sinking to her knees. She pulled the veil from her face.

"*Dane!*" she called out loudly, moving her hands about hoping he would see her there, as he once had through mirrors.

"Dane...please...look at me! I am here! *Please...see me!*"

Suddenly he stopped talking to Stephan and cocked his head towards whatever water source he was near.

"*YES! DANE... I am here!*"

He stood and moved closer. She saw him full now in a black sweater, heavy winter coat, and tight jeans, black waves framing his face. Oh, by Sakkana's power he was beautiful—her heart ached terribly for him. She leaned forward, placing her arms full in the thick liquid, as if she could reach in and grab him. He was looking right at her now, then he gazed another way, and back again. In the light blue of his eyes she saw both sadness and hope, but not recognition.

He could not see her.

"DANE!" she screeched. "I am here!"

He shook his head, shrugged and turned away, moving back to Stephan. He sat again by the fire, but kept his gaze out to the water. He sensed her. No matter how hard she concentrated, however, he did not see her. All discretions from the past faded.

She needed that key!

"Don' leave, Dane," she said, tears choking her words. "I will get tae ye. I promise!"

The image flickered and faded and she was once again looking into a shallow pool.

She sat back onto the sand, frightened and alone, weeping for the love who existed in another dimension.

January 10, 2017

*"A true friend is someone who is there for you, even when he'd
rather be anywhere else."*
-Len Wein

Dane and Stephan
Lake Michigan

Just as Stephan had wished, they rented a new RV and made
camp beside the lake. The season was late and they had the place
all to themselves. To assure complete privacy, they had paid
extra—the camp manager stared at them as if they were in a
modern version of 'Brokeback Mountain.'

Now they sat outside by the lake on a night that smashed
meteorological records for the coldest night so far this season.
Stephan, who enjoyed camping, made a bonfire by the water.
Though a born New Englander, Dane had lived too long in the
south and was no longer accustomed to the cold. Dressed like an
Eskimo, he huddled by the fire, yet kept an eye on the lake—just in
case.

"It's fucking cold out here!" Stephan, a native South
Carolinian, complained. He blew air out, captivated by the frosty
mist of his own breath.

"This was *your* idea," Dane reminded him. "You should have
chosen a warmer lake, like Okeechobee in Florida."

Dane lifted a bottle of rum from the ground where he had
placed it by his booted feet. He cracked open the top, took a long
swig and handed the bottle to Stephan.

His friend, barely visible beneath a parka-like coat, scarf, gloves and ski pants, lowered his hood, long red hair spilling out about his shoulders, and took a hefty swig.

"I don't feel any warmer," complained Stephan. More of a pot smoker than a drinker, Stephan shivered.

"Give it a moment." Dane, donned in a winter jacket, black sweater and his jeans, sympathized. He, too, shivered against the lake winds.

"Do you have a plan?" Dane asked. "Besides freezing to death?"

"We're here. Let's see where this leads us," said Stephan. He guzzled more rum before handing the bottle back to Dane.

He took a sip, recapped the bottle and set it down.

"We need to—" Dane stopped, cocked his head towards the lake.

"What is it?"

"Shh. I thought I heard something."

"The sound of my teeth chattering," Stephan joked.

"No..." Dane stood and walked toward the water that gently licked at the shore. "I could swear I heard a voice."

"You're drunk." Stephan stood and joined his friend at water's edge.

"No, I'm not. Listen."

Both men went silent for a moment.

Wind blowing over the water howled and brought with it a light snow. Dane listened intently, trying to hear over it. He looked to the water, black and trembling with the wind. After a few minutes he shook his head, disappointment touching his heart.

Stephan looked at him."What did you hear?"

"I-I don't know... my name. I thought I heard someone call my name."

"I don't hear anything but the wind... and it's fucking cold!"

"Must have been my imagination. Wishful thinking I guess." He moved away from the shore. "Let's go in."

"About time!" Stephan said through chattering teeth. He grabbed a bucket, dipped it into the water and poured it over the campfire until it sizzled and faded.

-Twenty-Three-

Kaeplan

He had not seen Meirah all day and he grew worried. She had not met him for lunch or dinner, and in the time she had been in Almareyah she never missed a meal with him. He had always made certain to provide not only fresh blood, mostly animal to keep her suspicions at bay, but sometimes human in order to appease her palate. He also provided a wide variety of human foods, all her favorites.

Before leaving the dining hall, he asked Lenophis, "Have you seen Queen Meirah?"

The slave thought for a moment. "I believe she went out to hunt, Master."

"When?"

"I am not sure, Master. Isophia dressed M'Lady in her hunting attire. She did not say when, Master."

Kaeplan nodded. "Fetch Isophia to my work chamber."

Lenophis bowed. "Yes, Master."

Kaeplan walked to his work chamber and sat at the large oaken desk. He gazed over the strewn paperwork, thinking he should do a better job organizing his work. Orders for servants' chores and who would enter the Mortal Dimension for humans and when, plans to grow Almareyah, diagrams for new barriers. He knew where everything was and where he had left it, but as he stared at the mess something seemed out of place. Studying the papers carefully, he moved to grab a pen—a special pen he had brought with him from the mortal world. A Bic it was called. The slot in the desk where he always placed it was empty. The blank papers he kept in the only neat pile on the desk were in disarray.

Someone had been in his study! No one was allowed in his office, and all knew this fact. Quite clearly in fact. The one servant who had entered his office had been severely punished as an example to any others who wished to follow suit. Since then, no one had entered, nothing touched—until now.

A knock sounded on the door. "Come in."

Isophia entered, moved to stand before his desk.

"Have ye seen Queen Meirah?" he asked.

Though females had no physical voice, he could find what he wished to know within their minds. Only he and trusted male servants could hear them. Her voice filled his mind. Humans brought in for food were muted regardless of gender.

Isophia nodded.

"Did she go out tae hunt?" he asked.

Yes, Master. Keliah and I dressed her in her hunting clothing this morning, after breakfast.

"Have ye seen her since?"

She shook her head slowly.

Kaeplan sighed. "Go ask the others if they have seen her recently, then report back to me."

Yes, Master.

Once she was gone, he looked over the desk and in the drawers to make sure nothing else had been taken. The top left was locked. He opened it with a small key he kept hidden in the chamber. Opening the drawer, he released a sigh of relief. Within were battle plans to take over the Mortal Dimension, once he had built up a strong enough army. The human blood he allowed his citizens would assure they built up enough power to serve him well in a magical war against a non-magical dimension. Though he did not wish them to draw on too much strength, he allowed only small amounts per resident per day.

Kaeplan pulled the plans from the drawer and began to work on more detail; soldiers able to take down the strongest human forces and placements for their locations.

An hour went by and another knock came at the door. He tucked the plans back into their hiding place and locked the drawer.

"Come," he said, sitting back casually.

Isophia entered once again.

"Well?" Kaeplan said impatiently.

She was last seen in the Village, Master.

Kaeplan sat forward, tense. "Are you sure?"

Isophia nodded.

"Tell Lenophis to search for her. Check the Village, and the Pyramid. *Now!*"

Isophia nodded quickly and hustled from the room.

Meirah was a resourceful one, this fact he knew well. Growing up together in Mikaire, she always found ways to subvert authority. If she discovered the Village Square... Or worse, the Pyramid!

Not 30 minutes later another knock came to the door. "Yes."

Lenophis entered, bowed. "M'Lady has been found wandering the castle, dirty and disheveled."

"Bring her tae me here."

Fifteen minutes he waited. Finally, the door opened and Meirah entered. Kaeplan was not prepared for what he would see. Though her hair was clean, unlike the rest of her, it appeared as if she had been in a strong wind. Her hunting attire was torn with spots of dried blood marring the material.

"Where have ye been?" Kaeplan asked her, ignoring her appearance, trying to keep his annoyance in check.

"Hunting."

Kaeplan stood and walked to her. He flicked some dust off her tunic, played with a thread that hung from her torn sleeve. "Where were ye huntin'? Did ye find anything?"

"No," she answered. "I never left the castle."

He looked into her deep emerald eyes, and behind them he could see her lie. Her pupils had grown wider and deception pressed behind them as if trying to escape. He had spent enough years with her to know when she fibbed. He drew in a deep breath and released it slowly in an attempt to calm the anger building in his gut. And he was well aware she sensed his anger. Time to let it go—for now. If she had not seen the Pyramid, he did not want to give away his hidden food chamber.

"Have ye eaten?" he asked.

"No."

"Then go. I will have blood brought tae yer chamber."

Meirah turned to leave…

"Oh… Meirah…" She stopped and looked over her shoulder at him. "Ye would not have seen a pen would ye? It's missin' from my desk."

"Oh," she turned back to him. "I am sorry." She reached under her loose tunic and into the small pocket of her breeches, pulled out his pen, placed it on the desk.

"What did ye need a pen for?"

"My journal," she responded. "I like tae write and quill and ink is so cumbersome, would ye admit?"

Kaeplan nodded, unsure if she told the truth this time, for her eyes this time told nothing.

"May I go?" she asked.

Kaplan nodded.

Later in the evening, in his bedchamber, and after he had ordered animal blood brought to Meirah, he readied himself for bed. He pulled his night dress over his head and pulled down the bedcovers when yet another knock came to his door. Grumbling at the constant interruptions of the day, he moved to the door and opened it.

Pheneus, one of his many slaves, stood in the hallway. "I thought you would want to know, my Master, word came of an unfamiliar woman in the Pyramid earlier. She watched as a dead human was replaced. She wore Village robes, but Keplis had never seen her before. Head dress and a veil, but her eyes… Green like the verdant fields. She watched him, but he said he never saw her feed."

Kaeplan nodded. "Thank ye. I will be sure he is well compensated…and ye as well. On the morrow ye can choose any human of yer likin' tae drink from—more than three sips."

He bowed deeply. "Thank you, Master. You are most kind." He bowed once more before leaving.

"Damn it, Meirah!" Kaeplan slammed a fist onto his bed. "So, ye found the Pyramid after all, did ye."

That annoying Meirah resourcefulness. If it had not been for that quality, which he had found so alluring when they were young, she never would have fallen for the first mortal, Sir Kori Blackmore.

Kaeplan blew out his candle and climbed under the covers. Sleep eluded him, however. Meirah needed to learn she could not run amok in his dimension! Right then he made the determination that, no matter what it took, he would get hold of that vile mortal husband of hers.

The next morning, Kaeplan rose early and called a meeting of his top guards and most trusted slaves. They would keep a close eye on their 'Queen,' he told them. Follow her. Keep her away from the outside barriers.

Later in the day, breakfast with Meirah was quiet. Both seemed too busy in their own thoughts to talk much.

Finally, Kaeplan broke the silence. "So, what do ye plan tae do today?"

Meirah shrugged. "Be shadowed by yer slaves and guards?"

Kaeplan sat up straight. "Why would ye say this?"

"No reason." She glanced towards the guard standing by the door. The one who is never there.

She knew! He would have to move fast.

Once breakfast was over and Meirah returned to her chamber per orders, he hurried to the Pyramid, two guards as his company, using the castle's barrier direct to the Main Water Portal. No longer could he wait. She would find a way out—unless he brought Dane in!

Dane and Stephan
January 15, 2017

Dane stood at the water's edge, watching the waves lap at the shore.

"Hey!"

Dane turned to see Stephan come up behind him. "We have been here a week! Maybe it's time to go home."

"May I remind you it was your idea to come here?"

"I know, but it's snowing and the weather predicts heavier snow tonight. Lake effect snow can get pretty nasty here. Maybe I *should* have chosen Okeechobee."

"*Now* you wanna go to Florida?" A week of seeing nothing,

hearing nothing played poorly on Dane's mood.

"At least it's warm."

Dane shook his head. "No. I don't know. I can't go home without her."

"I'm not asking you to, Dane, but the lake is icing over. I doubt the portal will open in ice."

"You can't know that! Besides, what if she shows after we leave? There's no water during the trip to Florida. You go, Stephan. I will stay here."

"You are a stubborn son-of-a-bitch, Dane Bainbridge! C'mon already! You rarely come into the RV anymore and you barely eat. You'll die out here and I can't allow that! No matter what lake we go to, if she can, she will find us. Hell, if water is like mirrors, you could sit in front of a bathtub!"

"You said a larger body of water was our best chance, and you were right."

"Well, maybe I wro—" Stephan stopped, went still. His eyes were transfixed to the icy water.

Dane turned, following Stephan's gaze to the lake, the gray from an overcast sky, and the promise of more snow. "What?"

"I thought I saw—" Stephan started.

Then Dane saw it, too. A veiled image, as if a thin layer of ice covered it. But the red hair came into view first. Dane's heart began to race. Meirah! She had found him at long last. He ran into the icy waves, ignoring the frigidity on his feet...

"Dane! No!" Stephan hollered. "It's not—" Again, his words were interrupted.

As the image cleared, a flash of the past raced through Dane's mind—a red-headed man coming through his bedroom mirror.

"It's Kaeplan! Stephan... *RUN!*"

Dane barely got the words out when his red-headed foe, along with two men in matching uniforms materialized onto the shore. Guards to Kaeplan? What was going on?

There was no time to react. The men accompanying Kaeplan moved too quickly; one snatched Stephan, the other Dane.

Stephan struggled. "Let me go!"

Dane, however, knew this would lead him not only to his wife, but Adrian and Bruce. He let himself be taken. No fear of pain or torture could keep him from finding Meirah. He was led, with no argument, into the frigid lake as the snow grew heavy and the wind picked up.

Ice. Wind. Water. Then a gel substance that made it difficult to move. Before he could so much as blink, they stood on a sandy shore. Ironically the hot moist air soothed his frozen cheeks.

Dane knew without being told that he now stood in a new dimension... Kaeplan's dimension, he presumed. And somewhere within, Meirah awaited. He would find her. Rescue her. Get her back. And ask her forgiveness.

He watched Kaeplan carefully... as Stephan, too, materialized into the pool and was taken onto the shore, shivering and frightened. Dane would pay attention to every move Kaeplan made, to every detail of this new dimension—and find a way out. But first he needed to find his wife and his friends. His only regret was that Stephan had been dragged into this mess as well.

Each guard held tight to Dane and Stephan's arms, leading them with no shackles or binds of any kind. Bold move. But, they were strong and now within a new realm, there was no way to get back to the Mortal Dimension. If they ran, they'd be killed. Experience told him this, and he hoped his tales of Mikaire would prevent Stephan from attempting escape.

They were led through a door with no opening. Kaeplan's touch was all it took to make it disappear, and they were within a dark damp hallway lit by a torch on the stone wall. Magical barriers—a way to get from one place to another in an instant. Dane had seen many in Mikaire, but rather than geological relocation, these were indoors and brought them from one hallway to another.

The last hallway ended with a floor-to-ceiling tapestry depicting a gross interpretation of a bleeding man. Kaeplan pulled the large fabric aside; just a wall to Dane's eyes. But he knew these dimensions—nothing was ever as it seemed. Sure enough, one touch from Kaeplan and there appeared a dark entranceway. They all stepped in. As the tapestry fell back into place behind them, all went black. Unsure of his footing, Dane halted.

"Move!" bellowed a guard. In the dark he could not see which one spoke, but the close proximity of the voice to his location told him it was the guard who held him.

Dane took a tentative step forward, felt for the next step with his toe, but only empty air greeted his foot. He felt rather than saw the guard lower down... A staircase. In the pitch dark. Carefully, he stepped down. He heard a thud just ahead and Stephan called out, "Ow!" He had not noticed the step either.

"Hey, Kaeplan, did you forget humans cannot see in the dark?" he teased.

"Still cocky," echoed a voice well ahead and beneath them.

More stairs.

Dane felt for each step before letting his weight fall onto it, though he was sure the guard who held such a tight grip on his arm could easily hold his weight if he slipped. No need to damage the goods yet. That was Kaeplan's job for later.

Down several flights of stone steps, the last of which finally flickered with the light of a couple torches, and into a large room, bright in comparison as torches lined every wall. They moved through this room to a door, which was actually a door, latch and all, and Kaeplan opened it, walked in as they were nearly pushed through the threshold.

The stench hit Dane first, and as his eyes adjusted enough to see beyond shadow, before him was a dungeon. Much bigger and boasting more gadgets and devices of torture than he'd ever seen in Mikaire or anywhere else.

"You really thought this one through, Kaeplan," he said, keeping any fear that might seep through from his voice.

Kaeplan turned to him with fire in his eyes. "Ye're no' getting' out this time!"

"Meirah will find me," said Dane with a deliberately cocky tone. "We have a connection. She can sense me, she'll know I'm here," he lied, hoping somehow there would be a measure of truth to his words.

"She can no' get in here, obtuse human. This room is protected by magic even she can no' sense nor conquer. I learnt a thing or two in Mikaire—and in yer mortal world. This time *I* am in charge. *I* am the Master o' this dimension! Meirah does no' know this room exists, and neither will she ever!"

Dane forced a confident giggle. "I beat you before, asshole. I'll beat you again!"

Just then, he heard a weak, nearly inaudible voice from the cell to his left.

"D-Dane?" He looked to where the voice spoke his name and saw in the dark a lump of a blanket in the corner. "I-Is that you, *Curva?*" The figure cocooned in the blanket moved.

"Adrian?" Dane started towards the cell, but was halted by a solid hand on his arm.

"Y-Yes... help us, p-please." Adrian sounded so weak.

"Us?" Dane asked. "Adrian, where is Bruce?"

Kaeplan sighed loudly. "*Enough!*" He turned to the guard who held him. "Put that beast with his friend, remove his coat and sweater. Don't want him to get too cozy. And chain him well."

"And this one, Master?" asked the guard holding Stephan, as he removed Stephan's coat and sweatshirt. Stephan had grown pale and silent, his gaze darting about the room at each of the torture devices.

"The Rack!" said Kaeplan.

Stephan came around then. "*Rack?!*" But the guard had already dragged him to the flat platform and was wrestling him onto it, wrists and feet bound so quickly Stephan held no hope of escape.

Dane was brought into the cell and chained to the wall with the same efficiency.

"Hold it!" Kaeplan called out suddenly, making all stop and look. "Take his ring!"

Dane's eyes widened. "No!"

The guard moved to his left hand and with no way to fight him, his wedding band was easily removed. The guard exited the cell, handed the ring to Kaeplan with a respectful bow.

"This is getting old," Dane mumbled with an exaggerated sigh. He had escaped Mikaire. He would escape here. Despite Kaeplan's assurances Meirah would never find him, he held onto the hope that she would.

"Enjoy yer reunion," laughed Kaeplan. "Soon ye'll all be dead!" He turned a belligerent gaze to Dane. "Except *you*, Mr. Bainbridge. I will be requirin' yer blood for my plan."

"Plan?"

"Ye shall see. Oh... and don' worry on yer friends. They will be gone soon enough. And Meirah... well...ye might see her again... *IF* I allow it."

Kaeplan and his minion guards shuffled from the dungeon,

taking their winter clothing with them, the door slamming behind them.

The situation hit Dane then and he released his air of confidence. It was exhausting. Apparently Kaeplan had indeed learned from Mikaire and remedied where Sakkana fell short. Fear he would not get out of this one swarmed through him like a pissed off hive of bees. He gazed over to the lump under the blanket. He needed to keep up appearances, if not for himself, for his friends.

"Adrian?"

The blanket moved, slowly rising like a ghost from a grave to a sitting position, a blond head peered out the top. Dane stifled a gasp. Adrian was always slender, now his gaunt appearance, sunken cheeks and pale complexion made him unrecognizable as the drummer and friend he had known for over a decade.

"H-Hello, *Curva*."

"Are you alright?" asked Dane, unable to hide the concern in his tone.

A chuckle, then a moan. "Not exactly."

"What did they do to you?" Though he was sure he knew the answer.

"The... Four-Star treatment."

"They took your blood," said Dane, all too aware of the ritual time dimensions required.

"Th-They did more than that." Slowly, laboriously Adrian rose to his feet, leaned against the wall for support. He let the blanket lower beyond his emaciated waist to his hips.

Dane gasped despite trying to hold it in. Losing weight Adrian could not afford to lose was the least of his problems. His skinny arms were lined with the scars of being bled multiple times. They were bleeding him out like a cow at slaughter.

It took a lot of work to keep his thoughts to himself. He truly feared for Adrian's life. Though in Mikaire he himself had been bled, beaten and flogged, he was never in such a state as he now saw his friend. And they had taken *all* of his clothes, not leaving him with a tee shirt and jeans as Dane and Stephan were afforded. Just boots.

"Bruce! Adrian, where is Bruce?" Dread pitted his gut.

Adrian pointed forward with one weak and unsteady arm. Dane followed to where his friend motioned. All he saw was a tall wooden box, like a coffin, with a small slit in front.

"In there?" he asked, wanting to panic, but swallowing it back.

Adrian nodded before pulling the blanket back over himself and sliding back down the wall to sit.

He turned his attention to the coffin-box Bruce was in. "Bruce?"

No reply.

"*BRUCE?*"

Nothing. No sound nor movement.

Adrian spoke again. "I-I think he's dead."

"No," said Dane. "I can't accept that!"

"Hey!" Stephan called out. "Did you forget me over here? They're gonna stretch me." He fought against the impenetrable bonds.

Dane's gaze roamed over the contraption they called a Rack. He had seen them before—real ones. In a past life. This one, however, was not equipped with pulleys or ropes, nothing in which to stretch... anything. It was merely a slab of wood set at an upright angle with bindings for feet and hands. He gazed about the room and eyed each torture device, which he had seen in one lifetime or another. There were drawings of each in modern history books as well. None of these compared to the real thing. These were merely models, missing, for the most part, the worst of the torture aspect. As a matter of fact, they were more like the feigned equipment used by sado-masochists for sexual pleasure. Bondage without the discipline. And certainly lacking the pleasure.

If this situation were not so dire, he would laugh. Kaeplan had never seen the real thing. Apparently, he had spent too much time in the mortal world watching S&M porn movies.

"You have nothing to fear, Stephan. It's a fake, as are all the devices in this room. They couldn't harm a fly."

Adrian, just then, slumped to the decrepit straw-covered floor, the blanket falling away, leaving his naked body exposed to the chill of the chamber.

"Adrian?"

A weak Romanian accent responded, "Can't...get...up."

"Get the blanket, Adrian. You'll freeze."

But his friend said no more. He just lay there, unmoving. His long blond hair, usually so pristine, hung in dirty strands over his face. In the dim light, Dane couldn't even see if he was breathing.

"*Adrian*! Stay with me, buddy!"

A moan. But it didn't come from the drummer on the floor. Across the room. The box.

"Bruce?" Dane remained hopeful.

"I-Is that y-you?"

The voice was so small he almost missed it. "Bruce! It's me... Dane. Stephan is here, too."

The box moved ever so slightly. Dane sighed relief. He was alive...for now. He needed to keep them that way. Meirah would find them, he knew she would!

"Adrian...wake up, buddy. Bruce is alive!"

Adrian moved an arm down, one skeletal hand grasping the edge of the blanket to pull it up. "So...cold." He managed only to bring it to his chest when his arm went limp again.

They were alive, and that's what mattered. They had been bled to the point of exhaustion, near death, but he saw no evidence of torture. If history had taught Dane anything, the torture was being saved for him.

Meirah

All through lunch she remained quiet as her mind went over the map she had drawn. She planned to commit it to memory, just in case. Kaeplan knew she had taken his pen. Whether or not he believed her story about the journal was unclear. If he discovered the map...

"What is on yer mind, Meirah?" He asked, sipping his wine glass of blood slowly.

"Hmm?" She looked at him—the epitome of a flamboyant Wizard in his long robes of red and blue silk with gilded trim. His bright red hair was pulled back and braided down his back. He wore a crown of silver and gold. He made Sakkana look like a servant.

"Ye've no' said a word," he stated. "What is on yer mind?"

"Oh, nothin' really. I felt the Youngest One... eh, the babe, move." She tended to slip into Mikaire's language referring to age when she was with Kaeplan. Old habits die hard.

Kaeplan reached a hand across the table and placed it over hers. A shiver of repulsion ran through her and she wished to pull away, but she fought the urge. Better to retain the appearance of acceptance.

"What are yer plans for the day?" he asked.

Meirah shrugged. "No' sure yet."

"No huntin' this day?" He kept his hand on hers, used the other to lift his glass to his lips, letting the smooth blood slide down his throat.

Meirah shook her head, deciding to play along. "I can no' find my way out o' this castle. No place tae hunt."

For the most part, this was truth. She dared not return to the forest surrounding the village. After she had been discovered by a servant wandering the halls, dust and blood and scratches dotting her flesh and attire, Kaeplan had questioned her in such a way as to give the impression he suspected something more was behind her intentions. She needed no more suspicions to fall her way.

What she truly wished was to map out more of the castle anyway. Somewhere within, she knew Dane was nearby. She could not sense him, but her heart felt him.

"How 'bout this..." said Kaeplan. "Dress for huntin' and after I attend some business, we can hunt together. Meet me in an hour on the portico."

Meirah grit her teeth and nodded. "That sounds wonderful."

Twenty minutes later, attired in a muted green tunic and breeches, her usual hunting attire, Meirah exited her chamber. She would need to be quick, and discreet. She knew Kaeplan was having her watched and she kept her senses locked tightly on any feel or sound of another nearby.

Moving swiftly, she found herself once again at the end of the hallways with the tapestry of the bleeding man and the sword symbol at the bottom.

She gazed about and listened intently, her sensitive hearing on high alert for any footsteps that may come this way. She studied the tapestry. This hallway was empty; no shadow barriers as in the others, nothing. Only that damn tapestry. Her instincts tickled. There had to be something...

As she stared, hoping for a clue...anything, the wall hanging moved—a slight rustle as if a breeze touched it. But there was no wind and no way for a breeze to reach this hall. As the tapestry fluttered out, towards her, she realized then that whatever caused its movement came from behind it!

Taking up the bottom corner where the sword symbol existed, she lifted the heavy material away from the wall. Behind it, a door—black and open. Why did she not see this before?

The magic door within the pyramid came to mind. She had needed to touch it to make it work. Already open, she assumed someone had gone through, neglected to close the door behind them.

Taking in a deep breath for courage, she stepped through, allowing the tapestry to fall back into place behind her.

No light. She blinked to clear her vision and the stone steps came to her as darker shadow over lighter shadow. Careful of her footing, she slunk down the stairs as if hunting, making no sound. She came to a second landing and another set of stairs. Lit by torches, this one was much quicker for her to traverse. And when she arrived at a large room lined with torches, she paused to get her bearings. Deep beneath the castle she saw no reason for its existence. A door far at the opposite end was closed—but at least it was a door. Voices…she could hear talking within the room beyond. She closed in and listened.

Not wishing to simply open the door and reveal her presence, she placed an ear to the solid wood, just as she had done so many years ago when trying to find news of the mortal and who would bring it to Mikaire. She had been so young and naïve then.

She heard Kaeplan's voice. "Bleed that one first."

Then another, an American accent with a slight southern lilt. "No, please!"

Recognition struck her, but it was not Dane.

"Jesus!" she cursed under her breath. Kaeplan kept humans down here as well. But why? Was this where they were kept before taken to the Pyramid for his villagers to feed upon?

But it made no sense, even in Kaeplan's confusing world. She turned her head, as if listening with the other ear would clarify what she heard.

A moan of pain.

Meirah cringed.

And then another voice rang out from behind the door—a strong and quite familiar voice.

"Leave him alone! It's me you want."

Dane!

There was no doubt—her husband was prisoner within that room. She moved a hand to the door handle—a non-magical entrance. She paused only when she heard Kaeplan's voice again.

"I have special plans for *you*!"

Meirah could take no more. She pushed down the latch and the door swung wide. She stepped inside and what she saw made her cringe.

Almareyah

Dane

Seeing Kaeplan's minion slice open Stephan's arm brought to his mind memories he wished not to recall. *Not now!* He needed to forget the pain and tortures of his past and be strong for his friends.

"Leave him alone! It's me you want."

"I have special plans for *you*!"

The door opened then and to his surprise, though he shouldn't have been, Meirah barged into the room.

For a moment all went silent. Even Kaeplan was taken aback, amber eyes wide, mouth open. He had been so sure Meirah would not find his dungeon. Dane was not sure she would either, but his hope won out. He knew his wife—and she didn't disappoint.

Kaeplan moved at last. He approached Meirah with

apprehension. The over-confidence Dane had always seen fumbled. Meirah was Kaeplan's weakness… and Dane's strength.

"How did ye… What are ye doin'… How did ye find…?"

A small smile touched Dane's lips. Kaeplan couldn't even get out a sentence, he was so flabbergasted. He just wished Meirah had found them when Kaeplan was absent.

Meirah's face expressed her horror as she took in the room around her, its contents—and its residents. Once she'd gathered herself, Meirah rushed to the cell.

"*Dane!*" She grasped the bars and pressed herself close, reaching a hand in towards him. "Dane, I did no' know…"

"Meirah…" he interrupted. "I am so sorry. I swear nothing happened."

"I know, my love. I am sorry too. I—"

"*Enough!*" Kaeplan grabbed her arm, pulled her from the bars.

Meirah spun on him, pulling herself free of his grasp. "Ye betrayed me!" she screeched in his face. "Ye lied tae me! Ye never sent word tae Dane as ye promised, did ye?"

"Ye wish tae speak o' lies, Meirah? The Pyramid! The Portal! Ye lied about yer whereabouts, about wantin' tae birth here!"

Dane watched the exchange with vague recollection of a time when Meirah had been caught trying to free Sir Kori from a similar situation. It was that fire, that spark that made him love her more every day.

"I would no' have had tae lie if ye'd no' lied tae me! I no longer wish tae remain here. Ye set them free. *Now!*" Meirah bellowed, hands on hips.

Kaeplan's evil laugh rang through the room.

"Ye find this humorous, do ye?" she snapped.

And then his wife did something even Dane did not see coming. She hauled back and let a powerful right hook fly into Kaeplan's face. The crack could easily be heard as the bone broke and he dropped like a ragdoll. His hands came up to cover his bleeding nose. He whimpered and squirmed from where he knelt, his pristine robes sprawled around him on the dirty floor.

Meirah's fists were still held up like a boxer in front of her face, ready to strike him again.

Kaeplan gazed up. Through his hands, he hollered, "Don' just stand there, ye morons. Get her!"

The two servants standing by Stephan dropped the items they held, allowing Stephan's blood to splash all over the floor. They rushed at Meirah.

The guard who had held the bowl that caught Stephan's blood, a tall monstrous man, reached for her arm. She spun with a punch, but missed. Monster caught her wrist as it swung by his face. He pivoted around behind her, grabbed her other arm at the same time bringing them both behind her in a painful twist. She cringed.

Dane pulled uselessly on the chains that kept him from helping his wife as he watched the other servant, a stout man with scraggly hair, rush in. Meirah leaned back into Monster and kicked out with both legs. Her feet struck Scragmire square in the chest. He flew back with such force he hit the box where Bruce was imprisoned—and had not made a sound in several hours.

Meirah and Monster flew backwards from the impact of her kick, slammed into the cell bars behind them. They both crumpled to the floor. Meirah was free.

Dane cried out her name, but his voice was lost beneath the crash of splintering wood as Bruce's box hit the floor. The door opened, Bruce rolled out, coming to a lifeless halt next to Kaeplan, who leapt to his feet in surprise.

Dane gasped. His friend, if not dead, looked it. He lay on his side, his clothes so soiled and bloody as to be unrecognizable. His brown hair, wet with sweat and mats, webbed his face and beard, veiling his face from view. And the smell that wafted from the broken box; that of waste and vomit, sweat and rotted food, made Dane gag. He swallowed hard to prevent puking.

Meirah scrambled to Bruce, dropping to her knees beside him. One of the servants ran to the corner of the room, bent and retching. The other merely stood with his hand over his face, staring. Even Kaeplan made no move. Blood was smeared across his face, but had stopped flowing from his broken nose.

Meirah took Bruce by his shoulders and rolled him gently onto his back. Tenderly, she moved the hair from his face. His mouth and eyes were open, his face as pale as a bleached sheet.

Dane pulled with all his might on the chains as if pleading for them to release him. The pain in his wrists went ignored. Adrian crawled to the bars, his naked body exposed to the damp cold as the blanket fell away. He grasped the iron in small pale fists.

"*Bruce...*" he cried.

Stephan stared at the scene with glazed eyes as blood from the open wound on his arm trickled blood onto the floor.

Meirah bent over Bruce, and if the smell bothered her she did not show it. She placed an ear to his face, then his heart. She placed two fingers on his throat, checking for a pulse. Her shoulders slumped then and she sat back on her haunches, slowly shaking her head. When she looked up, tears streamed down her face.

"He's... gone," she whispered.

Adrian rattled the bars. "No!! Bruce! Please...*please*!"

Meirah gazed over to Dane, mouthed the words "I am sorry."

The fist that punched Dane's chest ached more than when Meirah's own fist had slammed into him at the hotel. In his mind, the entire scene was so surreal he expected any moment to wake. But he didn't, for this was no bad dream.

Adrian dropped to the floor of the cell, weeping loudly.

"Meirah," Dane said softly. "Stephan...please."

She shook her head then, as if coming out of a spell, and looked over to the red-haired man bleeding to death on the Rack.

Fluid and quick she stood, but as she made a move towards Stephan, Kaeplan grabbed her arm with one bloodied hand. She snapped a fiery look in his direction. He released her. She proceeded to Stephan, who was now unconscious. She lifted the leaf from the floor where it had fallen, and wrapped it snugly around Stephan's wound. The bleeding stopped, but he was not moving. She placed an ear to his chest. Dane held his breath.

Meirah pulled up. "He shall survive."

Dane released his breath.

Dane looked over at Bruce's body. Though they fought often, Bruce was his friend and business partner. And the best damn guitarist any rock band could hope for. In the past dozen years, they had formed Dark Myst together, rose to fame and fortune, and despite their differences, their constant head-butts over religion, songs and relationships, he loved Bruce like a brother. He was a good man, a great musician and a wonderful husband and father. How would Cailtlyn survive this loss, he wondered. At this point, she had no idea where her husband was or what had happened.

"Meirah," Dane whispered. She moved to the cell, past

Kaeplan who made not a move. "Someone needs to get word to Caitlyn."

Meirah bowed her head and nodded. She turned to Kaeplan.

"Let them go." Her tone was somber. "They need tae inform their friend's wife o' his passing. They need tae bring him home."

Kaeplan narrowed his eyes. "No. This is unacceptable."

Meirah's cheeks turned bright red. Such a powerhouse she was, especially when angered. She made Dane proud.

"Let them go!" she said a bit more forcefully. "I shall stay."

"NO!" Dane screamed, but Meirah put her hand up to silence him.

Kaeplan stood for a few moments in silence, contemplating his options. He glanced to his servants, both of whom stood by him now, ready to do his bidding.

"Bring his body to the Mortal Dimension." He nodded at Bruce. "Leave it where it will be found."

Monster reached down, grabbed up Bruce's six-foot, 200-pound body as if he weighed nothing. Bruce's head flopped back, allowing Dane too well of a view of his friend's pale face. The dead eyes stared at nothing as Monster exited the chamber. Dane knew then he would never see Bruce again. Guilt and remorse raked at his gut like razors. He couldn't stop thinking of their last fight, how he had hit Bruce in the face, the terrible things said that night.

"I'm so sorry, Bruce," he whispered as Monster disappeared through the door that closed behind him.

Adrian collapsed then, drawing attention from the somber death scene. *No, not another!*

"Adrian! Please, stay with us!"

Meirah wiped at her tears and straightened. She turned to Kaeplan. "Let me tend him."

Kaeplan shook his head. "I am no' lettin' ye in *there*. Ye'll free yer human."

"If I promise tae stay wi' ye—"

Kaeplan snorted. "Yer promises are worth nothin' tae me."

"I never lied tae ye, Kaeplan. No' as ye did tae me. Ye said I could move round as I pleased, that I was no' yer prisoner."

"Fine! But ye'll be locked in wi' him, and if ye try tae free him he will be executed immediately. Is that clear?"

Meirah nodded. "Agreed."

Kaeplan nodded to Scragmire. "Let her in, lock the cell behind her. Fetch her rags and warm water... And drinking water."

Scragmire bowed. "Yes, Master."

He unlocked the cell door, allowed Meirah inside, then closed and locked the heavy barred gate behind her. He exited the chamber.

Kaeplan turned away to follow behind, but stopped at the door, and turned. "Meirah... I do love ye."

Meirah grunted. "Yer kind o' love is based on jealousy, greed and hate. That is no' love, Kaeplan. It is obsession."

Kaeplan slammed the door behind him.

The moment he was gone, Meirah ran to Dane and threw her arms around him. He so wished he could return her affections. She buried her head in his chest and wept.

Through muffled tears, she said, "Dane. Oh... Dane. My husband. My love. I have yet again put ye in harm's way." Her weeping grew stronger. "And Bruce... I got him killed."

"Meirah..." Dane wanted so desperately to touch her. "Look at me."

She gazed up with tear-filled eyes.

"Stop blaming yourself," he said. "If anyone's at fault, it's me. If I had insisted you come on tour with me none of this would have happened. You saw him, I should have believed you."

Meirah pulled away, eyes cast to the floor. "He would have found me...either way. I should not have followed. I was... angry."

"And it's my fault you were in that situation...he would have taken me either way. He needs me as Sakkana did." Dane realized how hard he was pulling on the chains, the need to comfort her rooted so deeply inside that his heart ached more than the shackles on his wrists. "No, sweetheart. I could never live without you."

Meirah pressed herself against him, arms wrapping around his neck, she stood on tiptoes to kiss him. He bent his head down, rattling the chains in desperation. Her kiss grew deep and he moaned against her mouth. The terrible world around him, the cell, the chains, all of it disappeared. She reached her hands out and intertwined her fingers in his. Just to taste her was bliss... He felt himself becoming aroused, but didn't care.

Until a moan interrupted them.

"Get a room," came a small voice from the corner.

Meirah pulled back, a blush forming on her cheeks.

"You should go help him," said Dane, nodding towards Adrian.

"Oh Dane..." Meirah stepped towards him again, and kissed him once more.

He returned her kiss then pulled his head up. "Go help Adrian," he whispered.

Meirah nodded, and when she pulled back, the room grew cold. He wanted nothing more than for her to stay there, keeping him warm, smelling the sun in her hair. But he couldn't bear to lose another friend.

She knelt beside Adrian just as the door opened. A servant entered with a basket in one hand, a bucket in the other.

"Stand back!" ordered the servant, as he pulled a key and unlocked the door.

Meirah stood and backed against the wall. The servant opened the door just enough to place the items inside then slammed it closed, locked it. But he didn't leave, he merely stood nearby, watching.

"Give us privacy, please," said Meirah, moving to pick up the items.

"Master said I must remain here."

"Fine!" she said as moved back to Adrian and set the basket and bucket on the floor. She gathered what clean straw she could find and placed it like a pillow, carefully lifting his head.

"Ye'll be fine," she spoke softly like a mother to an ill child.

Dane's heart swelled with pride watching her tend to Adrian as she once tended to him. What an amazing doctor she would have made, Dane thought as she took up a rag, dipped it into the steaming water bucket, wrung it out and proceeded to sponge Adrian's cold body. As she warmed him, chest first, she took the blanket and placed it over where she worked to hold the heat in. Adrian's eyes closed gently, relaxed. Dane knew that touch... so gentle and patient.

As her soft and careful hands cleaned the sensitive flesh of his groin, the fuzz of short flaxen hairs, pain or no, Adrian grew erect. An autonomic response that all men endured. Dane swallowed back a twinge of unacceptable jealousy and looked away, towards Stephan. He was either asleep or unconscious. Relieved, he could clearly see the rise and fall of his friend's chest. Thanks to Meirah, Stephan lived. Perhaps no one else had to die.

As for himself, Kaeplan's words echoed in his mind; *I have special plans for you.*

Dane knew he'd probably not get out of this one alive. His luck had run out.

Meirah finished tending to Adrian's body, warming him with the water, swaddling him like a baby in the blanket, tucking it carefully around his body to assure the warmth not escape.

She reached into the basket and pulled out a cup and a pitcher made of ceramic. She poured the clear water and placed the cup to Adrian's lips, lifting his head gently so he could drink. He drank down three cups, and on the last bit that was left in the pitcher, she stood and moved towards Dane.

A loud ting sounded on the bars. She halted and looked to the servant.

"Only the blond one!" he ordered.

"But... he's thirsty and—"

"*Only* the blond one!"

Meirah sighed, looked to Dane and mouthed the words, "I am sorry."

Dane nodded his acceptance of the conditions. He had not been as long without water and Adrian needed it more. When Meirah returned, Adrian's eyes were closed. He'd already fallen asleep.

"He will be alright," she said to Dane. She moved to give Dane a kiss, but once again they were interrupted.

"Time to go, M'Lady!"

"Oh bullocks!" Meirah exclaimed before setting the cup and pitcher back in the basket, lifted it and the bucket, and moved to the cell door.

"Set them there," said the servant and she did as she was told. "Turn around." With a shrug, Meirah did as she was told and Dane noticed the expression of confusion on her face. The servant unlocked the door, pulled the basket and bucket out of the cell, set them down.

As the servant pulled a pair of manacles from his robes,

Meirah heard the rattle and turned back. "What are *those* for?"

"Turn around. Master's orders. You are to be brought directly to your chamber. I have orders to kill the mortals should you refuse or fight."

Even as the manacles were attached to her wrists behind her back, Meirah maintained eye contact with Dane. She was led away without fuss, not turning from him as the cell door was closed and locked. Only when she was led towards the exit did she have to look away, but before she walked out the door, she glanced back—and in the emerald of her eyes Dane saw a spark that gave him hope. And then she was gone, the door shutting behind her. He slumped against his own bondage, dropping is head so his hair hid the tears that ran down his cheeks.

Meirah

The door locked with a loud click. Inside her chamber she was as much a prisoner as Dane.

She rubbed at her wrists where the irons had held her so tightly. There was little to see or do, but wait. She sat on the bed, licked her lips. The taste of Dane's mouth still lingered. She wanted more, so much more. More than the few moments they'd had in the cell, more than the two years they spent as husband and wife. More than the many years since she had met Sir Kori Blackmore.

Through the years they had learned much. Enough to escape Mikaire, to take down that world until it existed no more. She needed a plan.

Her dilemma rested mostly on getting the key. She had seen the pendant around Kaeplan's neck. But was it the real key? In Mikaire, they had foreseen her plan to confiscate the key and had made a duplicate; a key that did not work. Kaeplan might use that information here as well. But, then she would also need to free Dane, Adrian and Stephan.

The loss of Bruce weighed heavily. Empathy and pain swirled through her for Caitlyn and baby Dane. Knowing mortals as she now did, she understood their need for closure. Burying bodies, or cremating them. Rituals of their own, a way to say good-bye. This concept had not existed in Mikaire. Once a resident passed on, the body was simply fed to the beasts of the forest. The cycle of life; feed those on whom they fed.

Once had she witnessed a human funeral. A friend of the band's had died of what was referred to as an overdose. Dane had explained to her how certain drugs—herbs made by humans to create powerful feelings of false bliss—could be deadly if consumed in quantities unacceptable to the fragile mortal body.

It had been a somber affaire; a lot of tears and sobbing, and a box containing the body of the deceased was present in what was referred to as a church. She had not understood the words spoken by the robed man at the pulpit. Something about powerful men named Jesus and God.

From there they had all piled into cars and drove slowly to a large plot of land dotted by stones with names and dates carved into them. She did not understand this ritual that ended in the body being placed into the ground to rot away forever; no use to anyone.

A knock at the door interrupted her contemplation. She looked up as the jingle of a key and the lock clicked. The door opened. Kaeplan stepped in and the door closed and locked behind him by another she did not see.

His clothing was fresh; robes of a light blue lined with gilded flowers. On his head was a crown of gold. Wizards did not wear crowns, but Kaeplan saw himself as not just a wizard, but a king as well. His face was clean and fresh with no indication of their earlier altercation.

"I see my fist left no lasting damage," she said, squinting her eyes and wrinkling her nose.

"Ye're might lucky I have a magical healer here."

Meirah couldn't contain the derisive snort that sounded from her throat.

"Did ye find pleasure in harmin' me?'

"I only wish I had done more damage."

"We are bein' honest now?" Kaplan stood his distance, arms crossed over his chest.

"No reason any longer tae be otherwise." Meirah shook her head. "What is it ye want, Kaeplan? Why are ye here? Am I yer new prisoner?"

"That depends on you."

"I am listenin'."

"Ye know I can no' release yer mortal. I need him."

"Tae drain him as Sakkana did, only tae bring him back over and over…" Just saying the words ached her heart.

Kaeplan shook his head. "No. I have no' the power tae reincarnate."

"Then why? What did ye mean ye have special plans for him?"

Kaeplan stood silent for a moment. The amber eyes reflected deceit. Meirah no longer trusted his words, nor his actions.

When he approached her, his movements were careful, guarded. He sat beside her on the bed and when he spoke his words were soft and caring, reminding her of the Kaeplan of years long past.

"Why Meirah? Why betray me? I offered sanctuary and a wonderful life as a queen for ye and the Youngest One, even though it's the spawn of a mortal."

Meirah scoffed and twisted to look at him. "Yer words speak of paradise, but yer actions belie them. Ye want only for yerself, Kaeplan, no' I…nor my child."

"Is that what ye truly believe?"

"That is what I have witnessed."

"Meirah…" He reached a hand towards her, but she cringed back. He placed both hands on his knees. "Can ye no' see how much I love ye? I have loved only ye since we were Young Ones. Ye're all I have wanted all this time."

"Kaeplan." Her words were serious. "I have ne'er seen ye as a mate. Now I can no' even see ye as a friend. Too much has passed between us. Deceptions. Lies."

His youthful face fell into a frown and before he turned away she saw pain in his eyes. "What can I do tae make this up tae ye? Tae keep ye wantin' tae stay wi' me?"

"Ye wished for truth, Kaeplan. Set Dane free… and the others."

He balled the material of his robe in his hands. "If I let them go, ye'll stay wi' me?"

Meirah closed her eyes, pulled in a long and hard breath, released it slowly. Her next words she knew she would regret forever.

"Aye, Kaeplan. I'll stay wi' ye." She swallowed away a lump in her throat. "But... Ye *must* keep yer promise this time. I want Dane safe. Ye've killed his friend. If ye don' let him and the others free, I will make ye want tae kill *me*."

All Meirah wanted was for Dane to be safe, even if it meant her own life. His love for her offered more than enough pain for the dozen lives he had already lived. If she had to remain in Almareyah to assure his freedom, then so be it. She could find a way out in time. Kaeplan would never harm her.

"Please," she whispered, her face close to his. She placed one hand on his shoulder, the other on his chest, placing a palm over the chain visible from beneath his robes.

He closed his eyes at her touch. Taking that opportunity, she fingered the chain before pulling it gently out, exposing the small sword pendant. Kaeplan's eyes snapped open. He grabbed her hand.

"What are ye doin'?"

"Yer necklace," she said, her voice innocent and soft. "Is this the key from Mikaire?" She played daft. She took a risk in pulling it from its hiding place, but she had to be sure.

He yanked it from her grasp, tucked it back under his robes. Before he did, however, she received the information she needed to know.

"Um, aye," he stuttered, caught off guard. "The imitation. I believe yer mortal took the real pendant when ye both destroyed Mikaire."

But this key was no imitation... Just as the real key that had finally opened the portal to the Mortal Dimension to set Dane free from Mikaire, this one boasted a small red stone at its top. And she saw its sparkle before Kaeplan removed it from her hand. The fake key had held no light.

Meirah played along. "Aye, that he did."

Dane had worn the pendant for a long time after Mikaire... a reminder he was safe and no one could take him again. But after a year or so, he'd placed it in a drawer and it became a forgotten relic.

Kaeplan stood. "If ye promise tae stay, I shall free yer mortal and his friends."

"And I need tae be there... Tae make sure ye keep yer word.

No more deception."

Kaeplan thought for a moment, then nodded. "Agreed."

Mortal Dimension
January 26, 2017

-Twenty-five-

"A broken heart is the worst. It's like having a broken rib. No one can see it, but it hurts every time you breathe."

Caitlyn
Charleston, SC

Two weeks passed with no word from Bruce. Last she had heard from her husband he had gone back to Vegas to help Dane search for Meirah.

Even when on tour, not a day passed when Bruce didn't call her. She had called the police in Vegas weeks ago. They'd told her a Dane Bainbridge had reported his wife missing around the same time. Not new news. She loved Dane and Meirah like family, but she wished they had not included Bruce in their adventure, even though he told her it was his idea to go along.

Caitlyn had to assume they had found their way into whatever dimension they suspected Meirah had been taken into… the only reason Bruce would not call.

And so, she had been keeping busy caring for their son, fans of the band, and even the media who had heard the news of the band's possible break-up. That alone made her want to shut off the phone, but she needed to keep the line open in case Bruce called.

So, when the phone rang late that evening, she sighed, assuming another reporter had gotten their private number. She answered anyway.

"Mrs. Beaufort?" said a male voice on the other end.

"Yes..."

"This is Captain Smith, of the Charleston Police Department. Can you open the gate please, we need to speak to you."

Caitlyn's heart jumped a beat. "Why? What is it?"

"We are just outside. Please, open the gate and we will come to you."

Unsure if this was a reporter trying to find a way in, she moved to the window and slid open the shade. Down on the street, she could see a police car waiting outside the gate... and a cop holding a cell phone standing outside it.

She almost dropped her phone. "D-Did you...did you find my husband?" she didn't want to hear the answer. If the police were there, it was bad news.

"We're not sure. Please. Go to the door so we can talk."

"O-Ok..." She hung up the phone and went downstairs. Her legs wanted to give out, but she just kept telling herself nothing was wrong. Bruce was with Dane in some other dimension in time... a place the police, or anyone else in the "real" world, would never believe or understand.

She pressed the gate button and went to the front door. She opened it just as two officers exited the car and approached her. For some reason she didn't understand, her legs went numb.

"Mrs. Beaufort?"

Why was he asking her name again? "Yes." Was it her imagination or did her voice sound shaky?

"We need you to come with us."

Was she under arrest? "Why?"

"A body was found that fits the description of your husband. You need to make a positive identification."

"A b-body?" That meant dead. No, it certainly wasn't Bruce. He was in some weird space in time.

"Yes, ma'am. Please..."

"I-I um... I have a son... I need to..."

"Do what you need to find care for him, we'll wait."

From there, her motions were on auto pilot. Her mind continued to convince her it couldn't be Bruce, yet her body had gone numb all over, as if her subconscious was trying to prepare her for the worst. She called the nanny, promising extra pay, and then dressed in a light pink blouse that was Bruce's favorite, and a skirt. She slipped her feet into flat pumps and told Lisa, the nanny, who arrived within several minutes, that she would be right back.

She knew Lisa asked a bunch of questions but if she answered she couldn't remember. Nothing from there on out was held to memory; not the drive to the hospital, nor the doctor or the long walk down to the morgue. All of it happened, but to someone else. A movie she fell asleep watching, or a book she'd read. But not to her.

Even as she was led into a cold room lined with steel drawers did it not feel real. Nor as the Coroner opened one of those drawers and she could see the covered body within. She didn't even realize she had been fisting the material of her skirt so hard that she tore a seam.

When the sheet was pulled back, she was sure the man that lay there could not be Bruce. The beard was too long, he had been stripped of his clothing and the long dark hair was dirty and matted. Could be some homeless man, she told herself, but deep within she knew.

"Is this your husband?" asked the police officer.

She wanted to shake her head no, but found herself nodding. When she opened her mouth no words escaped.

A hand touched her arm, and she wasn't sure why until she realized her knees were buckling. And she was crying. No, this was not Bruce, it couldn't be! But it was. She saw the distinctive mole on his upper right breast. The one she always circled with her finger when they were lying in bed talking or after they made love. Though the hand still held onto her arm, she briefly saw the floor before everything went black.

Almareyah

-Twenty-Six-

Dane, Stephan and Adrian

Everything hurt. Long ago he'd lost feeling in his arms, but his stomach ached and twisted and he had to fight to remain standing on sore feet, or else fall forward again. His wrists were raw from the manacles and the pain spread down his arms to his chest. He gazed at the straw beneath him. Though musty and soiled, he would give anything to lay in it and sleep.

After they had moved Bruce's body, Adrian went quiet, though he could still see his friend quivering beneath the cocoon of blanket Meirah had wrapped him in.

He looked over at Stephan. His friend was waking, slight moans issuing from pale lips.

"Stephan?" Dane needed to talk to someone, anything, to keep his mind off the pain.

There was no response.

"*Stephan!*"

The blue eyes blinked open and the long red hair shifted as his head moved. "Ohhh, my head…" He came awake suddenly then, leaned forward as far as the bindings would allow. "Bruce?" he cried out.

"You didn't dream it, buddy," said Dane. "He's gone."

His head flopped back onto the hard wood of the rack. "Oh, God! I was sure I'd tied one on and this was all a drunken nightmare."

"'Fraid not," Dane said sadly.

"Adrian?" Stephan strained his head forward again.

"He's ok. Meirah tended to him. He's asleep."

"So, she really was here?" Stephan tilted his head to look at the leaf wrapped around his arm.

"Told ya she'd find us."

"But we're still here."

"They took her. She'll find a way…" Dane hesitated. "She will…she will find another way. She knows we're here. She will get us out. I know she will."

"But what if Kaeplan—"

"No," Dane interrupted. "He won't hurt her."

"How can you be so sure?"

"Because I've been through this before—"

"And you were killed—eleven out of twelve times."

"It's the twelfth time that matters."

"This is not the same world. And now that she's tried…" Stephan let the sentence run off, allowing Dane to fill in the blanks.

"Have faith, Stephan."

"Faith was Bruce's department. And look what happened to him!"

All went silent then. What more could be said? Dane had no answers. But he held unshakable trust in his wife, even if Stephan didn't. He was sure she'd leave him for Kaeplan after what had transpired between them at the hotel. But she hadn't. She hated Kaeplan more now than ever before. He saw the sparkle in her eyes, felt it on her lips. No matter what, their love was forever and she would never stop trying until he was free. Even if he had to live yet another dozen lives.

If there had been a clock in the room, the tick tock would have been loud and obvious. Stephan and Adrian both slept, but he couldn't. He'd start to nod off, but the agony in his shoulders woke him up.

To keep himself awake, he wondered on this anomalous dimension in time. It was real enough alright, but he couldn't quite understand it. In Mikaire, one year had equaled 32 years in the human world. In only a few short weeks he'd grown a full beard and his hair was at least 2 inches longer. He guesstimated he'd been in Almareyah only a day, or was it two? His face itched with hair growth, but only a bit more than at home. So, the time difference, he figured, must be close to the mortal world's.

This was good news, as he wouldn't miss too much time once they returned—and they *would* return. Though apprehension knocked at his nerves, he kept it tucked safely away.

The click of a door latch drew him away from his thoughts.

His hope that Meirah had come to rescue them was shattered when Kaeplan entered, fresh and clean with no indication of a broken nose. He wasn't alone. Five of what must have been stock from Kaeplan's giants of guards piled in behind him.

No one spoke. One of the guards, tall and slender with a scar that cut across his face, moved to Stephan. Two others, one wearing a gold choke-like necklace that resembled a fancy dog collar, the other with hair so white it glowed, approached the cell. The other two remained on either side of Kaeplan like bookends. When he moved, they moved. They were all well-armed with swords and knives at their wastes.

As Scarface removed Stephan's bonds, Dog Collar and White Head entered the cell. Dog Collar unchained Dane's arms and feet, keeping his movements guarded. Dane's hands dropped to his sides and he would have crumpled to the floor if Dog Collar had not caught him and held him up by one arm. White Head picked Adrian up, blanket and all.

Dane leaned on Dog Collar, though he didn't want to. He couldn't help it. His feet hurt so bad, his legs weak and his body so exhausted he wasn't sure he could stand much less walk.

All Dane could do was rub the raw flesh of his wrists and shake his hands to try and return the blood flow. Out of all of them he was in the best shape, though he had to piss like a racehorse. His bladder hurt from holding it, but dignity had kept him from soiling his jeans, especially in front of Kaeplan.

"Can I pee, please?" Dane asked, trying to maintain politeness despite his circumstance.

Dog Collar glanced to Kaeplan, who nodded. With all the muscle he brought with him, Kaeplan was confident Dane wouldn't try anything.

As he took a step away from Dog Collar, however, he felt the buckle of his knees. But the strong arm caught him again.

"I can do this," said Dane, embarrassment winning out over

exhaustion. He pulled away and stumbled to the corner of the cell where Adrian had made his bathroom.

Dane turned his back on the men and fumbled at his zipper with fingers that barely worked.

Relief at last! But, he barely got the zipper back up when he felt the sharp tip of a sword touch his back through his tee shirt.

With swords and knives pointed at them from every direction, they moved as a group from the room. Once within the larger torch-lit room without, Dane noticed the lack of stench he'd stopped smelling in the dungeon. No scent of urine, feces, blood and death. The air was gratefully warmer too.

White Head set Adrian onto his feet and to Dane's surprise, Adrian stood on his own, blanket held tightly around himself.

They all stopped within the large room and the guards surrounded them in a circle. On a stone bench lay what appeared to be piles of rags. As Dane contemplated this odd exchange, Kaeplan spoke at last.

"Remove your outer clothing."

"Excuse me?" Dane said.

"Do it! Or my guards will run ye through!" And he meant it.

Adrian dropped his blanket. The man Dane knew as an incredible drummer could not possibly have been the skeletal waif that stood shivering, naked, dirty. He wanted to grab the blanket and cover Adrian again, if only so he didn't have to see such emaciation. Instead, he pulled off his own tee shirt.

Never one to be shy, Dane felt exposed and uncomfortable as he unzipped his jeans, this time unable to turn away from anyone, and removed them and his boots. Even his socks needed to be removed. Stephan did the same, looking as uncomfortable as Dane felt.

Naked, all three men stood with hands over their privates, looking to one another in questioning. How Adrian could stand, with no meat on his bones and having had no real food in who knows how long, was unclear.

As rock stars, they were not shy men where nudity was concerned, but this was not the typical circumstance. The large guards stood by, looking at them like they were cattle before starving men.

Dog Collar, White Head and Scarface then walked to the back

of the room and each grabbed one of three buckets Dane had not noticed until then.

What the hell...

The contents of the buckets were tossed onto each of them. Cold water!

"Holy shit! Mother of fuck!" Dane exclaimed as Stephan swore under his breath and Adrian cringed back.

Dane shook the water out of his hair. Stephan tossed his back. Adrian let his hang before his face. They all stood shivering in confusion.

"You all stink!" said Kaeplan. "I won't have my people smellin' ye!"

The guards gathered the rags and approached them.

Dane stepped back. "Oh n-no... No man touches my naked body. I am *not* gay!" He glanced to Adrian. "No offense."

"N-None taken." Adrian shivered. White Head began to towel Adrian down. The Romanian drummer, who could scarce stand didn't argue nor move.

Scarface moved to Dane without hesitation as Dog Collar dried Stephan. As he did so, he removed the leaf from Stephan's arm. Stephan looked in awe at the barely visible scar. None of this was new to Dane, but seeing his friend experience the magic for the first time reminded him that it hadn't been all that long ago since he'd marveled at the same.

As Scarface dried him, Dane looked over at Kaeplan. "The only one I've let bathe me, ya know, is Meirah."

His statement produced the response he'd hoped for. Kaeplan's cheeks turned as red as his hair. If he was going to die in yet another time dimension, he'd at least leave a little heat behind.

"Yep," Dane teased. "Meirah and I bathe together *all* the time, our naked bodies pressed together... making love...in the water."

Kaeplan shook with unexpressed rage. He waved a hand in the air dismissively. The guards—who must have loved doing the duty of a servant to three mortals, all because their wizard was afraid of said mortals—replaced the towels and lifted robes. Each man was dressed in a robe, which felt like satin, but were a plain egg-white in color with no fancy gilded flowers or hems.

Dane refused to stop teasing. "Meirah loves the water, and having wild crazy sex in the water—oh...wait. This dimension is entered through water, isn't it?"

Dane laughed as the robe was tied around his waist, forward and around then tied in the back like a Japanese Kimono. "Now every time you see water, Kaeplan, you can envision Meirah and I... together! Something *you* will *never* experience!"

Dane could almost see smoke pouring out the wizard's ears beneath his flaming red hair. His face was twisted in rage, lips pursed, body tense.

"Wait," said Dane, getting the attention of all in the room. He looked directly at Kaeplan. "You're a virgin, aren't you?" He laughed. He could see Stephan in his peripheral vision making a "cut" expression across his throat with his hand. But Dane was having too much fun.

"Meirah told me about the lack of sex in these dimensions. Ohh, that means you are all virgins." He glanced around the room at the five guards who stood expressionless. Unlike Kaeplan, who he could see, was about to explode. "You poor things. Ya know, in the Mortal Dimension, we can have all the sex we want."

He almost missed it, but just caught the look on Scarface's somber face. Jealousy. But it was gone in an instant. He was getting to them all. Good. Let them suffer for a change.

"Give it up, Kaeplan. Meirah will never be the one. She despises you! You'll *never* have her...she united with me. No matter what you do to me, she will never be yours!" Dane snarled the last two words harshly. "***You lose!***"

Less than a second. That is how long it took for Kaeplan's sword to be free of its scabbard, the tip touching Dane's throat. Finally, a reaction he could understand.

Between clenched teeth, Kaeplan hissed, "*one...more...word,* Mortal, and I shall—"

"You'll *what*? Kill me? What of those *special plans* for me, eh? Do you think in all the lifetimes of torture and death I endured in Mikaire *you* can possibly do *anything* that has not already been done, you spineless, dickless piece of dog shit!?"

With a howl, Kaeplan whipped around and threw the sword across the room. It zipped past White Head's face and landed with precision, stuck in the wood of the dungeon door—right smack in the center. Dane was impressed, though he'd never admit it.

"*Get them to the Pyramid!*" Kaeplan screamed to the guards.

As Scarface took Dane's arm, Kaeplan stepped close to Dane. "Ye think I can no' have her?" he whispered harshly. "This is *my* world and I can have what and whom I wish—whenever I wish it!" He grabbed his sword and stormed out of the room.

As the guards pushed them all forward and out of the room, Stephan stared at Dane.

"What?" Dane snapped at his friend.

"What if he rapes her...or worse?" asked Stephan.

"Then I'll kill him. Even if I have to return from the dead to do so. Meirah is strong. She won't let him touch her."

"You sure about that? He's pretty pissed."

"He deserved it! With all the women in this world, he thinks he can have *my* Meirah?"

"I think he sees it the other way around."

"He can see it any way he wants. She's with me."

Stephan sighed as they were herded through another shadow barrier and down yet another hallway.

Kaeplan

Once well enough away from the dungeon and the Hot Room, Kaeplan leaned against a wall and allowed his breath to find him. Rarely was he ever alone anymore, and though being the wizard of his own dimension was a lifetime dream, not all was ideal.

Watching Sakkana in Mikaire, he'd witnessed what appeared a life of comfort, luxury and dominance. Magic, power, attaining all he desired. He had not seen the underbelly of the beast... and its name was Dane Bainbridge.

In his dreams, Meirah was always at his side, ruling with him, not against him. She would have a child—their child, and they would live a life of grandeur together.

Damn that mortal!

Unfortunately, he had been correct about Meirah...she would never be his. Not willingly anyhow. And the little one inside her was Dane's... even thinking it made him shudder and want to kill someone. He had almost killed Dane in the Hot Room, but at the last second he'd flicked his wrist in such a way to avoid hitting anyone.

The beast was corrupting his every plan to bring Meirah in as his guest, let her have the child, then win her over with the perfect life. She was never to know he had Dane here! The bastard's only purpose was to be the Ritual in the Village Square, kept secret from Meirah, where he would kill her mortal and be done with it. Once Dane was dead, Kaeplan's world would have been complete. Now, however, he needed a new plan... and advice. Sheathing his sword, he made his way to his Seer.

An Hour Later

The Seer, a lowly looking old man with long white hair, looked at Kaeplan in deep thought.

"Well?" Kaeplan asked impatiently.

"M'Lady has a powerful bond with this mortal that even magic cannot break."

"Aye, I know this." Kaeplan sighed. "What can I do?"

"The baby binds them." The Seer took a sip of his tea.

"An aberration," Kaeplan whispered, more to himself than the Seer.

"Half human. Half magical." He set the tea cup on the table between where they sat.

"What can I do?" Kaeplan repeated his earlier question.

"The answer lies within you."

"What is that to mean?" Kaeplan's frustration grew. "Give me an answer."

"You have the answer. You've made the decision."

"Elaborate!" Kaeplan snapped. "Please."

"As long as the babe lives, she will never be yours."

Kaeplan's eyes widened. "You want me to kill a baby?"

"You already have."

"But I have no'. I do no' understand."

"Visit the Apothecary."

"Why...?

"Because you were going to anyway."

30 Minutes Later

Rarely did Kaeplan walk the streets of his Village alone, unattended by guards. But the best he left to watch the mortals.

Residents bowed as he passed, then fell to their knees in worship. Kaeplan reveled in the attention, keeping his body straight, his eyes forward. Let them grovel. Let them worship. They would not exist if not for his power.

An old woman, barely able to keep to her knees, reached a shaky hand out to touch his gilded robe. Had a guard been present, she would have been flogged for such disrespect. But he was alone and needed his people to see he was not the monster Dane made him out to be. He bent and took her hand, lifted her gently to her feet. Villagers watched as he leaned to kiss her cheek.

"Thank ye," he said in a manner most contradictory to his station.

The old woman beamed. Cheers and cries of gratitude reached his ears. He bowed to them all before straightening again and continuing to his destination.

He knew this small act would ripple through the villages, making for stronger followers. His mood lifted to a respectable level, and he began to feel hope enter his heart yet again.

Kaeplan moved across the road, the crowd parting for him, bowing as he passed.

Above the glass door a wooden sign simply read 'Apothecary.' He entered and closed out the din of worshippers behind him.

The store was small and clustered with shelves that held many small bottles, labeled and priced. Along the ceiling beams above, herbs hung drying. The place held a pleasant odor, relaxing and soothing to the senses.

Kaeplan approached the long wooden counter. No one was present, but he assumed the potion maker was in the back. On the counter sat a silver bell. Kaeplan lifted it up, shook it. The high pitched ring echoed around the store. For the first time since creating Almareyah he felt like an ordinary citizen. He did not like it.

From the back room came a voice "Be there in a minute."

Kaeplan glanced to the door. A mob had gathered outside the store. He hoped none would enter. This business was his alone.

A few minutes later, the Apothecary, whose name was Helious, a squat man with straggled grey hair that touched his shoulders, entered from the back, brushing dust from beige breeches.

"What can I do for—" He halted as he looked up and saw his Master standing there. "Oh my... Master, such an honor." He bowed deeply.

"Please... rise," said Kaeplan. "I am in need of a potion."

He stood straight. "Yes, of course... anything you wish."

Now this was more like it.

"I need something tae end a pregnancy wi'out harmin' the mother."

Helious stared at Kaeplan a moment as if sizing up this unique request. "M-Master?"

"Ye heard me."

Helious seemed to snap out of some spell. "Oh...oh, yes. I have just the thing." He scuffled off to the other end of the counter and bent, began shuffling noisily through clanking bottles.

Kaeplan glanced wearily to the door. Most of the mob had dissipated, returning to their mundane lives serving him. Only a few remained, looking in, curious as to the nature of their Master's visit here.

Though Almareyah had no media as in the Mortal Dimension, gossip spread like a flooding river nonetheless.

Kaeplan slid behind the counter, startling Helious as he stood and turned, small vial in hand.

"Oh... um..."

"In there," Kaeplan nodded to the door to the back room. "This is secret."

"Of course. Of course." Stuttered Helious.

They moved to the back room. Once away from the prying eyes of the public, Kaeplan motioned to the vial. "Is that it?"

"Y-Yes, Master. Just a drop should not harm the mother, but kill any living thing within her."

Kaeplan snatched the vial from Helious's hand, dropped it into the pocket of his robe.

"Is this...um..." Helious stuttered, "for M'Lady? I hear she carries the babe of a mortal."

His confidence was unnerving. Kaeplan drew his knife, held it to the Apothecary's throat as the small man's grey eyes widened in surprise.

"None o' yer concern... Nor anyone else's. Is this clear?"
The Apothecary bobbed his head up and down quickly.
"Good!"

-Twenty-Seven-

"Deception may give us what we want for the present, but it will always take it away in the end." -Rachel Hawthorne

Kaeplan

He arrived at the Dining Hall early and took his seat at the head of the table. Meirah's place was set. As he awaited her arrival, he fidgeted, taking up a plate, moving it to another location, replacing it with a bowl. He lifted the candelabra, moved it nearer to Meirah's setting, changed his mind and moved it farther away. The shadow fell on the pitcher of human blood—the special pitcher—Meirah's surprise. He sat down as he heard footfalls approach. Drawing in a deep breath, he sat up straight.

The double doors groaned open. A servant accompanied Meirah in.

Kaeplan smiled and stood. She was dressed as he had ordered; burgundy dress with sleeves the length of which touched the floor. Very similar to the dress she had worn for the celebration in Mikaire; the engagement that never happened.

"Ah, Meirah. Your beauty radiates." He held the back of her chair for her.

She paused before sitting, a glance of suspicion tossed his way.

Kaeplan retook his seat, motioned to the servant who lifted the pitcher, filled Kaeplan's glass, then hers.

He lifted his glass. "A toast."

Meirah took her glass warily. "To what?"

"Freedom for your mortals—and your continued visit here wi' me."

"Once ye free Dane and the others, ye mean…"

"O' course!"

They clinked glasses. Kaeplan drank, eyeing Meirah over the rim of the crystal.

Meirah hesitated.

"Drink," said Kaeplan. "'Tis quite a surprise."

She placed the crystal to her lips, paused again. Kaeplan motioned for her to drink. She sipped, then downed the entire glass.

"Is this human blood?" she asked, staring at the empty glass.

"Aye, it is. Do ye love it?"

"It has an odd taste, like…"

"Like the blood of more than one human? Quite the delicious mix, don' ye think?"

"Yes, but—"

"Then enjoy." He grabbed up the pitcher, refilled her glass. "Drink."

A smile played at her lips. Human blood was quite intoxicating when one did not drink it often…except to wizards, who could easily tolerate it. But this mix of two human's blood made her, he knew, feel almost giddy. Like a strong liquor. The red liquid disappeared in one long swallow.

The servant placed plates of Meirah's favorite human food between them. She ignored it. After pouring herself and drinking one more glass of blood, her smile grew broad. She gazed at the glass with eyes soft and warm with stupor, a grin of satisfaction.

"I had forgotten—" She reached for the pitcher but it was empty. "Aw, all gone." Her smile faded.

Kaeplan watched Meirah with a constant grin. His plan was going better than expected. She appeared quite intoxicated and when her favorite dish of eggs was served, she turned them down.

"I think I would like tae retire early tae my chamber, Kaeplan."

He stood. "Are ye feelin' ill?" he asked with genuine concern. He had no notion that the special blood would have such a quick reaction.

"Nae, I am fine, I forgot the effects of human blood is all."

"I shall accompany ye."

Once at her chamber, Isophia and Keliah took over her preparation for slumber. Kaeplan left, a smile on his face for a plan well executed.

Meirah

Meirah woke screaming. Agony. Pain, like a sword sliced through her abdomen. She sat up, her hands moving instinctively to her belly. The pain was so intense she had trouble catching her breath. *What is happening?*

Sweat broke out on her forehead. Help…she needed aid. The castle slept. The coverlet fell to the floor as she thrashed.

Swinging her legs off the bed she slid to a stand, but her limbs were numb and weak. She crashed to the floor. At a crawl, she found a table, grasped the edged, hoisted herself up. Bent forward, she warbled to the door. Locked. She banged weakly on the door. "H-Hel…"

The floor came up to greet her and all went dark.

When Meirah woke, she was in her bed. Daylight streamed through the windows. No pain, but incredulous fatigue still weighed her down. Someone stood by the bed.

"Dane?"

In response gentle hands held a wet rag to her forehead. As the world cleared, Isophia's face came into focus.

"What happened?" Meirah's last recollection was having dinner with Kaeplan the night before.

Human blood. Two humans. Now that she was sober, a recollection struck her mind. The blood. It tasted vaguely familiar but not. She'd drunk the blood of one human long ago… Dane's blood. The strongest of all. But his had not held this impact.

"What did Kaeplan do?" she said weakly.

Isophia didn't answer. She couldn't. But her face told of a sadness she couldn't verbally express.

The door opened then. A male servant she did not recognize entered and she attempted to focus on the items he carried.

She tried to sit up. Gentle hands forced her back down.

"You must rest, M'Lady." He placed a cup to her lips, which she at first refused. But then she smelled it...water. She took a few sips.

The pain returned, but only in her memory. She reached down to her abdomen.

"The baby?" Fear coursed through her. The small swell that had been there was gone. "Ohh, by Sakkana, *No!*"

Twenty-Eight

Almareyah

Caitlyn

She wrung the water from her hair and brushed off her clothing as she stepped onto the shore. From what she could tell so far she was alone. Not what she had expected to find, however, though she wasn't really sure what she would find. She could see little through the dense trees, which consisted mostly of palms and other tropical fauna, and a path leading to... who knew where?

She touched the knife at her waist, wishing she could have brought a better weapon. One of Dane's swords, or a gun. But Bruce never believed in keeping guns in the house and she was not about to go to Dane's house for a sword. Edna surely would have talked her out of her plan. To her nanny, she had simply explained that she needed to visit a sick relative. Lisa had tried to talk her out of it, stating she was in no condition to travel, Bruce's funeral having been only four days prior, and bringing up the fact the police were still in the middle of their investigation into what they referred to as a kidnapping and homicide. But that was exactly why now was the perfect time do go. She had assured Little Dane had enough care and informed all the caretakers she would be back in a few days, maybe longer.

She started down the path through the trees and brush. The sun above was bright and warm.

Within a few minutes, she was sweating. She removed the sweater she wore and tied it around her waist. A few more minutes' walk and she removed her jeans, donning now only the shorts she wore beneath. She had not known what to expect for climate, so she had layered her clothing. She folded her jeans and sweater and hid them beneath an odd-looking tree she did not know the name of—just in case she found her way back or needed them. Carrying them was far too much of a burden and she had not brought any packs. She placed the knife in the belt of her jean shorts, close to where she could easily grab it.

Within ten minutes, she stopped and stared at the strange anomaly before her; A wall. A small path ran between the wall and the forest she had just stepped out from.

"We are definitely not in Kansas anymore," she whispered, and when she gazed up at the sun to get hold of her bearings, she realized it was not the sun at all, but a humongous light merely imitating sunlight. That explained the lack of humidity in a tropical forest. The entire area was one huge room! She started down the wall in search of a door. After all, where there was a wall there had to be a door.

She knew from Dane that Mikaire had run on a different line of time and it was possible more time might pass in the 'Mortal Dimension' than where she was. But she couldn't be sure as Dane and Stephan had not been seen since they left to find Meirah, Bruce and Adrian.

Just the thought of her husband made her weak, so she had to push it aside. Be strong.

She observed the room around her as she followed the wall, a smooth limestone with an occasional Egyptian Hieroglyph. Quite odd, but interesting. With her Bachelor's in ancient architecture, Master's in ancient language and several smaller degrees in random other studies, all acquired before she had met Bruce, she knew seeing this place would hold endless fascination—so long as she kept her wits and didn't get herself killed.

Caitlyn studied the Egyptian Hieroglyph on the wall, trying to recall that chapter in her language studies. Water, it was the symbol for water.

"No shit," she said aloud.

The next symbol was the Hieroglyph for portal, or doorway. Again, no kidding, she thought.

"C'mon, give me something I can work with!"

Down the long length of wall, she spied a door at long last. Around it were more Hieroglyphs. How sneaky, to give clues in a long dead language. She read each symbol carefully, but was sure she got them wrong, until she realized in horror what they said: DEATH ROOM.

She grabbed the latch of the door and paused. She was not sure she wanted to know what was on the other side. Taking in a deep breath, she clicked the latch, opened the door. On its other side she found herself in a hallway lit by torches. The place reminded her of an ancient stone castle. And then, another door.

She opened it slowly and paused when she heard voices on the other side. She peered out the crack in the door.

From her vantage point she couldn't see much. Two men were there dressed in tunics and breeches, similar attire to Meirah's preferred dress. They were pointing this way and that as if trying to make a decision.

It was then she noticed many others in the room—but they were not walking, nor talking. Their backs were to her, but she could see now they were tied up like animals. She quietly cracked the door more—causing a bit more of the scene to come into view. More people tied to poles. All were sparsely dressed; most of the women in underwear and bras, or underwear alone. All the bound men were completely unclothed, one wore boxer shorts.

"What the..." she whispered.

Her gaze halted on one particular man with long red hair, tied up to the far right of where she stood. He was unclothed, but his head was bent forward, hair covered his body like a soft waterfall, only inches from brushing the ground. Something about the tangled red hair, the slender body... Familiarity.

One of the dressed men who had been speaking to the other walked to the red-head, grabbed a fistful of hair and brought his head up, tilted it to the side. Caitlyn stifled a gasp. *Stephan*!

The man opened his mouth wide...fangs, like Meirah's only longer, sharper. Caitlyn stifled another gasp as he bit hard into Stephan's throat, which caused him to flinch and release a weak moan. He was still alive.

The other man moved about the room, looking carefully at each bound person. Caitlyn's gaze followed the half circle of prisoners. She recognized no others, but as her gaze swept the people, one bound man caught her attention. He was so skeletal as to appear dead. Dirty matted hair at first looked to her eyes as brown, but when her gaze halted on him, she noticed he was blond.

She could not see his face for the hair falling over it, but she was sure that was Adrian.

Panicked, she looked through the crowd once more. Nope, no Dane.

Oh God, they killed him.

The man who bit Stephan stopped, removed a rag from his pocket, wiped his mouth as if he were sitting at a fancy dining table. He then stopped before a short pole made of marble, a small Egyptian obelisk. Caitlyn watched as he erased something then took up a crayon that hung beside it and wrote on its top.

His friend was still looking at each person with hungry indecisive eyes.

"Hurry and choose," said his friend impatiently. "We need to get home before dark."

"It's difficult," said the other.

"Just pick one! They're only humans. Doesn't matter which."

"Why do we get the left-overs? I want the one Master Kaeplan saved for himself. His blood must be amazing!"

"Well, you cannot have that one! He is being prepped for Ritual. Just take the one I drank from... the redhead... I hear he and that one..." he motioned to Adrian, "came in with the strong one."

"No, that one has some hair on his face, it's repulsive. And this one..." He looked Adrian up and down. "How can he have any blood? He's a skinny twig. Can't taste very good."

"Just choose already."

Caitlyn understood then. Dane... Kaeplan was holding him, the strongest blood, to drain during some macabre ritual to keep his world alive.

"Fine!" said the man still searching. "I'll take this one..." He walked to a young woman dressed only in a small pair of lace panties. "She looks yummy." With no more hesitation, he sunk his fangs into one of her breasts. She cringed into the bonds, her mouth opened wide as if to scream, but nothing came out. He stopped, repeating his friend's motion of wiping his mouth then writing on the obelisk.

As they turned and walked away, Caitlyn heard them chatting. "I want more..."

"You can't have more, unless you want to endure the

wrath...."

And then they were gone, exiting out the large doors at the other end of the circular room.

Caitlyn peered around. No others, just the bound humans. She moved slowly, guardedly, into the room and padded to Stephan. His head had dropped again. On the obelisk was written the number 4.

What in the hell does that mean? She thought, until she noticed 4 sets of fang marks on his neck, chest and arms. The number of times he'd been fed on by these beasts.

What kind of sick son of a bitch...

"Stephan," she whispered.

He groaned, face still hidden by his abundant hair.

Caitlyn touched his shoulder, shook gently. "Hey, Stephan, wake up." She reached under his chin, lifted his face to look into his eyes. The dark blue orbs were glazed, confused. He stared at her as if she were a delusion.

"It's me, Stephan... Caitlyn. I need to get you out of here."

"C-Caitlyn?"

"Yes, I am really here. Wake up, we need to get you out before anyone else arrives."

"But... B-Bruce..."

Her heart clenched, stomach knotted. "I know... I can't think on that now or I will not have the strength to free you."

She pulled her knife and proceeded to saw at the ropes that held his wrists, but it was taking a hideous amount of time, the ropes were so thick and strong. She could untie them faster, she reasoned. They were tied tightly, but quilting and needlepoint became a hobby while she was pregnant, and untying knots was a strange gift of hers. He leaned forward again, unable to hold himself up, but that only made untying the knots more difficult.

"You need to snap out of it, Stephan. I can't get the ropes."

With a groan, he fought to stand upright, slackening the ties just enough. Once he was free, he stumbled forward. Caitlyn caught him, but despite his thin stature, he was still too heavy for her.

He stared out at nothing.

"Are you with me, Stephan?" Caitlyn asked, nerves pitted in the depth of her gut.

He nodded, swaying. "Dizzy."

"Blood loss. Can you stand? I can't carry you, and we need to free Adrian."

He forced himself to a warbling upright position. Caitlyn placed a hand on his arm. Once he steadied himself, she released him and moved to Adrian. Stephan warbled along behind her.

Adrian by this time was leaning hard forward. Caitlyn noticed the number on his obelisk: 9.

"Stephan, help me, please." She began to work on the bindings.

Stephan looked down at himself, as if realizing for the first time he was naked. He pulled all his hair forward in an attempt to hide his junk, but as long as his hair was, it didn't quite reach.

"Stephan! Please, no time for modesty—hold him up!"

Stephan stepped beside Adrian, slipped one arm behind him and wrapped it around the skeletal waist. "Jesus Christ!" he exclaimed. "There's nothing to him. Is he alive?"

"He's unconscious but he won't be alive for long if we don't get him out of here."

Caitlyn freed one arm, which flopped lifelessly to his side. Stephan groaned at the dead weight that was suddenly leaning against him.

"I'm too weak to hold him up, light as he is," said Stephan as Caitlyn freed the other arm and Adrian flopped like a rag doll against Stephan's chest. "Ugh!"

Both of Stephan's arms went around the small waist. He shook as he labored to hold his friend up. Caitlyn bent and untied his feet, fortunately the ropes there were loose, just enough to keep him in place.

"You got him?" Caitlyn asked.

"I-I think so." Though his grip tightened, his own state of being weak with blood loss rendered him too frail to move while holding the emaciated form in his arms. "N-Not sure how long I can hold him."

"Stay here!" Caitlyn said before moving away to a woman nearby who wore only panties, and was very much awake, watching with brown eyes framed by fearful white.

"You'll be okay," Caitlyn assured her. She easily untied her and the girl rubbed at her red-rimmed wrists before crossing her arms over her bare breasts. "Stay with me, ok? I'll get you out. I know the way."

The girl nodded quickly.

Caitlyn moved down the line to another.

"What are you doing?" Stephan asked in a brash whisper. "We need to get out of here!" His gaze darted about nervously.

Adrian slipped slowly from Stephan's grasp, to where he now held his naked friend under the armpits.

Caitlyn worked on the ropes of a tall and muscular man, naked, his bald head and face covered in brown fuzz. His obelisk read 1. He had strength still.

"We need help."

Caitlyn knew she couldn't free all of the close to two dozen people in the room, so she chose only those who still held strength. The girl she freed aided her, which made the job go faster.

"Only the ones who can stand and walk," she ordered as the bald man also began freeing others.

Once they had untied seven people, Caitlyn looked to the rest. "I'm sorry," she said to the remaining prisoners before moving back to Stephan and Adrian, the free prisoners following her as if she was the Messiah.

Adrian moaned, slowly coming around. He sagged in Stephan's weak arms, knees bent, nearly touching the floor. Stephan couldn't move with the weight of Adrian pressing him down.

Caitlyn looked over at the bald man she had freed. "What's your name?"

Her question received no verbal reply, merely a shake of his head.

"H-He's been m-muted," said Stephan, fighting to retain his hold on Adrian.

What kind of sick... Caitlyn looked once more at the stranger. "Can you carry him?" She motioned to Adrian.

The man nodded and with no hesitation, he took the burden of Adrian's limp form from Stephan.

"Thank you..." Stephan breathed heavily.

The man hoisted a naked Adrian onto one shoulder like a sack of flour.

"The Portal out is this way..." said Caitlyn.

She led her newly-formed entourage to the door from which she had entered. Above it, she noticed for the first time a sign, written in English and a language she did not know.

CASTLE RESIDENTS ONLY.

Odd. She reached for a handle that was not there. "Shit," she muttered under her breath. "How do we get out of here?"

She placed her palms against the wood grain of the door; smooth like glass. It didn't budge. Perplexed, she turned to her freed prisoners. Slowly, she shook her head as they all stared at her for direction.

Kaeplan

He watched Meirah, lying so still in her bed. Gently, he fingered a lock of her dark red hair. So soft. So close to his in color.

"Oh, Meirah," he whispered, "What an heir we shall create together."

She moaned, her eyelids fluttered.

"Meirah, my love."

Her eyes opened and she stared at him with no recognition.

"Ye'll be fine," he said.

Slowly she sat up. He placed his arms around her not only to feel her near him but to steady her.

"K-Kaeplan?"

Hearing her speak his name thrilled him. He'd had a servant give her a glass of water laced with *rumious*, which grew in abundance in Almareyah. It tended to cause some confusion, but its most endearing quality was complete compliance. She was his at long last. Yes, he had wanted her to come to him on her own, but barring that...

The herb worked.

He ran a hand over her back, fingering the material of her night dress. Arousal became imminent. She had healed quickly from the birth of her still-born baby—Dane's last legacy. Kaeplan smiled. It was time to create his own heir.

Meirah's body was warm against his and he moved a hand to the laces of her garment. As he loosened the strings, however, an alarm reverberated through his mind and interrupted him in unwelcomed sonorousness.

His hand moved from her laces as he released a frustrated sigh. The alarm rang again, filling his mind with the unpleasant vibration. Bideus must have returned with a new human.

"I am sorry, my love, I must go. Duty calls."

"Take me with you," begged Meirah, taking his arm, emerald eyes pleading.

She wanted to be with him!

He smiled, nodded. He helped her up from the bed. She was surprisingly steady.

"How do ye feel?" he asked with genuine concern.

"Well enough tae remain at yer side."

If only Mikaire had possessed such an herb, he'd have been with Meirah long ago. The ultimate test of its power, however, was yet to be discovered.

Caitlyn

She walked about the vast room, resisting the urge to free the rest of the prisoners. So far, their luck held and no one had come in and discovered them. There had to be another way into the Portal room.

She returned to the door, where those she had freed awaited. She felt around again, sure she had missed something. So busy in her attempt to open the door, she did not see the two who approached from behind.

"Who in the name o' Sakkana are ye?"

Caitlyn spun in sync with the others. Standing behind them was an unfamiliar man. He held an air of authority in his demeanor and of royalty in his gilt clothing. Beside him, was...

"Meirah?" Caitlyn moved towards Dane's wife. Hands grasped her arms; she had not even noticed the two who flanked her.

"Kaeplan!" she said, realizing now who this authority figure was.

Meirah, dressed only in what looked like a nightgown covered by a blue robe of lace and silk, stood beside him like a queen defending her king. As the wife of a rock star, Caitlyn had seen that drugged look too many times. The bastard had managed to find a way to keep Meirah subservient to him.

"Ye know me, and ye are…?" asked Kaeplan.

"You *murdered* my husband!" She struggled against those who held her, but their grip was too strong.

Kaeplan paused a moment. "I have killed many humans. I can no' be sure which was yer husband." He paused, deep in thought for a moment before stating, "Hm… ah! The bearded one! Aye, that was an unfortunate accident, actually. He was due tae come here wi' the others…" He glanced to Stephan, who stood beside the large man carrying Adrian.

Caitlyn's anger warred within, threatening to get the best of her, but this would do no good. Briefly, she assessed the situation. Bruce had insisted she take self-defense courses, and atop her martial arts training, she used this knowledge to her advantage. She dropped her body weight like a boulder, causing them to loosen their grip. She spun, landing a groin kick to the one closest to her. He released her, humped in pain.

She spun to the other, landing a good right hook to his face. The moment she was free, she grabbed the knife at her waist and in one fluid motion was behind Kaeplan. She reached around, the knife coming to rest near his throat.

Meirah did nothing. Subservient, but not defensive.

"Open the door!" she snapped. "Now!"

Two guards forwarded on to her. She pressed the knife to Kaplan's throat, harder.

"I will slice him from nose to nuts if you try to stop me!"

Kaeplan placed a palm on the door and it faded away. A dark corridor awaited beyond.

"Just him!" Caitlyn referred to Kaeplan's minions. But they didn't back down. She dug the knife against Kaeplan's throat until he winced. He waved a dismissive hand to the guards.

With the knife held close to his throat, and the rescued prisoners standing close by to defend their rescuer, Kaplan had no choice but to lead all down to the Portal room and through the fauna to the pool.

Once at its edge, Caitlyn spun to stand in front of Kaeplan, knife held outward, tip touching the red mark she'd made on his throat. "Where's Dane?"

"Nowhere ye will find 'im," said Kaeplan.

"Bring him here!"

"No!" snapped Kaeplan. "Kill me if ye wish. Without 'im I shall die anyway."

Caitlyn looked at Meirah, who had moved with Kaeplan as if the two were connected by an invisible rope. "Please... Dane is your husband. Don't you want him back?"

No reply. Meirah shook her head slowly.

Drugs and... A spell!

"Meirah! Snap out of it!" Caitlyn snapped the fingers of her free hand before Meirah's face.

Meirah blinked quickly and her eyes cleared. "Caitlyn?" Her voice was small.

"Yes... Meirah, it's me. Dane needs you!"

Kaeplan slapped Caitlyn's knife hand away. "Enough!" He stepped between Caitlyn and Meirah, reached behind him and touched Meirah's arm, pushing her gently behind him. The visual between her and Caitlyn snapped. Caitlyn peered over Kaeplan's shoulder. Meirah's eyes once again hazed. Drugs, magic. Powerful.

"Ye may go," said Kaeplan. "All o' ye. I have what I need. All o' ye can be replaced." He slipped an arm around Meirah's waist as she took her place once more beside him.

The trees and bushes behind them rustled loudly as more guards piled into the room, to the Portal, to stand by their king and queen.

Caitlyn glanced to the others. Her body trembled with rage. *Bruce.* This bastard killed him. She raised her knife again, towards Kaeplan. Her hand shook terribly.

"Meirah," she said, keeping her eyes on Kaeplan. "Please...I know you're in there. He has Dane. He'll kill him!"

"That is enough!" said Kaeplan. "I said ye could leave. Go live yer human life. Forget this place. I'll no' bother ye again. Just... send back Bideus. I sent him to get a mortal... Or did ye kill 'im tae get in here?"

Caitlyn's gaze flamed at Kaeplan's. "You...killed...*my*...life! I care not of your Bideus. He was my key in here. Now... I want Dane and I will return your minion."

Kaeplan scoffed. "Bideus is nothing. I need Dane's blood. Kill

Bideus if ye must."

She took a step forward, but a hand on her shoulder halted her. Stephan stood beside her now…

"Caitlyn," he whispered. "Let's just go. We're outnumbered. We'll get Dane back somehow."

Caitlyn stood stiff, shaking. "You can't imagine what it's like to lose your soulmate forever," she snapped at Stephan, but her eyes drilled into Kaeplan's. "It's like living death!" She glanced over at Stephan. "You've seen how Dane is without Meirah."

"Caitlyn," said Stephan softly, "I am so very sorry about Bruce. I lost as well, we all did. But we must think of now. Adrian needs a hospital. Dane has handled himself in these worlds before. Trust he will find a way again."

Caitlyn's eyes found Kaeplan's once more and she allowed her rage and pain to bore into them.

"This is not over!"

Kaeplan

Allowing the humans their leave was a small price to pay for what he had gained. But what really plagued Kaeplan was Meirah. She had come around, if only for a moment, when the woman had spoken to her. He had gotten her back, but the incident made him realize his hold on her was not as strong as he needed. It was time to seal the bond.

Meirah was already in bed by the time he entered her chamber, which was dark save the single candle on her night stand. He watched her in sleep for a moment, reveling in her beauty. The smooth pale flesh. The soft hair that haloed her head and hung off the bed to touch the floor. Beside her bed, an empty glass sat. Good. She had drunk the drugged blood he had sent to her room earlier in the evening. She slept so peacefully, hands crossed on her chest. The candlelight revealed it then… her wedding ring. Time to rid Dane from her mind. Carefully, he slipped it from her finger, placed it in a pocket with his robe.

"Ye're free," he whispered. "And mine."

He slid out of his robes and climbed naked into the bed beside her. He moved his hand down beneath her nightdress, between her legs. Her heat brought him to immediate arousal. So nice. Warm, enticing. Perfect. He so wished to merely climb atop her, make love to her, conscious or no. But he was no animal, and he wished for her compliance. To feel her legs wrapped around his waist, to know she was all his.

Her soft supple flesh beneath his hand was like stepping into paradise. She was his paradise. And when he slipped a finger into her, she moaned.

"Aye, Meirah, I am here..." he whispered.

Her eyes fluttered open and she gazed at him through the flicker of the single candle by the bed. He leaned in to place a kiss on her lips. She complied, her tongue parting his lips, her legs opening with his touch. Gently, he moved to lay atop her. As her arms wrapped around him, he pressed his arousal against her. This was what he lived for, what he dreamed of for many years, what gave him the strength to survive so long in the human desert.

He pressed into her and as the moist heat of her surrounded him, he felt his climax near. He slowed himself, wanting this to last. Nothing compared to this moment. All the waiting, saving himself for Meirah was worth this. Euphoria took him to a place he had never before experienced.

Meirah arched her body against his, wanting more. Deeper he drew into her. Her cry of pleasure, her moan of climax and he could no longer hold back. He pressed harder, deeper until he felt the most wonderous sensation... he cried out and released into her a lifetime of longing, needing, waiting.

He slumped onto her, kissing her neck, not wanting to move away. "Oh Meirah, I do love ye," he whispered into her ear.

Meirah pulled him closer, and in soft loving words, she spoke. "I love ye too, Dane."

Dane

He came awake suddenly. He didn't know what woke him, but her name was on his lips as he did.

"Meirah!"

His voice echoed off the close stone walls around and returned to him, empty and alone. He sat up, opening his eyes to complete darkness. He was still in the tiny cell where he had been placed several days prior. This cage was much smaller than the other and though grateful he was not chained, he could only sit, stand or lie in a fetal position on the musty serge. Better than being chained to a wall, he thought, trying to find a single ray of light in the dark.

He grabbed the bars of the door that, even in the pitch, he knew was there. Each day, he was visited by one of Kaeplan's minions, bled, even flogged once, for what he knew not. His back flamed with fresh wounds over old scars. And he was scarcely fed. Once a day, his internal clock told him it was time, he was brought bread, water and one piece of fruit. Not enough to keep alive the rats and ants that crawled along the floor...and him.

There had been too much time to think with no one to talk to. He wondered what happened to his friends, the pain of Bruce's death still raw in his mind. But thinking only made things worse, so he'd stopped doing it. Most of the time, he merely sat curled in the corner of the cell, waiting for death, keeping the robe sashed and hugged tight to his body.

Dane tried to stand, but even using the bars for leverage, he was simply too weak. He sat back against the stone wall, which cooled his back. Fortunately, they had not taken the robe, and he kept it wrapped around himself like a blanket.

He had come to know by the grumbling in his stomach, when it was time to eat. So, when he heard a click indicating the opening of the lock to the room where his cell was located, he wondered what could be amiss. It was not yet time to eat, or be bled.

The light of a single torch lit the room. He lifted his head wearily, but still it took a moment for his starved brain to comprehend what he saw.

Kaeplan entered, and several guards stood behind him.

Kaeplan stared at him with disdain burning in his amber eyes. "Ye've some good friends, I must admit. Several tried tae free ye... *they failed.*" His maniacal laugh was eerie and disheartening.

Dane grasped the bars, forced himself with what little strength he could muster, to stand. "What did you do to them?"

"I set them free, o' course. So, ye need no' worry on them. They went home. Ye're alone."

"And Meirah?" The feeling that had awoken him returned. He

grasped the bars tighter. "No! *How dare you touch her*!" He knew now. He didn't know how, but he knew!

Kaeplan stood perfectly still and though he made not a single movement, Dane saw acknowledgement in his eyes… like a blow to his face he had not seen coming. It lasted only a second, then Kaeplan blinked it away.

"Get him out of there!" he bellowed to the guards.

Two guards moved forward with chains. Another opened the door, forcing Dane to release the bars. He almost fell, but two grabbed his arms, held him up. The others chained his wrists, hobbled his legs. As if in his weakened state he could do anything.

As they hauled him out of the cell, he dug his feet into the floor, halting before Kaeplan, gazing with utter loathing into his eyes.

"She saw *me* the whole time!" he said with satisfaction.

The guards shoved Dane forward, but not before he saw Kaeplan flinch.

He was led through a small dark hallway to a door with no handle. Kaeplan, ahead of them, pressed a palm to the surface.

The sudden bright light blinded him. Warmth. Sunshine. He squinted. They were outside, in a desert. Down a sandy path awaited a plain brown carriage hitched by two white horses. His mind flashed images of his own horses back home. His heart ached. He would never again see them. Bruce was dead. Meirah was under a spell. This is the end, he thought as they loaded him into the carriage.

As they drove away, Dane saw the world outside for the first time. A desert of eternal sand dunes and palm trees. As they moved away from the structure he'd been prisoner, it came full into view; not a castle, but a smooth white pyramid. An identical replica of the Giza pyramid in Egypt as it must have looked thousands of years ago.

And then it was gone; just like that, and they were surrounded by wooded forest. The air shifted from searing and dry to hot and humid in an instant. Crossing barriers in Mikaire should have prepared him, but this world was so different in so many ways. This time he was not surprised when they materialized into a village.

Just as he'd experienced for 12 lifetimes, just as in Mikaire, villagers swarmed the carriage, cheering and grasping. This was Ritual. Their lives would go on. His would end.

And not just at the fangs of some random wizard, but Kaeplan's. He would taste his revenge at last. Briefly, Dane wondered who he would come back as next time. And would Meirah still love him?

The carriage halted at what appeared to be the center of town. He couldn't see much beyond the swarm of villagers, but as his gaze swept from one face to another, the crowd began stepping to the side, parting like Moses and the Red Sea.

Another carriage arrived then, a fancy carriage of golden rims, blue and grey body, and curtains on the windows, pulled by two big black horses. They halted beside his carriage, and one of Kaeplan's servants hopped down to open the door.

Kaeplan stepped out, flanked by two guards. At least he came out to witness Ritual, unlike Sakkana who had remained holed up in his castle until it was time for him to drain Dane of his life.

Two guards dragged Dane from the carriage, lifting him up then placing him onto his feet. The sand was hot as opposed to the floor of the cell, which was always cold. He still wore only the robe he'd been given... how many days ago now? Four meals, so about as many days.

He was half led-half carried through the parting crowd to a pole that looked all too familiar. A whipping post, identical to the one in Mikaire that had been erected for his flogging after he had struck Kaeplan.

Oh man, not again! Why were these anomalous wizards so into flogging?

They shoved his back against the pole—he flinched at the pain, his back still raw and sore—and hooked his manacled hands above his head to a heavy iron ring. Briefly flittered a thought as to how they would flog him with his back to the pole. No, not the chest, he thought, how would he wear his stage costume? He wouldn't, he realized, for this was the end, of him, of the band, of everything. Oddly, he wasn't afraid. Too many lives of pain; he should have died hundreds of years ago!

The villagers encircled him like fans at one of his concerts. Once again, he was the star, but the conclusion would not end in an encore.

Kaeplan stood off to his left, but he held no whip, no knife, nothing. He simply kept his hands folded in front of himself. He wasn't looking at Dane, but there was something—his jaw was clenched. Tension apparent.

Had Dane's words at the cell gotten to him? Or was something else causing the infallible wizard tension?

Dane's attention was drawn from Kaeplan by commotion which hailed from the back of the throng. Villagers were moving again, parting aside as they had before. Another carriage, smaller but as fancy as Kaeplan's arrived. Over the din of the crowd he had not heard it coming. It stopped within a circle of gawking villagers. The door was opened by a servant, who then stepped to the open door, held out a hand. Dane recognized the delicate hand that reached out to take it.

Meirah stepped a slippered foot out and emerged like a queen, complete with sparkling silver tiara, onto the searing hot sands. Dane's heart skipped. Was she actually going to watch his death again? The sight of her walking through the crowd in a flowing gown of burgundy made Dane's chest ache. Every ounce of him wanted to run to her, hold her, press his lips to hers.

Shock value. Kaeplan was making sure Dane's torture would hurt more than on the outside.

Meirah stepped up to stand beside Kaeplan and the bastard had the audacity to kiss her lips.

Dane closed his eyes. But a poke in his side forced him to look. One of the guards stood by with a sword, making sure he saw it all.

As a servant stepped forth, knife in hand, Dane heard music. The crowd went silent and all he heard was a single song. But this was no song of Ritual as the one played in Mikaire. It was a song he'd written for Meirah. Piano, soft and melodic. He gazed about to find its source when he realized it came from within his own mind.

He looked over at Meirah, but she had not moved. She was, however, looking directly at him. Was she trying to communicate with him in some way? But this was not possible, as she would have to drink his blood for the bond to be complete, and she had not drunk from him in over a year.

Yet another interruption, another parting of the crowd ensued.

Now what?

A servant came forth, carrying something bundled in linen. He set the bundle at Dane's feet and stepped back.

Kaeplan looked at Meirah, whispered something in her ear, before stepping forward to Dane. He reached down and took up the bundle, unwrapped it. The last fold of cloth was removed and within was a tiny baby, pale, not breathing. Not moving. Dead!

What possibly reason would there be for showing him a dead premature child?

Kaeplan lifted the tiny lifeless form up to Dane. A little girl.

"Look familiar?" Kaeplan asked, an evil grin on his lips. It was at that moment, Dane noticed the sprouts of red hair on the tiny infant's scalp.

Oh God, no.... Dane glanced over to Meirah, then instinctively to her abdomen. It was flat, and not just from the cut of the gown she wore. She no longer carried their child—the dead baby was their daughter!

"NO!" Dane cried, unable and unwilling to hide the tears. He struggled fruitlessly against the bindings. "You...even you...wouldn't... *You killed my child!?*"

One blow after another. This was Kaeplan's torture. Destroy all he held close to his heart. He'd said he set Adrian and Stephan free, but had he? Or were their bodies the next to be paraded before him?

Mikaire's tortures of physical abuse were far preferable to this mental anguish.

Dane looked over at Meirah. She had not moved, but he knew her. Her emerald eyes were wide, brows slightly furrowed. In some way, even under whatever spell Kaeplan held on her, she felt the loss. Her hands wrung the material of her dress. She fought an internal battle of her own. Whether or not she was fully aware of what transpired here, he didn't know, but she felt *something!* And he knew now—somehow she had put their song into his mind.

Kaeplan handed the infant to a servant, who rewrapped it and took it away.

"Now ye know," said Kaeplan. "Yer legacy is dead, gone forever!" He stepped closer. "Sakkana strengthened the blood through Ritual in his own way. Destroying the spirit—this is *my* Ritual."

Kaeplan moved to turn away but stopped. "Oh…" He leaned close to Dane's ear. "She carries *my* legacy now!" Smiling, he walked away.

"*You… Bastard*!!" Dane was so angry, so distraught, he didn't care what was done, what was said, what happened to him. His breath came hard and fast, chest heaving with disgust and anguish. "I'll *kill* you!! You will *regret* this!"

Kaeplan waved a dismissive hand in the air and a servant stepped forth into his place. The sharp blade of a knife glinted in the sun. The servant opened the front of Dane's robe to the sash at his waist.

He squeezed his eyes closed to the tears and pain—from the loss of his and Meirah's daughter, from seeing Meirah walk away, and from the knife that sliced across his heart.

Meirah

Her heart beat so fast, she thought sure it would pound out of her breast. She wrung her hands against the dress to prevent them from shaking. She couldn't let Kaeplan see. Kaeplan's true identity had not been privy information, but as the last of the drugs he had given her wore off, she found herself standing in the hot sun—and Dane was there.

The night she had lost the baby pained her more than watching Dane die a dozen deaths before her eyes. She had been told the stillborn child was due to stress, the baby had been born too early. Lies!

As Kaeplan held the child up to Dane, all became clear. Did Kaeplan speak the truth about anything? Love. Aye, he loved her, but did he not think killing her child would go unnoticed forever? His methods of securing her as his mate were flawed, and she would be sure never again would he fool her.

She watched Dane, knowing somehow she had to reach out to him, let him know she was there. The evening before, she'd come round just long enough to switch the blood she was given each night with Dane's blood, kept in storage. She knew the scent of it, poured out the other, took his. This allowed a limited bond.

I am here my love. But he could not hear her. She thought for a moment, her mind still swirling. Then it came to her. Music! Dane's lifeline. She envisioned him at the piano. His eyes she saw in her mind; so light blue as to appear silver. His gaze drifted far away every time he played the love song he had written just for her. Long fingers, made for reaching keys on the instrument not as easily accessible to most.

The melody became real in her mind. Dane bent his head forward at the piano, long black hair waved over the keys as he played, face hidden, wrought in concentration, passion. And when he began to sing his voice was richer than gold, smoother than the tranquil waters.

Standing in Almareyah, she allowed the song to reach his mind. And he heard it, she knew. Expressive eyes hidden by lashes long and dark as the night came open, gazed to find the music.

The connection she thought gone forever had returned. *Hope.* In all her life he had been her one true love and she couldn't lose him again. Her husband needed her.

And as Kaeplan walked away, she looked to Dane as the knife sliced through the flesh of his chest, and she felt it as well. His blood poured into a golden goblet.

Dane

Three goblets of blood. They'd cut him deeper than usual this time. Kaeplan was there again, beside Meirah. The first goblet was brought to Kaeplan and he drank. Then the second. The third. They were on the fourth when the sky grew dark—no, not the sky, his mind, his world, his life.

Ritual usually lasted three days, to test the blood's strength, but Kaeplan didn't need to test it; he knew! Instead of drinking alone and from the source, he made this a spectacle for all in his world to see.

By the time they brought Kaeplan the third goblet and were filling the fourth, Dane faded. His body dropped, held up by arms that no longer felt attached. How much blood did the human body hold? Apparently, his was coming to the end.

He gazed over to Meirah, concentrated on her, focused on her. The emerald eyes stared back—and she was looking at him. She was there; whatever spell Kaeplan had placed on her was gone, but she was helpless to stop this. He wanted to die in her arms, as he had so many times before. Not hanging on a chain like a slaughtered pig.

The crowd was cheering. He could see them, but they sounded so far away. He fought hard to remain focused on Meirah, to *see* her, to never allow her from his mind, even after death.

Just give up. It's over. But still he fought to live. He had to get Meirah away from Kaeplan. In his next life—would he remember?

The hot sun grew cold. Thoughts that rampaged his mind grew fewer. The frigid breath of death whispered on the back of his neck.

Still he refused it.

A fifth goblet. His mind was heavy, sight grew dim. His head dropped, but he forced it back up. *Meirah! Keep looking at her.*

A voice entered his mind then, Kaeplan's gruff voice. *Give it up. She is mine now.*

The blood gave Kaeplan the bond to hear him, to feel him, but he was a wizard and the death of a mortal only strengthened them, so the death would not bring them down too.

He ignored Kaeplan's words.

Too weak to utter a word, he mouthed to her; *I shall see you soon, my love.*

Kaeplan's voice echoed once more in his brain. *You shall never see her again! No coming back this ti...*

Music! His and Meirah's song interrupted Kaeplan's words. She was letting him know she was with him.

Kaeplan snapped a look to Meirah. He heard it too... knew she communicated with him, but her eyes remained fixed on Dane's, and his on her.

Peace encompassed Dane then as death pounded at the door, would soon knock it down. No longer did he feel the hot sticky blood that ran down his chest and saturated the robe. No longer could he hold his head upright. But, just as everything began to fade for a final time, he saw Meirah move. To the shock of all, she ran to him.

He felt nothing now but the chains being unlatched, the manacles removed. Indistinct voices encircled him. As he dropped he felt warm gentle arms catch him, and then he was on the ground.

Through the blackness that came to take him he saw the emerald eyes staring down at him.

He tried to speak, to lift a hand, unable to do so.

"I am here, my love." She bent to place a kiss on his lips before death finally came through the door and all went black.

-Twenty-Nine-

"Do you remember the death of love?"
-"Tristan" by Pythia

Meirah

When Dane dropped, unable to hold his own weight, Meirah could feign ignorance no longer. Why did she let this go so far? She released a long held breath and bolted to his side. Kaeplan reached to grasp her but he missed. She caught Dane in her arms.

"Remove the binds!" she ordered the servant with the knife.

She held him tightly upright as he slumped heavily into her, head on her shoulder, hair falling over her like melting black ice. Shadows came over them, blocked out the scorching sun. She lifted her face and the wail she released made all step back.

"Get her *away* from him!" Kaeplan's command seemed far away.

The shadows returned. Someone released Dane's bindings.

He dropped to the ground, his weight bringing her down as well. Blood and sand stained her gown. She knelt beside him, his head in her lap as she had done so many times in the past.

No, not again!

She looked into the silver-blue eyes that still stared at her.

"Dane, I am here, my love," she whispered into his ear, hoping he would hear. A single tear ran off the side of one eye and dripped onto her hand. She reached down and kissed it off his cheek.

Music came into her mind then. Beautiful and sad. She saw

Dane's hands at the piano keys, playing a song just for her. And over the music, and the bellowing crowd, Meirah heard a heartbeat. Just a single thump. Then another moments later. Dane's heart. It worked to keep beating. Always the strong one, he still struggled for life. But he had lost too much blood, she knew. As the song in her head drew to its end, she bent to kiss his lips and when she raised her head, she saw the sparkle in those perfect, unique eyes that always spoke of love and devotion, fade over in death. The heartbeat halted.

He had not looked away from her the entire time, but now those eyes saw nothing. She reached up a hand and closed them as her own tears dripped onto his cheeks.

She reached beneath him, lifted his body into her arms and stood, her strength rooted from grief and anger.

Kaeplan bellowed commands that sounded from another place.

"Get her! Take him *away*!" Despite his frantic words, no one did his bidding. What harm could be done now? Their wizard had his sacrifice, they would survive.

Meirah stepped forward, the throng parted to allow her passage.

All at once Kaeplan stood before her. She halted. No words were exchanged. She looked him in the eye and the blue fire of her rage forced him back.

Meirah carried her husband's body through the sea of gawking villagers. She passed the barrier into the dunes, and they were alone. She trudged with no effort through the deep sands, past the Pyramid, into the heart of Almareyah, with no destination in mind. Instinct guided her. She would take him to a place where she could die beside him. Together. Forever.

Meirah was unaware of how long she walked. Time did not pass here as it did in the mortal world. No sense of it existed. Ironic in a dimension that resided on the veil of time. Merely a concept. As a being born of a magical dimension, she understood this well.

She did not think on it, though, but merely carried her husband's body away through the wind-swept dunes, palm trees and a small oasis with its body of fertile water. The barrier she crossed into went unnoticed.

Bushes with thorns like daggers that cut through her dress and flesh alike. Still, she paid no mind. Rock formations, grasslands, she noticed none of it, until...

Her emotions lost, body numb, she heard it before she saw it. Water. Not just any water—ocean water. In a dimension built behind a portal of water it made sense when nothing else did.

She carried Dane to the sandy beach. The waves grasped at her feet, which she realized for the first time were now bare; somewhere she had lost her slippers. Blood from the cuts caused by walking so long without them now pooled in the water around her and moved in and out with the frothing waves.

Such *power* the ocean held. She moved into the waves that tried to take her down with them. She halted, standing ankle deep in the salt water, feet sinking into the deep sand beneath.

Power.

Could the answer be so simple? The magic of this place was held in water.

At the edge of the lapping waves, she set Dane's body carefully onto the sand. His hair and robe waxed and waned with the tides. His exposed torso no longer bleeding, soaked in the water.

As a Mikairian the ocean had been but a dream. In the mortal world, it had been the first place Dane had taken her. If anything could renew Dane, the ocean could.

Meirah sat beside the body of her love, letting the ocean water wash over them both. She knew not what ascendancy this magical ocean held, nor if it could return life to the dead. She had to try.

She placed her palms on Dane's cold, still chest, over the gaping wound, and closed her eyes. And she prayed—not to any god, but to the waters she believed held the power to renew her husband's life.

"Please," she pleaded, "wash away this wrongful death borne o' greed. Bring Dane back tae life."

She opened her eyes. At first she saw nothing. But then slowly it ascended; an ambient light of blue cascaded and rolled with each wave. Each wax, each wane, the light grew stronger, brighter, until it encircled Dane's body. Meirah remained transfixed on it.

"Return him, please," she begged of the light.

The luminosity reached around Dane like loving arms. Meirah

stood and stepped back, watched. His body moved now, not of its own will, but towards the water. The light drew him into the waves until, slowly he disappeared beneath the salty waters.

Meirah stepped back into the water, heart pounding for his return. She waited, chewing on her fingernails, pleading within to see him walk back out, alive and healed. But the blue light faded then disappeared altogether and the water was as it always had been, soft frothing white waves lapped at her feet once more.

"No... please... bring him back tae me!" She started towards the waves.

A hand on her arm from behind both startled and excited her. Dane! She spun around.

The face was unfamiliar. Brown eyes encircled by the ravages of sun and age, grey hair that touched his shoulders, robes of beige, darker where the water soaked the hem. Not Dane.

"Who—" she began.

The stranger shook his head. "Your love has gone," he said simply.

"But... the water took him..."

"He has been returned." He stepped back and put out a hand. "Come..."

Meirah looked back at the water, shook her head. To the stranger, she asked, "How do ye know...?"

"Water is the most powerful force on earth. He has been taken, returned."

"W-Who are ye...?"

"I am Seer to Master Kaeplan."

Meirah cringed. "Then ye do *his* bidding! How can I trust—"

"I see paths as they shall come to pass. Please, M'Lady, come. You need nourishment. I will explain, but you must come with me lest the cold take you as well, not to your love but to a place you will neither like, nor belong."

He turned and began to walk up the beach. She did not follow. She glanced back to the water, which told her nothing, then to the Seer.

"Come, Lady Meirah."

She followed then, stepping away from the ocean that took Dane away.

Christine Church

-Thirty-

Kaeplan

"Ye know why I called ye here, correct?" Before him stood five village guards in the meeting chamber, which had been cleared of all furniture. Two servants stood by the door with mops and buckets. Two other guards stood nearby. The five before him held not a clue what was to befall them for their disobedience.

The village guards all nodded. Kaeplan looked at Terthioa and addressed him specifically. "Ye released the mortal's bonds. Ye allowed Lady Meirah tae take 'im. Why?"

Terthioa bowed. "Forgive me, Master. The mortal was dead. I saw no harm—"

"*No harm*? She took him! Now she is gone, missing. And it is all yer fault!"

"But, Master, I couldn't know—"

"*Stop!*" Kaeplan motioned to one of the castle guards. The guard stepped forth, handed Kaeplan a sword.

Terthioa's eyes widened. "Master, no, please… I will make it up to you, I will…"

A quick flick of the sword. His head rolled to land at the feet of the other village guards. They all stepped back quickly.

"No excuses!" said Kaeplan. "I canno' afford such disobedience in my world. All o' ye…" he addressed the other four village guards, "ye did nothin' as she took the mortal. I said tae get her, ye disobeyed. Now ye pay!"

Once all traitors had been rendered their punishment, Kaeplan left the servants to clean up. He wandered the halls of his castle with no destination.

He had not meant to kill the mortal. But the taste of such powerful blood and the knowledge he was taking life from the human who had so long ago stolen his love overcame him. He had destroyed his own plan to keep the mortal in lock-up as long as possible, feeding him only enough to keep him alive. He had been giving him water on which he had placed a spell to forget Meirah. Despite his magic, their bond proved stronger than he had anticipated. The staged Ritual was meant to test that bond, to show the villagers his power.

But he had failed.

He held plenty of Dane's blood in storage, but would need more. And yet he erred by drinking it all. Humans, so fragile. The only way they kept their species going was to over-breed and over-populate. They used the earth's resources with greed and gave no thought to consequences.

Kaeplan found himself standing before the closed door of Meirah's chamber. He grasped the latch, pulled. The door creaked open. No candle flickered within. No servant bowed upon his entrance.

He walked slowly to the bed. The coverlets were mussed as if she had only just arose. He lowered himself upon it, let his hands run along the linen sheets. He took up her pillow and discarded nightdress, hugged them close to his body.

"Oh, Meirah, my love. Where are ye?"

He breathed in their scent still fresh from her bed and the items tucked within his embrace, and fell asleep with her image playing in his mind.

Meirah

She awoke screaming. Disorientation played on her mind and she thought she saw Dane's ghost at the foot of the bed. As she came full into waking, however, it faded. She could not bring herself to recall where she was, for this was neither her bed at home nor her chamber in Kaeplan's Palace.

The Seer burst into the room. "Are you alright, M'Lady?"

Though she barely knew him, she threw her arms around him and wept on his shoulder. He held her gently and allowed her to release the pain.

She saw Dane and the blue water, so bright, take him away from her. He was gone. Dead. Kaeplan killed him, just as he had killed Bruce. It all weighed on her now—she wept for the loss of her husband, their child, Kaeplan's betrayal. Caitlyn's loss, the tortures, the lies. Everything. All she wanted was to go home to South Carolina and be with Dane again, as they had been before Vegas. But where was home now without him?

After what seemed an eternity, her tears spent at last, she pulled back, wiped at her cheeks.

"I-I am sorry. I-I should no' have—"

"Lady Meirah, you need not apologize."

She brushed long strands of hair from her face and eyes, gathered herself.

Seer stood. "Take a bath. You will feel better. Then meet me in the Living Chamber. I will retrieve you nourishment and we may talk."

"I am sorry," she said again, "about last night." She fixed one errant strand of hair after another. Useless. The salt water made it unruly.

Seer offered a smile borne of empathy and understanding. "You were overwhelmed. Exhausted. Clean up. There are fresh clothes in the chest. They should fit." He smiled, then stood, leaving the room and closing the door behind him.

Meirah did not wish to rise. Her body and mind craved peace from the pain and emptiness, and waking to a nightmare worse than the one she'd dreamt.

So many times Dane had died in her arms. Yet, before, she knew he would return and that knowledge kept her going, kept her sanity in check.

She knew Kaeplan held a cruel streak, a greed for power, and a hatred for Dane, but this…To flaunt their dead infant before him… before her!

She hated him when he had Dane tortured in Mikaire. Now, however, he had crossed a new barrier. She loathed him! She never wanted to see him again. She wanted him to suffer as Dane had, as she did now. She wished him dead!

After her bath, she felt slightly better, at least physically. She brushed out her wet hair, braided it. The cedar chest in which Seer had referenced held a variation of clothing neatly folded within. Where they had come from she cared not.

She chose a dress of blue velvet with black trim. Blue for Dane's eyes. Black like his hair. Long flowing sleeves and a small mid-line that cascaded out to a flowing skirt.

Once dressed, she slipped her feet into a pair of light blue slippers she found at the bottom of the chest to complete the ensemble. She met Seer in the Living Chamber.

He sat by a crackling fire reading. He placed the book down as she entered.

"Ahh, M'Lady. What a vision of perfection you are…"

He motioned to a large cushioned chair opposite where he sat. "Please."

Meirah straightened her skirt and sat by the fire, appreciating its warmth.

"Please, relax," said Seer. "I shall return shortly with a beverage to heal your inner ills."

He stood and disappeared through a doorway beyond.

Meirah gazed about the room. For an anachronistic dimension, it appeared quite modern—almost Mortal Realm modern, save electricity.

The room was bright, however; lanterns of an unnatural luminosity lighting the room. The chair in which she sat was made of the softest leather, plush and comfortable. Dark wooden panels lined the walls. A chandelier hung above, each candle lit, offering a soft ambience. One wall was floor to ceiling books. The other walls boasted paintings and tapestries… and one in particular caught her attention. The same exact tapestry of the bleeding man holding the key to the Portal, as she had seen in the castle.

The Seer returned to the room carrying a tray with a pitcher and two glasses. He set the tray on the table by Meirah's chair, lifted the pitcher and filled each glass. Blood. Human blood. She could smell the sweet aroma. He handed her a glass, took one for himself and sat in the chair opposite her.

Meirah brought the glass to her nose. Definitely human. But whose? Not Dane's…she would know if it was. Still, she paused in taking a sip.

"Go ahead, drink." Said the Seer. "There is nothing in it, I promise." He took a sip from his own glass to prove his point. "See? I know master Kaeplan drugged you to keep you compliant. But there will be no such foolery here."

The aroma that wafted into her senses enticed and she took a sip. "Whose blood is this?"

The Seer shrugged. "Just a human."

Meirah set the glass down. "I am sorry, but humans should nae be used like cattle. They are livin' creatures, like us, wi' feelings and lives."

"I meant no disrespect. Master Kaeplan supplies those of us on his Council with human blood only."

"And the villagers too!" she said in a snarky tone.

"Ah, you saw the Pyramid, then. Hm, yes. Your husband was human. I understand. But I have no other blood to offer you and you require nourishment. This blood will provide you with the best."

She lifted the glass again, took a sip. It certainly was delicious and her body screamed for its nourishment. Though she did feel guilt at taking it.

"The villagers do exist off the blood of the beasts in the forests. The small amounts they are allowed in the pyramid is merely a way for Master Kaeplan to show he cares for them—compliance without magic or drugs."

Meirah snorted. "Kaeplan cares for no one but Kaeplan."

Meirah took a bigger sip. The blood filled her, quenched her, relaxed her. She could feel each shrunken vein fill with its necessary sustenance. She drank it down.

The Seer refilled her glass. "You're dehydrated and you need this to go forward."

"Forward. Tae where?" She sipped at the second glass, feeling a mote better with each sip, physically anyway. The emptiness within could not be cured with blood.

"Wherever you need to go to get to the next step."

"And where is that?" she asked.

"That, M'Lady, is up to you."

"I want tae go home—tae the Mortal Dimension. Back tae Dane and our life as it was."

"Going forward does not always mean returning to the life we once led." The Seer drank the remainder of his glass and refilled it.

"I want nae other life than wi' Dane."

"If that is your destined path, so shall it be."

"*How?*" she snapped a bit harsher than she intended. "My husband is *dead*! Kaeplan killed him. Where can I go now?"

"Please, M'Lady, remain calm. I feel your anguish in my own heart. That is why I brought you here. Keep in mind there are many paths and only your actions will choose which one. Each fork in your road of life is a decision you and only you can make."

"Only if I can turn time back and prevent Dane's death..." she said softly. She drank more blood, then looked into the Seer's eyes. "Time... Is it possible to change time?"

The Seer shrugged noncommittally. "I don't know."

"But ye're supposed tae know all. Ye're a Seer! What does my future hold?"

"I can only see that which will come to pass. I cannot bring back the dead, nor can I choose your path for you."

Meirah gulped the blood in her glass. "Then what paths lay ahead that I may choose the correct one?"

"Only you know the answer."

Meirah's temper flared. "Ye said ye'd give me answers. Ye've given me naught but more questions! *What do I do?*"

The Seer sighed, sat back in his chair, holding his glass in two hands. He looked at her seriously. "You want my honest opinion. Not as a Seer but as a human may choose, though I am no more human than you? No matter what path you choose will have advantages and disadvantages, as all decisions in life."

"*But ye said ye'd give me answers!*" Meirah downed the blood and set the glass on the table so hard it cracked. Her heart pounded, hands shook. This round about was getting her nothing but frustration.

"We learn from our mistakes, but we cannot take them back, only move on ahead and find a road that will lead us closer to that which we desire... Unless we have already chosen it." He was so calm, sipping at his glass as if his answers made sense.

But they made no sense to Meirah.

The Seer set his empty glass down. "I will tell you this...Perhaps in your case, you need to travel a similar path and seek that fork in the road. Then choose the one you desire. That is all I can tell you."

Meirah wanted to strangle him.

"However," he said. "I can, if you wish, send you down a path I feel will be your best choice given your past. What you do with it and where you go will be up to you."

"Fine! Then send me down the path that will lead to Kaeplan's death and Dane's life."

"I cannot alter what has transpired. Where you go, where you find yourself depends not only on your direction, but on your husband's."

Meirah cocked her head. Finally, a different answer. "What does that mean?"

"Your Dane's path has been taken, but not chosen by him. His path may have led him back to where he most desired." Meirah shook her head. "He may not be dead, Lady Meirah. His path may have taken him back to life, but a different road than yours. Do you understand?"

Meirah gasped, sat up straight. "He could be *alive*?!"

"I did not say he was… I cannot know. He was taken by the magical waters… to where…" he shrugged.

"Oh by Sakkana's power!" Meirah rose quickly. "When the blue light came, I wished hard for him to return, to live!"

"Then it is possible the magic listened to your bidding… and returned him…somewhere. Whether or not he was returned in death or life…" The Seer shrugged.

Meirah turned and gazed at the tapestry on the wall. "That… there is one like it in the castle. I know no' what it means, but… Send me down *that* path!"

"As you wish."

-Thirty-One-

Mortal Dimension

Dane

For the longest time all was black and he was floating, weightless, bodiless. But he could hear the sonorous crashing of waves against rocks, like a hard music with no voice nor melody.

And the taste of it. Salt water washed over his broken body, filled his mouth. Then it was gone only to come again, and again.

His mind was hollow and empty. He tried to think, but that only resulted in a terrible pain that webbed through his head. The only thought the pain allowed through was a wonderment of his situation. Was he alive or was this death?

Voices then sounded over the melody of the water. Distant at first, but growing louder. Pounding of footsteps muffled on sand.

Then came the heat, though it was always there, he felt it now, searing his exposed back and buttocks. Closer voices.

"Call 9-1-1!"

Shade moved over him and he could feel rather than see those who surrounded him—those who spoke. Many different voices.

"Is he alive?"

"Oh God, look at his back! What happened to this guy?"

A gentle hand touched his throat.

"I feel a pulse. He's alive."

"Looks like he was whipped."

"Who would do such a thing? Did someone call an ambulance?"

"They're on their way."

"Look at his wrists… he was tied up!"

"Oh my God! The poor man."

"Tortured and tossed in the ocean."

"He's lucky to be alive."

"Turn him over."

"He's naked!"

"What... you never saw a penis before, just do it?"

Hands touched his side, rolled him onto his back. The sharpness of the light touched his closed lids. He tried to lift a hand to shade his eyes, but he could not move. Those who spoke shaded him once more.

"He's so pale!"

"Look at his chest. He was cut open!"

Someone closed in on him, he felt their breath on his face.

"Hey, buddy, who are you? Can you hear me?"

Dane nodded, though to what he was not sure. His head belonged to another. He had no body that he knew of—he felt nothing. Knew nothing. If he had a head and brain, it was not his.

"He's awake!" Yet another voice.

"Who are you? What happened to you?"

He opened his mouth to speak, but no voice came out. He was too weak. More came. He heard them.

"What happened?"

"This guy washed up on shore naked and messed up."

Shifting of shadow over his face as those around him moved.

"Move the hair from his face."

Fingers touched his face, his hair.

"Hey, I know who this is! I saw it on the news. He went missing awhile back."

"Who is he?"

"Some rock star. They said he had been kidnapped a couple years ago, tortured and returned."

"Looks like someone has a real grudge on this guy."

Distantly, a familiar wailing sounded.

"The ambulance is coming, buddy... you'll be okay."

"What's his name?"

"I don't remember, but he's famous."

"Maybe we'll get a reward for finding him..."

The shadows disappeared and another, more distant voice—one of authority—echoed through the air and into his addled brain.

"Step back, everyone!"

He tried to open his eyes, but the weight kept them closed. Did he even have eyes?

"Look! He's waking up!"

"Please folks...step back!"

The shuffling of feet faded. He wanted to speak, but to say...what? No thoughts resided in his mind, much less words.

Though he felt those who touched him, heard the voices, confusion dominated everything else. Something was placed over his face that allowed him to breathe more easily. A sigh. Then blackness. Sweet nothing.

His next awareness was a wailing siren, then movement. Not his own, but a road beneath a vehicle. An image flashed through his mind—the sway of a bus. A television he could not concentrate on. A sofa. A bottle of rum. The flash came and went so quickly he could make no sense of it.

And then another voice. "You'll be okay."

The peace of nothing took him once more.

Next time he woke, he was able to open his eyes. There was light, but it was dim. He heard a steady beeping sound. The smells were different—sterile. No water. No burning sun.

Distant voices came to his ears.

"He's coming round." A feminine voice.

He blinked away the haze until the images cleared.

She leaned over him. Strawberries and clean linens. Dark brown hair, blue eyes.

"Hey," she said softly. "Glad to see you awake."

He opened his mouth. Nothing came out.

"Oh...wait," she said.

He watched her movements. She wore a pink shirt, no sleeves. She lifted a pitcher and poured clear liquid into a cup. She picked up the cup and placed it before him. "Here. Drink this." She placed the cup to his lips.

He took a sip. Cool and refreshing. He drank more.

"Slow down, sailor," she said. "You don't want too much at first." She removed the cup.

He groaned, wanting more to soothe parched lips. Finally, a

word choked from his lips. "Thirsty."

"I know, sweetie," she cooed. "But too much at first is not good."

He reached for the cup, but it was no longer there. "More..." His voice was rough and raw.

She placed the cup to his lips once again. "Just a little."

The water went down more smoothly this time.

He cleared his throat. "Thank you." Still rough but better.

After a few more sips he sat back against the upright bed. "What happened?"

"You don't remember?" she asked.

He concentrated. "Um... an ocean, water." He cleared his throat again. She handed him the cup half filled with water. He drank a few sips. "Then...people around me. They were talking. One said something... he knew who I was, had seen I was missing. There's more, but..."

"It's okay, sweetie. You will remember. You've been through a lot. I'm sure Edna, Adrian and Stephan will be thrilled to come see you..."

"Who?"

Her brows furrowed and she cocked her head. "Edna, Adrian and Stephan... Your friends."

Such a confused tangled mass of emotions and feelings with a sparse memory thrown in once in awhile. None of it made any sense. He shook his head slowly.

The woman sat back on the chair she had placed close to his bed. "Do you recognize me?"

"Ummm..." He focused on her face. Though she appeared familiar, a million faces all ran through his mind at once and he couldn't place her among the crowd. He decided to take a jab in the dark. "Are you... my girlfriend?"

Her shoulders slumped as she sighed. "No. I am not."

"I'm sorry, I see so many faces in my head but I can't place them."

"No worries, this is normal after a trauma."

"Are you a nurse?" he asked, but her clothing told him otherwise.

Her eyes sparkled. "One of many jobs... well, an assistant. Until I met Bruce."

"Is he your boyfriend?" he asked.

She cast her eyes down in sadness. "No... he, uh... he was my husband. He passed away."

"Oh, I am sorry... I-I didn't know."

She shook her head, wiped away a tear and straightened, nodded. "It's alright. I have to ask... do you know who *you* are?"

Good question. The pain in his head returned as he fought to remember. "No."

Caitlyn

Amnesia. Not uncommon after a major trauma. Caitlyn hoped it was only temporary. Though she had asked Adrian and Stephan the details of Bruce's death, Adrian had not been conscious enough to remember, and Stephan was too traumatized to talk about it. The autopsy had revealed a combination of dehydration, starvation and blood loss as the cause of death. Somewhere in Dane's mind the answer was there.

"I will be right back," she told him.

Caitlyn stood, placed a comforting hand on Dane's arm and offered him a smile before she left the room and approached the desk.

"I need to speak to Mr. Bainbridge's doctor."

Several minutes after the page went out, Dr. Cooper approached Caitlyn.

"I know amnesia is common after a trauma, but he doesn't even know who he is, and he seems to be in great pain every time he tries to remember."

'There is no sign of brain injury that we can see so far, but we plan to do a CT scan anyway. We did find something interesting in his EKG and heart tests, however."

Caitlyn cocked her head, indicating more.

"It looks as if Mr. Bainbridge's heart stopped for quite a time, which could have resulted in brain damage, dependent upon how long the episode lasted."

"He was ... dead?"

"We only know that his heart stopped. We'll know more after tests. If the heart stopped for too long, it causes lack of oxygen to the brain. If there's brain damage, it may be temporary or permanent. We simply won't know without more tests and time."

"That is why he has no memory. What can I do to help?"

"Talk to him. Remind him. Anything familiar may help reverse the amnesia if his brain is not too badly damaged. Frankly, just by the tests we've done so far, he shouldn't be alive now, much less talking. He should be comatose."

Caitlyn grabbed her phone to dial Edna and the others, but she couldn't help wondering why Dane died and returned and Bruce did not.

After speaking with Edna, Adrian and Stephan, she returned to Dane. He was still awake, gazing about the room in confusion, as if trying to figure out where he was.

"Hi again," she said, taking her seat by his bed. "Dane."

He looked at her. The cup was still in his hand but empty. "Your name—Dane Bainbridge."

"Dane...Bainbridge," he said, but his empty eyes told her he didn't recognize his own name.

"You're the lead singer in a rock band called Dark Myst."

"I am a singer..." His face scrunched in concentration.

"My name is Caitlyn Beaufort. My husband, Bruce was the lead guitarist in your band."

"Bruce... he died? How?"

Not a subject she wished to discuss at this time. She shook her head. "Let's concentrate on you now."

"Thinking is exhausting."

"I understand. Your friends are coming. They might help you remember."

Dane nodded. "Dane...Bain...bridge," he repeated as if trying to recognize his own name.

Long ago, before she'd met Bruce, amongst her many occupations and jobs, she worked for a short stint as a nurse's assistant. She had seen an amnesia case only once. She recalled that stress only made it more difficult to remember. What Dane needed now was family, friends, loved ones. As soon as he was well enough, he needed to go home to the familiar. But for now...

"Dane, do you remember Meirah?"

Dane

Meirah! The name echoed through his mind, but was drowned out by an excruciating pain that rendered him blind. He placed a hand against his head, squeezed his eyes closed.

He shook his head slowly. "I-I can't..."

"Are you ok?" asked the woman beside him... what was her name? Caitlyn. Yes, that was it.

He nodded, opened his eyes. The pain was gone.

"Are you in pain?" she asked with concern.

"Only when I try to think too hard."

"Sleep now. I am going to the cafeteria."

Dane closed his eyes and relaxed. He heard Caitlyn's footsteps, the door open, then close.

Water. The buoyancy kept him afloat just beneath the surface. Yet he didn't drown. He drifted. A female voice echoed in his mind. "Bring him back tae me!"Blue light was everywhere. A sense of calm, a peace he'd never before experienced. He let the calm take him.

Dane opened his eyes. He was still in the hospital room. He was alone and all was quiet but for the beeping of the machines. His chest ached. Not a physical pain, but an unfathomable emptiness. He needed to understand what it all meant, was desperate for memories, answers.

"My name is Dane Bainbridge," he said to himself. The name meant nothing. "I am a singer in a rock band called Dark Myst."

Nothing.

"Meirah." He repeated the name spoken earlier by Caitlyn. The pain was sharp and spread through his head, replacing confusion with memory. He let the name go and the pain faded.

The door to his room opened then. Several entered; Caitlyn, a tall skinny man with long blond hair, a stout older woman, and another man with long red hair. They approached him.

"Your friends are here, Dane," said Caitlyn.

The blond spoke first. "Hey, *Curva*. Ve thought ve had lost you forever." An accent. Not American.

Curva? His mind replayed a distant scene. A bus. A large television. A movie playing on its screen. And this man...he sat beside him, talking. What was he saying?

Dane motioned to the blond. "You. I-I see you in my mind. We're in a bus. It's not clear, you're talking to me. But...it's blank."

The blond offered a grin of straight white teeth. "You remember me?"

Dane nodded. "The accent. Something...you're not American."

"No. From Romania. Sometimes you call me Dracula." He giggled nervously.

"Dracula. Yes. Are you a vampire?" said Dane, smiling.

"No, *Curva*" he laughed. "I am drummer. My name is Adrian Ionescu."

"Yes... for our band, Dark Myst. She...eh, Caitlyn told me."

"Do you remember the band?" asked the red-head.

Dane shook his head. "Bit and pieces come to mind every now and then."

"I'm Stephan Gale. Do you remember me?"

Dane thought hard. Stephan. Stephan, he repeated in his mind. He looked up at the red-head. "Water. Camping. We went camping?"

Stephan laughed. "Well, sorta... but it's good you remember."

"Things are coming back," said Caitlyn. This amnesia should only be temporary then, which is excellent news. The doctor said your CT scan showed no brain damage."

Everyone was smiling when Dane noticed the stout older woman standing in the back. Her face for some reason was more familiar than the others. A name slipped from his lips. "Edna."

With a huge grin, she came to the bed. "Mr. Dane. Yas remembers me?"

"I do... I want to go home. I miss the animals. The horses, my cats... Wolfe..."

Edna's grin dropped like a boulder from a cliff. "Mr. Dane... Wolfe, he—"

"He died, didn't he?"

"Near a year ago now."

Caitlyn cleared her throat. "Don't force yourself too much, Dane. You need rest." She glanced at the clock. "Visiting hours are almost over anyway. We'll see you tomorrow, okay?"

She bent, kissed Dane's cheek. Adrian and Stephan both took his hand with a light squeeze and big smiles. Edna also took his hand. "Y'all come home soon, k?" Dane nodded.

Once they had left, he lay awake in the bed, thinking... and trying to remember who Meirah was without a headache interrupting his thoughts.

Caitlyn
A Week Later

"Get rid of it all!"
Caitlyn stood in the hallway of the hospital. Edna and Stephan had come once she called them to inform them Dane was well enough to return home.

"All of it?" asked Edna. "There is a lot."

"I know. But Dane remembers everything now... except her. Somehow, she's been erased from his memory. This is a good thing. He can go on with his life, but if he sees too many reminders of Meirah he may remember. And he is better off *not* remembering."

Edna shook her head. "Do ya know how much of her is in that mansion?"

"I know it will take some work, but he won't fully recover if he remembers her. All evidence of Meirah's presence must be removed. *All* of it! Portraits, photos, clothes—everything. Get Adrian to help, too."

"He went away with a boyfriend... needed time," said Stephan.

Edna glanced at Stephan who shrugged.

"She has a point," he said matter-of-factly. "Dane was a horrible wreck two years ago when he returned from Mikaire and thought she was dead. Then this time as well. With her, he is stable and reliable in is work. With no memory of her, he's... normal. No visions in his mirrors to worry on, and no anguish that he may never see her again. I can deal with the sex-crazed rock star, but the brooding Dane..." He shook his head.

"I'll help," said Edna. "We done got one night to rid him of all memories that Meirah ever existed."

The task proved more daunting than Caitlyn imagined.

Stephan, Edna and Caitlyn went from room to room, looking through everything. Open boxes sat in each room of the mansion, and one by one they were filled. In the den they removed photos of Meirah taken within the last year, replacing them with photos of the band and others from his life before Meirah. Some were from Stephan's own collection, others they found around the house.

They boxed up all of Meirah's clothing, which filled three large boxes as Dane bought her everything she desired. They replaced the empty closet space with items from Dane's drawers and his band costumes, which had been in his trunks that usually remained within the band's equipment trucks.

Memories of Meirah were everywhere; wedding albums, food Edna knew were her favorites, blood in bottles, even music in the studio of songs he had written for her. Concert song line-ups were replaced with new ones that omitted those songs.

In the bathrooms, all of her brushes, shampoos, shower gels, toothbrush and more, were all boxed and replaced with Dane's toiletries.

Once they were confident all evidence of her had been removed, they had filled ten large moving boxes full.

"Put these somewhere he will never find them."

Meirah

The flicker of the small candle did not reveal much around her, but allotted her some semblance of vision. But, of what...? Thus far, all she saw were smooth walls that she could easily touch if she were to stretch out her arms. A hallway; and it seemed to go on forever. This was the path she had chosen. Where it led, she did not know, but she kept the Seer's words in her mind to recognize the forks in the road and follow the one that felt most comfortable. Right now, she considered turning back and returning to the Seer's home. But she doubted she could. The door behind the tapestry, just as the one in the castle, was a magic door. As Kaeplan alone could open the castle tapestry door, only the Seer could open the one in his home.

She walked for so long, searching for even the smallest shadow barrier or doorway, she hardly noticed the candle's light growing dim. Eventually, it burned and went out.

"Shit!" She dropped the useless stub and continued on in complete darkness. Gaining proper footing without seeing or knowing where she was or what lie ahead was daunting.

Meirah stumbled. Not over any object, but over her own feet. Vaguely, she wondered how blind humans could walk with such confidence. She needed that confidence now as she righted herself and took another tentative step forward.

Even if this dark hallway led her to the dungeon, she could find her way back into the castle from there. Where she would go after that was unclear.

Onward she walked, to a future unknown. She stumbled once or twice, but found her feet and continued. Life itself was unclear. Many never found their path in the mortal world. But as a magical realm being, paths were generally set. Perhaps she needed to stumble through the dark to find a clear and brightly lit path. She understood the metaphor behind the Seer's words now. Had he deliberately given her a candle he knew would lead her into darkness?

She almost missed it; a lighter shadow amongst the black.

"Finally," she whispered.

The barrier brought her to a familiar hallway. She was in Kaeplan's castle. She truly hoped this was not her destiny. Using the image in her mind of the map she had drawn out—which she did not have with her—she followed the corridors of the castle to her bedchamber, keeping her senses aware of any presence of another. The last thing she wanted was to run into one of Kaeplan's servants, guards, or worse Kaeplan himself.

She entered the chamber, closed and locked the door behind her. She flopped down on her bed with a sigh. Pulling the coverlet up to her chin, she felt some measure of normalcy. At least this was her bed, for what it was, her chamber.

Her body ached, but not as badly as her heart. The Seer made it sound so simple, finding the path destined for her. But she knew what she wanted, where she needed to go, but not how to get there. One small step in the dark. One small step forward.

Images of Dane floated through her mind of their own accord, and she allowed them in. If this was all she had left of him, then so be it.

For the first time in her life she contemplated taking her own life. In death, she could see Dane again… perhaps. At least she would find peace at long last. No pain, no sorrow, no Kaeplan. Her death would hurt him, and if that was the only way to do so…!

She drew the covers over her head. He would still live, even if she did not, wreaking his havoc on the Mortal Dimension. No, she conceded. She needed to find a way to harm him as he did to Dane, and to her. Killing him was too good for him, even if she was able.

As she lay there, drifting into a much needed sleep, her mind formed a plan, and somewhere within it the correct path came to her.

-Thirty-Two-

"I'm ready to accept the challenge. I am coming home." –Lebron James

Dane
February 27, 2017

Returning home felt strange. Dane walked into the foyer, spying his own house as if for the first time. The marble floor, the massive staircase, the den, parlor, all of it—as if he were trespassing on another's territory. Returning from tour after months away never felt so unfamiliar, yet familiar at the same time.

Edna and Caitlyn came in behind him, almost running into him as he stopped suddenly.

"Mr. Dane?" asked Edna. "Are yas alright?"

Dane nodded. "I feel like I've been gone for years."

"Do you remember it all?" asked Caitlyn. She moved to stand before him, looked quizzically at him.

"I believe so," he said, looking about.

He offered her a smile, then moved on to the parlor. He strolled slowly, taking in that which should be familiar, yet seemed bizarre. The large fireplace with the painting above it of knights in battle. The swords. Copies of originals he had used in most of his lives.

He stopped at the shining black grand piano near the turret windows swashed by lace curtains. A cat lay on the leather-cushioned piano bench.

"Hey, Mr. Scott," he cooed. The cat stood and rubbed against him as if he had never left. Dane ran his hand over the soft head, the clipped ear that indicated he had been rescued and neutered.

The cat followed as Dane ran a hand over the polished wood of the instrument. Within, he wondered where his career would go next. Without Bruce, would the band be able to continue on? Would they find a new guitarist or break up?

A thought for a different day.

He sat at the bench where the cat left a warm impression. A song entered his conscious mind. Piano and violin. A song he'd written over a year earlier.

From the corner of his eye he saw Edna and Caitlyn watching him curiously.

He placed his fingers on the keys. The song came to him from his heart. The music flowed to his fingers and he began to play. He closed his eyes.

Long red hair, emerald eyes, watched him play. A bright smile.

He stopped suddenly as a sharp pain shot through his skull. He cried out, placed his hands on his head.

Caitlyn was there in an instant, gentle hands on his shoulders. "Dane!"

He opened his eyes, looked up into her concerned face. Edna stood beside her, worry on her eyes. "I'm ok," he reassured them. "It's gone now."

"What happened?" asked Caitlyn.

"Not sure. I was playing. Then I saw…I'm not sure what I saw. Flashes of…someone. Red hair. Green eyes. Then pain, excruciating pain. But, it's gone now."

Caitlyn and Edna glanced to one another enigmatically.

Dane stood and stepped away from the piano. "Am I forgetting something else… something important?"

"No, sweetie," cooed Caitlyn. "You're tired. It's been a long road. You should get some sleep."

Dane glanced to the grandfather clock in the corner of the room. "It's only 5 in the afternoon," he countered, then said quickly, "My horses—I want to see them."

"Dane," Caitlyn stated authoritatively, "The horses are fine. They're in the pasture grazing. You need rest."

"I slept in the hospital."

"I know, but trust me… hospital rest and home rest are very different."

Dane yawned, either by suggestion or because…"Maybe you're right." He turned to Edna. "They are alright? The horses? Kobeejo… he hasn't had any laminitis? The weather's been—"

"The stable crew has taken proper care o' them, I made sure. No heat in the hooves, nothin'. He's fine. Just as when yar on tour."

"Oh, God. Shit!" Dane exclaimed suddenly. "Tour! We never finished the…" He stopped and looked to Caitlyn. "Bruce. I am so sorry for what happened."

Caitlyn swallowed hard, eyes closing briefly before once again meeting his gaze. "Not your fault."

"But if he hadn't followed me—"

"Dane! You didn't cause this. *They* did."

All of his past lives, no one ever before followed. Bruce had, tried to rescue him from the vampires in the other dimension. And he lost his life for it. Adrian and Stephan had also followed. They escaped as he did. How he did, however, was fuzzy. All he could recall was water, a blue light, then people, a beach, the hospital. He couldn't help thinking about it, wondering about it… wanting to remember it.

"I'll bring yas a tuna sandwich," said Edna. "In bed."

Dane's thoughts faded. Better not to think too hard, lest the pain return. "Yeah. Yes… I'd like that I think."

Caitlyn placed a hand on his arm. "C'mon, I'll help you."

"Thank you, Caitlyn, but I can find my way to my bedroom. You should go. See your son. You've spent too much time with me, not that I am not grateful…I am."

Caitlyn pulled her hand away and nodded. "Alright. I will come see you tomorrow."

Just as everywhere else in his home, the bedroom seemed empty and foreign. Dane stood in the center of the room, gazing about, trying to find familiarity. He turned to his own reflection in the large antique bureau, startling himself in the process.

"Oh, it's you," he said to his own reflection, realizing he sounded daft. He stared at the mirror, memories flooding in from Mikaire, his time spent there, all the lives he had lived and lost to a blood-drinking wizard, the unicorns, the strange creatures, even Kaeplan, who had come to take him into Mikaire the last time.

His gaze swept the mirror's frame. There was something else there, but it would not surface. A reflection of...someone. How had he gotten out of Mikaire? He recalled the concert with the enormous mirrors. He feared them, but why? He'd passed out after seeing... Something.

Then Mikaire. He recalled it all...being in the cell, even as Sir Kori. The tortures. The Ritual. Enduring a terrible flogging for hitting Kaeplan. Fighting Kaeplan at the Main Mirror. Then he was...pushed out. Pushed, but by whom?

Dane shook his head. So many memories existed but in between there were gaps he couldn't fill.

"You're just tired," he whispered once again to his reflection, as he removed his shirt.

So sad to look at. He'd lost a lot of weight and his ribs protruded grossly He ran a hand over the scar on his chest, cut like a canyon through the sparse hairs. Yet another mark of his many torturous lives.

He needed some good sleep in his own bed. The California King enticed him. His cat, Lucy, begged for attention. She hated when he was away. She preferred sleeping on his chest.

"Hi Lucy, it's ok. I'm home now."

He stripped off the jeans Edna had brought him while he was in the hospital, climbed into bed. Lucy was on his chest before he could even lie down. She rubbed against his nose as she always did when she missed him, purring loudly. He settled in and placed his hands on the soft body as she curled up under his chin. The vibration of her purr lulled him to sleep.

Meirah
Almareyah

Frantically she searched through the desk. She knew she had placed it there, but it was not where she'd left it.

She threw pens and papers to the floor. "Where are ye?" she asked no one. She had searched everywhere and was on her second look when a voice interrupted her.

"Is this what ye're lookin' for?"

Startled, she looked up from the chaotic mess she had created.

Kaeplan stood at the threshold, and in his hand was her map. He waved it around as if taunting her.

"That is *mine*. Give it back!" she snapped.

He looked at the map. "Why would ye make a map o' the castle?"

"Why do ye think? I did no' want tae get lost in this maze." She thought quickly.

Kaeplan nodded slowly, but in his amber eyes sparked disbelief at her words.

"May I have it back?"

He unfolded the map carefully, though she knew he had already seen its contents.

"What are ye doin'? Ye're no' goin' tae find anything...it's just a map o' the castle."

"Just a map o' the castle," he repeated. "Then why is there a star by the entrance tae the Portal Room? It is no' in the castle." He studied it further. "Oh, and um..." He squinted at the page. "Are those tiny drawings o' humans in the Pyramid?"

"So...?" she paused. "Ok, so I saw the humans ye have tied up there. Ye allow yer villagers tae feed from them! Why? In Mikaire—"

"*This is no' Mikaire!*" He took a corner of the map and began to tear it.

"No!" Meirah took a step towards him, but halted as he tore the map in half. Then again, and yet again, until the map was naught more than confetti. He tossed it at her, tiny pieces falling on her like paper rain.

"Fine!" She lifted her head, gazed at Kaeplan. "I have it memorized anyway."

"Then why would ye be lookin' for it so viciously that ye'd tear up the room?"

"Because it is the *only* thing here that is *mine*! And ye just destroyed the last piece of me that existed in this place."

It was also the first piece of my plan.

Kaeplan's expression softened. "Meirah, I am sorry—"

"**No**! Ye don' get tae apologize, Kaeplan. Especially no' for a piece o' paper after all ye've done... after ye killed..." her voice cracked. She cleared her throat. "After the death o' my child in this place... and ye killed my husband. Ye took everythin' from me—*everything*!!" A single tear trickled down her cheek, but inside she wept deeply.

"He would no' remember ye anyway!" Kaeplan blurt out, then clamped his lips shut.

"What?!" Meirah's stare bore into him. "What did ye do?"

Silence.

"*Kaeplan!*" She shuffled through the litter to stand before him. "WHAT-DID-YE-DO?!!"

He sighed abruptly. "Meirah, ye have tae know...I did no' mean tae kill 'im. I lost as well."

Her hand flew. She slapped him hard across the cheek, then again. "How *dare* ye!" *You* lost?! **YOU** lost?!"

Her hand came up again, but he caught her wrist before her palm could make contact with his face again. The anger and pain that roiled within her gut made her stomach churn with sick.

Kaeplan released her.

"Meirah. Ye have tae believe me. I ne'er meant tae hurt ye."

"But ye did! In the worse way possible. Ye lied tae get me here, then—" She swallowed hard as blood and tea fought to come up.

"Meirah... ye look pale. Please, lie down." He reached for her, but she slapped his hand away.

"*Do no' touch me!*" she hissed.

Her stomach turned again. She walked past him, sat on the bed avoiding his gaze. She put her head in her hands, rested her elbows on her knees. Kaeplan's footsteps drew close.

"Meirah," he said softly. "I really did mean for ye tae have the child here. That was no lie. And I did no' mean tae kill yer mortal. I needed 'im, his blood. I was only goin' tae take what I needed, but...humans. So fragile."

Meirah cleared her throat, swallowed. Without looking up, she said, "The reasons matter not. I can never forgive what ye did." Slowly, she raised her head, looked direct into his amber eyes. "I *hate* you! Do ye hear me? I loathe ye more than I did Sakkana for takin' Sir Kori and makin' me watch his death—and all Dane's lives henceforth. He did it tae keep his world alive. But *you*... Ye did it all for selfish reasons. All o' it!"

Kaeplan opened his mouth to speak, but she cut him off. "And ye drugged me so I would be compliant tae ye! For all I know, ye killed the baby too."

Kaeplan's gaze dropped to the floor, he shuffled his feet. Meirah knew him. She rose slowly to stand before him. "No! Y-You did no'... Ye killed my child?! *You killed my baby*?!"

"Meirah, I—"

"What! Ye did no' *mean* tae?!" All at once clarity seeped into her conscious mind. She stepped back, her incredulous stare bore into him. "Ye SLIME! Ye drugged me tae keep me from the horrible truth of what ye did...Ye raped me!! Ye killed Dane's child so ye could replace..." She shook her head, her hand instinctively moving to her wedding band. With a gasp, she glared at the empty finger. "*Ye took my weddin' ring*!!"

"Meirah, I had yer best int—"

"*No!*... I remember. Ye climbed into my bed." She pressed her palms against her temples, against the headache that formed quickly. "I can no' believe... But ye did."

Lowering her hands she looked dead into his eyes...Fearful eyes that could no longer hide the lies, deception, murder, rape... "If I am wi' yer child..." she shuddered at the thought, "I will kill it! And I will kill *you*!!"

With strength borne of scorn and rage, she grabbed Kaeplan by the lapels of his robes, lifted him off the floor. Now she saw true fear in those deceiving eyes. She shoved him with such a force he flew back across the room, hitting the opposite wall, cracking a wooden beam. He dropped in a heap of blue robes, fiery hair and flailing arms.

He lay for a moment, unmoving. She hoped she had killed him. But the groan told her he was only stunned. She moved at him again. The fire within burned so fiercely she did not know herself what she was capable of doing... and she did not care!

As she reached him, he raised a hand. "Please!" he moaned. "I am sorry. Please..."

"I told ye... *Ye get no apology*!" She kicked him then, a sharp blow to his ribs. He crumpled forward, forehead to the floor. She kicked him again, sending him once again into the wall... a loud crack. She could not be sure if it was him or the wall. He rolled like a ragdoll onto his back. His eyes looked up at her in a haze of agony, begging for her to stop. Blood trickled from his mouth, which was open in an unspoken plea.

Her foot came down on his face. This time she knew the bone crunching crack was not the wall. He screamed, his hands coming up to his bleeding, broken face. Blood spewed onto the floor, blue robes turned crimson. She lifted her foot for another, hopefully final, blow, when she saw it. How could she have forgotten... From beneath his robes dropped a necklace... the pendant. *The key!*

She bent to grab it when the door behind her slammed open. Before she could reach it, strong hands grasped her, pulled her backwards.

"No! I need it... I need to get out!" she wailed.

Screaming, she pulled and twisted, tried to free herself. Her stare remained transfixed on the key. More hands on her. The hiss of a sword unsheathed. Still, she kicked, struggled against the bondage of hands. The flash of a sword passed by her face to her throat.

Then a small pained voice, a muffled plea. "No, please."

The sword pulled away, but the hands did not.

Then she saw them... the guards. Two that held her. Two that aided the bleeding Kaeplan to his feet. His knees buckled. They dragged him out the door along with the key.

They shoved her backwards then. She landed on the soft bed, still kicking, fighting. The door slammed closed. She bounced up, ran to the door, tried the latch. Locked.

Like the Banshee of human myth, she howled out in anger and need, banging on the solid door. Her cries were lost in the vast emptiness of the castle walls.

Her strength spent, she slid to the floor, weeping.

Dane

He held the tiny baby in his arms. "My little Meirah," he said in a soft voice meant to comfort. She looked up at him with light blue eyes that sparked silver and green. On her head, a tuft of red hair. Pride swelled in his heart. Love filled his soul. *My daughter.*

The dream changed then. No longer was she swaddled in his

arms. Strange hands took her away.

"I need her," he pleaded.

He looked again, but now she was at his feet, lying lifeless on an open cloth of linen. The blue eyes were closed. She wasn't breathing. His daughter—*dead*.

Pain clenched in his stomach. He woke. The pain was real, but there was no baby. He opened his eyes. His bed. His room. Lucy lay against him, stirred when he moved. She uttered a small groan of dissatisfaction.

"Sorry, Lucy."

He sat up. The image from the dream haunted his mind and emotions even into the waking world. A baby. *His* daughter. But he had no children. Just a dream. But, was it? So often his dreams reflected incidents from past lives and nightmares of what may be, he had stopped thinking of dreams as 'just dreams.'

He climbed out of bed, grabbed his jeans from the floor and slipped into them, noticing the tuna sandwich on his dresser, which Lucy apparently discovered first, for it lay on the plate as if a starving cougar had come across a weak gazelle.

"Thanks, Lucy, that *was* my dinner."

He grabbed a brush off the bureau and brushed his hair out, gazing once again at the mirror—that damn mirror that was giving him the real feeling he was missing something important. A daughter. To his knowledge he didn't have a daughter. He let his mind wander back to Almareyah. He had been bled there. He died there. He knew that now. So, he wouldn't have any memory of his trip back to the mortal world. He assumed Kaeplan sent his body back as he had with Bruce. He thought back to Mikaire, as far back as Sir Kori. Details came back easily...Yet still, so many gaps dotted his memory. Like the trip from the Main Looking Glass to the wagon that had brought him into Mikaire and the cell. He remembered all those who stood around him, but something happened there... what was it?

He set the brush down, still staring into the mirror, not looking at his own reflection, but beyond. He saw a hand... a female hand. It reached for his armor, touched him. He looked to see the girl then...

Pain webbed his mind. He shook the thought away as he sat on the bed. Lucy leapt into his lap, purring as he pet her short black and white fur.

Dane skipped forward. The cell. The one he called Black Hair. As Dane worked through the memories, certain moments drew in the pain. Always where there should be…someone. Each life, each memory, produced the same result. Memory gaps were unacceptable after a bout of amnesia almost made him forget everything.

He brought himself back to the whipping post in Almareyah. Before they bled him, a tiny bundle was shown to him. The linen it was swaddled in was opened. A baby—so tiny. Just as in his dream. He had recalled something in his sleep and finally it came to him.

"Oh, my God!" He stood quickly. Lucy leapt onto the floor. "I had a daughter."

But, she was dead. Stillborn? Killed? The most important question of all he needed to know was; who was the mother? He flipped through the pages of his life searching for a clue. Nothing. Then a name from the dream popped unexpectedly into his mind— Meirah.

'Do you remember Meirah?' Caitlyn had asked him when he was in the hospital. Nowhere in his mind could he find the mother of his daughter, Meirah.

Must have been one of the women he'd bedded throughout the years, he reasoned. So many, he couldn't remember them all. But the pain he had felt at seeing the baby's dead body meant this was once a significant aspect of his life.

For now, however, it just wasn't there. No memory. Amnesia. He'd worry about it later.

The mansion was dark as he walked through the hallways from his room. He'd slept into evening. He glanced at the large clock in the hallway as he flipped on a few lights to avoid tripping over cats. 9pm. He'd slept four hours.

He was famished, having never gotten his tuna sandwich. He moved towards the kitchen, but as he passed the den, voices greeted his ears. He stopped at the threshold.

Edna and Caitlyn sat opposite one another near the cold fireplace, talking quietly and sipping wine.

It was Caitlyn who noticed him first. "Dane, you're awake." She set down her wine glass and stood. "Please, come in, we were just talking."

He entered the den, lit dimly. An ambiance of comfort and home struck him and for the first time in a long while he felt its peace. His favorite room, the den. Filled with technology and entertainment, this was where he found solace when the life of a rock star became daunting.

"Please." He motioned for Caitlyn to sit and she complied.

"How ya feeling, Mr. Dane?" asked Edna.

"Good. Rested. Hungry."

"I left ya a tuna sandwich."

"Lucy ate it," he chuckled.

"Oh, I shoulda thought... I'll make ya another," said Edna, rising.

"No, please. I'll get something." Edna shrugged, sat back down.

Dane turned to leave, but stopped, turned back.

He glanced to each of them. "I need to ask you guys something." They both nodded.

"I know there's something important I've been fighting to remember."

Caitlyn sat forward. "Um, what is it, sweetie?" She took a gulp of her wine.

"Meirah..."

Caitlyn choked on the wine. Edna's brows lifted. Caitlyn wiped away a dribble from her chin, coughed then settled. She motioned for him to continue.

"You asked me in the hospital if I remembered her."

Caitlyn swallowed hard, nodded.

"I know who she is," said Dane.

Caitlyn gripped the wine glass. "Y-You do?"

"Yes. You no longer need to protect me from her memory. I know you didn't want me to remember..."

"Dane, you have to understand..." Caitlyn defended.

"It's ok," he said softly. "I understand now. You didn't want me to remember her death. You didn't want me to hurt more. But I remember what happened."

Caitlyn cleared her throat, glanced to Edna, who asked, "What d'ya remember?"

"That I had a daughter. I think Kaeplan killed her. But I can't remember who the mother was. I know the baby's name was Meirah."

Caitlyn and Edna both sighed and looked confused at the same time. Caitlyn set down her glass, stood. "Dane, let's get you something to eat." She placed a hand on his arm, but he didn't move.

"There are gaps in my memory all over the place. My head pains me when I try to recall. But you both know..." Caitlyn's hand fell away from his arm. Dane looked from one concerned face to the other. "What am I missing?"

Edna bit her lip. Caitlyn stared at him, her expression serious, but in her deep brown eyes he saw a flicker, which revealed information held back.

Caitlyn touched his arm again. "Let's get you something to eat," she repeated.

"Tell me first. You can't deny there's something else. You must know who the mother was..."

Edna stood. "Mr. Dane, ya been through a lot." She stared at him with those motherly eyes he knew so well.

Caitlyn weighed in. "You really need more recovery time. We'll tell you what you need to hear once your mind is better prepared."

Dane cocked his head. "What is *that* supposed to mean?"

Caitlyn sighed, once again removed her hand from his arm. "It means that the headaches you're getting are a sign that your mind is not yet ready for certain memories to return. Listen to them. Give it a few more days. Don't try to force it and it will come."

Dane scoffed. "You're not going to tell me, are you?"

Caitlyn gazed seriously into his eyes. "In good time. When you're ready. For now you need to eat."

Caitlyn and Edna

"That was close," said Caitlyn as she leaned on her idling car out in the driveway.

Edna's car idled behind hers. One last chit chat before heading home. The time was late and Caitlyn needed to get home to her son. Since Bruce's death, the nanny was working overtime.

Though she needed to tend to things in her own life, she also knew how critical this phase in Dane's recovery was, so she and Edna had made him a nice dinner of shrimp and vegetables and left him to eat and watch TV in the den.

"I reckon he'll remember the truth... eventually," said Edna.

"We have to play our cards right," Caitlyn opened her purse, took out a cigarette, lit it. At Edna's glance to the smoke, she explained. "Since Bruce died. I know it's not healthy. I don't smoke in the house, but it helps me relax." She drew in a deep drag, let it out with a contrite sigh.

"Now what?" asked Edna.

"I haven't used my psychiatry classes in a long time, but I think I can still play a mind." She sucked on the cigarette as if it were a lost lover.

"What's the plan?" asked Edna.

"We lie. If we make up something believable, hopefully he will stop trying to recall the gaps in his memory."

"He thinks he had a daughter named Meirah. The name is there." Edna reached for the cigarette, took it from Caitlyn, took a drag and handed it back. At Caitlyn's confused look, she said "What? I smoke sometimes too. I've been known to smoke a joint or two when Dane had some in the house."

Both ladies shared a hearty laugh.

"Wish I had one now," said Caitlyn. "Bruce was so against... well, everything."

Seriousness overcame their expressions then. Caitlyn cleared her throat.

"About the baby... Where did that come from?"

Edna shrugged then said, "Meirah was pregnant."

"I wonder..." Caitlyn thought back to what she recalled of Kaeplan and Almareyah. "That memory is more than likely real. Either Meirah's stress caused her to stillborn or—"

"Kaeplan killed Dane and Meirah's child," Edna finished, horror registering on her face.

"Then paraded it in front of him!" Caitlyn shook her head, dropped the cigarette and snuffed it with her shoe.

"Beast!" exclaimed Edna.

"That he is! But whatever we come up with, we must all be on the same page with Adrian and Stephan."

Edna nodded. "Agreed."

Kaeplan
Almareyah

Pain webbed every part of his body. His face felt as if it had imploded, every breath agony to his ribs. Kaeplan lay on his bed, holding a cold wet cloth to his face as his servants worked to rid him of his blood-stained robes.

Lenophis drew a sharp breath once all the clothing was carefully removed.

Eyes swelled shut, Kaeplan could not see the damage. "Tell me what you see."

"It…it looks bad, Master. You will need the Apothecary… and the surgeon."

"Then fetch them!"

As the servants shuffled off to do their Master's bidding, Kaeplan suffered in his dilemma. Meirah's fury had been fiercer than he had ever imagined. He had seen it many times in the past, especially where the mortal was concerned, but this time she would have killed him had the guards not entered. And her brilliance at discovering her plan… How would he gain her love now? Drugs, spells. She had conquered them all. And his ego suffered along with his body. Throughout his life, he had held few regrets. Now they plague him like the locusts he had seen during his time in Egypt.

Kaeplan fell asleep thinking about what to do with Meirah when the door opening startled him awake.

He heard the servant's voice. "The surgeon and Apothecary are here, Master."

Dane
South Carolina

He drifted in and out of sleep, still seated in the large suede stuffed chair in the den. The only light in the room was from the flicker of the television. News. He watched it through half closed lids, until the next story aired. The news anchor, a petit blond woman in a black and white dress, stood before a set of mahogany double doors.

Sleepily, he thought, *those look like the doors on my house,* seconds before a knock sounded out front.

He sat up straight. *Who could be here at this hour?*

Too tired to care, he stood, stretched, and moved through the gallery into the foyer. He sighed and opened the door. He regretted it immediately.

The lights and a camera pointed at his face and he squinted, threw an arm up at the sudden assault.

"What the f..."

The blond news lady shoved a microphone in his face. "Mr. Bainbridge," she said, "were you kidnapped by the same people who had taken you in 2014?"

She glanced to the cameraman, motioned to Dane's chest, whispering frantically, "The scars... get the scars."

It took Dane's addled mind a moment before he realized he wasn't wearing a shirt and the gash that killed him was plain across his breast. He crossed his arms over the scar.

"Uh," he stuttered, ill prepared for an interview, particularly this time of night. Hell, they probably knew more than he did.

Oh hell... He stepped outside to stand directly in front of the news lady. Her brows raised in surprise at his compliance. She was used to doors slammed in her face, but Dane figured this a good opportunity to dispel myths and shed some good lies across the board.

"Yes, I was." Dane said without hesitation.

"Do you know who took you?"

"No. But the scene was similar. I was able to escape again."

"And they tortured you again?" She glanced to his chest, where much of the scar was invisible behind his arms.

"Not as badly as last time," he said, giving only what they wanted. He still had not had time to conjure an interesting story.

"They took your band mates as well? Were they the ones who killed Bruce Beaufort?"

The mention of Bruce took him aback. Guilt and pain entered his heart.

"Yes," he said sadly.

"You told the police you didn't know who took you. Did they take your wife as well? Has she been returned?"

Wife?? Now it was his turn to look stunned. Time for an interview of his own. As the news anchor placed the microphone to his face, he snatched it. She stepped back in surprise. The cameraman zoomed in.

"What do you know of my wife?" Dane asked, desperate for an answer to what had been missing in his memory. He tilted the mic to her as if their roles had been switched.

Her mouth open, she stuttered. "Um... Not much. She disappeared before you did."

"What was her name?" He asked, staring intensely into her plain blue eyes.

She glanced to the cameraman and mouthed, "what was her name?" The cameraman shrugged.

Dane returned the mic to himself. "You seem to know so much about my disappearance. So, what is my wife's name?" He shoved the mic in her face.

She signed CUT to the cameraman. He shut off the camera and lowered it. She turned back to Dane, took back the mic, but didn't speak into it. They were off the record now.

"Mr. Bainbridge, I'm only here to report on the story of *your* disappearance. I don't know personal details. Just what I received from the police reports about you."

"You didn't learn the name of my wife then?" Dane asked. Though his words were calm, his insides shook like an 8.0 on the Richter scale.

She shook her head. "Only that you'd been taken two years ago under mysterious circumstances and it happened again. But this time your friends and wife disappeared too. Later, Bruce Beaufort was found dead in the Vegas desert. The autopsy showed he died of dehydration, starvation and blood loss."

"Then you know just as much as I do," Dane snapped. He turned, opened the door, walked back into the house, slammed the door.

Back in the den, he flopped down into the stuffed chair. The live broadcast showed the news anchor returning after the commercial that aired after she'd cut the cameraman off. They stood in his yard. She was talking, reiterating what he had said on camera. She mentioned something about his amnesia. He flipped the TV off.

He had hoped to get some answers, but was more confused now than before. Wife? He couldn't recall ever having gotten married, much less that she had been taken by Kaeplan as well. Obviously, he had a wife and a child, a daughter, whom Kaeplan murdered. Did he murder his wife as well and the pain of losing her repressed his memory to the point of pain when he tried to remember? There was only one way he was going to get the answers.

Meirah
Almareyah

Locked in her chamber, there was little to do but think, weep and clean. Cleaning helped keep her mind off the weeping. She replaced papers and knick knacks that were strewn all over and around the desk and floor. As she picked up the confetti that was once her map, she wondered how she would get out of Almareyah. She had planned to use the map to find the proper barrier to the village. She had told Kaeplan it was all in her memory, but that was only half truth.

She could recall certain corridors and where they led, but how she had found her way to the tunnels and then the village blurred in her mind along with dozens of other details.

If only she could find a way back to the village, perhaps she could find those who had shown pity, sympathy for the death of her daughter. They had not been drugged as she was... Killing an infant and using it to break Dane's spirit—a plan that backfired—had touched the heart of many; villagers, servants and guards alike. They had aided her in taking Dane's body away, despite Kaeplan's commands to the contrary.

At the time she had been too distraught to notice, but as she went over that day in her mind, she truly had seen sympathy, even pain, on the faces of so many who were supposed to be loyal only to Kaeplan. Surely, he had over-stepped a boundary that had turned at least some against him. If only she could escape this prison, get to the village, hold an audience, convince them of Kaeplan's cruelty... With his people rallying against him, surely he would have to set her free.

Done with her task of cleaning the room, replacing items to their proper place, she stepped back and surveyed her work. But, as she gazed about, a shimmer of faint light sparkled from under the desk. She'd missed something. She reached beneath the desk and grasped the object.

"Ow!" She pulled back quickly. A single drop of blood welled up on her finger. She sucked it away.

Bending forward, she peered beneath the desk. A letter opener, shaped as a small sword. Sharp at the tip. She reached under and took it by the handle. A weapon. Small, but useful if used correctly.

She changed into her tunic and breeches, hid the letter opener in her waistband, and waited.

Kaeplan

He rose from the bed and gazed into the mirror that stood opposite the room. A servant moved forward and helped him into a fresh robe. He smiled at himself, quite pleased.

His face no longer bled. No cuts. The process of healing had been excruciating, especially fixing his broken nose, but the surgeon's skill and the Apothecary's magic potions had produced desirable results. He swore he even appeared younger, more attractive. Bright red hair hung down his shoulders in smooth waves, high cheekbones accented features that made him feel like a male model he had seen in the Mortal Dimension... The epitome of exquisiteness.

Once his crown was placed atop his head, he tuned to all in the room. "Ye've done well. Now, please leave me."

Once all had shuffled from his chamber, Kaeplan preened himself like a proud bird. He had to see Meirah and needed to appear perfect. He straightened, drew a deep breath, took on the air of the ruler and wizard he was... She would not take that away from him. She would not destroy his life, his world, as she had done to Mikaire.

His main and most powerful blood source gone, the time had come to determine his next move. Almareyah being a simple work in progress, he had no Council yet, as Sakkana had, so this was up to him alone. If Meirah refused to stay with him, he would do away with her. Insistence on betraying him rendered her naught but a liability.

He loved her. Deep within he understood her reaction, her pain. Her anger. But, as ruler of Almareyah he could not abide her actions. If she allowed him to make it up to her, if she complied, her life would be spared.

With no real plan in mind, he left his chamber and headed towards Meirah's room. He wished to rule with her beside him, but if he could not...

Two guards stood alert outside Meirah's chamber. They bowed low as Kaeplan approached.

"Open the door," he commanded.

One, trusted for his duty and alliance, pulled the key from his waist and placed it in the lock, turned. His hand moved to the latch, but he stopped and turned to Kaeplan. "Do you wish us to accompany you, Master?"

"That will no' be necessary," said Kaeplan, though within he wished they would, but he wanted to be alone with Meirah, to talk with no other ears nearby.

He bowed, opened the door.

"Remain close by," Kaeplan whispered to the guard then entered the room, his caution on high alert, glancing about to be sure she didn't stand in wait. Then he entered, the door closed behind him.

Meirah sat on her bed, head bowed.

"Ye changed yer clothes," said Kaeplan.

"I am more comfortable," she said, voice muffled as she did not lift her head. "Ye know I loathe dresses."

"Aye. Ye've always been... unconventional."

She looked up as he approached her. Streaks of dried tears lined her face. "What d'ye want, Kaeplan?" she asked dryly.

He moved a few steps closer, halted with several feet still between them. She appeared calm now, harmless enough. Softly he spoke, keeping his words short and to the point.

"What can I do tae gain back yer trust and forgiveness?"

Meirah closed her eyes and merely shook her head without speaking.

"There must be...*somethin'*," he pleaded.

She looked down again, shuffling her feet, pushing dirt and dust along the floor. "Let me go home," she whispered sadly.

Kaeplan sighed and took a chance, sitting beside her on the bed. Though she would never believe him, he did feel badly for what had happened to her. Though the mortal's death was his ultimate goal, eventually, he did not wish it like this, nor to harm her. Carefully, he spoke.

"What then, Meirah? What is there for ye now? An immortal in a mortal world. Yer husband is gone—"

Her head snapped towards him. "Aye, thanks tae *you!*" she snarled.

"I am sorry," he stated sincerely.

"Ye've said that. It changes *nothing!*"

"Meirah, I love ye still. Even though ye tried tae kill me, I love ye. Even if ye hate me... I love ye. I ne'er meant—"

"Ye've said all this," she interrupted.

Kaeplan let out an exacerbated breath and dared to shift a bit closer to her. "I shall make it up tae ye. Ye belong *here*. In a magical dimension. Meirah, we're no' like mortals. What would ye have if ye went back?"

"Friends who do no' lie and betray me!" She was getting worked up again. He needed to bring the conversation back to an even level.

"And if I promise no more lies. Rule beside me. Anythin' ye wish, it is yers..."

Through clenched teeth, she hissed, "Bring back my husband and child!"

Kaeplan bit his lip. That did not help, and he knew his answer surely wouldn't.

"I can no' do that. But I can offer ye a better life here. Luxury. Yer e'ery need fulfilled. I will no' touch ye without yer permission. I promise with all my being." He placed a hand over his heart. "What d'ye want that I can make possible?"

"There is *one* thing..."

Kaeplan offered a grin. "Anythin', my love?"

She looked up at him then and he saw the flames in her eyes far too late.

"Ye can *die!*"

Her movement was so quick he did not see the sharp blade in her hand. She thrust it towards his heart so fiercely it went through his hand, the blade slicing his robes and just touching the flesh underneath. Kaeplan screeched and rose quickly, pulling away. He grabbed the blade and painfully ripping it out of his hand, tossed it across the room with a clatter. If his hand had not been over his heart...

He cried out. "*Guards!*"

The door burst open. The two guards who'd accompanied him to the chamber rushed in. With no further command, they took Meirah by the arms and waist, holding her back as she continued her fight to get at Kaeplan.

He stood aside, out of range of her kicking feet, holding his bloody hand with the other.

"Lock her up!" he ordered.

"*No!*" she screeched.

"Ye make bad decisions, Meirah. Ye need time tae think on them. Perhaps time in the dungeon will change yer way o' thinkin'!"

He nodded to the guards, who dragged a screaming Meirah from the room.

"And fetch the surgeon!" He called out behind them as Meirah's screams echoed back to him. Each word rent his heart.

"*I will kill ye, Kaeplan! Mark my words!*"

Long after her wails faded, Kaeplan remained, though his hand hurt something terrible. Another robe ruined by her anger. On the bed her nightdress lay unfolded. He snatched it up, wrapped it tight around his hand.

He sat on the bed, the pain in his hand making him feel queasy. He closed his eyes and found himself back in Mikaire so many years ago. Yet almost as if it were yesterday. Young Ones, playing Xulus 20, their favorite game, out on the moors. The sun on the moors played off the red in her hair. Her laughter chimed like a songbird in his ears. Ah, the Meirah of their youth. The tight tunic and breeches she wore allowed him such a view of her shape.

Though not yet a woman, budding breasts beneath her wet tunic always gave him a rise he needed to hide.

Now she was a woman, and blossomed into a perfect flower. Such a shame the mortal pulled the pedals from his rose. The untouched *wild roske of Mikaire* was lost to him forever.

If only he could turn time back on itself, before the mortal stole her heart. Before Sir Kori had come through the Main Looking Glass!

Kaeplan arose quickly, ignoring the sway and dizziness that overcame him. Meirah thought she had lost? He had lost more. His love, his ultimate source for blood to keep Almareyah alive. Dane was dead… Kaeplan needed that strong blood, the ultimate source Sakkana reincarnated, for he had found no other better. Yet it had been the reincarnations that gave Dane and Meirah the power and the knowledge to break Sakkana's spell and free themselves. If Dane had lived, he'd have done the same to Kaeplan. Sakkana had been far stronger than Kaeplan was now, and he was still bested by a dozen lifetimes of strengthened blood and knowledge the human had obtained.

Kaeplan refused to die. Refused to let his world die. Sir Kori did not hold the same knowledge, yet held the strength in his blood. And that was what Kaeplan needed. Not Dane, but his first incarnation—the knight who had erroneously stumbled into Mikaire. But was it possible?

An idea came to him, but he would need advice. He would first see the surgeon, then make his way down the shadow barrier to the Seer's home.

-Thirty-Three-

"Sometimes by losing a battle, you find a new way to win a war."

Dane
March 5, 2016

"Thank you," he said and hung up the phone. He grabbed up the travel bag he always took with him on the road, opened it. Quickly, he took inventory of his supplies. It was all there. The tour had been cut short, so he had not used up the usual toiletries that traveled with him everywhere.

He glanced at the clock. Two in the morning. He had a few hours yet. He'd be gone before Edna arrived.

Once downstairs, he left the travel bag and his suitcase—stocked with various weather clothing—in the foyer and walked to the den. The roll top antique desk sat beneath several open windows. A breeze fluttered the sheer curtains over the desk. He pulled up a chair, grabbed some paper from the top shelf, a pen from the holder and prepared a letter. He sat thinking, staring at the blank page. What could he say? She'd be furious. She'd call Caitlyn.

His mind's eye conjured the last image he'd seen of Bruce; the lifeless body, dead eyes, pale bloodless skin.

"What are you doing, Dane?" he asked himself. He set the pen down on the paper, stood, and decided to go out to the barn.

The horses were in their stalls, casually munching their hay. The back doors to the paddock were closed and for a moment he wondered why the stable hands had closed them in on such a warm night. A rumble of thunder in the distance reminded him. A big storm was coming in. Spring storms could be especially fierce in South Carolina. Just like the New England Nor'Easters he'd grown up with.

Camelot, his black Andalusian gelding, moved from his net of hay and poked his head over the stall door. Dane rubbed the soft fur of the horse's face.

"Sorry, buddy, no late night ride tonight. Daddy has to go away again."

As if understanding his words, the horse placed his muzzle on Dane's shoulder. A twinge of guilt rippled through him.

"I know, Cammy. I've been gone a lot. But there's a storm coming, I can't take you out, You spook, remember?"

The horse nuzzled his arm. Dane hugged the large head. Even as the rumble became a bang that shook the windows in the barn, Camelot didn't flinch.

"Hear that?" Dane cooed softly. "You'd throw me and I don't like walking back a mile in the rain."

Camelot nuzzled closer, as if he knew, as if he remembered the night his master had taken him on a midnight ride. The moon had been full that night, but the rain came in suddenly. The trail became slick. But it wasn't the rain, or the fall, that plagued Dane's mind now. It was the *reason* he had chosen to ride that night. He'd needed to purge an unsettling thought from his mind. But…what was it?

Earlier that day two years ago, Bruce and Caitlyn, who was still pregnant, had come to visit. Another unfinished tour. Dane had passed out onstage. But why?

"The doctor said it was exhaustion," he told his horses. "But…" He glanced over at his older grey and white Paint, Kobeejo, who was ripping hay from the net as if it was his last meal.

He looked back to Camelot. "I was onstage," he said, as if his horses would provide the answers he sought. "I saw… something. But, what?" he asked, thinking aloud. "Mirrors. They had replaced the stage set with huge mirrors. I hated mirrors."

Again… why?

"The stage set had not arrived due to a blizzard."

Dane glanced from one horse to the other. Camelot, having given up on getting a ride or a treat from his owner, went back to his hay net. "You guys aren't going to tell me the answer, either, are you?"

Dane turned around. Behind him—a mirror. "This was not there back then," he said, working things out aloud.

He stared at his own reflection. Long black hair tied back, silver-blue eyes reflected back at him as if gazing into them could provide recollection.

Mirrors!

He had avoided them most of his life. Something about them unsettled him. The mirrors onstage. He'd seen something. Something that disturbed him, made him feel overwhelmed. Caused him to lose consciousness.

"Wait a sec," he said to his own reflection rather than to the horses. "Bruce saw it too... that's why he and Caitlyn had come over that night."

But Bruce was dead. Caitlyn knew something, but refused to divulge.

"Sonofabitch!" he called out, just as a loud crack of thunder and a bright flash rocked the barn.

When he'd come home from the hospital, he'd rested, but then... that was when Kaeplan took him through the mirror. But how did he know to avoid mirrors? Before that day he had never seen Kaeplan before.

"Okay... I was onstage, I saw myself in those blasted mirrors. I saw the audience. And then, in the middle of a song, I saw..."

Pain shot through Dane's head just as his mind was about to allow the memory in, causing him to drop to his knees on the barn floor. He pressed his hands against his aching temples. He remained there for several minutes, forcing his mind to go blank, for every thought throbbed.

Camelot's nicker brought him back. He opened his eyes and stood. The pain was gone, but he had no more answers than before. Once again, he could only attribute this memory gap to the amnesia. The clock on the barn wall read 3:05 am.

"Shit! I have to go!"

He gave each horse a half a carrot that he kept in the small fridge, which pleased Camelot to no end. Then he exited the barn, shoving the door closed against wind so strong it worked against him. The sky streaked with electricity as he dashed through the downpour back to the mansion.

As he entered the back door to the mud room, a white hot flash of lightning lit the world, followed immediately by a crash so loud it shook the door as he pulled it closed. Hand still on the handle, he paused. The door. It had been smashed. Needed to be replaced. Why?

Dripping wet, Dane sighed at all the blank memories. Everything reminded him that he had forgotten.

No time. He had to change clothes.

Back in his bedroom, he removed his wet clothes, and grabbed a fresh pair of jeans from the laundry basket. With no thought, he quickly pulled a tee shirt from his bureau drawer and moved to the bathroom to dry his hair. He pulled the binding from drenched locks and let the black waves fall over his shoulders.

No time for another shower, he unfolded the tee shirt. On is front, a logo for Dark Myst. He paused, ran a finger over the silk-screen letters. His band. His career. His life. Would they come back from the death of their lead guitarist and founder?

Dane sighed, dressed, combed out his hair, placing the hair tie around his wrist to put it back up once it dried, then headed back downstairs. As he reached the gallery, his cell phone, which he'd placed in his travel bag, rang.

"Who the hell…?" It was 3:45 in the morning!

He grabbed the phone from the side pouch. He didn't recognize the number. "Hello?"

A pause, then an automated message came on the line. Due to severe weather, his flight was delayed 3 hours. He pressed the END button and tossed the phone onto his travel bag. That left very little time between departure and the time Edna would arrive.

His earlier headache left him feeling drained. *Fine*, he thought, *I'll rest for an hour then leave.* He walked to the den and slumped into his stuffed chair, reclined it back and closed his eyes.

He woke at 6:25 am. His flight was at 8. With no time to write the letter he had planned, he scribbled a quick note.

Gone away for a bit.

I'll be fine. Don't worry.
Please care for the critters.

Dane

He took the page and put it on the fridge with a magnet. Then grabbed up his travel bag and suitcase and headed out to the airport, to catch his flight to Las Vegas.

Kaeplan
Almareyah

Though he did not need to, he knocked on the door of the Seer's home. The door opened. The expression on the Seer's face reflecting his surprise at seeing Kaeplan there.

"My Lord, what an honor! Please…come in."

"Good afternoon." He entered into the living chamber. A fire burned and crackled in the fireplace, the room warm and inviting with the scent of wood and herbs.

Though he never told anyone, Kaeplan loved going there. The sound of the ocean nearby reminded him of Meirah in better times. How she had always spoke of seeing an ocean, for Mikaire had none. One of the reasons he created a water dimension.

"What brings you here, M'Lord?"

Kaeplan took a seat by the fireplace, reveling in its plush comfort.

"Tea?" asked the Seer. "Or blood?"

"Nothin', thank ye. Please, sit. I am in desperate need of advice."

The Seer sat across from Kaeplan but did not relax back. He leaned forward, elbows rested on his knees as if expecting to leap up at any moment.

Kaeplan got right to the point. "Is it possible to travel back in time… or to change time?"

The Seer's brows furrowed deeply.

"I know it sounds ludicrous," said Kaeplan, "Perhaps it's no' been done. Can one travel through time?"

"May I inquire as to the nature of this strange request?"

"Ye know what has happened?" Kaeplan asked.

"I do."

"Then ye know it was no' my intention tae kill the mortal."

The Seer nodded. "You wish to return to the point where the mortal is still alive and prevent is death?"

"I *needed* that blood!" Kaeplan expressed hardily. "However... returning to that point in time will not change certain facts that need not have occurred in the first place."

At the Seer's confused glare, Kaeplan elaborated. "Sakkana could bring life back tae the dead. I can no'. Howe'er, if I can travel back tae Mikaire—before Sir Kori came through the glass—the power o' his blood would be mine fore'er. It would assure my immortality, the life o' this dimension. I could have her back." He whispered the last sentence as if thinking aloud rather than to the Seer.

The Seer leaned back in the chair at last. He tapped a finger to his lips as if in deep thought.

Finally, he shook his head. "I've never heard of it done with success. It would take great power—far more than even Sakkana possessed.

Kaeplan sighed. "So I have no' the power tae do it? Without Dane's blood I shall ne'er possess such power. I have doomed myself."

"Wait," said the Seer, sitting forward again. "I did not say it cannot be done."

"What do you mean? How?"

"I am saying it would take the culmination of great power you would need to attain... and even then it is not a sure thing. You would need the strongest blood from a magical being with power such as yourself."

Kaeplan thought for a moment. "Another wizard?"

The Seer shrugged. "Perhaps, but getting that power would take more power. Do you understand?"

"I think so..." Kaeplan paused, his mind whirring with thoughts and ideas. "Thank ye. I believe I know now what I need tae do."

Mortal Dimension

Caitlyn and Edna

Edna still held the note in her hand when Caitlyn came into the kitchen.

"What is it, Edna? What's wrong?"

Edna handed her the piece of paper. "He's gone."

"Shit!" Caitlyn placed the paper on the center island.

"Maybe not tellin' him about Meirah was not such a good idea."

Caitlyn refused to think the worst. "He didn't say where he went. Maybe he went to CT to visit his parents?"

"I'll call!"

Several minutes later, Edna hung up the phone. She shook her head. "He went back to Vegas, I guarantee it."

"He wants answers," said Caitlyn. It made sense. She had seen the news broadcast that had taken place on Dane's doorstep. He'd questioned the news lady about his wife's name. He knew it all began in Vegas, that Bruce had been found in Vegas.

"I am sure you're right, Edna. Apparently the baby named Meirah wasn't satisfying enough. He knows now he had a wife, thanks to that nosey reporter."

"Do we go there? Look for him?" asked Edna, biting her nails.

"Let me call Stephan. He may have some answers. Then... if we must..."

Dane

The walk through the desert to the puddle was farther than he remembered—although these days his memory was unreliable. Why did he even go out there to begin with? To find Bruce and Adrian? No. He'd gone with Stephan to the lake for that.

In his mind it was clear… Bruce and Adrian being taken under and to another dimension by Kaeplan of Mikaire. That still didn't answer why they went there in the first place.

Thinking made Dane's head ache, along with his feet for walking such a distance.

The night air was chilly. Dane drew up the collar on his down-filled coat. He kept winter clothes for the when he would visit his parents in the winter. Just as Dane began to believe he had gone the wrong way, passing the water hole, his flashlight beam shone on a palm tree and some bushes. That meant water, an oasis.

The pond!

Once by the small pool he found a location where he could sit and watch without being seen. Not that he knew exactly what it was he was looking for… a way in?

Answers.

He removed his backpack and dropped it to the ground, flopped down beside it.

The night grew increasingly cold. Each breath created a fog that dissipated in the light breeze circling around him. He untied the sleeping bag from his backpack, unrolled it. He climbed inside then pulled a bottle of wine, a knife, and a granola bar from his pack. Then he waited.

It wasn't the Nevada desert that surrounded him. The heat and the sun pounded on his bare skin. He felt aflame. Then he saw the whipping post. He tried to holler out, but he had no voice. His hands were bound above his head. The strands of the whip looked to him like snakes ready to bite. His heart ached. With his eyes he pleaded to those who surrounded him.

His gaze halted on a woman. Her ginger hair was braided neatly and the burgundy dress she wore swept the sands. He needed to get to her. He begged for her to see him, but the emerald eyes gazed down.

"Please," he said, finding his voice at last. "Help me, Meirah!"

Dane struggled to rid himself of the bindings that held his body.

He was trapped, sweating. He came awake fully. Daylight pounded on him, hot and searing. The sleeping bag served to bind him in its heat.

He wriggled out of the bag, simultaneously pulling out of his coat. In the process he kicked an empty wine bottle, sending it careening across the sand. The wind lifted his discarded granola wrapper and took it away.

Finally free, he stood and removed his sweatshirt. The tee shirt beneath was soaked in sweat. He pulled it off, allowed the hot but dry wind to cool him a moment before he found another in his backpack and slipped into it. He'd prefer to be bare-chested, but in this sun he'd bake to a crisp.

He packed up, found the granola wrapper and shoved that in too. Then he headed back to the hotel. Though he'd nodded off, he doubted he had missed anything. His sleep had been restless and short. Such an odd dream. He saw his daughter grown—red hair. He knew it was her because he had called her by name. Perhaps her mother also had red hair? He simply couldn't remember.

Once back at the hotel, he removed the brown contact lenses he wore to hide his eyes, showered, changed, cranked the a/c and lay on the bed. He would sleep the day, eat, then head back out to the oasis, refreshed and ready for another night, this time staying awake. Kaeplan sent servants to the mortal world only at night to grab mortals for blood, so more than likely he wouldn't miss anything during the day.

That evening, Dane found the water hole much more easily. Just as the night before he set up and waited. This time the bottle of wine was replaced by a thermos of tea. He needed to stay alert and awake.

The night trickled on. He had no cell service out there, which was fine as he wanted no interruptions or calls. He used the phone to play games until the battery indicated it was getting low, so he shut it off to save the rest of the battery, just in case. The time was 1:52 am. He propped himself near a grouping of fronds and watched through them. The moon reflected off the small pond and lit the area fairly well, so he would clearly see anyone coming though the Portal.

Several times his eyes drooped and he had to force himself

awake. He was pretty sure no one had come through the Portal the previous night. But Kaeplan kept a steady stream of humans, judging by what Caitlyn had seen and this water area seemed the most popular with him.

Despite his best efforts to stay awake, he nodded off just before dawn, leaned against a palm tree just beyond the fronds that served as his watch blinds.

He was awakened by a noise he couldn't at first comprehend. But as he came awake, he realized it was the splashing of water. Sliding silently over to his fronds he peered carefully through. A man in servant's clothing rose up from the pond like Jesus walking on water. His hair was black, like Dane's, brown intense eyes gazed about as if making sure he was alone. Dane knew these beings could see in the dark, so he slowly replaced the fronds without making noise, but heard footfalls near. The servant was heading in his direction. Carefully, slowly, he reached for his knife, held it tight in his hand.

The man passed right by Dane's hiding blind. Dane leapt from the brush, grabbed the man unsuspectingly from behind, the blade to his throat.

"Remove your clothes!" Dane commanded.

The servant hesitated.

"Now!" Dane reached his free hand to the servant's waist and withdrew the knife there.

The servant, taken by surprise and knowing he was not in the position to argue, removed his servant's robes and tunic, dropped them to the sands, leaving him in just his breeches. The chilly night made the man shiver.

"Turn around," Dane ordered.

The servant spied him suspiciously, eyes wide. Slowly, he turned his back to Dane, who had both knives held to him, one on each side of his throat. Dane knew how fast these beings could be... One move and he'd kill the man, servant or no.

Once he saw the back of the servant's head, he lifted the largest knife and slammed the hilt down hard on the back of the man's head. He went down in a heap on the sand. Dane removed rope from his backpack and tied the unconscious servant tightly to a palm tree, wrapping the rope securely around his body, and leaving his hands in his lap, bound the servant's wrists. Dane dropped a few bottles of water beside the unconscious man.

He placed the knives in the waistband of his jeans, gathered up the robes and tunic and slipped them on.

The key! The servant had to hold it in order to get through. Searching the robes, he found a small pendant hidden within a secret pocket inside the robe.

"Stay here," he commanded to the unconscious man. "I'll be back when I have my answers."

Making sure he was well dressed as an Almareyan servant, he walked to the Portal, and paused. He had weapons, his eyes were hidden by dark contacts, his hair was in a ponytail, he was well dressed as a servant of Almareyah. No telling who he'd run into on the other side. The rising sun cast tendrils of orange and red light over the desert as he released a staggering breath and stepped into the water.

The hand that grasped his arm took him by such surprise, he reacted on instinct. He drew one of the knives and spun on his captor, tearing his arm from the man's grasp, ready to slice him open.

At the last second he realized he knew this person who interrupted his plans.

"Stephan!" He shouted. "Jesus Christ, I almost sliced you in two. What the hell are you—"

His friend wasn't alone. Caitlyn, Adrian and even Edna were there, watching with wide eyes as if they didn't recognize him.

"What in hell are you all doing here??"

Edna brought up the rear, huffing and sweating despite the chill air. "We... we can't let yas go!"

Dane ignored his housemaid. Anger at their audacity bubbled within, but he swallowed it back.

He looked at Adrian, pale and hardly fit for such a trek. "Shouldn't you be resting?"

"Not when we worry you'll get yourself killed."

Edna stepped in. "I can't lose ya again, Mr. Dane."

Dane put the knife back in his waistband.

"Um..." stuttered Caitlyn, staring at the servant, still out and tightly secured to the tree. "Who is that?"

"Where do you think I got the clothes?"

"You're just going to leave him tied to a tree in the desert?"

Caitlyn asked in astonishment.

"For now. If I let him go, he will follow me back to Almareyah and alert them to my presence. I have to go in as him. Besides, I left him water. I'm not a beast, ya know."

"Don't they need blood?" asked Stephan.

"These vampires can go a long time on just water. He is not human. He'll be fine."

"Ok," started Caitlyn, tearing her gaze from the servant back to Dane. "But that doesn't excuse you going in there alone…"

"I cannot stay here! Don't you understand? I need answers. I know there's more to this, but when I try to remember the pain is unbearable. The answers are through this Portal." He motioned to the water. "When I find the answers, I will return."

"No," said Caitlyn, softly. "You won't."

"I know how dangerous this is, Caitlyn. I'm prepared… And none of you can change my mind. There are too many gaps that need filling."

"Because…" Caitlyn said sadly. "If you find the truth, you won't want to return."

"Look… My heart is empty and I know filling it means returning to Almareyah even if it means my life. I can't live like this anymore."

"We'll tell yas everythin'," said Edna quickly.

Caitlyn placed a hand on Edna's shoulder then. Her expression rang sadness. "He's right. I see it now. He will never rest until he sees the truth for himself. Us telling him won't break the spell."

"I will go, too," chimed Stephan.

"No!" snapped Dane. "You almost died last time. I won't have anyone else's blood on my hands. I have to do this… alone." Dane glanced to Edna. "Care for the cats, the horses."

"Of course… always." She stepped forward and hugged him. "Please be careful and come back to us, Mr. Dane."

"I will. I promise." He glanced to each, gazing quickly into their worried eyes. "You're all good friends."

Dane turned then and stepped into a swirling pool of blue light. He'd seen it before. He took a deep breath, held it then leapt.

Blue light surrounded him, water hugged his body. Weightlessness. Then he was out, standing atop a swirling pool. He released his breath. The room was warm and dry and all around him was desert, palms, and sand. The Portal Chamber. He raised the hood of the robe to hide his face, checked his pockets and jeans beneath the robes. Everything was there; knives, key... He removed the key pendant, held it above the water.

"Um..." How did one close the damn thing? He thrust the small sword towards the water like Spiderman flinging a web. "Close!"

Nothing.

In Mikaire he'd never had to close the Portal, only open it, and that was done by imaging with all your heart where you wished to go while holding up the pendant. But he was already where he wished to go. He squatted down and touched the key to the water. *"Close!"*

Nothing. The blue light continued swirling on top like a colorful fog.

Dane stood, sighed.

"Is there a problem?"

Startled, he spun to find a guard standing a couple yards behind him. Quickly he lowered his head to hide his visage beneath the shadow of his hood. "Um, my key is not working."

The guard stepped towards him, Dane placed his free hand into the robe, touched the knife handle.

"Where is the mortal?" the guard asked, looking around.

Dane's mind drew a complete blank. He shook his head slowly, keeping his face lowered, but looking up with his eyes, thankful for his brown contact lenses. His real eye color was unique for a mortal, much less an immortal.

"You couldn't get one... Or you were afraid?" asked the guard.

"I, um... I couldn't find one. Strange world, all sand, no people."

The guard sighed deeply. "Here... give me your key."

Reluctantly, Dane handed it over. He didn't want to... what if the guard decided to keep it? But not handing it over would be worse and the guard had already begun to look at him in suspicion. The guard took the key, mumbling.

"I don't know why Master Kaeplan sends amateurs to do such an important task. He won't be pleased. He needs many mortals now, not just one. I hope you are not on the Retrieval party for

271

tomorrow."

He placed the key over the water, chanted:

Deep in the watery pool,
Almareyah's power will not fool,
For none without shall see,
Once the Portal is closed with the key.

The pool water stopped swirling and the blue light faded. The guard turned to Dane, handed him back the key. "Better get this back to Master Kaeplan straight off. And learn that chant!"

Dane nodded. "I shall."

The guard walked away, disappearing into the jungle in the direction from where he had come. Dane chose not to follow. He feared running into the guard, or worse, many guards who might recognize that he is not one of their own. Better to avoid as many as possible.

He gazed about the massive room that seemed more like an indoor solarium of sand, trees and of course water. An oasis, just like the one he'd come through. He'd been here before, but then he had seen the room through eyes of fear. He'd been searching for something—or someone. Now he gazed through quizzical eyes that sought answers to a seemingly unsolvable riddle.

As he walked, searching for a door, or a barrier, anything, he recited the chant in his mind until it, naturally, became a song. He would not forget it again.

He ran his hands along the smooth limestone as he kept himself wary of movement, guards or servants. Nothing on one wall, so he started down the next. He had begun to believe there was no other way out but to follow the guard when a flicker of dark and light near the end of the wall caught his eye. It was then that Caitlyn's words relayed in his memory.

"There's a room where humans are kept tied up for citizens to drink from. On the other side of the room is a door with a sign that says CASTLE RESIDENTS ONLY. From that side, only one of Kaeplan's minions can open it. Beyond is a small hallway lit by a torch, then a door into the Portal Room. On the wall with the door back out are Egyptian Hieroglyphs. The Hieroglyphs above the door read 'DEATH ROOM.'

Reversing her direction, he moved cautiously down the wall, searching for the Hieroglyphs, and when he saw them, he followed. He came to the door at last, grateful it was actually a door...with a latch. He stepped through it and found himself in a dark stone hallway, the light of a single torch flickering on the wall. He followed to a solid wood door. This must lead to what they call the Death Room, he thought.

He was not at all prepared for what he saw when he entered. So many humans! The scent of blood, sweat and suffering heavy on the humid air. Each was tied to poles, which made Dane's mind recall his own horrors with poles. His stomach churned and he hiccupped back the nausea. Most moaned in pain. Many stared as if they could see nothing. Others stood stock still or leaned forward against their bonds. All were scared to death.

So transfixed he was on the people and their suffering, he didn't hear the guard who came up beside him. He was all at once there. Just a slight move, barely noticeable, Dane's hand moved instinctively to his knife hilt.

"What are you doing in here, Servant?" asked the guard. As before, Dane looked through the shadow of the hood. The guard's hair was blond, just touching in his shoulders and he kept his hands on his hips in authority. Dane eyed the sword at his waist.

They weren't alone, he realized in horror. Three villagers entered from large double doors near the front of the room. They spoke amongst themselves before dividing up to their desired humans.

"Answer me, Servant," said the guard. Though his voice was quiet, Dane could hear anger in his tone. "Why are you here?"

Dane kept his head angled down, but raised his eyes to this new blond guard. "I am new," he said.

"Are you lost as well?"

Dane glanced to the villager closest to him, not because he was ignoring the guard, but because something odd about him struck Dane's attention. He was average looking enough; male, about Dane's age, dark short hair, but his clothing... An odd mix of generations. Khaki pants, a tunic and leather boots. Just as in Mikaire, the men had no facial hair. He found that odd, as Kaeplan created this world based on his time spent in the Mortal Dimension.

His gaze moved to another man. His bright red lips were wrapped around the wrist of a human female. His eyes closed in the ecstasy of feeding. His tall slender body reminded him of Adrian, his clothes as well were unmatched; Tight jeans, also a tunic, and sandals. Light brown hair was tied back in a ponytail.

When Dane had been bled at Ritual, all the villagers were dressed in robes, similar to the one he now wore. Ritual robes. They'd done the same in Mikaire, but the everyday attire, though anachronistic, had held no hint of the mortal world.

The guard was speaking, snapping his fingers in front of Dane's face as if to break him of a spell. Dane dragged his gaze back to the guard.

"You must have been made only yesterday," said the guard. "Go back to the castle now. Servants are not allowed in here. You can find all the human blood you want at the castle."

The time had come. The opportunity present. His hand wrapped around the hilt of the knife. Just a precaution. He had to ask, though, even if he risked revealing himself.

"I heard a name," he started. "Meirah. Do you know this name?"

The guard let out a hearty laugh, mouth open to reveal impressively long sharp fangs. Dane offered a closed-mouth smile. His lack of fangs, even small ones, would surely give him away. He was actually surprised the guard in the Portal Room had not smelled his human blood, but in here, with so many humans, he was hidden.

Finally, the guard's laugh faded. "Even the newest castle servants know the name of Master Kaeplan's wife!"

Wife! Kaeplan's wife's name was the same as the deceased baby the wizard had paraded before him? Something was not adding up. Questions built in his mind faster than he could find answers.

Meirah. A flash of red hair. Emerald eyes. And then agony. Dane's hands rose to his head as if he could press the pain away.

"What ails you, Servant?" The guard's voice cut through the pain.

"My head."

"Get to the castle straight off then. Master Kaeplan's Apothecary keeps herbs to cure such ails within the ward."

The ache faded, but Dane feigned its continuance. "Can you help me there? I am blind with this pain."

The guard sighed. "This should take but a moment. Come with me." He touched Dane's arm as if to aid him in walking. The guard led him to the door with the sign indicating only castle residents were allowed—back the way he had come!

The guard touched the handle-less door and it faded as if it was never there. They moved together through the black entrance. Just when Dane was sure they would return to the Portal Room, the guard halted half-way down the hallway with the single torch. Through the flickering light Dane saw it for the first time; A shadow, but not a shadow for nothing within the hallway could cast such a shadow. How could he have missed it? Yet, as the guard turned toward it, Dane followed. A barrier. There was a moment of black then another hallway lit by torches. And windows. They were inside the castle.

The guard stopped and turned to Dane. By now, he was sure he would not be recognized, for even if a description of him was known by all, they'd be looking for silver-blue eyes. Still, he kept his hands on his head over the hood to hide his hair. Just in case.

"Follow this hall to the tapestry. Take a right, then a left at the statue and you will find the Ward Chamber. There is a sign. They will help you. I must return to the Pyramid."

Dane nodded. "Thank you."

He started down the hall, keeping an eye on the guard, who turned and disappeared through the wall. He was alone at last—and in the castle. If there were answers, he would surely find them here.

He straightened, no longer needing to feign a headache, and strode at a good pace down the hallway until he came to the tapestry. He studied the gruesome image. The bleeding man, then, at the bottom corner, the key symbol. He reached in his robe pocket and produced the key. *Of course.* Just like Mikaire. This key held the answers he sought. But in what way?

Dane stared at the tapestry, looking up and down, sure the image would tell him what he needed to know. He had seen this image before… Seen this tapestry before. He'd forgotten. Yes… this was the way to the dungeon where Bruce died.

Dane repressed a shiver at the sudden memory. No reason to

return there! He turned right and made his way to the Ward, but did not go in. The tapestry came once again into his mind. He shook his head. He couldn't get in anyway without Kaeplan's magic touch.

Yet, he retraced his steps back as if his feet moved on their own. But this time, as he rounded the corner to the left, he caught it in his peripheral vision. Just a slight movement, easy to miss. The tapestry actually moved. It was so slight as to be unnoticeable to anyone not looking. He'd learned quickly in this world that even the slightest anomaly, the most minute shadow, shift or flicker of light could be a barrier, to lead to a new destination.

He grasped the bottom of the tapestry, lifted and ducked underneath, expecting a wall yet finding nothing, not even light of any sort. The magic door was open!

Recalling the steps, he took a tentative step forward. And misjudged the step in the dark. He went down hard, hitting a step, then another as he tumbled down the first set of stone steps. His hands flailed for something to halt his decent. Finally, he came to rest on the second landing.

Lying on his back, he took shallow breaths, each producing a pain of its own. Slowly, he sat up. Nothing broken, he accessed. Minor pains plagued his arms and outer thighs. But at least now he saw light. The torch illuminated the next set of steps.

Dane raised his aching body, carefully standing to avoid the areas he knew would show quite a bit of bruising later on. Using the dim light now available, he carefully traversed the stairs to the bottom. Finally, level floor. He took a step forward into the well-lit chamber and halted quickly.

Memories pounded his brain of he, Adrian and Stephan forced to remove their clothing, "bathed" with cold water then donning robes. They had been taken out through a shadow barrier rather than up the dark steps. The last ones Kaeplan had taken out of this room… and he forgot to close the magic doorway behind the tapestry; the only reason Dane was able to enter it. Or was Kaeplan in there now?

He looked to the dungeon door on the other side. Suddenly he was shaking and sweating. His feet did not want to move forward. Why did he need to go in there anyhow? He began to turn away, to find the shadow barrier, or to return to the stairs. Something within halted him. Curiosity perhaps? No. A feeling, so strong he couldn't ignore it. Taking in a deep breath, he forced his feet to move to the door, his hand to grab the handle, turn it...

He stepped through the threshold with dread pounding in his heart. No Kaeplan, but his gaze immediately fell to the box where Bruce had been held prisoner, still smashed on the floor. Though no one was there, he saw it in his mind; his friend's body, pale, lifeless.

There had been a fight that caused the box to tip. Kaeplan was there. Guards. And then—his mind blanked out.

Before the agony in his head, which he had begun to recognize, returned he forced his gaze away from the box—and found himself staring at the dark cell where he had been chained. No light reached it, but every detail was clear in his mind. Pain and suffering hung thick in the air. Reluctantly he approached the cell, needing to confront his demons. Needing to scratch the itch of curiosity and unanswered questions that led him here.

The chains where he had been bound. Adrian huddled naked in a blanket.

Too much too soon, he began to turn away, to leave this room of horrors where he had lost his friend, the guitarist of Dark Myst, when movement caught his peripheral vision. Something in the darkest corner of the cell. Must be a rat, he reasoned. But he could not turn away. The same corner where Adrian had huddled in fear.

Very little of the flickering torchlight reached to the cell, but yet he saw a face appear slowly from the darkest shadows. Someone was in there!

He concentrated, seeing the pale complexion, long tangled red hair... Emerald eyes. He was at the bars before he realized he had moved. He saw her face then... He felt a twinge of pain in his head, but it did not grow to the usual agony. The smooth contours of her cheeks. The ruby lips. His heart skipped a beat.

She stood slowly, walked to the bars. Once again he hid his face beneath the cloak hood.

But he couldn't stop staring into those eyes! So green, like a cat. And familiar.

"Did ye bring me blood?" she asked weakly.

That voice. He had heard it before. He knew her, somehow. He tried to remember.

The agony arose. He grabbed his head, his knees buckled. Then he was on the floor.

She spoke with concern. "Are ye alright?"

Time leapt backwards all at once. He was Sir Kori Blackmore. There was a girl, young, curious. Red hair, green eyes. She approached him without fear, touched his armor.

Past lives flashed by his memory. The pain intensified, but he couldn't control nor stop the rushing flood. He was sure his head would explode. Memories of past lives—and she was there. She was always the last one he saw before the dark took him. And then...

Dane's life, his past flashed like a stampede through his mind. He saw her in his mirrors. But she was an illusion. Mirrors onstage. He passed out after seeing her. Then they were together in Mikaire. A fight to break a spell. A monster. A cave. He made love to her in the dark. A large mirror. Kaeplan fighting them. The end of Mikaire! Then she was at his parent's house. Pregnant. His child.

Dane writhed on the floor as the agony of remembrance held him captive. Each memory flowed as one. And then a name: *Meirah.*

A dead baby. Not Meirah. A daughter. His... and Meirah's. Wife. She was his wife. The baby was theirs.

Dane cried out in his agony. "Make it stop!" The pain webbed out from his head to engulf his body. He was paralyzed with it. Tears streamed down his face.

A tour. A fight. Sabrina. Meirah's anger. Her face—so hurt. Then she was gone. Desperation to find her plagued him deeply. Stephan and a lake. And then... This dimension. Almareyah. He was flogged for no reason. Bled. A spell. Pain everywhere. And then—nothing. Next he remembered he was in a hospital. Blank slate. No memories. Slowly, all returned. All except.... Her.

The pain and suffering faded slowly. He was lying on the dirty musty floor of the dungeon, his arms covering his head. As the agony abated, the memories that had been taken from him returned. His questions found their answers.

He sat up then, and grabbed the bars in aid to stand. His legs were weak. Head lowered, he took in deep and shallow breaths.

Slowly he raised his head. She stood before him, confused. Delicate hands held the bars, watching him. *Meirah. His wife.*

"Meirah," he whispered.

She nodded. She didn't recognize him behind the hood. Gathering his wits, he reached up and removed the brown contact lenses, lowered the hood.

Meirah gasped, took a step back. "No... Why... Why are you impersonating him?" Her voice was filled with panic.

Dane moved closer, letting the light fall on his face, his silver blue eyes. He pulled his hair from its binding. "Meirah... My love."

"Dane?" Her voice was small, unbelieving. "But you... you're dead."

He had heard that statement before. Martha two years ago. She had seen her dead brother in his eyes.

"No, Meirah. I am alive."

"Oh my... Dane!" she cried out, rushed to the bars and placed her hands over his. Their fingers locked. And between the bars their lips met.

The warmth of her touch, the sweet taste of her lips, light as bright as that which had brought him back to life filled his every molecule. Once again they were lost in one another—a bond deeper than love, deeper than the spell that forced him to forget. Nothing in his world, or hers, could keep them apart

So lost in one another, neither heard the footsteps that came up behind Dane. He was jerked backwards fiercely, agony pounding his head and back as he hit the wall and fell to the floor in a swirling storm of dust and robes. Before he could make sense of what happened, pain webbed through his scalp as he was dragged to his feet by his hair.

As his feet touched solid ground and the room stopped spinning, he saw a face. Anger flared in the amber eyes before morphing into a twisted gaze of confusion.

He was released so quickly, he stumbled back, grabbing the edge of the Rack Stephan had once been tied to and regained his balance. He shook his head back to reality and looked at his attacker.

Kaeplan stood before him, expression marred by complete and utter surprise.

"B-But," the wizard stuttered. "You're *dead*."

"So I've heard." Dane rubbed the back of his head where a knot had begun to form.

"I saw yer body," Kaeplan murmured.

"I guess you're not the only wizard in this world," Dane countered in an attempt to give himself time to act.

"Ye're no wizard!" Kaeplan snarled, apparently insulted.

Dane slipped a hand under the tangle of robes, wrapped his hand around the hilt of his knife.

"I returned from the dead... And not as someone else, as Sakkana so often achieved. Even he couldn't pull that off. Neither can *you*!" He pulled the knife, pointed it at Kaeplan's throat. But the red-haired bastard in the gilded robes called his bluff.

Kaeplan stepped back and cried out. "GUARDS!"

Before Dane could blink, two large guards rushed like freight trains into the Dungeon. They were at his sides in less than a second. The knife was knocked from his hand, his arms pinioned behind him—he had forgotten how fast and strong these magical blood-drinkers were. He didn't even bother to fight back.

Vampires!

"Put him in with her," Kaeplan snarled to the guards. "But be careful. He is sly and cunning." He pulled a set of jingling keys from beneath his robes.

Kaeplan looked strictly at Meirah then. "Step back or he will die again—this time permanently." Meirah obliged, backing to the wall behind her.

As he saw the wall with the chains coming at him, he simultaneously felt the robe of the servant yanked from his body. He had barely enough time to put up his hands as he hit the wall, arms, hands and face first. Once again, he felt his body give to the solidity of the stones and met the fetid, dirty floor.

Lying there, he moaned. "Why must these walls be so hard?"

All at once Meirah was sitting beside him. She reached around him, helped him to sit up. Gently, she placed a hand under his chin, lifted his face upward.

"Ye're bleedin' my love." She looked at Kaeplan. "Let me tend him."

Kaeplan snickered. "This is no' Mikaire! Ye'll receive no such clemency here."

"Ye're a *beast*, Kaeplan," she snarled.

Kaeplan scoffed. "Call me what ye will. I see clearly now. Yer mortal was meant tae return—tae do *my* bidding. This is as it was meant tae be."

"What does *that* mean?" she asked clearly agitated.

Kaeplan sniggered. "Time, my dear Meirah. Time is bendable. He..."Kaeplan nodded towards Dane, "...is the key to it all. I did no' think it possible. Now I know... It *is* and will be."

Laughing, Kaeplan turned away. He tossed the servant's robe to one of the guards. "Go fetch him!" he snarled.

The guard bowed and moved to the door. Kaeplan followed. Before crossing the threshold, however, Kaeplan turned to Meirah once more.

"Ye'll be mine. No' now, but as the hourglass flows backwards, yer mortal will serve me... and ye'll ne'er have known of his existence!"

The door slammed behind Kaeplan and his guards. The single wall torch flickered, faded, then grew bright again.

Time may have moved more slowly in this dimension, but to Dane it crawled slower than a snail. Even with Meirah at his side, a sense of foreboding plagued his every waking moment.

Most of the time spent in the cell, they talked or simply held one another in silence. Neither understood Kaeplan's cryptic message, but instinct and knowledge told them both the wizard had stumbled upon something big—something that would change, or erase, their lives forever.

-Epilogue-

A week later

"I called ye here because I now have the means tae see our plan become a reality."

Kaeplan looked over at Uchillies who sat for a moment, twirling strands of his long white hair through slender fingers.

Finally Uchillies nodded. "Then you acquired the source of power you need?"

"I did." Kaeplan smiled.

"And you have acquired the necessary requirements?"

Kaeplan nodded. "I have bled him daily for the past week. My Alchemist has collected the herbs ye stated we need. And I have the spell memorized. Wi' yer power and mine, we can make this happen."

"And once you've turned the hourglass?"

"I will find ye. Our power will be unrelenting. Together, we shall turn it all 'round. None can stop us."

"Do not get ahead of *this* wizard, Kaeplan," Uchillies motioned to himself, grey eyes sparked with white glowing specks, fangs so long they protruded from closed lips. "I render my powers for this task, but do not dare forget our bargain in return."

"I promise."

Uchillies was what Kaeplan needed—an old wizard with powers beyond all the others.

Several weeks before, Kaeplan had travelled to Vertemps, one of the longest lived and oldest Dimensions in existence, it had survived for thousands of human years. A Dimension beyond glass—so close a neighbor to Mikaire as to touch one another at the edge of time.

Together, they could destroy the wall that separated Almareyah and Mikaire. Mirror and Glass. Their combined powers could proposedly turn back time.

"Let us get started then." Uchillies stood, held out a hand. Kaeplan took it and the bond between them was completed. "Tonight. Midnight. We begin."

In his chamber, Kaeplan searched for clothing that would fit into Mikaire's world. He had not yet been a wizard there, and so he needed to fit into the Mikaire of the past. Searching chests and wardrobes, he found a tunic and breeches that matched Mikairian style and colors.

Once donned in attire worthy of the son of a Committee member, he moved on to the Alchemist's holding room. He gathered all the blood he had collected from Dane throughout the past week, leaving the mortal so weak he teetered on the brink of death. If he did indeed die, however, it no longer mattered. Soon Dane Bainbridge will never have existed.

Kaeplan met Uchillies in the Portal Chamber at precisely 11:30 pm. He had positioned guards at every entrance into the room with orders to kill any—even villagers—who attempted entry. Soon, they would no longer exist anyhow.

They set up the necessary Ritual items near the pool before standing together at its edge.

Kaeplan looked over to Uchillies "Ready."

A large iron pot, placed beside the Portal, held the necessary herbs.

"The key," said Uchillies

Kaeplan removed the pendant he had taken from Dane, placed it over the Portal and both chanted quietly.

The thick water swirled, blue light indicated it was open. The water turned to crimson.

"Now," said Uchillies.

Kaeplan poured the pitcher of Dane's blood into the cauldron of herbs. Explosion, flames, smoke flared bright.

"Go!" said Uchillies.

Kaeplan drew a deep breath and leapt into the chaos of crimson waves. He could not breathe nor move. Life as he had known flashed backwards in a split second.

Almareyah, the human desert, struggling with a dying Mikaire, serving Sakkana, playing with Meirah as Young Ones—and then voices, excited and desperate, came to his ears.

"A mortal has come across the Main Looking Glass!"

The spinning of backward progression halted all at once. Dizzy, Kaeplan found himself sprawled on the dirt ground. Someone halted and helped him to his feet.

"Exciting, is it not?" Then the man rushed off, leaping into a wagon pulled by... juspettes! The Mortal Dimension called them unicorns. He remembered that.

Mikairian villagers ran around him like a rushing river around a rock. The clothes. The beasts. He was home! He was in Mikaire.

Villagers hopped into wagons lined like soldiers ready to bring them to this spectacular event. Kaeplan hopped onto one that passed by and settled into the straw beside an Older One who offered him an exuberant smile.

As if he had not grown up with it, he watched in fascination as they crossed the Village barrier into the forest. He wondered where Meirah could be. He had not been there the first time. Now he watched each detail as if seeing Mikaire for the first time. Such a strange feeling; being back in a world that, by his time, had long been destroyed. Gone due to the mortal Sakkana chose to reincarnate, ignorant that its strength and knowledge would grow, until it possessed the power to break spells and escape—killing Sakkana and destroying Mikaire. No one in this time had this information—except him. And with that power held the knowledge to change the past.

Continued in Book Three

Beyond Broken Glass

Like Vampires?

A unique series unlike any other!

Fate of the True Vampires
Sands of Time
The Early Scrolls
Blood Moon
Love's Tragedy

16159877R00172

Made in the USA
Middletown, DE
29 November 2018